THE
MOST PLEASANT HISTORY
OF
ORNATUS AND ARTESIA

A Prose Romance

Publications of the Barnabe Riche Society
Volume 16

Series Editor
Donald Beecher

"Ornatus and Artesia."
From a late seventeenth-century edition of *Ornatus and Artesia*
in the Newberry Library, Chicago. By permission.

Emanuel Ford

THE
MOST PLEASANT HISTORY
OF
ORNATUS AND ARTESIA

**Edited with
Introduction and Notes
by**
Goran Stanivukovic

Dovehouse Editions, Inc.
Ottawa, Canada
2003

This book has been published with the help of a grant from the Humanities and Social Sciences Federation of Canada, using funds provided by the Humanities Research Council of Canada.

National Library of Canada Cataloguing in Publication
Ford, Emanuel
    The most pleasant history of Ornatus and Artesia / Emanuel Ford (Foorde) ; edited by Goran Stanivukovic

(Publications of the Barnabe Riche Society ; v. 16)
Includes bibliographical references.

ISBN 1-895537-79-7 (bound)
ISBN 1-895537-72-X (pbk.)

I. Stanivukovic, Goran V.   II. Title.   III. Series.

PR2276.F53M67 2003   823'.3   C2002-906046-X

For orders write to:

Dovehouse Editions Inc.
1890 Fairmeadow Cres.
Ottawa, Canada, K1H 7B9

For information on the series:

Editors: Barnabe Riche Series
c/o Department of English
Carleton University
1125 Colonel By Drive
Ottawa, Canada K1S 5B6

Typeset in Canada: Carleton Production Centre
Manufactured in Canada.
Cover: "A Difference of Opinion." Sir Lawrence Alma-Tadema, 1896.

To My Parents

Table of Contents

Preface   8

Acknowledgments   9

Introduction

   The Author   11

   The Date   15

   Sources, Influences, and Intertexts   17

   Ornatus and Artesia and the Story of Romeo and Juliet   24

   Geographical Romance: Phrygia and Natolia   26

   Genre   32

   Style   34

   Plot   38

   The Book Market and Critical Reception   40

   Eloquence, Love, and Narrative   54

   Gender Disguise and Sexuality   64

   Property, Lineage, and Government   79

   The Text and Editorial Procedures   87

Bibliography   93

The Most Pleasant History of Ornatus and Artesia   107

Textual Annotations   245

Preface

The publication series of The Barnabe Riche Society has been established to provide scholarly, modern-spelling editions of works of imaginative literature in prose written in English between 1485 and 1660, with special emphasis on Elizabethan prose fiction. The program allows for works ranging from late medieval fabliaux and Tudor translations of Spanish picaresque tales or ancient Greek romances to seventeenth-century prose pastorals. But the principal goal is to supply much-needed editions of many of the most critically acclaimed works of the period by such authors as Lodge, Greene, Chettle, Riche, and Dekker, and to make them available in formats suitable to libraries, scholars, and students. Editorial policy for the series calls for texts carefully researched in terms of variant sources, and presented in conservatively modernized and repunctuated form in to order make these texts as widely accessible as possible, while respecting the substantive integrity of the originals. Each edition will provide the editor with an opportunity to write a full essay dealing with the author and the historical circumstances surrounding the creation of the work, as well as with its style, themes, conventions, and critical challenges. Each text will also be accompanied by annotations.

The Barnabe Riche Society is based in the English Department of Carleton University in Ottawa, and forms a component of the Carleton Centre for Renaissance Studies and Research. Its activities include colloquia, the awarding of an annual prize for the best new book-length study dealing with English Renaissance prose fiction, and the editorial management of the series, backed by an eleven-member international editorial board. The society invites the informal association of all scholars interested in its goals and activities.

Acknowledgments

Several institutions were helpful during my work on this edition. I would like to thank The Folger Shakespeare Library, the Huntington Library, and the Newberry Library for generous fellowships and an inspiring working environment without which the research for this edition would not have been possible. I am grateful to the University College of Cape Breton for a small start-up research grant that helped me begin this project, and to Saint Mary's University for a Senate Research Grant that enabled me to complete this work. My research in Britain was supported by a grant from the Social Sciences and Humanities Research Council of Canada, for which I am very grateful. I also wish to thank the Bodleian Library for providing me with a copy of the 1682 edition of Antonius and Aurelia (Douce, A.271.), the British Library for permission to use their copy of Ornatus and Artesia as my copy text, and the Huntington and Newberry libraries for granting me permission to reproduce illustrations.

Many individuals answered my queries, offered advice and encouragement, and read parts of the manuscript. I am grateful to John Bartlett, Peter Blayney, Susan Brock, C.N.L. Brooke, John Brunton, Mary Campbell, C.P. Courtney, James Daybell, Carmine Di Biase, M. Morgan Holmes, Don Hughes, Natasha Hurley, M.J. Jannetta, Henry Jenzen, Alan Jutzi, Joseph Khouri, John Kerrigan, Arthur F. Kinney, D.J. McKitterick, R.W. Lovatt, Lori Humphrey Newcomb, Mark Nicholls, Christine Mason, Alison M. Pearn, Thomas Rendall, Mary Robertson, Paul Salzman, James Schiffer, Jonathan Smith, Alan Stewart, Laura Syms, Kevin Taylor, Paul Werstine, Stanley Wells, Pamela Wetzel, Suzy Wochos, Heather Wolfe, and Laetitia Yeandle. In particular, I am indebted to Donald Beecher for graciously extending several deadlines, for reading a number of drafts of the manuscript, and for sharing his enthusiasm for Ford's romance with me. I am indebted to Ronald Bond for supporting my work from its beginning; Elizabeth Hulse for reading my manuscript scrupulously; Mary and Richard Keshen for giving me their house, a comfortable study, and two desks during two consecutive summers; Constance Relihan for expressing interest in this edition from the day I began my work on it; and Tony Telford Moore for inspiring me (unknowingly) to try my hand at editing and for never allowing me to forget how difficult that task is. Vaughan's help came just when it was most needed, for which I shall always remain in his debt.

Goran Stanivukovic
Saint Mary's University, Halifax
2003

Introduction

The Author

"The only life we have of Ford is the history of his books," wrote Philip Henderson, who, in 1930, produced the first modern transcript of *Ornatus and Artesia*.[1] His remark is still valid today. Scattered references to Emanuel Ford's works appeared well into the nineteenth century, but very little is known about the man. While the surname Ford was relatively common in Devon—John Ford the dramatist, for example, was a Devonshire man—the name Emanuel was less so, providing some hope that he might be found through the consultation of English parish records.[2] In the register of the parish church of Kenn, Devon County, for example, there is a record of one "Emanuell Ford or Andrew" baptised on 3 November 1562. This may or may not be the author. But if it is, and the date of the baptism is a few days after the birth, then he would have been in his late thirties when his romance *Ornatus and Artesia* was published. An alternative candidate is the "Emanuel Fourd" who matriculated as a member of Trinity College, Cambridge in Lent Term 1584–85, perhaps the same Emanuel, but more likely another (age 22 is late for

[1] From the Preface to Ford's *Ornatus and Artesia* in *Shorter Novels: Seventeenth Century* (London: J.M. Dent and New York: E.P. Dutton, 1930), p. 2. Henderson's transcript is inaccurate in many places.

[2] Alternative spellings of Ford were Forde, Foord, Fourd, and Fourde; of Emanuel there were Emmanuel, Emmanuell, and Emanuell.

11

matriculation). The published register of the members of Cambridge University states only that *this* Ford was "presumably" the romance author,[3] and Helmut Bonheim, for one, argues that Ford did matriculate to Trinity.[4] But Ford's name does not appear in the Trinity College buttery books at the time he would have been an undergraduate. Perhaps he matriculated without taking up residence. Or perhaps he moved to another college, which was not unheard of, although there is nothing in the university records to bear this out.[5] The fact that the "Fourd" of Trinity College is listed as sizar suggests that he was a man of limited personal means who, in part, paid his way at university by performing menial tasks for a fellow or a wealthier undergraduate.[6] Should this sizar be Ford the romance writer, then it could be that, as a commoner, he had to earn his living, perhaps by trying his luck as a professional writer in the potentially lucrative market of popular romance.[7] Thomas Nashe, also a sizar, was a student at St. John's College from 1582 until 1588 (B.A. 1586). Speculation is free as to whether the paths of these two writers crossed. In any case, a university education would not have been

---

[3]See *Alumni Cantabrigienses: A Biographical List of All Known Students, Graduates and Holders of Office at the University of Cambridge, from the Earliest Times to 1900*, compiled by John Venn and J.A. Venn (Cambridge: University Press, 1922), p. 157. For a similar entry, see also *The Book of Matriculations and Degrees: A Catalogue of those who have been Matriculated or been Admitted to any Degree in the University of Cambridge from 1544 to 1659*, complied by John Venn and J.A. Venn (Cambridge: University Press, 1913), p. 258. The entry reads: Fourd, Emanuel. Trinity. S(izar). L(ent) 1584–85.

[4]Helmut Bonheim, "Emanuel Forde: *Ornatus and Artesia*," *Anglia* 90 1,2 (1972), p. 47.

[5]Johnstone Parr, "Robert Greene and His Classmates at Cambridge," *PMLA* 77,5 (1962), p. 542.

[6]For the role of sizars, see James Bass Mullinger, *The University of Cambridge from the Royal Injunctions of 1535 to the Accession of Charles the First*, Vol. II (Cambridge: University Press, 1884), pp. 399–400.

[7]For example, Robert Greene, who was a sizar at Cambridge less than a decade before Ford, entered the literary scene in the late 1590s and was soon to became a professional writer, earning his living by publishing romances and other works of popular literature.

essential to Ford's achievement. All of his works were written at least a decade after the name "Fourd" appeared in the university records, and a good elementary education would have served for the few classical allusions and Latin tags that occur in his works. Following a different lead, there is an Emanuel Ford who married Margery Raddon in the parish church of Offwell, Devon County, on 21 June 1596. But again, this may or may not be Emanuel Ford the writer.[8] This, so far, is the best that can be made of the matter.

The date of Ford's death and the place of his burial are likewise unknown.[9] He could have died at any time after writing his last romance, *Montelyon*. Publication dates are of no particular help insofar as the earliest surviving copy of this work, now in the Huntington Library (STC 11167), bears the date 1633 (Salzman 352), but by all indications it was written more than a third of a century earlier. (That earlier editions do not survive is no surprise given that such popular literature was often read to pieces

[8]There is also the name and signature of one "Emanuell fforde of Honyton," a gentleman, which appears in a manuscript land deed dated 7 September 1655. The deed, consisting of one membrane, is now in the Folger Shakespeare Library in Washington, D.C. (shelfmark: Z.c.9(214)). The deed, however, is too late for the writer, because Ford would have been ninety three at the time of signing it. Yet, we might speculate about the deed's possible connection with the writer's family, whether to his son or grandson. Further pieces of archival evidence relating to the "Emmanuel Ford" of Honiton include his will of 1656, and a note affirming his affiliation with the Honiton Grammar School, possibly as a governor or trustee. Both the will and the note are in the Westcountry Studies Library in Exeter. The note about Ford's involvement with the Honiton Grammar School is in the Charity Commission Reports. It is unlikely, however, that this is the same Emanuel Ford as the one baptised in Kenn because the date of the will is too late and the reference to a wife named Bennet (not Margery) would suggest that it is not. But the will written in 1656 can be linked to the deed at the Folger written in 1655. It might refer to the same person, for, at that time, it was common to have wills and deeds composed in short proximity. My research into the archives in Devon, London, and Cambridge—places associated with the author—have yielded no further information.

[9]Henderson (2) believes that Ford died in 1607, but there is no material evidence to support that statement.

and discarded then as it sometimes is now.)   Paul A. Scanlon (152) speculates that the first publication date was 1599, within weeks or months of the appearance of *Parismenos* (the second part of his first work, *Parismus*), published that same year, or late in 1598. In a similarly circumstantial way, the *DNB* states that Ford "flourished in 1607," but this, the date of the second edition of *Ornatus and Artesia*, is no guarantee that the author was still living.[10]

Ornatus and Artesia is itself difficult to date precisely, given the absence of an entry for it in the Stationers' Register and the lack of a title page in the single surviving copy of the earliest edition, although clearly it was written and presumably published between 1595 and 1599. For want of precise evidence, scholars must fall back on two conflicting clues, the first, a reference to the work by Francis Meres in 1598 — whether seen in manuscript or in a printed edition is unclear — the second, Ford's observation in his "Epistle to the Reader," that he had "taken but one flight" before writing or publishing *Ornatus and Artesia*, suggesting that it was the second of his endeavors in the genre, following *Parismus*, published in 1598.[11]

These publication dates together invite us to think of Ford as one of the "Elizabethan prodigals," the term by which Richard Helgerson refers to Lyly, Lodge, Gascoigne, Greene and Sidney — all of whom were aspiring writers of prose fiction.[12] His tastes were clearly aligned with the vogue for romance. There is some evidence that Ford's works were appreciated throughout the seventeenth century. The title of his last romance, *Montelyon, Knight of the Oracle*, was adopted by John Phillips, one of John Milton's nephews, who published almanacs under that pseudonym between 1660 and 1661. Finally, in the 1640 edition, one R.K., in a poem "In Praise of the Author," thanks Ford for "offring at

---

[10]This copy is in the Bodleian Library (Douce, A.p. A27).

[11]Francis Meres, "School of English Literature, Painting, and Music, up to September 1598," *An English Garner: Critical Essays and Literary Fragments*, ed. J(ohn) Churton Collins (Westminster: Archibald Constable), 1903, p. 23.

[12]Richard Helgerson, *The Elizabethan Prodigals* (Berkeley: University of California Press), 1976, pp. 1ff.

free cost, / His Talent for our hearts delight."[13] But the strongest testimonial lies in the numerous reprintings throughout the seventeenth century. *Parismus* went through twenty editions during the 122 years following its first printing.[14] Ernest Baker goes so far as to state that for popularity Ford, for a time, lead the pack: "Sidney ran him close in sustained popularity . . . otherwise none of the early novelists or romancers had anything like such a hold on generations of readers."[15]

The Date

No entry for *Ornatus and Artesia* appears in the Stationers' Register.[16] The imperfect copy in the British Library[17] is generally assumed to be the first one printed, but its missing title page leaves

[13] Emanuel Forde, *The famous historie of Montelyon, knight of the oracle* (London: B. Alsop and T. Fawcett, 1640) (Folger copy STC 11167.2).

[14] Douglas Bush, *English Literature in the Earlier Seventeenth Century* (New York: Oxford University Press, 1952), p. 535.

[15] Ernest Baker, *The History of the English Novel*, Vol. II, *The Elizabethan Age and After* (New York: Barnes and Noble [1936], 1966), p. 124.

[16] This absence does not mean, however, that the book was not "licensed." It was not uncommon for printers to "license" and yet not enter their work. The names of printers and publishers appear on the title pages of these four early editions of *Ornatus and Artesia*, suggesting that the books were published legally — that is, that there was no effort to conceal the printer's and publisher's identity. Omissions in the Stationers' Register often suggest the printer's desire to save money, for while he might pay the six-pence fee to obtain his licence, he would save the additional four pence paid to the clerk of the Stationers' Register for recording the fee in the register. Particularly for works belonging to the "cheap-print culture," such as *Ornatus and Artesia*, that practice would not have been uncommon. See Cyndia Susan Clegg's reference to Peter Blayney's view on the matter in her *Press Censorship in Elizbethan England* (18). For a more recent account of the manufacturing of books in Renaissance England, and for the relationship between producers and retailers of books, see also Peter W.M. Blayney, in "The Publication of Playbooks," *A New History of Early English Drama*, ed. John D. Cox and David Scott Kastan (New York: Columbia University Press, 1997), pp. 384–422, esp. pp. 389–92.

[17] STC 11168.

the matter open to some question. In the *Short-Title Catalogue* (3, 47) the first publication date is pushed back to 1595, although rightfully followed by a question mark. What is certain is that the work was in existence in some form by 1598 because Francis Meres mentions it among the some twenty-two romances he alludes to in *Palladis Tamia*.[18] That there are several "naturalist" allusions uniquely in common with Lodge's *A Margarite of America* published in 1596, that date may be suggested as the earliest period in which *Ornatus* was written. But Ford's own "Epistle" holds the most pregnant clues. He states therein that *Ornatus* was his second effort in the genre, but that he had been urged to publish the work in haste — recent work, presumably, that he called "summer fruit" for not having had time to ripen. His promise is, however, that should *Ornatus* be found faulty, he had his earlier and more seasoned work, held back from publication, ready to publish the following winter to make amends. If that first work is *Parismus*, with or without the second part, published singly or together in 1598 or early in 1599, it would appear that the publication of *Ornatus* should be dated to 1598 or 1597 at the earliest: written second but published first. That would allow Meres to have seen it in print. Nevertheless, the description of *Ornatus* as a second "flight" has led others to think this was also his second romance to be published, hence in 1599, this being the calendar year for the Year of Grace, 1598.[19] In keeping with

---

[18]Meres mentions *Ornatus and Artesia* together with twenty-two other romances which, he claimed, should have been censored because they were "harmful to youth." See Meres, "School of English Literature, Painting, and Music, up to September 1598," p. 23.

[19]Critics often take the difference between the Year of Grace and the calendar year for granted. Yet this difference is especially important in our establishing, as closely as possible, the dates of books, such as *Ornatus and Artesia*, which were not entered in the Stationers' Register and which lack the preliminaries. For a brief discussion of the difference between the Year of Grace and the calendar year in the context of establishing dates for early books, see Blayney, "The Numbers Game: Appraising The Revised STC" (in Cox and Kastan, ed.). Blayney reminds us that the starting point for the Year of Grace, which had been adopted in England since the thirteenth century, marks "the feast of the

this widely endorsed dating, the first edition will be referred to as [1599] in the discussions and annotations to follow.

Sources, Influences, and Intertexts

Like other Renaissance romances, *Ornatus and Artesia* is a collage of literary influences. The sources that Ford might have drawn upon are not always clear, largely because they are so interwoven among themselves. Patently clear, however, is that *Ornatus and Artesia* is the product of a literary culture in which the eclectic emulation of sources for style, structures and motifs was the norm. Similarities with Robert Greene's *Pandosto* (1588; 2nd ed., 1592), for example, suggest that Ford may have been influenced by the success of Greene's romance and that he regarded it as a model for *Ornatus and Artesia*. But this is merely a self-evident beginning. Such borrowings are not mechanical but inspirational. Ford enters Greene, as one of several, as a less experienced writer in search of procedures and characters for framing his own configuration of adventures.[20] But such inspirations as these regarding plot motifs, style, and character types, not to mention genre and ethos, are always matters of negotiation concerning the degree to which they are treated as community property. Even the names of particular characters suggest Ford's debt to other fellow romance writers.[21]

Annunciation three months after Nativity." That point, Blayney continues, "marked the day on which the number changed, and that number had nothing to do with the calendar" (p. 385). I thank Paul Werstine for drawing my attention to Blayney's essay.

[20] Among those similarities between *Pandosto* and *Ornatus and Artesia* are the imprisonment of the main hero-princes (Dorastus in *Pandosto*, Ornatus in *Ornatus and Artesia*) and the reconciliation of warring parties (Natolians and Armenians in Ford's romance, Pandosto and Egistus in Greene's); in both romances the main hero changes his name to enable him a safer access to his beloved. In both, the love between the main characters materializes outside their native lands in order to avoid obstacles created by their families (the parent's prohibition in Greene, a family feud in Ford).

[21] He may have derived the name Sylvian from a prince in disguise, Silvian, in part II of *Palmerin of England* (entered in 1581 and published in 1596). The name Silvia (Silve in *Amadis de Gaula*) was common in

Ford's more notable allusions can be traced, in tell-tale fashion, not only to the Greek romance in general, but to the *Palmerin* and *Amadis* romances, and to Sir Philip Sidney's *Arcadia*. Again, Ford's borrowing is at the level of romance ethos, while taking inspiration, at the same time, for the generic designs of his episodes.[22] Comparing Ford with Sidney, Mary Patchell points out some specific similarities between the *Arcadia* and *Ornatus and Artesia*. Ornatus's temptation "by the beauty of the sleeping Artesia" (99) is similar to Musidorus's infatuation with the sleeping Pamela, while Artesia's refusal to subject herself to Lenon who has abducted her (ch. XI) is analogous to Philoclea's rejection of Cecropix. Patchell surmises, too, that the rebellion of Helotian peasants in the *Arcadia* may have furnished the episode of the peasants' storming of the king's palaces in *Ornatus and Artesia* (99). But the war between the Phrygians and the Armenians (ch. XIV and XV) seems to have been influenced, not by the rebellion in the *Arcadia*, but instead by the war between Mitylene and Methymene from *Daphnis and Chloe* (books 13–17). One can see the indeterminate intertextualities at work. Although Ford's use of *Amadis de Gaula* and the *Arcadia* are intricately combined throughout *Ornatus and Artesia*, asserting which part of Ford's

Renaissance romances, especially for the second most important female character in both the *Palmerin* and *Amadis* cycles. The hag's name, Flera, in *Ornatus and Artesia* may have derived from Florea, the jealous, malcontent, and evil daughter of the queen in *Palladine of England*, which came out in 1588. See *The famous, pleasant, and varitable Historie of Palladine of England*, tr. A[nthony] M[unday] (London; by Edward Allde for John Perin, 1588; STC 5541). Munday's adapted translation from French was done from Claude Colet's translation of the anonymous romance *Florando de Ingliterra*.

[22]The passages of erotic titillation and voyeurism, such as Ornatus's gazing at Artesia's breast while she is cooling off in the shade (ch. I), might derive from *Daphnis and Chloe*, where, in book 3, Lycaenion spies on Daphnis and Chloe. The pirates' plundering of Phrygia (ch. X) may have been inspired by the Tyrenian pirates' looting of Daphnis's country. The pirates' kidnapping of Artesia (ch. XII) and her separation from Ornatus are analogous to the motif in the *Arcadia* (I.1).

romance was influenced by *Amadis de Gaula* independently of the *Arcadia* and which came through the *Arcadia* is not easy to do.[23] Turning to the Greek romances, Ornatus's arrival in Natolia after shipwreck (ch. IV) resembles Clitophon's arrival in Sidon after the shipwreck in Achilles Tatius's *Clitophon and Leucippe* (I.1).[24] In that same work (VI.21), Leucippe rescues her virginity from the pirates much as Artesia does from Luprates (ch. XI). Subsequently, the captivity episode and Artesia's imprisonment with Ornatus (ch. XIII) may have been inspired by the imprisonment of the lovers in the *Aethiopian History* (VIII.x). Yet the cultural and narrative background for this episode could also have been the numerous printed and oral accounts of the Turks or pirates attacking Christian ships and taking men and women as captives in the eastern Mediterranean during the sixteenth century.[25] These episodes appeared in the travel narratives that burgeoned on the English print market in the late 1590s.

Ford's habit of borrowing specific, dramatic moments from the repertoire of stock actions in Greek romances suggests that he is more interested in action than the ideas, the manner rather than the matter, embodied in these classical romances. *Daphnis and Chloe*, one of the most popular of Greek romances, could well have furnished Ford not only with a few specific structural elements but also with a plot featuring a small number of characters and a narrative that induces erotic contemplation.[26] Further ideas for episodes may have been adapted from *Amadis de Gaula* (*Amadis of France*), which Ford could have consulted in the French

[23]Mary Patchell, *The 'Palmerin' Romances in Elizabethan Prose Fiction* (New York: AMS Press, 1966).

[24]Wolff, *The Greek Romances in Elizabethan Prose Fiction*, p. 311.

[25]As Roma Gill suggests, "Mediterranean history of the sixteenth century is rich in accounts of Turkish sieges and stratagems." See *The Complete Works of Christopher Marlowe*, ed. Roma Gill, Vol. IV, *The Jew of Malta* (Oxford: Clarendon Press, 1995), p. xi.

[26]This characteristic of *Daphnis and Chloe* is noticed by Giles Barber, in "*Daphnis and Chloe*," 10. *Daphnis and Chloe* appeared in English in Angel Day's 1587 adapted translation of Jacques Amyot's French translation; it remained popular (and the only available version) throughout the sixteenth century.

version of 1559, or more likely in the 1572 abridged translation by Thomas Paynell.[27]

The disguising of male characters in female clothes has a long tradition in romance, starting with the Hellenistic Greek writers. Their practices passed on to sixteenth-century Italy. In canto XXII of Ariosto's *Orlando Furioso*, two knights disguise themselves in women's clothes to obtain access to their ladies. But in his female disguise as Sylvian, Ornatus more closely resembles Pyrocles disguised as an Amazon and renamed Zelmane in book I of *Arcadia* than Ariosto's disguised knights. The cross-dressing motif in Sidney, however, might have come from *Amadis de Gaula*, where in book IX Florisel dresses himself as a shepherd to woo Silve. In the same book of *Amadis de Gaula*, Agesilan, enamored of Diane after seeing her picture, dresses himself as the Amazon Daraide, and after a shipwreck, reaches Galdap. This adventure, too, is analogous to Ornatus's arrival in Natolia following shipwreck, disguised as a woman.[28] But again there is the incertitude concerning priorities to be assigned to sources.

The cross-dressing motif, coupled with the topos of the shipwrecked youth, also brings to mind Barnabe Riche's novella, "Of Apolonius and Silla," in *Riche his Farewell to Militarie Profession* (1581).[29] The shipwreck and disguise sequence in Ford's work is, in fact, an inversion of the situation in Riche. Ornatus pretends that he is shipwrecked before he takes service with Artesia. Riche's Silla takes ship in pursuit of the duke who has abandoned her, and after wrecking on his shores, assumes the guise of a boy page in order to gain service at his court.

[27] *The Treasurie of Amadis of Fraunce* (London: H[enry] Bynneman and Thomas Hacket, [?1572]. Entered as trans. by "Thomas Panell," 1567–68; STC 545).

[28] For Sidney's indebtedness to *Amadis de Gaula*, see Victor Skretkowicz's introduction in *The Countess of Pembroke's Arcadia* (*The New Arcadia*), pp. ix–xx.

[29] Another edition of Riche's work, published around the time when Ford was likely to have been at work on *Ornatus and Artesia*, appeared in 1594 (printed by V. S[immes] for T. Adams).

An examination of Ford's sources points to a pastiche effect.[30] The principal narrative source of *Ornatus and Artesia* is the story of Florisel of Niquée (Niquea in Paynell's translation) in books ten and eleven of *Amadis de Gaula*. This is a narrative of a prince in love with Princess Arland who disguises himself as a woman and lodges with a shepherd in order to be near the beloved, who, like Ornatus, becomes the object of another man's desire. Unless Ford knew the story of Florisel of Niquée from a French version of *Amadis*, however, the only available sources would have been either Sidney's adapted version of the story in the *New Arcadia*, published in 1593, or Paynell's adaptation of a few extracts of orations from books 1–13.[31] That ambiguity involving sources adumbrated above persists even here. Paynell's translation was, in any case, the only English version of books 10 and 11 of *Amadis de Gaula* available at the time.[32] His abridged version of these episodes is, principally, a collection of the epistles, orations, and lamentations that appear in *Amadis de Gaula*, which, again, accounts for the priority gained by these features in Ford's work.

---

[30]Ford may have found the idea for the name of the central female character, Artesia, either in the story of Phalantus and Artesia in *Amadis de Gaula* — that story is not included in Paynell's adapted translation — or in books I and III of *Old Arcadia*, where the story is developed and attention is focused on Artesia's character. Ford's Artesia, however, is a character independent from both Sidney and *Amadis de Gaula*. While Sidney's Artesia treats love very superficially and is not in love with anyone but is only satisfied with paying lip-service to Phalantus for the benefit of reaching Amphialus (book I), and while in Sidney's romance she is an evil character given to plotting and treachery (in book III), Ford's Artesia demonstrates a more developed philosophy of romantic love. She is constructed not only as an ideal romantic heroine but as a psychologically independent female character.

[31]See Patchell, *The* Palmerin *Romances in Elizabethan Prose Fiction*, p. 99.

[32]The next full translated adaptation of books 2–12 appeared in 1592 as *The second booke of Amadis de Gaule*, tr. L. P[Pyott] (London: [A. Islip] for C. Burbie, 1595; (STC 542). Books 2–12 were entered in 1594, which (as the publication date) is too late for us to assume that Ford would have known them. One can only speculate, of course, that he may have known the *Amadis* romances in French.

Ornatus and Artesia, in relation to sources, then, is most accurately described as a plot derived, whether directly and indirectly, from the *Amadis* in conjunction with Sidney's adaptation and Paynell's partial translation — Sidney for the narrative design, and Paynell for specific letters and orations.

Although the general structural "disposition" of the story of *Ornatus and Artesia* is modelled primarily upon Sidney, Ford borrowed the conventions pertaining to the letters exchanged between lovers and the long orations on love from the *Palmerin* and *Amadis* texts. The emphasis on the exchange of letters, rather than eclogues — a recurrent feature in other romances by Ford — foregrounds this epistolary romance tradition. Undoubtedly it was attached to the emergent place of fashionable letter-writing in Elizabethan culture generally, as reflected in the growing number of manuals for teaching the art. These manuals specialized in models for "occasional" letter-writing — such set circumstances as the lover's praise of the beloved, the lady's reply, and the persuasion of a lady to marry, creating a kind of interface between social practice and fiction.[33] The fashion for such letter-writing was given further impetus through the novels of Matteo Bandello, which were very popular in England, especially after the appearance of William Painter's and Geoffrey Fenton's translations.[34] Epistolary fiction was a significant development of the age with roots in Aeneas Sylvius Piccolomini's fifteenth-century masterpiece, *De duobus amantibus historia*, translated into English as early as 1550 as *The History of Two Lovers*, and George Gascoigne's equally paradigmatic and influential *Adventures of Master F.J.* (1573–75). By removing the eclogue from romance, which differentiates *Ornatus and Artesia* from the *Arcadia*, Ford enhances the laws of plotting and makes his characters more

---

[33] Among the most popular of such manuals were Angel Day's *The English Secretorie* (London: Richard Jones, expanded ed., 1592), William Fullwood's *The Enimie of Idlenesse* (London: Henry Bynneman for Leonard Mayland, 1568), Nicholas Breton's *A poste with a madde packet of letters* (London: T. Creede for J. Smethicke, 1602), and William Fiston's *The welspring of wittie conceits* (translated from Italian; London, 1584). I am indebted to James Daybell for drawing my attention to Fulwood's, Breton's, and Fiston's works.

[34] Pruvost, *Matteo Bandello and Elizabethan Fiction*, p. 229ff.

psychologically independent (however rudimentary that psychology may appear to modern readers).[35]

In addition to the influence of Greek romance and its Renaissance imitators, there is a prominence of classical mythology. The myth of Pyramus and Thisbe from Ovid's *Metamorphoses* (IV.54–201) puts in an appearance, and the legendary story of Atalanta and Hippomenes is interwoven as a parody in chapter VIII in the episode in which Ornatus, dressed as Sylvian, delays the pursuing boar by throwing overripe apples in its path. In fact, given that the story of Ornatus and Artesia is one of victory (amorous and heroic) and escape, the myth of Atalanta and Hippomenes functionally fits the relationship between Ornatus and Artesia prior to their marriage ceremony. Likewise, the parting of the protagonists in chapter XV may have been modelled on the departure scene in Ovid's story of Ceyx and Alcyone (*Met.*, XI.537–48) in which Alcyone watches Ceyx sailing away. This generic situation may also echo the parting of Procris from Cephalus in the story "Cephalus and Procris" in George Pettie's collection *A Petite Pallace of Pettie His Pleasure* (1576). Moreover, the stories of Pyramus and Thisbe, Cephalus and Procris, and Ornatus and Artesia all originate in the same fictional *topos*, namely the story of the emotional suffering and tragedy of the young as a result of parental interference in their love leading to separation and the trials of absence.

The story of Pyramus and Thisbe was related in the Renaissance to the story of Romeo and Juliet, and both were associated with debates about the dangers of marriage based on the free choice of a mate. George Whetstone, for example, writes that "where Beautie, Loue, and Free choise, maketh the Mariage, they may be crossed by Fortune, & yet continue faithfull. Pyramus and Thisbe, Romeus and Iuliet, Arnalt and Amicla . . . were dispossest of their liues, but yet unstained with dishonesty."[36] The analogy between the story of Ornatus and Artesia and those of

---

[35] Already in Sidney, pastoral narrations and eclogues are meant to sound like performances (for example, for the court in exile), suggesting to Paul Alpers the author's "discomfort" (*What Is Pastoral?*, p. 348).

[36] George Whetstone, *Aurelia. The Paragon of Pleasure and Princely Delights* (London: Richard Iohnes, 1593), sig. H4ᵛ, STC 25338.

Pyramus and Thisbe further situates Ford's fiction in the tradition of the Renaissance debate about Fortune's role. Sylvian's insistance that it was "their parents' cruelty, but not their love" (ch. v) that drove those mythical lovers to their death, together with the fact that Ornatus and Artesia not only overcome obstacles to their courtship but death itself in order to marry, demonstrates a very real resistance to the influences of Fortune.

Ornatus and Artesia and the Story of Romeo and Juliet

The echoes of the love story of Romeo and Juliet in *Ornatus and Artesia* call for a brief assessment of Ford's possible indebtedness to Shakespeare or to other readings of this famous story. The enmity between the two noble families, the Montagues and the Capulets, and the clandestine love that arises between their children are analogous to the situation in *Ornatus and Artesia*: the old feud between Ornatus's father, Allinus, and Artesia's father, Arbastus. (The feud is over the death of Renon, Allinus's brother, believed to have been murdered by Arbastus's men.) J.J. Jusserand takes the Shakespeare connection for granted, not only in this, but in *Parismus* as well, concluding that "had his purpose been to show his contemporaries the height of Shakespeare's genius by giving, side by side with it, the measure of an ordinary mind, he could not have tried better or succeeded less."[37] This is the aside of a bardoloter ambiguously caught between admiration for Ford's success with the common reader and his disdain for Ford's literary achievement. In essence, Jusserand meant that Ford "succeeded more" not "less" in proving the ordinariness of his mind beside the Shakespearean genius. The potential influence of *Romeo and Juliet* on Ford's fiction is hardly surprising given the play's success on the boards. The play was in fact pilfered by many.[38] Nevertheless, the feuding-family motif, per se, was by no means specific to Shakespeare, allowing that even the Shakespeare-Ford axis is as provisional as the other source attributions.

[37]Jusserand, *The English Novel*, p. 195.

[38]*The Shakespeare Allusion-Book*, I, p. xxxv. This source does not refer to Emanuel Ford.

There are fewer echoes of the Romeo and Juliet story in *Ornatus and Artesia* than in *Parismus*, making the matter of sources even less clear. That Ford refers to reading, not watching, the story suggests that he may have had in mind one of the printed versions, whether Arthur Brooke's poem, or the Englished version of Bandello's *The Tragical Historye of Romeus and Juliet*, first printed in 1562. This translation went through two more editions (1567 and 1587) before Ford wrote *Ornatus and Artesia*. Linking the names of Pyramus and Thisbe to Romeo and Juliet in the context of a family feud and the tragic fate of young lovers, as René Pruvost shows, seems to have been common in English Renaissance prose fiction printed between 1562 and 1583, as in Bandello's version of the story,[39] and in George Pettie's *A Petite Pallace of Pettie His Pleasure* (1576).[40] The effect in Pettie, as Robert Maslen observes, is to rank "the contemporary novel alongside Ovid's fables" much as Ford does in reinforcing a popular narrative through alignment with a canonical exemplum.[41] In addition to the possible printed sources, a long tradition of the story of Romeo and Juliet in Renaissance oral culture might have contributed to Ford's knowledge of the story, as well.[42]

Nevertheless, to rebalance the options, Ford was writing closer to the date of the early productions of Shakespeare's play and to its 1597 memorial reconstruction printed in quarto, than he was even to the third edition of Brooke's translation, published in 1587. The play was first performed between 22 July 1596 and 17 March 1597, and Ford may have seen it in London. In 1598 John Marston, in *The Scourage of Villanie* (Satire 10), refers to a

[39]See Pruvost, *Matteo Bandello and Elizabethan Fiction*, pp. 13, 16, 44, 71–72, 75, 84, 93–94.

[40]See Bullough, *Narrative and Dramatic Sources of Shakespeare*, I, p. 374.

[41]Robert W. Maslen, *Elizabethan Fictions: Espionage, Counter-Espionage, and the Duplicity of Fiction in Early Elizabethan Prose Narratives* (Oxford: Clarendon Press, 1997), p. 190.

[42]For the history of the Romeo and Juliet story in the Renaissance, see Chambers, *William Shakespeare*, I, pp. 345–56. For different versions of the Romeo and Juliet story and their adaptations in Renaissance England, see Bullough, *Narrative and Dramatic Sources of Shakespeare*, I, pp. 269–76.

performance at The Curtain.[43] Thus the earliest production of *Romeo and Juliet* and the first written record of a performance of it fall around the time when Ford would likely have been working on his romance. The play was also mentioned in Francis Meres's *Palladis Tamia* (1598), which came out shortly before *Ornatus and Artesia* was published. That is as much as can be ventured.

Geographical Romance: Phrygia and Natolia

Although it cannot be argued definitely that the eastern Mediterranean geography of *Ornatus and Artesia* was influenced by Renaissance geography or literature concerning travel in the Levant, or by the descriptions of the countries of Asia Minor found in the geographical and ethnographic writing of Ford's time, there are some obvious similarities between what he says about this region and his contemporaries' knowledge and cultural depiction of it. Renaissance maps and their impact on the writer should be seen as part of a larger cultural context within which his romance originated, rather than as direct sources that determine the settings of his fiction. With that caveat in mind, it becomes instructive to point out that Abraham Ortelius (*Theatrvm orbis terrarvm*, 1570, fol. 52) locates Phrygia within Natolia; the map in the 1560 edition of the Geneva Bible shows it stretching westward to the coast of the Sea of Marmara.[44] Robert Stafforde, a Renaissance geographer, says that "Natolia, or Asiaminor [*sic*], is limited on the West with the Archipelago, on the South with the Mediterranean Sea, on the East with the Riuer Euphrates, and on the North With Pontus Euxinus [the Black Sea]" (G3^{r}-^{v}).[45] In Ford's literary geography, Natolia figures as one country, but in ancient times it was known as a large region composed of a number of smaller independent countries, including Phrygia. The boundaries that constituted Natolia were either unstable or non-existent when Renaissance cartographers drew their maps of the region; hence in Ortelius and Mercator Natolia is represented as one country, and this is how Ford represents it as well.

[43]Chambers, *William Shakespeare*, I, p. 346.

[44]*The Geneva Bible*, a facsimile of the 1560 edition, ed. Lloyd E. Berry (Madison: University of Wisconsin Press, 1969), sig. 69^{v}-70^{r}.

In an extended and episodic account of the fame of Phrygia and its demise under the Turks, Richard Knolles frequently refers to wars between various countries of Natolia, including Phrygia and Armenia, locations that also appear in *Ornatus and Artesia*.[46] Among fiction writers, Ford is the only one who uses Natolia, and with the one exception of *Parismus*, where it is substituted with Getulia, it features as a central location in all of his romances. Since Natolia was held by the Turkish armies, in the Renaissance imagination it became a logical setting for the clash between Christians and Turks, and for displays of power, heroism, and militant masculinity. That *Ornatus and Artesia* might have been considered during its time as part of the growing literary interest in the eastern Mediterranean can be seen in the Folger Shakespeare Library copy, which survives in a contemporary binding, bound together with four other fictional histories and romances printed in the seventeenth century. What these texts have in common is their connection with Turkey and the eastern Mediterranean. Whoever put them together may have considered them in some way related.[47]

The same cultural geography that appears in Christopher Marlowe's *Tamburlaine* and reflects his "fascinated interest in the geography of the Middle East"[48] also underlies the narrative of *Ornatus and Artesia*. Upon hearing that "[p]roud *Tamburlaine* intends [to conquer] *Natolia*" (1.1.53),[49] Orcanes, king of

[46]Richard Knolles, *The Generall Historie of the Turkes* (London: Adam Islip, 1603), sig. M4^r.

[47]The short-title contents read "1. The admirable adventures of / Clodoaldus, / 2. That Life & death of Almansor a Mahometan King / 3. The His[tory]: of Ornatus & Artesia / 4. Pheander the Mayden Knight / 5. The pilgrim of Casteele." (Folger 4294, copy 2). The texts in this volume were printed in 1634, 1627, 1619, 1617, and 1623 respectively. The volume, which bears the initials "B R," could have been bound for the owner, which was the case with books bearing initials.

[48]N.W. Bawcutt, ed., "Introduction," *The Jew of Malta*, The Revels Plays (Manchester: Manchester University Press; Baltimore: Johns Hopkins University Press, 1978), p. 5.

[49]*Tamburlaine*, Part II, in *The Complete Works of Christopher Marlowe*, ed. Fredson Bowers, 2nd ed., Vol. I (Cambridge: Cambridge University Press, 1981). All quotations from Marlowe's play are from this edition.

Natolia, in part II of *Tamburlaine* (1592), describes the importance of his kingdom: "the Center of our Empery'/ Once lost, All *Turkie* would be overthrowne: / And for that cause the Christians shall have peace" (1.1.55–57). And the military alliances that Orcanes proposes in his encountering with Tamburlaine — "we will march from proud *Orminius* mount / To faire *Natolia*, where our neighbour kings / Expect our power and our royall presence, / T'incounter with the cruell *Tamburlaine*" (2.2.2–5) — are similar to those in *Ornatus and Artesia*. In chapter XIII, for example, Allinus seeks help from Turbulus, the Armenian king, to counter Thæon, the usurping king of Phrygia, who is seen as a menace to Natolia. Thus *Ornatus and Artesia* engenders the same kind of fascination with the political geography of the Mediterranean in general as in Marlowe's *The Jew of Malta* and Shakespeare's *Othello*, and more particularly with the near and middle East following the trend set by Marlowe's *Tamburlaine*.

In the Renaissance, Phrygia was considered poor and subjugated by the Turks, even though the country had once been an important trading post on the major commercial route to Smyrna. Herodotus suggests that Phrygia was also known as the country of a most ancient people with a distinct non-Oriental culture and civilization.[50] In his English translation of Ortelius's Latin descriptions of these geographical locations, W. Bedwell expands his original by referring to "[t]he miserable estate and condition" of Natolia and Phrygia.[51] By contrast, Ford's allusion to the "rich and renowned country of Phrygia" is part of the romance convention based on situating stories in either ancient or mythical lands and giving them historical resonances, in this case linking Phrygia to ancient Troy. In Ford's Phrygia, Troy's heroic past is replaced with a mixture of romantic and chivalric adventures and with piratical abductions of men and women in love. In creating such a narrative of piracy and abduction, Ford blends the Hellenic with the piratic eastern Mediterranean of the

[50] See *Euterpe: being the second book of the famous History of Herodotus*, trans. B.R. (London: Thomas Marshe, 1584), STC 13224.

[51] Abraham Ortelius, tr. W. Bedwell, *Theatrum orbis terrarum. The Theatre of the World* (London: Iohn Norton, 1606), fol. 112, STC. 18855.

Renaissance. He, moreover, associates the country with the war for just rule, while both his fictional Phrygia and Natolia are lands of commerce, trade, and wealth. As places of danger and pleasure, the Natolia and Phrygia of *Ornatus and Artesia* are fantasy lands with an historical name and a loosely defined past. Ford's interest in Armenia, though small, may not be altogether insignificant. The many fanciful beliefs of the sixteenth and seventeenth centuries included the idea that Armenia was one of the three "competing locations" for the earthly paradise (the other two were Mesopotamia and the Holy Land) according to the commentators on Genesis.[52] Hence it often features as a background for romances. As one of the earliest Christian nations to fall to the Turks, however, Armenia was a place whose decline suggested, in the cultural fantasy of the Renaissance, subjugation by the Turks. Echoes of this culturally imagined Armenia, one in which paradise and politics converge, resonate in *Ornatus and Artesia*. Complicating these echoes is a literary tradition in which the eloquence of Edenic bliss often characterizes the language of courtship and the topography of romance narratives,[53] and in which romance involves war. We see this interlacing of cultural and literary traditions in Ford's ambivalent location of the romantic narrative on the threshold of Armenia. From his Armenia come both the peacemaking ambassadors and the unruly bandits who help Allinus in battling the Natolians.

Set in an historical context in which English merchant ships are threatened by Moorish pirates and in which Phrygia and Natolia are at war, *Ornatus and Artesia* illustrates how romantic fiction evokes both the past and contemporary realities: the English interest in the trading routes and markets of Turkey and the anxiety over pirates who threatened the trading routes of the English merchant ships and their enterprises. Broadly speaking, then, one might argue that, much like Asia Minor in Sidney's

[52] Jean Delumeau, *History of Paradise*, p. 160.

[53] For the *topos* of paradise in romance literature, see Ernst Robert Curtius, *European Literature and the Latin Middle Ages*, tr. Willard R. Trask (New York: Pantheon Books for the Bollingen Foundation, 1953), pp. 82–83, p. 244.

Figure I.   Map of Phrygia.
George Sandys, *A Relation of a Iourney begun An:Dom*, 1610,
sig. A3^r, detail, RB 93571. Reproduced by permission of
the Huntington Library, San Marino, California.

New Arcadia, Ford's Natolia in *Ornatus and Artesia* stands for "a
fallen but aspiring world of warfare and love."[54]

The reference to the war between Natolians and Armenians
in *Ornatus and Artesia*, though a product of Ford's literary imagination, evokes an historical reality, namely that most of Asia
Minor was dominated by the Turks following a series of historical events leading to its fall from Christian hands, events
that are well documented in such works as Knolles's history of
the Turks. When, for instance, Ford writes about how Turkish

[54]Elizabeth Dipple, "The Captivity Episode and the *New Arcadia*,"
Journal of English and Germanic Philology 70:3 (July 1971): 426, 418–31.

pirates were helped by Armenian pirates and Saracens in their conquest of Phrygia and in the ruin they caused there, his narrative echoes precisely the kind of military support among the infidels that the Turks received from various vassals and subordinate nations when they embarked on the conquest of Asia Minor and Armenia.[55] The defeat of the Armenians and the restoration of justice and a new rule in Phrygia not only fulfil a generic requirement of romance, a shift from political unruliness to harmony, but they also create the fantasy of restoring order in a region threatened by unruly infidels, especially Turks and Saracens. At first glance, the influence on eastern Mediterranean geography in Renaissance romances may not be very different from its presence in ancient romances. In both, this topography suggests the exotic, a place in which miracles are possible and mysteries abound, while, at the same time, reminding readers of the current political and historical realities gripping this region.

The deployment of eastern Mediterranean geography in *Ornatus and Artesia* and other geographical romances becomes a form of literary archaeology and anthropology that excavates for its popular readership the long-lost lands and cultures of the pre-Turkish Asia Minor of antiquity and early Christianity. This nostalgia for the Aegean coast of Asia Minor can be seen as a version of the Renaissance recovery and reshaping of the classical past, of its history and cultural values.[56] Links with the historical and geographical context of the eastern Mediterranean make

---

[55]One of the most popular sources for the Renaissance knowledge of Turkish history and the geography of Asia Minor and the Levant was Richard Knolles's encyclopaedic work entitled *The Generall Historie of the Turkes*. Knowles describes how Cutlu-Muses "subdued . . . a great part of Armenia" with the help of his sons, kinsmen, and soldiers gathered from various parts of Turkey (B6^r). It seems that romance writers in their narratives imitate this sort of military alliance.

[56]It might also be seen as the early modern fantasy that the Saracen empire be defeated and converted to Christianity. This fantasy is satirized, for example, in *The Tragical History, Admirable Achievements and Various Events of Guy of Warwick, Written by B.J.*, printed in London in 1661 but, as Helen Cooper argues, possibly dating back to the early 1590s. See Helen Cooper, "Did Shakespeare Play the Clown?," *Times Literary Supplement* (April 20, 2001): 26.

Ornatus and Artesia a romance in which the cultural discourses of space, politics, and alterity are woven through a narrative of sexual and emotional maturation. Historical geography becomes in Ford's romance a domain "of interest and pleasure,"[57] in that the narrative that evokes them situates both interest and pleasure beyond the preoccupations of the author's own world.

These multifarious influences, sources, and intertexts ought to be seen as signs of a moment in English literature, for during the 1590s there was an urgent need to absorb foreign traditions and influences and to shape them into a new national literature; this national "program" has been called "the *mundus* of English culture."[58] The dense web of interwoven sources, echoes, and influences makes the narrative of *Ornatus and Artesia* "an art of manipulating complexity."[59] Thomas Greene refers to a large number of cultural and stylistic influences, imported and acquired into one culture and reshaped in the form of a "broad and disorderly semiotic universe" (*The Light in Troy* 20), resulting in a new body of literature which, around the 1590s, was important to the formation of a national literary canon, as well as to an increase in literacy and to the vernacular as the language of literature. *Ornatus and Artesia* expands the genre of romance by incorporating elements of contemporary culture, ideologies and domestic affairs, by making use of geography and travel literature, and by creating literary extensions of the relationships between the nobility and the nascent middle-class, kinship, and patriarchy.

Genre

The narrative style and tone of *Ornatus and Artesia* make it part of the tradition of neo-chivalric romances — romances which, like Sidney's *Arcadia*, embody "a nostalgia for Elizabethan heroic

---

[57] Michel de Certeau, *The Writing of History*, Trans. Tom Conley (New York: Columbia University Press, 1988), p. 9.

[58] Thomas M. Greene, *The Light in Troy: Imitation and Discovery in Renaissance Poetry* (New Haven and London: Yale University Press, 1982), p. 20; emphasis in the original.

[59] de Certeau, *The Writing of History*, p. 7.

values."[60] Those romances gained in popularity during the last two decades of the sixteenth century when the rise of national sentiment under Queen Elizabeth was strong. As a chivalric romance, *Ornatus and Artesia* incorporates a number of generic literary traditions. On the one hand, it is a story of danger, adventure, abduction, shipwreck, captivity, and war. These characteristics bring Ford's creation close to the Greek romances of Heliodorus and Achilles Tatius. On the other hand, the narrative of *Ornatus and Artesia* deals with the various stages in the emotional and sexual maturation of two young heroes. One might argue, then, that Ford's romance is a kind of Renassaince *Bildungsroman*, one that includes "sexual awakening, sexual conflict, and the resolution in love . . . toward the rewards [of] . . . romantic love and marriage."[61] The affective experiences of lovers are the gist of Renaissance romances. The story includes an individual's experience with homesickness, the pain of separation, and the thrill of finding a lover believed to be lost, fears for the missing beloved, the pressures of solitude and social exclusion, sadness due to separation from friends, the resolution of will and strength of character to endure dangers and threats to life (and chastity), physical resistance to evil, emotional and sexual maturity, and an enduring hope for reunion with the missing lover.

These generic features had already been prepared for by the new orientation in romance fiction toward civic and personal, rather than chivalric, concerns, and they had been affected by the style of late sixteenth-century fiction. The "profane story" of *Ornatus and Artesia* belongs fully to this novel ethos. Margaret Tyler tells the reader of her translation of Diego Ortuñez de Calahorra's *Espejo de cavalleros* that this new form of writing has for its "purpose . . . to animate . . . and to set on fire the lustie courages of you[n]g gentlemen, to the aduancement of their line."[62] Even though Tyler wrote this comment some twenty years before *Ornatus and Artesia* appeared, her words

[60]Salzman, "The Strang[e] Constructions," p. 113.

[61]Jan Cohn, *Romance and the Erotics of Property: Mass-Market Fiction for Women* (Durham: Duke University Press, 1988), p. 153.

[62]*The Mirrour of Princely deedes and Knighthood*, trans. Margaret Tyler (London: Thomas East, [1578]), A3[r], STC 17978.

anticipate Ford's preoccupation with masculinity, virility, matrimony, and social advancement, together with such issues as lineage, wealth, travelling and trade, the conflict between Christians and non-Christians in the Levant, and Renaissance English culture's apprehension over piracy, violence, governing, and politics. Therefore, Ford's romance can appeal as an heroic tale, a patriotic work, and an erotic romance all at once, making it a new Elizabethan amalgam emerging from a conflation of forms.[63]

Style

Ornatus and Artesia reveals the propensity of Renaissance fiction to absorb neologisms and archaisms, and to indulge in a complex playfulness involving tropes and figures. Despite this linguistic richness, however, its style is not excessively euphuistic, nor is it overly ornamental, though the syntax is at times cumbersome. In fact, in the testimonial note at the end of *Parismus*, one of Ford's contemporaries, L.P. (very likely Lazarus Pyott, the pseudonym of Anthony Munday), says that Ford's "stile" is "(though plaine), yet so pleasing" (Gg3[r]).[64] The relative absence of euphuistic ornaments, especially after the first two chapters, makes for a quick-paced narrative that enables Ford to focus on plot. Nevertheless there are euphuistic touches, among them the reference to the mythical bird Celos, the bird of forgetfulness, Artesia's allusion to the flower called heart's ease (ch. II), and the references to the mythical and exotic herb artas and the bird akanthus; these are residues of an older tradition that here create stylistic ornateness. Artesia's "euphuisms," particularly those occurring in chapters II and V, convey her inability to find the causes of her grief in the absence of love. Debating with

---

[63]In *Ornatus and Artesia* we see how, "[i]n assimilating some heterogeneous and divisive material, the new [Renaissance] fiction sought to explore areas of friction and conflict among competing sites of authority." See Robert Weiman, *Authority and Representation in Early Modern Discourse*, ed. David Hillman (Baltimore: Johns Hopkins University Press, 1996), p. 120.

[64]Quoted from Emanuel Forde, *Montelyon: Knight of the Oracle*, a modern edition, ed. Anne Falke (Salzburg: Institut für Anglistik und Amerikanistik, Universität Salzburg, 1981), p. xxv.

Adellena about the nature of love in chapter II, for example, she concludes that it "is but a vanity that troubleth one's cogitations," and that only a fool "will love so deeply without hope or reward." In chapter V, when something has stirred her feeling upon first seeing Ornatus, she is not able to articulate that new feeling; balanced phrasing and the either/or of antithesis become the perfect vehicles for expressing the novelty of infatuation:

> Is love of such a force to draw one into these extremes? Then may I compare it to the herb artas found in Persia, who being but holden in the hand causeth a heat through all the body. . . . It may be he [Ornatus] hath hired her [Artesia] to do this [ask Adellena to convey his love to Artesia] and thereby I may be deceived, yielding to pity when there is no cause, and with the bird akanthus ready to come at every call.

But generally, as Ford's story develops and his characters mature through experience, the artificial and impersonal style becomes more individual and free of rhetorical clichés. Later, when Artesia rejects Lenon's love, the style has lost its earlier euphuistic ornateness:

> I know not how to accept of your love, being yet so far from knowing what it is that if I should but dream thereof my heart would be out of quiet. Besides, many cares continually attend the same, and my mean estate so far unworthy thereof, with innumerable other discontents and cares that I should make myself subject unto, . . . Therefore, I entreat you to settle your love elsewhere more agreeable to your estate and fancy, for I shall think myself most fortunate if I never fall into that labyrinth of disquiets, but will, during my life, labor to keep myself free from love's bands. (Ch. V)

The affective situation is the same as in chapters II and V — the refusal of love is the effect of the inexperience of it. But, after she has had several meetings with Ornatus, Artesia's language becomes more direct and natural. In the "Epistle," Ford has already announced this change in the style, telling his readers that his "unpolished history . . . wanting the ornament of eloquence fit for rare invention, presenteth itself in his natural and self-expressing form, in well applied words, not in tedious borrowed phrases." In *Ornatus and Artesia*, figurative language gives way to the plain. The syntax, likewise, begins to match the realism of

the action and the characters' behaviors. In chapter IX, for example, Adellena's swift report is a matter for syntactical efficiency:
"Adellena, brooking no delay, which in those affairs was dangerous, stood not to imitate of those griefs . . . but with all haste
returned to Artesia," to tell her that Ornatus has been banished.
Such developments parallel the withdrawal from the euphuistic
and the artificial generally in the prose of the 1590s.

   That change, simultaneously, was a reaction to a specific type
of ornamentation that characterized John Lyly's *Euphues*: an excessive use of tropes and figures in all manner of contrasting
rhetorical situations.[65] It was accompanied by a series of argu-
ments by contemporary rhetoricians, now recommending that
writers master styles up and down the registers of prose expression, simply designated in classical terms as the low, the
middle, and the lofty. In *The Arte of English Poesie* (1589), George
Puttenham says that a "[p]oet [should] follow the nature of his
subiect, that is if his matter be high and loftie that the stile be
so to, if meane, the stile also to be meane."[66] Non-fiction prose
and fiction — usually Sidney's *Arcadia* was quoted as an example
of the latter — were considered lower genres because their subjects were not high. They dealt with human desires (not politics,
law, or religion), and hence called for a plainer style, with only
occasional indulgences in the middle style.

   The rhetorician John Hoskins, for example, considered plain
style a virtue of the language. In *Directions to Speech and Style*
(1599), he says that to write in the plain style "is not to be curious
in the order . . . but both in method and word to use," and
he defines the style as "diligent negligence." Hoskins's major
advice is that style "followeth life, which is the very strength and
sinews, as it were, of your penning, made up by pithy sayings,
similitudes, conceits, allusions to some known history, or other
commonplace."[67] To follow life in telling stories, he suggests, is to
use rhetoric and to emulate or copy earlier, presumably ancient,
references and texts; this concept is what was at the center of
the humanist practice of imitation. Such use of rhetoric was

---

[65]Staton, "The Character of Style in Elizabethan Prose," p. 198.

[66]Puttenham, *The Arte of English Poesie*, p. 149.

[67]Hoskins, *Directions for Speech and Style*, p. 7 (emphasis in original).

INTRODUCTION 37

particularly suited to fiction, which contributed to the expansion
of vernacular literary prose (a new genre) and the demand to
adapt ordinary speech to the new uses of art in such prose.[68] It is
Lyly who, in *Pap with a Hatchet* (1589), reacts against his own style
in *Euphues* and defends the "old vaine," that is, low style, that
was less excessive and varied in ornamentation.[69] In practice,
Sidney, Greene, and Anthony Munday had already absorbed
some of those debates in their new fiction when Ford appeared
on the literary scene. His insistence on argument, not ornament,
is a clear sign of the new style in prose fiction.

Ford very often "followeth life" in his style in *Ornatus and
Artesia*. Compared to other romances, including the *Arcadia*, it
contains numerous examples of realism. In chapter III, a chapter
brimming with examples, Artesia is troubled by her first experiences of love. She tries to deflect some of her thoughts by picking
up a book to read. Unable to concentrate, she puts it back ner-
vously and attempts to sleep again, but forgets a burning candle.
Soon after, in a moment of rage, she tears up Ornatus's first letter,
but then picks it up again and pieces it together. In chapter X,
Ornatus uses the occasion of the shipwreck to grab a plank and
hit Luprates so hard on the head that his brains fall out — realism of a sort. In chapter XV, in the episode of the war between
the Armenians and the Phrygians, Ford describes how so much
blood was shed that the earth on the battlefield turned red. And
in chapter X, while in Flera's custody, Artesia first refuses to eat
but then realizes that eating will give her the strength she will
need to escape captivity. While these and other similar episodes
of realistic detail are meant either to produce a sensational effect
or to individualize the action, in other instances, such insets are
attempts to create psychological verisimilitude. Thus in chapter IX, Ornatus reflects back on the episode in which, after having
defeated Alprinus, he does not tell Lucida what has happened.
Ornatus says that

---

[68]Morris William Croll and Harry Clemons, eds., "Introduction," in
Euphues: The Anatomy of Wit and Euphues and his England by John Lyly
(1916; rpt. New York: Russell and Russell, 1964), p. lx.

[69]John Lyly, *The Complete Works*, ed. R.W. Bond (Oxford: Clarendon
Press, 1902), pp. 3, 396.

being alone by himself, having the wide world to travel into, but never a friend to go to, void of fear but not of care, he studied whither to direct his journey. Sometimes his conscience accusing him of too much disloyal dealing towards Lucida, in betraying her virtues by his dissimulation, in telling her Alprinus was living, when he knew it to the contrary. (ch. IX)

Such examples reveal how Ford uses the structure of his romance to represent a character's inwardness and to provide glimpses into consciousness itself. They are instances of how plain style best conveys the affective situation. The plain language of this passage is the language of self-reflection.[70] Ornatus's "dissimulation" to Lucida is part of the intrigue action of the plot, meant both to complicate the action and to move it forward. It enables Ornatus to leave Natolia in disguise, aided by Lucida, without drawing attention to Alprinus's absence.

The plain style, at the same time, may reflect a renewed acknowledgment of the roots of narrative in oral traditions. This "residual oralism"[71] of prose fiction, as Walter Ong argues, reflects the non-literary and still largely oral basis of Tudor English, and it also echoes the oral delivery and dissemination of earlier romance literature. Such conventions were characterized by a lack of amplification, elaborate argumentation, and divisions of proof. Orality and plainness in prose represent a joining of strengths.[72] Ford's fiction, therefore, may be looked upon as a representative example of the drive to accommodate that residual orality to the emerging print culture.

Plot

Although fortune plays some part in the plot of *Ornatus and Artesia*, it does not control the entire action as it tends to do in Greek romance. In Ford, characters have a controlling agency of their own, and the episodic nature of their stories is far less arbitrary in causal and motivational terms than it had been among

---

[70]Northrop Frye argues that reality is "for romance . . . an order of existence most readily associated with the word identity." See *The Secular Scripture*, p. 54.

[71]Ong, "Oral Residue in Tudor Prose," p. 149.

[72]Ibid., p. 151.

the Hellenistic writers. There are fewer characters, now related by overarching desires, the principals working mutually by intimations of a shared future, one which is not merely assaulted by misfortunes, but which, through the many episodes, seeks its own definition and resolution. Just as the hero and heroine must labor for their respective securities in a hostile world, each must labor to know the other's mind. Such a commingling of interiority and exteriority gives new meaning to the episodic, a new sense of self-determination, and stronger thematic design to the typically fragmented parts. In this way, Ford controls the episodic excesses of the romance genre he inherited.

Ornatus and Artesia opens in an atmosphere of hatred, mistrust, delusion, and suspected murder that foreshadow the tragic. The plot, divided between Phrygia and Natolia, is based on circumstantial reality, characterized by kidnappings, disguises, intrigues, wars, voyages, shipwrecks, and temptations — all of them obstacles to the heroes' "struggle for felicity."[73] This struggle begins when Ornatus discovers Artesia uncovered and sleeping in the shade of a tree. The birth of his love is the beginning of his wandering and searching. Their separation is maintained by a sequence of outside forces — storms, shipwrecks, pirates, abductions, war, and rivals. The first part of the plot, set in Phrygia, features disguise and escape and only brief encounters between the lovers. These adventures serve to test the quality and sincerity of their love. Artesia's friend, Adellana, plays a crucial role in arranging times and places for the lovers' trysts, and in carrying messages between them. Deferred marriage and prolonged courtship allow Ford to represent love, courtship, and sex as stages of maturation with their own protocols of behavior.

In Natolia, the plot is complicated by the war between the Phrygians and the Natolians, and by Ornatus's involvement in the battle against the usurping king of Phrygia. The shift in location from Phrygia to Natolia occurs only after the love between *Ornatus and Artesia* has been sufficiently confirmed to allow the narrative to move in new directions. The war against Thæon, which occupies much of the "Natolia" segment, is a rebellion against an immoral ruler, against injustice and crime. The plot,

---

[73] I borrow this phrase from Kinney, *Humanist Poetics*, p. 363.

which culminates with Ornatus's victory over Thæon, therefore demonstrates the victory of law over lawlessness. It also helps us measure Ornatus's self-advancement by his growing virtue in courtship and war. His experiences are necessary rites of passage in the self's pilgrimage toward glory and self-perfection. They test the constancy of his character.

Such romance narratives pose challenges for modern readers: as Lorna Hutson points out, the problem "emerges out of a conviction that if we find ourselves unable to imagine what reading strategies these narratives are inviting, it is because we no longer need to learn through reading what they are trying to teach us."[74] We intrench ourselves in our modern perspectives. But if we look at the plots of Renaissance fiction as conceptual structures that offer models for pragmatic action, and as imagined strategies for private causes, then in the rhetorical fiction of *Ornatus and Artesia*, patience, hope, endurance, and self-control, which have their equivalents in the rhetoric of humanist virtue, are presented as qualities of private and political virtue.

The Book Market and Critical Reception

The history of the critical reception of *Ornatus and Artesia* is connected to the expanding book market in Renaissance England. Locating *Ornatus and Artesia* within the context of that market helps us to see the history of Ford's romance in a new light quite different from the viewpoint of Ernest A. Baker, who assesses Ford's place in the history of English fiction as follows:

> To those who are interested in the vagaries of the herd instinct in matters of literary taste, Forde's enormous vogue furnishes material for a generalization which is not yet out of date. It is a curious incident in the literary history of the English, but has little to do with the history of English literature, unless in an indirect way, since it might be argued that the demand for rubbish is a deterrent to those who would write better.[75]

This assessment can, in fact, be turned on its head once it is accepted that "herd instinct" matters, and that the tastes of the

[74]Hutson, "Fortunate Travelers," p. 84.

[75]Baker, *The History of the English Novel*, Vol. II, pp. 124–25.

common reader have a place in history. The success of *Ornatus and Artesia* (the "curious incident" of Ford) should be seen as the result of a specific moment in early modern culture when the new literary tastes of the emerging mercantile-class reader started to have an impact on the book market and the production of popular fiction.

Ornatus and Artesia appeared at a time when an economically advanced England considered chivalry an ideal of the past, yet preserved a nostalgic longing for just such old-fashioned things. To be sure, the new mercantile class was preoccupied with civic ideals, with honor derived from social achievement, not from inherited right, including success in the domestic commercial market and on the overseas trading routes. The chivalric romance by these standards was a form of "pure escapism."[76] But for that same mercantile class, romances that celebrated chastity and marriage participated in contemporary issues and values; here was a way to join old procedures to new considerations. *Ornatus and Artesia* should also be seen as a product of the time in which the idea of civic nationalism was linked with the emphasis placed on the achievement of the "middle class," and in which the household and marriage were the units on which the order, wealth, and stability of the early modern state depended.

Ornatus and Artesia was printed in the heyday of the English printed quarto, namely the years between 1583 and 1640, when the guaranteed sales of commercial fiction enabled the emergence in England of both the professional writer such as Robert Greene, and the popular amateur, such as Emanuel Ford.[77] Thomas Creede, for example, not only had a monopoly on publishing Ford's work, but his printing house had a big output of other marketable prose, in addition to "quarto fiction," including practical works in husbandry and books of piety.[78] Records show that between 1595 and 1600, Creede's shop was particularly busy

---

[76]Spufford, "Portraits of Society," p. 234.

[77]Arthur F. Kinney, "Marketing Fiction," in *Critical Approaches to English Prose Fiction, 1520–1640*, ed. Donald Beecher (Ottawa: Dovehouse Editions, 1998), pp. 45–61.

[78]The earliest surviving copy of *Montelyon* bears the colophon of Bernard Alsop, but it can be still regarded as part of Creede's production.

printing fiction, encompassing everything that Ford was known to have written.[79]

The expansion of the market for fiction was made possible by a significant growth in literacy.[80] David Cressy calls this cultural shift "the educational revolution of 1560–1640."[81] The new literacy among the non-élite classes led to an increase in popular literature of a kind that reflects the aspirations and tastes of the "common" reader. At the end of the sixteenth-century, chivalric and romantic stories once directed toward aristocratic readers were adapted to the new class of readers. *Ornatus and Artesia* belongs to this moment.

Who read *Ornatus and Artesia*? Who bought it? One answer hails from gender criticism. Suzanne W. Hull argues that *Ornatus and Artesia* and related "recreational literature" was essentially "women's literature" because women are prominently featured

Alsop was Creede's partner who took over the business when Creede retired or died in 1617.

[79] My evidence derives from the second, revised and enlarged, edition of the STC. The romances printed in Creede's printing house include Henry Robarts's *Pheander, the Mayden Knight* (1595) and *Honours Conquest* (1598), *Hugh of Devonshire* (1600, 1612), and Robert Kittowe's *Loves load-starre* (1600); in 1597 and 1599 he shared the printing of the second part of Ford's *Parismus*, and in 1598 he also shared the printing of two parts of Anthony Munday's translation of *Palmerin d'Oliua* (1596); Thomas Nashe's *Pierce Penilesse* (1595), Robert Greene's *Alphonsus, King of Aragon* (1599); two anonymous romances, *The Historie of the two Valiant Knights, Syr Clyomon and Clamydes* (1599), and *The Honour of Chivalrie, Set Downe in the Historie of Don Bellianus* (1598).

[80] Halasz, *The Marketplace of Print*, p. 4; Keith Thomas, "The Meaning of Literacy in Early Modern England," in *The Written Word: Literacy in Transition*, ed. Gerd Baumann (Oxford: Clarendon Press, 1986); Lawrence Stone, "Literacy and Education in England, 1640–1900," *Past and Present* 42 (1969): 69–139. Newcomb, "'Social Things'"; Spufford, "First Steps in Literacy."

[81] Cressy, *Literacy and the Social Order*, p. 52. I use the term "popular" here in the somewhat anachronistic sense of including different groups of non-élite readers — men and women below gentle status — while not excluding the élite readers.

in the stories.[82] Helen Hacket concurs.[83] But there is no consensus on the matter insofar as Caroline Lucas urges that Ford did not write for women on the very grounds that men, not women, are central to his stories, concerned as they are with chivalry rather than love, leaving this approach an unpromising one.[84] Although traces of book ownership are sparse and tenuous, the few that remain in the form of handwritten marginalia suggest that romances were owned and read by men and women alike. The Folger copy of Richard Parry's *Moderatus* (1594), for example, bears the signature of Elizabeth Watson (sig. X3^r).[85] But a more extensive example of a male reader of romances is found on the last leaf of the Huntington copy of *The treasurie of Amadis of Fraunce*, a romance originally written in Spanish, where Thomas Chardelowe not only acknowledged owning the book but also wrote a short, mocking poem about it.[86] The dedication of *Ornatus and Artesia* to Bryan Stapleton of Carleton, a gentleman in

---

[82]Suzanne W. Hull, *Chaste, Silent, and Obedient: English Books for Women, 1475–1640* (San Marino: Huntington Library, 1982), p. 78. Anne Falke, in "Medieval and Popular Elements in the Romances of Emanuel Forde," pp. 249–51, also suggests that *Ornatus and Artesia* was meant to be read by women.

[83]Helen Hacket, *Women and Romance Fiction in the English Renaissance* (Cambridge: Cambridge University Press, 2000).

[84]Lucas, *Writing for Women*, p. 49.

[85]STC 19337.

[86]*The moste excellent and pleasaunt Booke, entituled: The treasurie of Amadis of Fraunce*, translated out of Frenche by T. Paynell (London: Henry Bynneman for Thomas Hacket, [?1572], STC 545):

Thomas Chardelowe ownd this book
goud give him grace on it to look if I it lose
and you it find I pray now be not
so unkind but give to me my booke
againe and I will please you for
yor payne the rose is read the leafe
is grene god pleasure our noble
king and queene but as for the
Pope god send him a roope and
a figge for the king of Spayne   (sig. R2^r).

the county of York, is not evidence enough to argue that Ford's
book targeted only men, and double-gendered prefaces in Robert
Greene's romances, for example, suggest that they were meant
to be read by both men and women.

The development of the book industry, itself, may proffer the
most telling evidence about fiction and the common reader. Romances were printed in blackletter, suggesting a "down market";
one conclusion might be that such imaginative literature was not
valued highly, compared, for example, to the Bible and legal
books.[87] But such categories are rarely so neat. The presumed
alignment between "lower" classes and popular romance is not
easily generalized. Peter Burke suggests that the line which
separates upper and lower class engagement with common literature is not a clear one.[88] Nevertheless, the lingering blackletter
formatting of *Ornatus and Artesia* perseveres as a marker of material designed for artisan readers, owners of shops, apprentices,
householders, and secretaries.[89] Thus Charles C. Mish contends
that "the steady stream of black-letter romances . . . indicate[s]
the conservativism of the middle-class reading public, which, indifferent to the claims or directions of the development of fiction,
continued to consume stories not only old-fashioned in content

[87]For example, in the dedicatory epistle to Walter (spelled Gvalter)
Borough in his translation of the second book of *Amadis de Gaula*, the
translator, "Lazarus Pyott" (i.e. Anthony Munday), clearly suggests that
his translation should be considered leisure reading, not worthy of a
prominent place in a young gentleman's study. He says: "although it
[this book] deserue no chiefe place in your studie, yet you may lay it
vp in some corner thereof, vntill your best leasure will afoord you some
idle time to peruse these abrupt lines of an vnlearned *Souldiour*, who
hath written plaine English, void of all eloquence" (sig. A3^{r}–^{v}).

[88]Peter Burke, *Popular Culture in Early Modern Europe* (New York:
New York University Press, 1978).

[89]Assessing Ford's work, Helen Hacket, for example, argues that
Ford's "derivative and formulaic" romances written in the late 1590s
"were aimed from the outset at a less aristocratic audience than the
Arcadia." Hacket, *Women and Romance Fiction in the English Renaissance*,
p. 128.

but old-fashioned in appearance."[90] Mish identifies this popular audience as one "at the same time insensitive to aesthetic considerations and desirous of an inexpensive book."[91] To this debate on the progressive-reactionary tastes of the common reader, there is no easy solution. But in brief, there is the simple fact of the many works of popular fiction from the period, presented in the form of episodic adventures surrounded by romance conventions which simultaneously champion "modern" attitudes toward love and marriage projected into fantasy settings and wish-fulfiling encounters, and packaged in cheap black-type editions, many of them made rare today by the first early-modern throw-away culture. Even so, the readership for *Ornatus and Artesia* and other popular romances was likely to have been both élite and common, male and female.[92] A rumor circulated that Edward de Vere, the Earl of Oxford and lord great chamberlain of England, was among the readership of romances.[93]

Ornatus and Artesia was printed at the peak of what Alexandra Halasz calls "the marketplace of print," the proliferation of the book trade, especially of "baggage books," such as romances, ballads, chapbooks, and pamphlets.[94] Ford calls his effort a "silly present" (sig. A3^V) and *Parismus* (part II) "simple work" (sig. A3^r). Similar derogatory terms such as "silly toys" and "trifle things" were frequently used by writers and critics to refer to their "baggage books," ambiguously intimating both false modesty and a very real sense of inferior status. That it was also an "alternative literature" represents a different point of critical departure, literature "written from a social perspective at variance with the dominant ideology."[95] This "popularization of the sophisticated [aristocratic] romance in the 1580s and 90s" inevitably gave rise to concerns among the élite that literacy might empower

[90]Charles C. Mish, "Black Letter as a Social Discriminant in the Seventeenth Century," *PMLA* 68 (June 1953): 629.

[91]Ibid.

[92]Newcomb, "'Social Things,'" p. 753.

[93]Wright, *Anthony Mundy*, p. 43.

[94]Halasz, *The Marketplace of Print*, esp. the chapters "Print Matters" and "Figuring the Marketplace of Print."

[95]Margolies, *Novel and Society in Elizabethan England*, p. 4.

commoners and that cheap fiction might cause a decline in moral values.[96] In terms of literacy, in fact, the middlebrow class of readers was becoming the dominant one, even when élite classes were the better educated. As Laura Caroline Stevenson's statistics show, when it came to mere literacy, the educated and aristocratic readers "were outnumbered [by literate commoners] approximately three to one."[97] Thus the authority of the privileged and stable highbrow religious and courtly discourses were challenged, as Halasz observes, by "the proliferation and variety of discourses in the marketplace of print" (4). It is in this light that one can interpret Meres's and Ascham's denunciations of the cheap and erotic romances that proliferated in the print market of Renaissance England.

The early success of this work as witnessed by its many editions is a significant and eloquent fact, not merely of popularity, but of a very real capacity to fulfil tastes and reward desires. No one familiar with the mixture of the romantic, the heroic, and the humorous in *Ornatus and Artesia*, or with its gamut of styles, would be bored by Ford's work. Judging by the number of printed copies and by recorded references, part I of *Parismus* was the most popular of Ford's romances. According to the "Epistle to the Reader," after his first attempt at publishing, he was somewhat hesitant about having *Ornatus and Artesia* printed. He did not think highly of this work, since, in the "Epistle" to *Parismus* (part I), he says, himself, that he "published this history at the entreaty of some of [his] familiar friends," and had "no intent to have it printed" — or so he said. This self-effacing humility and the urging of friends was a typical rationale for a gentleman who resorts to the crassness of the printing press. John Frampton, in his dedication to Edward Dyer, presented his translation of *The Most Noble and Famous Travels of Marco Polo* (1579) in precisely these terms. The initial popularity of *Ornatus and Artesia*, one that lasted for over a century, stands in stark contrast to Ford's low self-appraisal. Eight editions had been printed by 1700 and

[96]Salzman, *English Prose Fiction, 1558–1700*, p. 100.

[97]Laura Caroline Stevenson, *Praise and Paradox: Merchants and Craftsmen in Elizabethan Popular Literature* (Cambridge: Cambridge University Press, 1984), p. 57.

six abridgements (some of which were reissued several times) were published before the eighteenth century.[98] Compared, for example, to Cervantes's *Don Quixote*, which went through seven editions in all its English translations in the seventeenth century, the success of *Ornatus and Artesia* was remarkable. It was still popular when the sentimental novel of the eighteenth century came into vogue.[99] Meanwhile, its success in America may also be seen as an effect of a major revival of, and changing views towards, romance, which flourished in the eighteenth century.[100] Ford's contemporaries were rather critical of his work. In what is probably the first recorded reference to the *Ornatus and Artesia*, Francis Meres warns his readers that the book should be censored because, together with twenty-two other prose romances on his list, it is "no less hurtful to youth than the works of MACHIAVELLI."[101] Why this recommendation for censorship?[102] It appears to have arisen over the mixture of violence and erotic titillation that Roger Ascham alludes to when he dismisses the *Morte d'Arthur* for its "open mans slaughter and bold bawdrye: In which booke those be counted the noblest Knightes, that do kill most men without any quarell, and commit fowlest aduoulteres

---

[98]The other abridgements are 1669, 1683, 1684, 1688, 1694, and 1700.

[99]Morgan, *The Rise of the Novel of Manners*, p. 6.

[100]This revival led, for example, to the publication of Charlotte Lennox's burlesque romance *The Female Quixote* (1752), Thomas Wharton's *Observations on the Fairy Queen* (1754), two editions of *The Faerie Queene* (1758), and Bishop Hurd's *Letters on Chivalry and Romance* (1762).

[101]Francis Meres, "Sketch of English Literature, Painting, and Music, up to September 1598," *An English Garner: Critical Essays and Literary Fragments*, ed. Edward Arber and Thomas Seccombe (Westminster: Archibald Constable and Co., 1903), p. 22.

[102]The condemned romances on Meres's list include: *Palmerin de Oliva*, *Primaleon of Greece*, *The Mirror of Knighthood*, *Guy of Warwick*, Richard Johnson's *The Seven Champions of Christendom*, Robert Parry's *Moderatus*, *The Black Knight*, Henry Robarts's *Pheander, the Maiden Knight*, Anthony Munday's adaptations of *The Stories of Palladin and Palmendos*, and *Bevis of Hampton*.

by sutlest shiftes."[103] The "bold bawdrye" or, as one modern
critic calls it, the "low-keyed titillation" of *Ornatus and Artesia*,
not its violence, may be one of the reasons for Meres's denuncia-
tion, if his deprecations were more measured and selective than
a global blacking of an entire genre.[104] A closer look at the list
reveals Meres' particular dislike for all things derived from the
Iberian *Palmerin* or the French *Amadis* cycles of chivalric romance,
both of which came into vogue in the 1580s. Or, in the case of
Bevis of Hampton and *Guy of Warwick*, he targets the chivalric
chapbook versions of medieval heroic romances. Some of those
works are also dismissed as "stinking lies" (sig. D1^r) in Thomas
Tomkis's university play *Lingva, or the Combat of the Tongue and
the five Sences for Superiority* (1607).[105]

There is, moreover, the violation of mimesis that occurs in romance narratives insofar as the impossible is represented as if it
were possible. In this way, a rejection is justified on epistemo-
logical grounds tantamount to an assault on fiction in general for
its inability to represent truth. In Francis Kirkman's *The Unlucky
Citizen* (1673), for example, an apprentice youth who encounters
troubles and misfortunes while living in London claims that in
"reading *Montelyon Knight of the Oracle* and *Ornatus and Artesia*,
and the famous *Parismus*, I was contented beyond measure, and
believing all I read to be true, wished myself Squire to one of

---

[103] Roger Ascham, *The Scholemaster* (1570), rpr. London: Bell and Daldy
(1863); reissue, New York: AMS Press, 1967, p. 81. I have silently edited
the long "s."

[104] A.C. Hamilton, "Elizabethan Romance: The Example of Prose Fiction," *English Literary History* 49 (1982), p. 292.

[105] In his work *Lingva: or the Combat of the Tongue. And the fiue senses for
Superiority*, Tomkis attacks the following romances: *Myrrour of Knighthood*, *Beuis of Southampton*, *Palmerin of England*, *Amadis de Gaule*, *Huon
of Burdeaux*, *Sir Guy of Warwick*, *Garragantua* (sic), and *Gerillion*. Tomkis
attacked romances again in his comedy *Albvmazar*, printed in 1615. The
conventions of romance, such as disguise, the shepherd's life, exotic
locations, incredible adventures, and the rhetoric of female chastity, are
mocked in the anonymous play *A most pleasant Comedie of Mucedorus*,
published in 1598.

these Knights."[106] This youth reports a similar enthusiastic dis-
orientation and willing conflation of realities in seeing Marlowe's
Doctor Faustus, "especially when he travelled in the Air, saw all
the World, and did what he lusted" (10). Traveling, lusting, and
doing what one desires — daring manifestations of youth, individual freedom, temptation, and anxiety — often go together in
Renaissance romances to the dismay of the puritanical and the
literal minded.[107] For Ascham, the prowess of the romance hero
was in conflict with the humanist concept of education based on
the mastery of the liberal arts toward the creation of the loyal citizen and the courtier in conjunction with the "new" society based
on peace, harmony, and Christian justice.[108] Both humanists and
religious conservatives did not consider "glory" a virtue, such
as it was celebrated in war and passionate excess. The Puritan,
Richard Baxter complains that young people are "quickly corrupted and ensnared by Talebooks, Romances, Play-books, and
false or hurtful History."[109] Ben Jonson, too, in a meditation upon
the mutability and permanence of art, dismisses romances, won-
dering whether a poet's work must be doomed to perish, as if he
had "compil'd from *Amadis de Gaule*, / Th' *Esplandians, Arthurs,
Palmerins*, and / The learned Librarie of *Don Quixote*" (29–31).[110]
Later critics have maintained the attack on romance on similar
grounds, namely for their immorality, violence, and the violation of verisimilitude. With subtle contempt, the nineteenth-
century French critic J.J. Jusserand notices little variation in types
of events and adventures in Ford's "novels," all of which, he says,

[106]Francis Kirkman, *The Unlucky Citizen* (London: Anne Johnson for
Fra[ncis] Kirkman, 1673), p. 11, Wing 638.

[107]See Adams, "Bald Bawdry and Open Manslaughter," pp. 34–37.

[108]I borrow this phrase from the title of Susan Dwyer Amussen's book
An Ordered Society: Gender and Class in Early Modern England (Oxford:
Basil Blackwell, 1988).

[109]Richard Baxter, *A breviate of the life of Margaret, wife of Richard Baxter*
(London, 1681), sig. A2ʳ, Wing 1194.

[110]"An Execration upon Vulcan" (1640), in *Ben Jonson*, eds. C.H. Herford Percy and Evelyn Simpson. 11 vols. (Oxford: Clarendon, 1947),
VIII: 203–04.

contain "the same improbable monsters and wonders, and the same licentious adventures."[111]

There have been positive critical views of *Ornatus and Artesia*, however. Francis Kirkman, who avidly encourages his readers to read romances, in the preface to the second edition of his translation from the Spanish of *The Famous and Delectable History of Don Bellianis of Greece, or the Honour of Chivalry*, published in 1673, states: "[r]ead the Historyes of *Parismus* and *Parismenos*, *Montelion Knight of the Oracle*: And *Ornatus and Artesia*," which he "place[s] together, being all three written originally in *English*, by one Person, who indeed composed them very Ingeniously."[112] Kirkman's preface is both one of the few Restoration responses to Ford's work and a witness to the popularity of his and other Renaissance romances in the late seventeenth century.

The general favor that *Ornatus and Artesia* enjoyed both before and during the Restoration held into the eighteenth century. A popular abridgement, *The Famous, Pleasant, and Delightful History of Ornatus and Artesia*, published in 1688, went through two more editions by 1700. This abridgement follows the usual model for such reductions in preserving only the main plot line of the original. There was, as well, an anonymously published text, *The Most excellent history of Antonius and Aurelia* (1682).[113] This work, which does not identify Ford as the author of the text on which it is based, attempts to pass itself off as original work. Only recently has the provenance of *Antonius and Aurelia* been identified.[114] Plagiarism is perhaps an inverse form of endorsement which others in that age may have recognized, and hence there is no solution to the anomaly presented by this hoax in light

---

[111]Jusserand, *The English Novel*, p. 98.

[112]Francis Kirkman, *The Famous and Delectable History of Don Bellianis of Greece, or, the Honour of Chivalry: Containing His Valiant Exploits strange and dangerous Adventures, with his admirable love to Princesse Florisbella, Daughter to the Souldan of Babilon* (London, 1673), Wing 632A.

[113]The copy of this abridgement is in the Bodleian Library (Douce, A.271).

[114]Gaunt, *The Most Excellent History of Antonius and Aurelia*.

of the fact that the source text was still in circulation and bearing Ford's name.[115] Critical reception of *Ornatus and Artesia* in modern times has varied from lukewarm enthusiasm to near hostility. Consider the following comments: Ford's work "is not unhealthy, it satisfies no morbid cravings, offers nothing in the way of wish-fulfilment or opportunities for emotional orgies, the story is the opposite of exciting, the characterisation is so unpronounced and abstract as to give no scope for day-dreaming, and the style is sweetly detached and strictly unsentimental."[116] Coming from Q.D. Leavis, this "series of negatives" is meant to sound like a sign of "respect" for a writer with "an innocence . . . that no novelist after Richardson could exhibit."[117] The sort of innocence that Leavis attributes to Ford originates in his lack of pathos. Instead, Ford "cooly proceed[s] with the business of getting on with the plot" (90). For Leavis, the virtue of his romances lies precisely in the absence of pathos that often characterizes the genre. She further argues that Ford "turned out popular romances . . . that are by no means dreary but add to their originals a lively charm" (89). His "fresh innocence," she continues, "had a certain delicate beauty that the succeeding age replaced by hardy cynicism" (90), forgetting that Ford's era was also the age of "hardy cynicism" on the part of Marston, Riche, Lodge, Donne, and Jonson. A long opening passage from *Ornatus and Artesia* provides Leavis with an example of that "delicate beauty" in Ford's prose. Ornatus first sees Artesia while hawking and becomes mesmerized by her beauty. This is one of the most lyrical moments in the work,

---

[115]Another abridged edition of *Ornatus and Artesia* is in the Newberry Library (Case Y. 1565 F75) and is entitled *The Famous, Pleasant, and Delightful History of Ornatus and Artesia, Containing their Crosses and Success in Love, Caused by Prince Lenon, Son to Theon King of Phrygia* (London: for B. Deacon, [n.d.]); it was probably published in the late 1690s. It consists of eight chapters of plot summary, and contains a woodcut that represents Ornatus and Artesia as a Cavalier gentleman and lady respectively.

[116]Leavis, *Fiction and the Reading Public* (London: Chatto and Windus, 1932), p. 89.

[117]Ibid., p. 90.

a moment in which the narrative slips into a series of conventional clichés through which love was expressed in Renaissance
literature. These formulas included a catalogue-blason of the
beloved's body, trait-by-trait, and the lover's dream of desire, a
dream induced by his gazing. Although Leavis' criticism of Ford
is neither systematic nor substantial, it is significant because she
was the first modern critic to draw attention to Ford's work and
to suggest his importance in the development of fiction.

Margaret Schlauch's view is equally deprecating. "With
Forde's output we find ourselves in one of the blind alleys of
early modern fiction. Yet . . . these romances of his were often
reprinted and must have been widely read. They made their
contribution to the vogue for 'heroick' romances . . . later in the
17th century."[118] Of all Elizabethan imitators of what she calls
neo-chivalric works — hybrids of Greek and French romance —
she singles out Ford in what might seem a compliment to a
popular minor writer. But his apparent failure to influence his
successors appears grounds for a final dismissal. At the other
end of the spectrum, Jusserand, in his brief account of Ford, goes
so far as to say that "there was [up to the eighteenth century]
a far greater demand for [Ford's romances] than for any play
of Shakespeare."[119] He brings us back to the statistics of print
production as the marker of greatness and success.

More recently, Ford's method of characterization has been rejected as too simple, although the compositional and generic
features of his fiction, especially in *Ornatus and Artesia*, have
received more positive evaluation. Ford's heroes have been
called "wooden" because they "never fail, are never embar-
rassed,"and because "external action replaces any psychological analysis (even in the love scenes), and dialogue expressing
ideas of choice is entirely excluded."[120] But this statement is too
strong. Even though Ford's characters are not developed with
great psychological depth (they never are in romances, because,

[118]Margaret Schlauch, *The Antecedents of the English Novel, 1400–1600
(from Chaucer to Deloney)* (Warsaw: Polish Scientific Publishers; London:
Oxford University Press, 1963), p. 174.

[119]Jusserand, *The English Novel*, p. 193.

[120]Davis, *Idea and Act in Elizabethan Fiction*, p. 165.

to a greater or lesser degree, characters in romances are types, not individuals with independent psychologies), in *Ornatus and Artesia* there is a clear departure in character development: unlike the main characters in Ford's other works, both the hero and heroine in this work demonstrate a certain degree of psychological sophistication.

Ford has also been praised for some originality in his plotting. He "likes to introduce a baffling situation suddenly, to leave it in partial suspense, and to reserve development and explanations for a much later point in the story."[121] *Ornatus and Artesia* in particular has been considered a good example of the neo-chivalric romance in the vein of medieval romances,[122] and a work in which extreme emotions, such as love, honor, revenge, greed, and ambition, are treated with a certain amount of psychological realism, though not explored in greater depth.[123] Anne Falke dismisses "the sublime and ridiculous nature of physical love" (252) as a principal feature of the work's "situational comedy" (251). Yet the subtle eroticism of *Ornatus and Artesia* is part of the larger moral purpose of the romance — it titillates in order to allow the writer to construct the narrative of the hero's continence and to enable him to elaborate the topic of the defence of chastity on which much of the Renaissance literature of courtship focuses.[124] The frequent interruption of the narrative with letters exchanged between *Ornatus and Artesia*, in which the protagonists' emotions burst out, has led critics to consider *Ornatus and Artesia* a precursor of the eighteenth-century epistolary novel.[125] Characterizing most of these views is the implicit degree to which they take for their standards the achievement of the modern novel, with its emphasis on novelty of plotting and the interiority of character, searching always for their presence as the only criteria of

---

[121]Schlauch, *The Antecedents of the English Novel*, p. 172.

[122]Falke, "Medieval and Popular Elements in the Romances of Emmanuel Forde."

[123]Bonheim, "Emanuel Forde," p. 55.

[124]See my essay "Sexuality and Humanist Romance."

[125]Klein, *Der Romanbrief in der englischen Literatur vom 16. bis zum 18. Jahrhundert*, p. 154. Loiseau, *Le récit dans le roman d'Emmanuel Ford*, pp. 16–21.

excellence in such "precursors" as *Ornatus and Artesia*. But an appreciation of Elizabethan-style romance requires a greater effort in historical and aesthetic imagination, joining how we read for pleasure and experience with the ways they read to these same ends. So viewed, romance addresses itself to a rich array of desires and anxieties inscribed in the procedures of the genre, closer as it is than the novel to the symbolic and the allegorical in its quests and encounters and its overarching designs of separation, trial, endurance and reward. Romance is a genre of its own, half way between myth and the most concrete and contemporary forms of social representationalism. Measuring that mimetic place in relation to the Renaissance social "moment" and its salient questions is the leading critical challenge.

Eloquence, Love, and Narrative

Throughout *Ornatus and Artesia* the protagonists struggle to overcome obstacles to their love and to find the language that will express that love. Moreover, the resolution of such narratives of desire depends upon the characters' acceptance of the ways in which they have both articulated and achieved maturity. The eloquence of love in *Ornatus and Artesia* embodies the Platonic idea of virtue (*arete*) as a state of mind that accompanies actions. Plato asserts that "every action accompanied by a part of virtue is virtue . . . that every action accompanied by justice is virtue" (*Meno*, 79C).[126] In Platonic ethics, then, virtue in action is only possible if it accompanies justice. At the same time, for Ford, courtesy generates virtue, as Artesia says of Ornatus: "His courteous mind is the fountain of all virtue." The process carried out by the characters in *Rosalynde*, namely their movement through "various stages of preparation from general, flexible, impersonal, qualitative concerns of rhetoric to substantial, applicable, causistic fiction"[127] could also be said of the characters in *Ornatus and Artesia*. The lovers' reunion in Phrygia embodies the victory of virtue in love and politics over the usurping rule of improper desire.

---

[126]Plato, *Laches, Protagoras, Meno, Euthydemus*. I owe this reference to Arthur F. Kinney, *Humanist Poetics*, p. 383.

[127]Kinney, *Humanist Poetics*, p. 381.

In *Ornatus and Artesia*, from the outset desire is countered by self-control. When Ornatus lulls Artesia into sleep with his lute music (ch. V), the narrative of seduction mixes eroticism with the rational aestheticization of seduction. Seduced by music, Artesia blithely slumbers while Ornatus

> left off his play to surfeit himself with beholding her sweet beauty, in which he took such delight as almost ravished his senses, sometimes thinking whilst she slept to imprint a kiss upon her sweet ruddy lip, but fearing thereby to wake her and lose that delightful contemplation, he desisted, beholding each part of her visible form, which was most divine, his mind was affected with inward suppose what perfections her hidden beauties did comprehend, which his fancy persuaded him he did in conceit absolutely contemplate.

The emphasis in this set piece is on the voyeuristic nature of the gaze, which, here related to the ocular origin of love, is also linked to the neoplatonic idea that love enters the heart through the eye; but the topic is also Ornatus's self-control. The sublimation of eros entails that desire is now directed to his mind ("his mind was affected with inward suppose") and that what first appears to be the subject of lust (Artesia's body) is soon elevated to the level of contemplation.

Until Artesia first expresses her love for Ornatus, which happens shortly before the wedding ceremony, its intensity is measured by her actions and her ability to overcome external difficulties through moderation and effective eloquence. She says that Sylvian can do anything to her "that shall not disagree with modesty" (ch. V). But Artesia does not know that Sylvian is Ornatus, and, as far as she is concerned, she is engaged in a clandestine exchange of kisses with another person. The affair is not just a titillating artifice, for Ornatus seems to be aware of its implication. He "marvelled that all this time she spake not of him, which he devised to urge her to do by many occasions" (ch. VI). What Ornatus's reaction suggests, in fact, is that immature and inexperienced love is subject to error. Throughout *Ornatus and Artesia*, love is confronted not only with temptations, but it undergoes transformations as well. In the recognition scene (ch. XIII), when Ornatus casts off his pilgrim disguise, Artesia's joy of recognition, couched in the language of union and followed by the lovers' embraces and kisses, gives a new dimension to their love. As the narrative develops, the characters also develop, and so does their rhetoric, conditioned as it is by delayed gratification. While subjugation to Ornatus involves the subordination of Artesia's love, the loss of her independence also means, in her words, gaining "a true friend." Love unity expressed in terms of bonds of friendship was an element of the Renaissance philosophy of love, derived in part from Greek ethics. In a Renaissance treatise that weighs love against friendship, the speaker speculates that love-as-friendship is a condition of mind: "this loue is confirmed eyther by gifts or by studie of vertue, then goeth it from a passion, to a perfect habite."[128] Such an aspect of the mind leads toward constancy ("habite"), a goal that is translated in fiction as a matrimonial unity that sanctifies passions. Artesia's love-as-friendship is also based on mutuality, on likeness.[129] A similar appeal occurs in the relationship between Alprinus and Lucida, although Lucida's subordination to Alprinus is made part of a larger argument about love's virtue and its constancy. Her love is constant despite the fact that Alprinus has killed her brother. Alprinus's crime is only forgiven because of his honorable deed, his killing of the large boar that has menaced the citizenry. From a literary and cultural point of view, the issue here is not so much female subordination to male rule or the author's misogyny; it is how, in humanist fiction, virtuous and honorable acts erase hostility and enable the bonding of virtuous people.

Both Artesia's and Lucida's love speeches use rhetorical pathos as an emotional appeal to their lovers from whom they are frequently separated. Pathos is the technique through which passion is conveyed, and by giving structure to the expression of the self, as Kibédi Varga argues, it enables us to "reconstruct the

---

[128] *A philosophical discourse, entituled the Anatomie of Minde*, T[homas] R[ogers] (London: I[ames] C[harleswood] for Andrew Maunsell, 1576), sig. D2ᵛ, STC 21239.

[129] Pettie says in the story of "Icilius and Virginia," "true love and faythful friends is to will and to nill one thinge, to have one object of appetite, and to have like effect of affection . . . love may bee sayd generally to proceede of the similitude of manners." *Pettie, A Petite Pallace of Pettie His Pleasure*, p. 104.

system of the traditional psychology."[130] The critical danger here is to read these speeches, especially Lucida's, as the writer's misogynistic subordination of women and to ignore the fact that, in this instance, the emotional basis of pathos is a desire for unity, an appeal for emotional equality, not a scheme for a disproportionate power relationship. As its narrative of an arduous resistance to temptations suggests, *Ornatus and Artesia* challenges the Renaissance women's subjugation to men by exploring the freedom of its characters to choose their mates and by allowing the lovers to prove, through action and eloquence, their readiness for the love union. In *Ornatus and Artesia* and other popular romances of the Renaissance, the positive portrayal of women was, as Louise Schleiner argues, "the fictional world's counterpoise to Euphuist misogyny."[131]

When Artesia asserts her independence in resisting the advances of men who are neither honorable nor virtuous, whose love she explicitly rejects, her subordination to men is clearly denied. When not yet fully assured of Ornatus's love, she rebukes his advances: "It is in vain to use many words; neither am I like to those that will at the first seem coy but afterwards yield. But I desire you to be satisfied with that which I have already said, that I cannot love." The problem is, however, that the narrative warrants something different: Artesia turns out to be what she has just said she is not. At first she is coy, but before the nuptial rites, she yields to Ornatus and loses her virginity. And yet Ford does not allow her virtue to be suspect. When Artesia yields, she does so only after Ornatus has reciprocated her love for him — when, in other words, the narrative more or less ensures that her chastity will be respected and consequently sanctified by the nuptial rites. When love is equally shared and mutually desired, Artesia's subordination becomes a way in which mutuality of pleasure, rather than an admission of the loss of personal independence, is described.

[130] A. Kibédi Varga, "Rhetoric, a Story or a System? A Challenge to Historians of Renaissance Rhetoric," in *Renaissance Eloquence: Studies in the Theory and Practice of Renaissance Rhetoric*, ed. James J. Murphy (Berkeley: University of California Press, 1983), p. 90.

[131] Schleiner, "Ladies and Gentlemen in Two Genres," p. 2.

As they mature in love, Ford's characters move from the rhetoric of polished but formulaic persuasion to a plain rhetoric of the mutual recognition of love. We see this evolution best in Ornatus's letters to Artesia. His persuasive rhetoric follows the hortatory structure of praise framed around the procedures of weighing options — that is, in Thomas Wilson's terms, a speaker's attempt to "persuade or dissuade, entreat or rebuke, exhort or dehort, commend or comfort any man . . . to aduise . . . that thing which we think most needful for him."[132] The expression of love, for example, in Ornatus's first letter, aimed at moving Artesia to love him, contrasts the pressures of existence against which the mental and emotional sides are in conflict ("Extremity maketh me overbold, and despair maketh me more desperate in uttering my mind. I cannot choose but say I love you . . ."). The emphasis in the letter is on the self's need to be in control of circumstances: "though you hate, I must love; and though you forever deny to love, yet will I persist in constancy, for the worst I can endure is death." In contrast to Ornatus's rhetoric of felicity,[133] with which he fills his letters to Artesia, and which assures not only consensual marriage but also social advancement and prosperity, stands Lenon's destructive amorous fury. In chapter X, frustrated that Artesia does not reciprocate his love, Lenon, "being come to the palace betook himself in his chamber raging more like a mad man than a passionate lover, sometimes swearing, cursing, and stamping, yielding so much to that mad fancy that in the end he vowed to obtain Artesia's love, though he hazarded his life, honor and good name." His emotional outbursts correspond to his uncontrollable behavior in attempting to court Artesia.

Episodes involving the love of *Ornatus and Artesia* differ from the episodes in which Lenon expresses his love for Artesia and the ones in which Floretus, Arbastus's brother and Artesia's uncle, falls in love with Sylvian, believing him to be a woman. On the structural level, these episodes are designed to test Artesia's virtue and the lovers' constancy, but they are meant as well to

---

[132] Wilson, *The Art of Rhetoric* (1560), p. 70.

[133] Like Lodge, Ford in *Ornatus and Artesia* "refuse[s] to lose hope in felicity." See Kinney, *Humanist Poetics*, p. 363.

show that the only alternative to honorable and virtuous love is desire based on the violation of justice, on dissembling, and on dishonor. There is a qualitative difference between Ornatus's love for Artesia and Floretus's love for Sylvian. When love is based not on virtue but on malicious calculations, "torment" and "scorching penury" result (ch. VI). We see this outcome when, for instance, Floretus speculates that Sylvian's poverty and social isolation will bring her to submission; such love is accompanied not by virtuous actions but by tyranny and usurpation. In contrast, Ornatus's virtuous actions prevent him from becoming a victim of disillusionment, despite the obstacles that repeatedly hinder him from reaching Artesia.

In order to obtain Artesia, Lenon hires Sylvian as a liaison while plotting to murder Ornatus; he asks him, disguised as a pilgrim, to keep her in custody in the green fortress; he seeks help from the pirates who abducted Artesia; he hires Flera to keep her imprisoned; and finally he lies to the court about his plot. Artesia's eloquent rejection (ch. X) of Lenon is a carefully constructed artifice aimed at downplaying her virtue, which is necessary here to dissuade Lenon from courting her. But the truth, plainly expressed to Ornatus (ch. XIII), is that Lenon's attention "is most hateful unto me and injury to you." Because she believes in love based on virtue and honor, Artesia's disappointment in Lenon, in a prince who resorts to such low means of assuring love, also represents a form of rejection of unvirtuous love. It is not his threats (rape) that she fears but his love ("not that he used her unkindly but that he loved her"). It is not just his brutality that she abhors but his intemperate desire ("not fearing his cruelty but his lust"). In rejecting Lenon, Artesia rejects lust, a kind of passion that lacks reason.[134] This and other rejections of improper suitors, such as Floretus and Luprates, suggest the extent

[134]In a treatise on the ethics of love, lust is described as "a desire raised against reason," and one that "in whomsoeuer it raignes, so killeth all good motions, that vertue can haue no place in the minde of him." *A philosophical discourse*, sig. C3ᵛ–C4ʳ.

to which Artesia has to fight for her independence in choosing a mate.[135]

What may appear as a random organization of narrative and as a monotonous repetition of orations and letters formulated around a series of rhetorical clichés represents, in fact, a way in which humanist romance fiction is structured. Coherence of time in the structuring of the episodes is not needed in order to make the fiction's argument plausible. Since one of popular fiction's roles is to be didactic, experiential, and ritualistic, it is the characters' actions that offer themselves for emulation. As Wesley Trimpi suggests, "The argument of fiction, as of rhetoric, is *implicitly* inductive — in the mind of the writer — but *explicitly* deductive in the work produced and in its effects upon the audience. In order to appeal most strongly to the emotions, the analysis of the given situation must select its premises beforehand so that the narrative argument may appear *as if* it had required no inductive process to arrive at the premises from which deduction might begin."[136] The rhetorical speeches and actions of *Ornatus and Artesia* work in this "explicitly deductive" way as iterative examples of virtue in action. Such consistency in their conduct is tantamount to an argument by repetition.

The eloquence of constancy, chastity, and continence and the shaping of narrative in such a way as to delay amorous pleasures until maturity of love is achieved are literary equivalents of the emerging social ideals in Elizabethan society concerning marriage as an endorsement of bonding, a means of containing the passions, and of creating mutuality in the family unit. Such protocols of love and courtship in Renaissance romances coincided with what David Cressy has called "the ritual dance of courtship," which included "mutual familiarization, clarification of intentions, and considerations of prospects . . ." and "usually involved . . . negotiation of privileges and opportunities, before sealing of consent."[137] Wooing through letters, as Cressy shows

[135]Constance Relihan argues that this is also the case with the romantic heroines of Lodge's, Greene's, and Deloney's fictions. See Relihan, *Fashioning Authority*, p. 19ff.

[136]Trimpi, *Muses of One Mind*, p. 299.

[137]Cressy, *Birth, Marriage, and Death*, p. 234.

through the example of Leonard Wheatcroft's amorous corre-
spondence, may have been "modeled on conventional romantic
literature."[138]

The narrative's emphasis on the preservation of chastity
through Artesia's defences against improper suitors echoes some
of the Renaissance controversies about women, especially the
tradition of attacks or defences, or even neutral writing about
women. Discussing the attacks, Linda Woodbridge argues that
they had the greatest influence in Renaissance prose fiction, the
genre, she says, that primarily targeted women.[139] It would be
too strong to argue that such a support of women's independence in their choices of lovers engenders a fictional fantasy of
freedom for women. But it is certain that Ford's narrative suggests strategies effective enough for them to resist any amorous
terms imposed on their personal and physical autonomy before
marriage. Even "accepting a marriage did not necessarily mean
embracing the excessively patriarchal nature of that union."[140]
Considered in this cultural context, Artesia's eloquent defences
of chastity do not necessarily have to be seen as the sign of a
threat to her purity, as an articulation of her anxiety over male
destructive power, but rather as the use of one power that she
has to assert personal autonomy.

By testing the characters' love and actions, *Ornatus and Artesia* participates, in a way different from that of the prescriptive
literature about women, in the shaping of the new ethics of love
and sexuality in Renaissance England. This new ideology of desire and marriage saw the family as a micro-state, as a symbolic
nucleus of the stable commonwealth, which was central to what
Martin Ingram calls "the quest for order" in Tudor England,
a quest that involved the consolidation of civic discipline and

[138] *Birth, Marriage, and Death*, p. 243.

[139] Linda Woodbridge, *Women and the English Renaissance: Literature
and the Nature of Womankind, 1540–1620* (Urbana: University of Illinois
Press, 1984), pp. 13–14.

[140] Theodora A. Jankowski, *Pure Resistance: Queer Virginity in Early
Modern English Drama* (Philadelphia: University of Pennsylvania Press,
2000), p. 170.

sexual morality.[141] Since Renaissance culture had strict views on prenuptial sex and illicit sexuality, the "new" humanist family depended on the control of pleasure in order to assure its usefulness for procreation. In both literary and non-literary humanist discourses on love and eros, the ideal of "an ordered society" depended on oaths of love and friendship and feelings of mutuality whose purposes were to celebrate marriage as a moral and social ideal.[142]

Yet this new ideology of passion and the relationship between a young man and a young woman promoted by *Ornatus and Artesia* contrasts with views circulating in marriage books.[143] The obsession with female chastity, continence, the duties of husband and wife, and the discipline of children discussed in the marriage conduct books by Henry Smith, Robert Cleaver, John Dodd, William Whateley, William Gouge, John Aylmer, and George Whetstone suggests the extent to which the issues of love, desire, and matrimony were central to the period's (male) ideas (and wishes) about private life. But their texts are "mirror[s] of the prescriptive literature," not entirely of the real condition of women, and propose a Protestant preacher's masculine ideal of women's behavior.[144] The ideal behavior of women described in

[141]Ingram, "Sex and Marriage: Laws, Ideals and Popular Practice," in his *Church Courts, Sex and Marriage in England, 1570–1640*, p. 126.

[142]I have taken the phrase "ordered society" from Susan Dwyer Amussen's book *An Ordered Society: Gender and Class in Early Modern England* (Oxford: Basil Blackwell, 1988).

[143]In her book about domesticity in Renaissance culture, Lena Cowen Orlin treats conduct books as reflections of women's condition. See her *Private Matters and Public Culture in Post-Reformation England*.

[144]For an account of a number of cases of women whose behavior did not conform to the prescribed ideals, see Alison Wall, "Elizabethan Precept and Feminine Practice: The Thynne Family of Longleat," *History* 75 (1990): 23–38. Some recent studies in the social history of the period shed a different light not only on the condition of women but also on the way in which the romance represents the role of women in love affairs. See Ingram, *Church Courts, Sex and Marriage in England, 1570–1640*; John Brewer and Susan Staves, eds., *Early Modern Concept of Property* (London: Routledge, 1995); Staves, *Married Women's Separate Property in England, 1660–1833* (Cambridge, Mass.: Harvard University Press, 1990).

them is a male fantasy, not a reflection of their real power or of the actual condition of genders and gender relations. If we look at matrimonial conduct books as texts that take some of a woman's power away from her, then we may consider *Ornatus and Artesia* to be a text that restores some of a woman's power, at least in the realm of courtship, love, and premarital desire. If, in relation to women, the conduct books are, in Alison Wall's terms, "dream[s] of submission and silence,"[145] *Ornatus and Artesia* is a fiction of eloquence and power — power that stems from chastity because the female has power as long as she is non-sexual. Nevertheless, the control of sexual energy as an ideal of sexual behavior remains one of the central demands of the Renaissance family, and in literature, especially romances, its equivalent can be found in the eloquence of mastery, self-control, and constancy. The insistence on Artesia's chastity and the control of Ornatus's sexual energy throughout *Ornatus and Artesia* affirm the stability of love until the plot ensures marriage and until fidelity and constancy are rewarded in the union of "a corresponding wealth and status."[146]

The new ideology of love and the family can be seen as a move toward the changing nature of patriarchy, or the rule of the father in the household. By leaving his father's house, Ornatus is exercising precisely that freedom to choose. And by deciding to face all hindrances to their love, Artesia is doing the same. In a treatise on marriage and the household, George Whetstone argues against "the reprehension of forcement in marriage," promoting instead a free choice of the future spouse: "The office of free choise, is the roote of foundation of Marriage, which consisteth onely in the satisfaction of fancy: for where the fancy is not pleased, all the perfections of the world cannot force loue, and where the fancy delighteth, many defects are perfected, or tollerated among the maried."[147] In addition, the marriage age

[145]Wall, "Elizabethan Precept and Feminine Practice," p. 37.

[146]McKeon, *The Origins of the English Novel, 1600–1740*, p. 256.

[147]George Whetstone, *Avrelia*, sig. U1[r]. Whetstone's argument against forced marriage is directed not only against paternal involvement but also against the crushing of freedom in the young as a result of such marriages. He says:

for young people was higher in Renaissance England than in most other countries of western Europe. In such a cultural climate, rituals of courtship, rites of virility, defences of chastity, and marriage contracts became important factors in the youth culture. Repeatedly in *Ornatus and Artesia* the crises of unilateral desire and the testing of mutual desire precede oaths of love and marriage, suggesting that romances move closer to reflecting a self-determined bonding of adolescents through their own moral and emotional judgment, in full opposition to parental authority and its policing of morals, exercised through arranged marriages. *Ornatus and Artesia* can be seen as an agent of the new ideology of love, and as an example of a text whose goal was to offer models for shaping the ideas about how to handle emotions and sex, how to enjoy them, and how to learn from them.

Gender Disguise and Sexuality

Many of the implicit attitudes towards gender and sexuality in *Ornatus and Artesia* are related to Ornatus' vestimentary disguise, a stratagem commonly employed in popular prose romances.[148] When Ornatus dresses himself "like a virgin of a strange country" in order to be near Artesia, the gender politics become potentially both complicated and humorous insofar as the hero "might well

---

I crie out vpon forcement in Marriage, as the extreamest bondage that is: for that the ransome of libertie is the death of the one or the other of the maried. The father thinks he hath a happie purchase if he get a rich yong Warde to match with his daughter: but God he knowes, and the vnfortunate couple often feele, that he byeth sorrow to his Childe, slander to himselfe, and perchance the ruine of an ancient Gentlemans house, by the riot of the sonne in Lawe, not louing his wife. . . . Pleasure yeelds no sollace to the sorrowfull, no more can forcement enforce the free to fancie. (sig. E3^r–E4^v)

The humanist values in the changing perspectives on love, eros, and marriage emerged in Renaissance England at a time when, as Christopher Hill suggests, "[m]arriage was delayed longer [in England] than in any other known [Renaissance] society." See Christopher Hill, "Sex, Marriage, and the Family in England." *Economic History Review*, 2nd series, 31 (1978), p. 445.

[148]See Winfried Schleiner, "Male Cross-Dressing and Transvestism in Renaissance Romances." *Sixteenth-Century Journal* 19 (1988), p. 605.

be esteemed to be [a virgin] by his youth." This narrative device
would seem to expose the hero's sexual identity to ambiguity
given that he slips into the disguise so effectively and persua-
sively that he might be courted as a woman, not to mention
deceiving Artesia after spending days or weeks in her intimate
presence. There would appear to be a need to negotiate between
the disguise as a conventional means for permitting characters to
go "unseen," and to gain forbidden entries, and the disguise that
by its own "essence" taints the character, or emblematizes some
latent ambiguity — implying that it is being used as a mechanism
for peering into the nature of Tyresian boundaries, "misplaced"
erotic desire, or an underlying androgyny even in the most outwardly masculine of males. Such prospects are tempting in light
of modern psychological enquiries, and it is intriguing to think
that earlier writers may have resorted to this narrative device to
express their own intimations in these matters. But ultimately,
hard evidence for the more enigmatic and psychological dimen-
sions are difficult to come by in such romances as *Ornatus and
Artesia*. A first line of understanding must remain, in any case,
the conventionalized fact of cross-dressing as an efficient means
for advancing plots and for developing deliciously ironic situations wherein lovers can spy on beloveds and take the reader
with them. Yet, the matter deserves further consideration in light
of the many recent critical studies of cross-gender dressing and
the prospects of ambiguous sexuality.

Mikhail Bakhtin describes cross-dressing as "a form-generat-
ing function"[149] by which he means that it serves as an element of
composition — which will prove to be fundamentally true. Yet
it is difficult to think that it does not have some bearing on content as well, not only through Ford's self-conscious playfulness
with gender disguise, but also because such disguise becomes
a stratagem through which man's behavior within the plot of
courtship is represented. Ornatus explicitly says why he main-
tains his disguise: "under the name of Sylvian I enjoy her sight"
which he desired more than anything. Yet he continues, paradox-
ically, that he sees her "but not as Ornatus, and so am I deprived
of her sight" (ch. V). This is playful, indeed, because his new

---

[149]Bakhtin, *The Dialogic Imagination*, p. 154.

identity alters his vision at a juncture where figurative expression and literal expression are easily confused. Who, then, is Sylvian? Is Ornatus altered by his disguise in anything but outward appearances? And who is "she" to Artesia, once "her" identity is made known? Repeatedly we are told that he was really good at this form of deception: "framing himself to such a kind of behavior that it was impossible to discern but that he was a woman indeed." The desire for a perfect verisimilitude, however, is challenged by the use of the female name and masculine pronoun attached to it, as when, at a banquet held at Arbastus's house, "*Sylvia* was kindly and worthily entertained, having *his* heart's desire" (my emphasis). The apparent name-gender disagreement may be a simple reminder of the double fact, and an indicator that Ford wanted that reminder foregrounded as a critical part of the reader's experience. Ford does not want the reader to "effeminize" the character by letting the disguise take over the man, and he found the solution to the name/pronoun anomaly simply by "masculinizing" Sylvia to Sylvian, even though, in speaking to Artesia, Lenon must continue to use the feminine pronoun, as when he says "I beseech you grieve not fair damsel for Sylvian, for no harm is done to *her*" (ch. IX), as an ongoing confirmation of his own deception.

The narrative that follows Ornatus's shipwreck in Natolia serves to reaffirm his masculinity, in case there was any doubt, by allowing him to exchange, for a time, his female dress for armor. "Sylvian" remains important in its flexible capacity to represent Ornatus in a variety of dramatic situations, concealing to others in the story yet disclosing to readers that this is Ornatus, sometimes as one whom Floretus takes for a prospective wife, sometimes when Arbastus must not know who he is. The narrative also insists on the form "Sylvian" whenever the cross-dressed Ornatus has to avoid seduction. Most pointedly, however, as far as Artesia is concerned his gender has not been compromised because Ornatus has resorted to cross-dressing, and the name he employs is of no importance. Thus in chapter VII, she says: "I know not by what name to call you when neither I know whether you are Sylvian or Ornatus, but which of both your words bear great show of true friendship, which I fear me is not grounded in your heart, neither do I greatly care."

In essence, such friendship is cherished whether from a man of one name or the other. Where disguise is concerned, the emphasis thus remains on function. Insofar as Floretus seeks a wife, for him Sylvian is a woman, separate from "her" masculinized name, on which the plot insists.[150] Artesia seeks a mate and therefore has to protect Ornatus from discovery; hence the narrative's playfulness with the grammatical markers of gender. Whether Sylvian is referred to by a masculine or a feminine name depends on who is speaking and on whether the narrative circumstances call for self-consciousness of disguise.[151] Thus, the meaning of Ornatus's disguise depends on what we *know* is happening in the narrative and on the characters' *knowing* that the disguise is necessary because of the hindrances to courtship.

Just as the pure functionality of disguise seems assured, however, a glance at certain Renaissance discourses on clothes and the projection of gender would seem to necessitate a completely new departure. What many of Ford's contemporaries appear to have taken for granted was that clothes signify the language of gender. Thus Philip Stubbes says of women who wear men's clothing or of men who cross-dress as women, "Our Apparell was giuen us as a signe distinctiue to discern betwix sex and sex, & therefore one to weare the Apparel of another sex, is to participate with the same, and to adulterate the veritie of his owne kinde."[152] For Stubbes a biased choice of clothes can both make

[150]Even deluded, Floretus shows a sign of suspicion at one point when, in chapter VII, he says that Artesia is with a "strange damsel Sylvian," meaning "foreign or alien," or "different," as if suggesting that something is not quite right with the person Artesia is with; Sylvian's "difference" has to do both with his performed foreignness and with his feminine disguise.

[151]The narrative complications in toying with this inversion of names contradict Mark Breitenberg's argument about the "the accuracy or transparency of apparel and language" in cross-dressing. See Breitenberg, *Anxious Masculinity in Early Modern England*, p. 152. For the cultural symbolism of clothing, see Ann Rosalind Jones and Peter Stallybrass, *Renaissance Clothing and the Materials of Memory* (Cambridge: Cambridge University Press, 2000).

[152]Philip Stubbes, *The anatomie of abuses* (London: Richard Jones, 1583), sig. F5^V, STC 23376.

and unmake the person, even to the point of dictating fundamen-
tal orientations. Ford seems to have broken with such a view,
one that was, in any case, conceived as part of a heated polemic.
Yet such views did establish themselves and became at least a
potential part of the perspective of the "common" reader. Where,
precisely, are the dividing lines between the semiotics of clothes,
the relativities of conduct, the ambiguity of pronouns, the reality
in the beholder's eye, the structuring of gendered behavior, and
the conventions of romance plotting?

Clearly, the moments in which the narrative endorses heteroerotic desire, and particularly those episodes in which Ornatus expresses his love for Artesia, sustain a full resistance to the
belief epitomized by Stubbes that the cross-dressed man lives
in peril of his masculinity. By default, in that regard, *Ornatus
and Artesia* arranges itself on the opposite side of the polemic.
But then could it offend with regard to a counter anxiety equally
expressed in that same cultural vortex? Consider that in the
year the romance first appeared, John Rainolds had written that
for men to put on women's clothing "is a great provocation of
men to lust and lechery: because a woman's garment beeing
put on a man doeth vehemently touch and moue him with the
remembrance & imagination of a woman; and the imagination
of a thing desirable doth stir up the desire."[153] Now to defend
the romance, it must be demonstrated to the contrary that Ornatus' feminine habiliments do not lead him to sensuality and
lust. On that score, the entire story is incremental but by no
means ambiguous. Ornatus is a man of remarkable sensuality in his raptures of erotic appreciation for Artesia, yet a man
of equally remarkable continence, honor and devotion in his
Frauendienst — the quintessential marker of his true masculine
self-control — who, nevertheless, for cumulative services in kind
beyond all expectation, in beating back predator after predator,
enjoys (generally, we must presume, to the readers' secret ap-
probation) a passionate preview of the nuptial delights. But this
is hardly confirmation of Rainold's presumption that women's
clothes have driven Ornatus to indulge himself uncontrollably in

[153]John Rainolds, *Th' overthrow of stage-playes* (Middleburg: R. Schilders,
1599), sig. N3^V, STC 20616.

women's erotic rites. The "argument" of this narrative has been entirely to the contrary, allowing only that matrimony is the proper reward for constancy, despite the stolen prelude. Therein lies a different economy of romance, namely that so much long-suffering, devotion, resistance, desire, and continence inspired by heteroerotic desire also finds its own natural culmination in the sexual embrace. The "bourgeois" romance is precisely this kind of exploit, teetering between the excessive and the contained in a world of teasingly disciplined desire. Northrop Frye holds that romance serves "mainly to encourage irregular or excessive sexual activity," leading to "escape" reading.[154] But escape into sexual fantasies is now less than half the story, for the fuse behind Ford's narrative is the legitimation brought to adolescent courtship — following the rites of passage that pertain to martial yet sensitive men and emotionally delicate, long-suffering, loyal, yet resourceful women — that is marked by public vows in the context of a political and social world.

Adellena is only a little surprised when, in chapter VI, Artesia reveals to her Ornatus's disguise: "Adellena was at first half astonished at her [Artesia's] speeches, but at last she perfectly remembered that it was he indeed, rejoicing most exceedingly to see him there, especially with Artesia." The narrative shifts away from the disguise and focuses instead on Ornatus's reunion with Artesia, entailing only that the unity of lovers is at stake here. These episodes do not turn on questions of effeminacy, but only on the structural demands of the plot.[155] A page earlier, when Ornatus reveals his identity to Artesia, the function of disguise becomes even clearer. Artesia's embarrassment is not a matter of his physical proximity while masquerading as a woman, but only the fact that he has heard her confessions of love for him. Functionally, the disguise has given to Artesia the time she requires to formulate her feelings, and a chance for Ornatus to know them, without a breach to her feminine discretion. She may be allowed to recognize, however, that his disguise has been a temporary intrusion upon her mental privacy. The technique has allowed

[154]Frye, *The Secular Scripture*, p. 24.
[155]Winfried Schleiner, "Male Cross-Dressing and Transvestism in Renaissance Romance," p. 610.

communication where an essential privacy and modesty was required, even while a situational irony prevails whereby Ornatus as a female companion is able to train his eyes and ears where hands cannot go, mixing innocence with experience.

When Ford pushes gender disguise to the point where titillation and play with gender boundaries cause anxiety, he does so in order to create comedy, suggesting that the cross-dressed body is a stratagem of narrative not only to deceive the innocent but to evade those with wicked intentions — a multidimensional mechanism of survival in a complex world.[156] In *Ornatus and Artesia*, one such moment occurs when, in chapter VI, Floretus falls in love with Sylvian, believing him to be a woman. "[F]air damsel . . . my heart hath long time been enthralled to your beauty, which I have refrained to utter, fearing to be refused. But knew you how faithfully my heart is devoted to your service, and with what torment I have concealed the same, you would pity me." Ford's comment on Sylvian's reaction is that he "had much ado to abstain from smiling to think how unfit he was to yield to such a reward as Floretus expected." This episode could be mistakenly read as incorporating elements of homoerotic desire in *Ornatus and Artesia*. But the smile quells all. The language of love in this episode places the emphasis, not on illicit desire, but on the power of love to so transform Floretus that he loses all judgment and political discretion. Ornatus is simply taken for a woman. Floretus does not rally to "her" for some quality of perceived manliness, and insofar as Ornatus does not feign reciprocation, even strategically, there is no transactional effeminization on his part. Gender is not under negotiation.

Ornatus's cross-dressing is also a source of parody, but one that redounds upon the myth he re-enacts rather than upon himself. On his way to find Artesia, Sylvian is charged by a "wild and fierce boar." Frightened, he runs, and when the boar draws near, he starts to throw apples behind him, thus feeding the boar, which overeats, abandons the race, and is killed. Sylvian cuts off the boar's head and tucks it under his arm as a trophy for

---

[156]In *Arcadia*, for example, Pyrocles is wooed by King Basilius, and in Pt. II of *The Myrrour of Knighthood* (c. 1580), the tyrant Argin orders Rosicleer, disguised as Lyverba, to undress.

Figure II.   Atlanta and Hippomenes.
Metamorphoses Ovidii. Illus. by M. Johan, Frankfurt, 1563,
sig. R1[r]. Reproduced by permission of the Newberry Library,
Chicago. Case Y 672 09456.

Artesia. Here, echoing Ovid's *Metamorphoses* (Bk. VIII), Sylvian
plays Meleager to Artesia's Atalanta.[157]

[157]In another version of the myth, in which she is the first to wound
the Calydonian boar, whose head she receives as a present, she embodies the female power that threatens an overbearing masculinity. Her
marriage to the effeminate Hippomenes therefore suggests a dialectical
union between strength and virtue, between two divided parts of the
self. Sylvian, feeding the boar with the apples while running away from
it, evokes both Atalanta and the maiden-looking Hippomenes. Thus
Ford's narrative suggests that the seducer's moderation empowers the
desired woman, not that masculinity is destabilized through its temporary female disguise. In his version of the myth, the cross-dressed hero
symbolizes the erasure of power relations between the genders implied
by Ovid's myth.

Figure III.   Atalanta's Race.
George Sandys, *Ovids Metamorphosis Englished*, 1632, sig. Q2 5ᵛ. RB62871.
Reproduced by permission of the Huntington Library,
San Marino, California.

This episode also carries overtones of the mythical race of
Atalanta and Hippomenes, the story of a fierce beauty who refused to be wedded and, in Golding's terms, a youth with "a
maydens countenance" (X.742; S5ᵛ), to whom Atalanta eventu-
ally belonged. Atalanta symbolizes both "an image of the self in
flight" and virtue pursued.[158]

This fantasy of woman's power, for Atalanta, is short-lived
insofar as Venus conspires to make her lose to the man who
takes her as a trophy in marriage. In parody, however, Sylvian as
a male Atalanta completes the fantasy conquest on her behalf by
defeating the boar and then by striking down the knight (caught
in his own quest) who seeks the boar's head as a necessary trophy.

[158]Jonathan Bate, *Shakespeare and Ovid* (Oxford: Clarendon Press,
1994), p. 56.

Figure IV.   Meleager and Atalanta.
Metamorphoses Ovidii. Illus. by M. Johan, Frankfurt, 1563, sig. N2^r.
Reproduced by permission of the Newberry Library,
Chicago. Case Y 672 09456.

This feat Ornatus executes through an act of male prowess in a female disguise. For soon after Sylvian continues his quest for Artesia with the boar's head in his possession, he comes across Alprinus (ch. IX), a knight on his way to kill the same boar. Ford pushes the issue beyond expectations for the sake of novelty in the plot and for achieving a grand comic effect. With an instant surge of Amazonian power, Sylvian

> suddenly caught hold on the Natolian's sword and drew the same out . . . thrust at him, and contrary to his thought, wounded him so deep that he left him for dead, wishing that he had not done that deed, but not knowing how discourteously he would have used him, let pass all further remorse, and casting off his woman's apparel put on the knight's apparel and armor, mounted the steed and, with the boar's head, rode back the same way he saw the knight come."

To the innuendoes concerning Atalanta we owe a fine new dimension in the structural projections of gender, whereby Ornatus can be his martial self in playing at women's games, completing for her in the course of things what she could not maintain for herself. At this juncture, we can lose ourselves in the multiplicities of contaminatio! Sylvian's forceful reaction against Alprinus's power may be seen merely as a male reaction to an arrogant male. But it can also be seen as a narrative trick, that of a powerful male disguised as a woman beating up on an unsuspecting knight who seeks from her, not her chastity, as we might expect, but a trophy he needs to save his own life.

The paradoxical in cross-dressing has attracted considerable attention among recent critics, even to the point of paralleling the peculiar biases of certain Renaissance writers, not so much that feminine habiliments possess, *ipso facto*, the bewitching powers to effeminize men or incite devious and perverse desires,[159] but to civilize men as an outward manifestation of an inward capacity to empathize with female longings, anxieties and experiences. In romance, gender disguises, as Louise Schleiner argues, "express a desire or need to partake . . . of the nature of the opposite gender," making male cross-dressing "not [the] highlighting . . . of differences between genders, but the convergence of genders."[160] Cross-dressing therefore becomes a way of "extending the personality [and] enlarging the self," not subverting it.[161] This is an emblematics, not of essentialist confusion and anxiety, but of understanding and mutuality. Cross-dressing is an imposed vantage point that prepares for a meeting of true hearts and minds. As Ford's fiction suggests, disguise does not imply a loss

---

[159]Commenting on Pyrocles's disguise as the Amazon woman Cleophila, Sidney says in *The Old Arcadia*: "this effeminate love of a woman doth womanize a man that, if you yield to it, it will . . . make you a famous Amazon." See Sidney, *The Countess of Pembroke's Arcadia (The Old Arcadia)*, p. 20.

[160]Louise Schleiner, "Ladies and Gentlemen in Two Genres," p. 10.

[161]Davis, *Idea and Act in Elizabethan Fiction*, p. 64.

of the self, as has been formerly suggested,[162] but a diversification of the self through experience. Roles do not confound life strategies, but extend the imagination.

One of the most striking examples of female disguise that does not affect masculine prowess is in the longest erotic episode in *Ornatus and Artesia*, the scene in which Artesia loses her virginity. This scene plays off the familiar scenario — it occurs in other prose romances of the period — of the hero's entry into the lady's chamber, his gazing at her asleep, her sudden awakening, her blush at seeing him standing above her, and their mutual recognition of a moment of emotional and erotic intensity, and the crisis they must confront in an economy of desire and contending obligations. The remarkable depiction of their delicately negotiated loss of innocence (ch. XIV) is a culminating moment, and one that Ford carefully calculated, no doubt, in relation to the traditions of romance in which writers rarely went so far. The scene abounds in descriptions of the movements and sounds that are part of a sexual encounter, thus creating an occasion for the reader's visual, voyeuristic participation in the narrative of lovemaking. When Ford says that Artesia "inwardly yielded, though outwardly she refused" Ornatus's sexual advance, the narrative epitomizes her feminine nature in its rhetoric of necessary innocence. Yet this episode of "low-key titillation"[163] is also an example of how, in fiction, love makes men brave. The positioning of this episode towards the end of the narrative of the long and laborious ways in which Ornatus has protected Artesia's virginity echoes the cultural situation in which many Renaissance young men did in fact protect the virginity of their chosen young women, "but only with a view to making them sacrifice it in the long run."[164] This episode is also a prelude to a much longer sequence of war episodes that celebrate Ornatus's male prowess. His feminine disguise clearly does not compromise his heroic masculinity.

---

[162]Gregory Bredbeck, for example, interprets Pyrocles's disguise as a "loss of some original unity or presence." See *Sodomy and Interpretation*, p. 103.

[163]Hamilton, "Elizabethan Romance," p. 292.

[164]Schindler, "Guardians of Disorder," p. 253.

The implication of cross-dressing for the plot of *Ornatus and Artesia* is further complicated by Ornatus's double disguise, which dominates much of the narrative from chapter X until the end, when Sylvian also disguises himself as a pilgrim in order to leave Natolia for Phrygia with a group of merchants belonging to Lucida's father. It is also important in chapter VI to enable readers to hear Floretus's intentions, when he confesses to Sylvian that he has killed Arbastus and plans to murder Artesia, thus ensuring her inheritance for himself. Ornatus's disguise is here entirely in the service of the narrative structure. Because Artesia still believes that Ornatus has killed her father, his separate knowledge of the truth about the murder enables further complications in the plot and justifies some of the characters' actions and behavior. The disguise will help Sylvian to rally three hundred of Allinus's men against Lenon's and Thrasus's army supported by the Armenians, and it will enable him, in chapter XII, to go on board Lenon's ship with Artesia bound for Phrygia.

Narrative strategy, not gender crisis, is behind so many other moments in which disguise plays a critical part. Thus, in chapter IX, Sylvian dresses in Alprinus's armor, and in chapter XIV, still hiding his identity before the victory over Lenon is assured, he borrows his friend Phylastes's clothes to address the Phrygians and urge them to stand up against Lenon. The same palmer's disguise is a stratagem employed not just by Ornatus but also by Lenon. In chapter XVII, the latter uses the same ruse to be smuggled into Phrygia. In fact, his disguise as a pilgrim has a more emphatic impact than Ornatus's cross-dressing at any moment in the narrative. When Ornatus pulls off the "subtle disguise that he wore, [he] knew him to be Lenon, at the first being half afraid to touch him for that they would have sworn he had been dead." Cross-dressing, then, is part of a larger strategy of concealment of identities upon which the wonders of romance so playfully depend.

Disguise in relation to sexuality in *Ornatus and Artesia* has relatively little to do with the debates about cross-dressing in Renaissance literature. While in the theatre boys cross-dress, in prose romances, it is adolescent and young adult men who do so.[165] This age difference accounts for some of the changes in the treatment of cross-dressing in romances, given that the period considered boys, as Stephen Orgel argues, as a sort of third gender, somewhere between men and women.[166] The maiden youth (or the maiden knight) of romances is more like an adolescent male or a young man who, while maturing, has not yet mastered self-control. This process of adolescent maturation involves an exploration of both maleness and femaleness, and male cross-dressing is a sign of that developmental process.[167] As a work that focuses on adventures, psychological and sexual maturity, and the public advancement of a young man, *Ornatus and Artesia* seems to be primarily interested in "the training of the developing male."[168] One might, in fact, argue that popular romances are, in a manner of speaking, fictional conduct books for the male youth who, caught in the period between adolescence and marriage, between being an adventurous youth and the responsible master of a household, has not yet matured sexually. Thus his "maiden countenance" is not a sign of his effeminacy that troubles the young man's sexuality, but a marker in the diversification of his social scope and understanding. If it is emblematic at all, it is so as an external indicator of the need to balance the comportment of the field with that of the boudoir.

This difference between social assumptions about boys and the literary fictions of male youth is crucial, because, in the case of *Ornatus and Artesia* (and in most other prose romances), gender

---

[165]Ford does not give Ornatus's age. Although romance authors typically do not give the age of their heroes, Nicholas Breton in his romance entitled *The strange fortvnes of two excellent Princes* (London: P. Short for Nicholas Ling, 1600), says that his hero, Prince Penillo, who is "of countenance milde, but not effeminate" (sig. B1^r–^{v}), is twenty-four (sig. B1^r). STC 3702.

[166]Stephen Orgel, *Impersonations: The Performance of Gender in Shakespeare's England* (Cambridge: Cambridge University Press, 1996), p. 103.

[167]On this point, see Louise Schleiner, "Ladies and Gentlemen in Two Genres," p. 1.

[168]I borrow this phrase from Guido Ruggiero, "Marriage, Love, Sex, and Renaissance Civic Morality," p. 19.

disguise is a matter of plotting expediency for the sake of adventure. Although in some treatises — those that offer moralizing versions of cross-dressing and that were inspired by objections to the use of boys in female roles in the theatre, as in Rainolds's *Th' overthrow of stage-players* — male cross-dressing is regarded with horror and abomination, but in practice it was seen as quite unthreatening.[169] David Cressy shows that in Elizabethan and Stuart England young men would cross-dress for May Day celebrations and the summer games, while the charivari or skimmington would "use cross-dressing to ridicule and discipline disorderly neighbours." Young men would also cross-dress during carnival and enclosure riots; they would don women's clothing to enter a forbidden place, or simply to be able to meet a lover, and prisoners cross-dressed in order to escape.[170] Apart from the fact that male cross-dressing was an element in the carnival festivities and that it occurred in the performances of morality plays in which men disguised themselves to impersonate women, what Cressy's research into the social history of male cross-dressing also shows is that when it occurred socially, cross-dressing took a form very similar to that which it acquired in prose romances. In all these social manifestations of festive cross-dressing, the disguise was "done for laughs," was "limited, temporary, and pragmatic, addressing the needs of a particular situation,"[171] and

---

[169] Arguing that "[a]ll men are abomination who put on womans apparell. . . . I call this refuge desperat, because your owne handling thereof doeth seeme to argue, that when you came vnto it, you did treade on thornes; and felt that you should bee pitifully pricked, if you stood long vpon it" (sig. N3ᵛ). With more fervor, Thomas Beard, in an adapted and expanded translation from the French, argues that male cross-dressing is "an act in nature monstrous, so very dishonest and ignominious" (sig. Z7ᵛ). The fact that he discusses the monstrosity of male cross-dressing in a chapter entitled "Of effeminate persons, Sodomites, and other such like monsters" (sig. Z7ʳ–8ᵛ) suggests a close link between effeminacy, sodomy, and cross-dressing, all of which are manifestations of transgressing masculinity. Thomas Beard, *The Theatre of Gods Iudgements* (London: Adam Islip, 1597), STC 1659.

[170] Cressy, "Gender Trouble and Cross-Dressing in Early Modern England," pp. 45–60.

[171] Ibid., p. 460.

not a sign of gender subversion. Even when authorities intervened, instances of cross-dressing, whether male or female, were treated "mostly [as] minor offences, more jests and pranks than challenges to the gendered social order, and their punishment was appropriately mild."[172]

Echoing a phrase coined by Mario Di Gangi, who talks about orderly and disorderly homoeroticism in Renaissance drama,[173] I would call this positive view of cross-dressing in fiction "orderly cross-dressing." It neither incurs anxiety nor implies sexual transgression. Rather, it is a stratagem of the narrative and, at best, a burlesque provocation to the masculine norm, not something that destabilizes that norm. Ornatus's orderly cross-dressing also suggests degrees to which early modern culture responded to the practice, and that those differences depended on the literary genre: they do not imply the same thing in Renaissance comedies as in popular romances, for even more so than in comedies, romances depend on high artifice and fantasy.

Property, Lineage, and Government

"Love plots [in early fiction]," Michael McKeon writes, "always concern . . . the socially significant event of marriage."[174] The social and economic contexts of love and courtship become increasingly important in the Elizabethan fiction of the late 1580s and 1590s as the influence of the new chivalric narratives took hold. With the rise of fiction centered on merchants and trade, especially in the works of Thomas Deloney, love and courtship are often represented in the language of mercantile exchange. Even though *Ornatus and Artesia* does not belong to that new genre of mercantile fiction, in it the topics of property, wealth, and trade intersect with the trials of courtship. The fact that all the lovers who attempt to court Artesia, including Ornatus, are fully mindful of her wealth and position indicates just how much

---

[172]Ibid., p. 461. What Cressy's findings also show is that there seem to have been more examples of women than men who were brought to court for cross-dressing.

[173]Mario Di Gangi, *The Homoerotics of Early Modern Drama* (Cambridge: Cambridge University Press, 1997), p. ix.

[174]McKeon, *The Origins of the English Novel*, p. 255.

the order of romance is surrounded and conditioned by matters of wealth and status.

The complications in the plot begin when Floretus plans to murder Artesia in order to prevent her from receiving her rightful inheritance from Arbastus, whom Floretus had just killed. When he presents his plan to obtain Artesia's wealth and marry Sylvian (ch. IV), Sylvian's response — "Arbastus's wealth . . . that is Artesia's by right. Then how can you possess the same, she living?" — anticipates one of the central themes of the romance's plot: women and property. Sylvian's rejection of Floretus's proposal on the grounds that it will impoverish him in material and emotional terms suggests the fiction's uneasiness with making marriage dependant upon a woman's property. Sylvian's indirect rejection of Floretus's love through a defence of Artesia's rights underscores the topic of the legality of a woman's hereditary wealth and her entitlement to it in marriage, in opposition to the Renaissance idea of the husband's right to his wife's property (ideas derived from Genesis 2 and 3).

Floretus's evil plan not only violates basic human justice because it involves murder, but also loyalty based on kinship, because, as Artesia's uncle, he is supposed to protect her inheritance. While he wants to "enjoy [Artesia's] heritage," Lenon is principally motivated by love. He says to Floretus: "I vow by heaven I will not take one pennyworth of Arbastus's substance from you, but freely give it you all. For it is not her possessions I regard, but her love" (ch. VIII). Yet the situation in which Lenon utters these words renders his declaration suspect, because he believes that Floretus will be responsible for his niece's heritage, including the just handling of the property. What Lenon does not know, however, is that Floretus has already concocted a plan to murder Artesia. A tyrant, Floretus is here represented as a figure who distorts a woman's right to property. He now wants to turn Lenon's proposal to his own advantage, believing that if Artesia loves Lenon, Lenon will be accused of murdering her, and then he and Sylvian "shall be quit of so cruel a deed, enjoy her heritage, and have an assured friend of Lenon whilst we live." The mastery of Ford's fiction in conveying meaning through the structuring of the narrative is seen in his juxtaposing of Floretus's and Lenon's intentions in the same chapter, suggesting how in different ways false lovers can plan to exploit women for the sake of property. Repeatedly in *Ornatus and Artesia*, threats to women are related to wealth and property.

The prominence of male violence in romances is one of the features of popular fiction of the 1590s. Lorna Hutson defines such violent actions as the "displacement of heroic masculinity,"[175] whose major concern is "the way in which it transforms the violence explicitly wreaked [in earlier chivalric romances] by men upon men, into a vengeance visited by the narratives themselves upon their heroines."[176]

The kidnapping of maidens, another form of violence against women in *Ornatus and Artesia*, is a romance convention that reaches back to the origins of the genre.[177] In the present work, such abductions are linked to the violation of property. A captured woman is a prize, equated to pirates' booty, as in chapter IX, when the pirates have "taken Artesia . . . and with her such wealth as they could find about them, having withal furnished themselves with the spoil of such cattle as fed in those places." The capturing of the pirates in chapter XII brings into the romantic narrative the theme of justice, including the restoration of property to its rightful owner: the narrative's heroine.

The violation of women and property can also take the form of the dispersal of the household—an act of social dislocation. Hence violation of property relates to threatened chastity by unruly masculinity—a double threat to the Renaissance *domus familia*, or family household. Thus in chapter X Lenon, "giving no credit to his speeches," lies to his father, King Thæon, saying that Allinus had murdered Arbastus, making Thæon disband Allinus's household.

> His servants were constrained to disguise themselves and travel into farther places of the country to live unknown. His lady was compelled to seek out a kinswoman of hers that lived in the country, of whom she was entertained, and there lived a poor life, far

---

[175]Hutson argues that this displacement characterizes much of the fiction between the 1560s and the 1570s.

[176]Hutson, *The Usurer's Daughter*, p. 115.

[177]This convention can also be traced back to the story of the seizure of the Sabine women by Romulus's men.

differing from her former life, which she took most patiently. And thus was Allinus's house defaced, his goods and lands seized upon, himself imprisoned, his wife in poor estate, his servants driven to wander from place to place, ready often to perish for want of succor, and all his dignity turned to misery only by Lenon's malice. (ch. X)

As a form of regal punishment for the misbehavior of a subject, the dispersal of the household is directly related to the dispossession of women and the abandonment of servants, taking in the threat to the noble household posited by commoners as well.[178]

The master-servant relationship also brings to the fore the romance's concern with the issues of rank and hierarchy, issues dependent on justice, as we see in the episode in which Ornatus scolds Thæon's servant for misbehavior. In chapter XIV, when Ornatus attacks Thæon for being an usurper, the king's servant is the first to apprehend and kill his master. Before Lenon has the servant punished for such treachery by having him tied to horses and torn apart, he spells out the enormity of his crime: "Art thou not one of his [Thæon's] servants? Hast not thou been maintained by him? Did he not trust thee with his life? Was he not thy king? Then how durst thou presume to strike thy master, be ungrateful to him that gave thee gifts, prove false to him that trusted thee and slay thy anointed king." Lenon's reaction to "this sinfulness of ingratitude" is more than just an example of concern with "traditional, hierarchical views."[179] The fact that he punishes his enemy's servant, who actually helps him defeat that enemy, suggests the narrative's preoccupation with the preservation of justice and rank against those who violate them. If we remember, too, that the "orderly family"[180] of Renaissance England included the care of husband and wife not just for their children but for their servants as well, and that husband and wife were responsible for correcting both their children's and

---

[178]At this point Ford's fiction echoes an event that appears to have been unusual in Elizabethan society: "In December 1599, when Essex returned from Ireland, Elizabeth 'dispersed' his household, a potential army of 160, requiring 'every man to seek a new fortune.'" Quoted from Orlin, *Private Matters and Public Culture in Post-Reformation England*, p. 7.

[179]Margolies, *Novel and Society in Elizabethan England*, p. 34.

[180]I borrow the term from Amussen, *An Ordered Society*, p. 96.

their servants' erring behavior, then the behavior of Thæon's servant is also a form of disobedience against the "orderly family," which is the focus of *Ornatus and Artesia*.

In these fictions, in which the romantic and the economic intersect, virtue is close to the humanist conception of the *vir virtutis*, to the sort of virtue that Lorna Hutson defines as men's "ability to overcome the vicissitudes of *fortuna* to master events and make them realize themselves as potential wealth, as good fortune."[181] This aspect of the humanist concept of virtue has roots in the writings of Plato. As Socrates concludes in the *Meno*, "virtue . . . is [the] ability to procure goods," by which he means "health and wealth." But this strand of virtue can be regarded as honorable only if it is tied to "justice and temperance" (78B–C). On his path to wealth and power, Floretus's plan to usurp Artesia's wealth represents an attempt to resist fortune. Ornatus's virtuous actions, however, make him a *vir virtutis* for whom the wealth and prosperity that come with marriage are assured by the very nature of his virtuous behavior.[182] Ornatus's ascension to the throne and his marriage make *Ornatus and Artesia* a profitable discourse, a fiction that offers examples of practical strategies which secure victory in battle, successful government, and a prosperous household for a young gentleman. The courtship plot and the prospects of household government at the end, as opposed to martial exploits, suggest that masculinity in *Ornatus and Artesia* is increasingly related not to the idea of heroism and military valor, but to *oeconomia* or a micro-commonwealth. Thus the narrative explicitly engages with the era's new understanding that a nation need not be forged on the battlefield, but can be moulded and strengthened through the stable government of the household and the protection of wealth and trade. This linkage raises the issue of the relationship between nationalism and masculinity in Ford's fiction, and it has implications

---

[181]Hutson, *Thomas Nashe in Context*, p. 53.

[182]The *vir virtutis*, Hutson argues, "stands as the ideal opposite to the prodigal: the one uses his inventive capacity to produce commodity for himself in spite of his fortune, the other collaborates with fortune in the consumption of his prospects and himself." See Hutson, *Thomas Nashe in Context*, p. 53.

for the popularity and reception of his romance in sixteenth- and seventeenth-century English culture. Ornatus's struggle against the vicissitudes of his world are an effort to pacify the rebelling crowds, and to rid Phrygia of Thæon's law and his usurped power. The establishment of a stable government, in short, is an extension of the ordered and stable household, symbolized in marriage.

Different forms of violence — the abduction of maidens, the plundering of Phrygia, war — are therefore directed not only against women, justice, and the state, but also against the family and, by extension, against lineage as well. Ford's fiction is concerned with virtue and "lineage culture."[183] In *Ornatus and Artesia*, these are regarded as necessary for achieving a "virtuous life" and establishing "peacable government." Because justice and the restoration of order in the lineage is based on the continuation of honor, matters pertaining to proper governing are made central to the narrative. This kind of virtuous and reasonable treatment of physical power in assuring that justice and order do not disrupt succession is best seen in Ornatus's rejection of violence. His moral dilemma, whether or not to kill an enemy (Lenon), is related to masculinity, and is to be contrasted to the traditional chivalric code which declares that killing an enemy is both just and desirable.[184] Ornatus asks:

> shall I now commit murder and endanger my soul by so heinous a sin? What will Artesia say if she [should] know thou art so bloodily bent and that thy heart is so hard as to shed thine own countrymen's blood? Ornatus, be well advised before thou do this deed and bethink of some other mean; avoid the danger thou art ready to fall into.

---

[183]Hutson, *The Usurer's Daughter*, p. 94. Hutson points out the concern of romances with "lineage culture" in keeping with the focus of chivalric romances and early humanist novellas upon cultural values.

[184]George Whetstone echoes the period's idea (inherited from the classics) that masculinity, death, and heroism converge, when he says that "manhood is most truely tried, by constancy in the trembling passage of death." See Whetstone, *The English Myror* (London: I. Windet for G. Seton, 1586; STC 25336), sig. A6^V.

The concern here is not just with this single act, but with the whole character of a virtuous man, a character that does not separate, as does the old chivalric tradition, the heroic from the romantic man. Ornatus's reflections on these concerns prepare him for noble actions through which power will be related to prudent reasoning and honorable agency.

Ornatus's musings about the war in Phrygia suggest that achieving virtue in this instance means stopping the war. "Ornatus's heart was vexed to see so much of his country's blood shed, that he entreated Phylastes to persuade the soldiers to give over, and himself rode betwixt the two armies with a herald, desiring them to stay their fury for a while." And the scene in which Ornatus and Phylastes coordinate their actions to control the crowd's passions by reminding them that Lenon and his father have done great harm to their country and their goods is more than an example of prudent military tactics. In resisting the violence of war, both men reject the old model of chivalric masculinity, instead promoting pragmatic agency and virtue over violence.[185] Ornatus's call for peace, justice, and the restoration of order in the kingdom is manifested in the form of virtue (*arete*), accepted by the ancient thinkers as a quality inherently aligned with the art of organizing a government. Classical writers described this kind of virtue as "learning" that "consists of good judgement in his own affairs, showing how best to order his owne home; and in the affairs of his city, showing how he may have most influence on public affairs both in speech and action" (*Protagoras*, 318E–319A). Ornatus's ability to move his countrymen to justice through rhetoric makes him a virtuous man, someone "excelling all other men in the gift of assisting people to become good and true" (*Protagoras*, 328A). At the time, when "[t]he entire chivalric revival is seen as a nostalgic anachronism and escapist fantasy of a decadent ruling class," as Richard McCoy describes

---

[185]Phylastes's and Ornatus's friendship, which is based on trust, is represented, for example, in chapter XIV, in the episode in which Ornatus dresses in Phylastes's clothes so as not to be recognized among the Phrygians whom he wants to pacify. This trust is assured through the symbolic signification of clothes.

Elizabethan chivalry,[186] Ornatus's pacifying rhetoric, set against masculinity wasted in war, his lament for the destruction of the country's wealth and nobility and the loss of freedom, represent an attempt to rekindle old heroic ideals of valor and honor in a new kind of knight: the Renaissance gentleman. Capturing Lenon and repossessing the realm from usurpation means the restoration of order and justice in Phrygia. Although Ornatus is the legitimate heir, the narrative of Ornatus's rise to the throne becomes a model of action for any ambitious youth seeking social advancement through honorable and heroic means.

The anxiety over usurpation, the interruption of lineage, and the perils of ancestral feuds among the nobility threaten to decimate their ranks, haunting the narrative of *Ornatus and Artesia*. Duke Ternus articulates this when he publicly addresses the Phrygians, exposing, in chapter XVII, the fact that "Thæon . . . was no way interested in the crown but by usurpation, and hath rooted out almost all that he knew to have any title of interest in our late king's blood — of which house Allinus's issue is the last by marriage of the lady Aura, niece unto our late king's blood." But the threat to political order comes not only from the fighting among the nobility, but also from social disorder, exemplified by the storming of Theaon's palace by the unruly multitude (ch. XI). The story of both Lenon's and Ornatus's rise to power shows how, in romances, sons and fathers are embroiled in struggles for sovereignty, struggles that require both "rhetorical cunning and political deviousness."[187] The crowning of Ornatus as king of Phrygia suggests that the crisis of heroic prowess is resolved in the favoring of son over father. Thus the old chivalric tradition is replaced by the judicious and pragmatic rule of the new generation.

The romance narrative of adventure, courtship, and marriage in *Ornatus and Artesia* appealed directly to the period's reigning ideology of social mobility and individual achievement, reinforcing perceptions of the household as a prosperous micro-state. It encouraged readers to imagine and think critically about the roles of men and women within the new mercantile world. Yet

[186]McCoy, *The Rites of Knighthood*, p. 15.

[187]Maslen, *Elizabethan Fictions*, p. 190.

at the same time, the romance narrative presented new ideals of individual achievement and social mobility, becoming a social allegory for the difficulties of achieving political stability and marital felicity.

The Text and Editorial Procedures

In preparing this modernized text, I have collated four editions of *Ornatus and Artesia*. The imperfect copy in the British Library, deemed the earliest (subsequently referred to as A), emended by the second edition (1607) in the Huntington Library provides the most authoritative source upon which to base an edition. Nevertheless, two later editons have been consulted, namely the 1619 edition at the Folger Shakespeare Library (STC 11169ᵃ) and the 1634 edition at the Huntington Library (STC 11170). Hence, all the variants to be found in the [1599], 1607, 1619, and 1634 editions (A, B, C, and D, respectively) have a potential bearing on the control text for this critical edition.[188]

The first surviving title page (and other preliminaries missing in the first) was printed by Thomas Creede in B.[189] It reads as follows:

> THE | MOST PLEASANT | Historie of Ornatŭs | and Artesia. | Wherein is contained the uniust Raigne | of *Thæon* King of *Phry-gia*. | Who with his sonne *Lenon*, (intending *Ornatus* | death,) right Heire to the Crowne, was after- | *wardes slaine by his owne Seruants, and* | *Ornatus* after many extreame mi- | series, Crowned King. | [woodcut] | LONDON | Printed by Thomas Creede, 1607.

The collation is 4⁰: A–R⁴.[190]

[188]The subsequent editions of *Ornatus and Artesia* are 1650 (British Library), 1662 (Houghton Library, Harvard University), and 1669 and 1683 (Beinecke Library, Yale University). Abridgements appeared in 1688, 1694, and 1700. See Esdaile, *A List of Tales and Prose Romances Printed Before 1740*, pp. 5–51.

[189]This copy (STC 11169) is in the Bodleian Library (Douce, A.p. A27).

[190]I give the collation for the ideal copy because we cannot know if the A gathering was ever complete (it may have consisted of three leaves only), because the whole of the A gathering is not missing from the extant copy, only part of it, and because page R4 is missing.

The initial letter on A1ʳ of A — a large ornamental letter of ecclesiastical design with decorative sprays (variation on Plomer 160)[191] — also appears in the 1607 edition. The woodcut in B, an emblem of Truth (Veritas), represents the image of a young virgin whose cape is being snatched by a male hand coming out of the clouds. The text around the emblem reads "Vir essit vulnere verita" (Man harms truth). The headpiece is a slight variation on one of the standard devices (Plomer 50). The tailpiece is an arabesque (Plomer 96). The same headpiece appears in both A and B. Throughout A and B the initial letters are the same, and in both A and B, the same arabesque printer's device appears as well (Plomer 96). The text is in black letter, also known as "English" type. When we look at these similarities in ornamentation, it would appear that A was set in Thomas Creede's printing house, just as the 1607 edition was. Nevertheless differences in catchwords, such as "tesia" (R1ʳ) prove that B was not reprinted from standing type, but from reset type.[192] Further to that point, in A the Epistle to the reader is printed in italics, while in B it is printed in roman type. Moreover, throughout B the turned letters are corrected. Further variants between them include the following:

page	line	A	B
B1ʳ	1	country	countrey
C3ʳ	12	she	shee
G3ʳ	19	vttermost	vtermost
J3ʳ	16	remain	remaine
N2ʳ	24	means	meanes

These and other similar changes are probably the result of differing spelling practices among compositors. Insofar as B (after the preliminaries) is a page-for-page reprint of A, there is no question but that it was printed from the earlier edition and not from the author's manuscript.

---

[191]Plomer, *English Printers' Ornaments*. The number given in parentheses refers to the device in Plomer's catalogue, not the page.

[192]This relationship would be highly unlikely given the (assumed) eight-year gap between the two editions.

Setting new editions from earlier editions rather than returning to manuscripts was standard printing-house practice.[193]
Creede's productions were no exception as can be seen in the
1596 and 1600 editions of Thomas Phaer's translation of *The thir-
teene bookes of Aeneidos*, the 1597 and 1599 editions of Nicholas
Breton's *The will of wit, wits of will, or wills wit*, and the 1596 and
1599 editions of Thomas Vicary's *The englishmans treasure. With
the true anatomie of mans body*.[194]

Edition C is a resetting of B with the usual corrections. The
title page follows the layout and text of B, except for the printer's
device and the name of the new printer, Bernard Alsop, to whom
Creede sold the rights.[195] There are significant adjustments to

---

[193]Using a previous edition for copy had advantages for the printer,
the principal among them that he could now use the printed copy to
set up the new type pages by formes, rather than seriatim. Setting by
formes can be much speedier if the printer has two or more compositors
working at the same time, one on the inner forme, the other on the outer
forme, for example. Indeed, using A would have meant that B could be
set up in any order whatsoever. In addition, there would be no need
for the somewhat awkward and time-consuming task of "casting off."
For printing practice and the use of previous editions in printing new
ones, see Philip Gaskell, *A New Introduction to Bibliography* (New York
and Oxford: Oxford University Press, 1972), pp. 338–51.

[194]Akihiro Yamada. *Thomas Creede*, 13. *Aeneidos*, set in roman type
and containing forty-two sheets, probably took seven weeks to print.
By comparison, the 1607 edition of *Ornatus and Artesia* took about two
weeks to print, the usual time for printing romances. We can conjecture,
however, that it may have taken even less time to print a romance
because it was customary for Renaissance printers to work on more
than one book at a time. By 1595, as Yamada argues (3–6), Creede,
who was an entrepreneurial printer, already had three workmen in his
printing house, one more than was common for an average-size house.
For the Renaissance printers' practice of working on books concurrently,
not sequentially, see also Peter W.M. Blayney, *The Texts of King Lear and
Their Origins*, Vol. I: *Nicholas Okes and the First Quarto* (Cambridge:
Cambridge University Press, 1982).

[195]This copy (STC 11169ᵃ) is in the Folger Shakespeare Library in
Washington, DC. Alsop was Creede's partner in 1616; in the following
year he took over Creede's printing house. See McKerrow, *A Dictionary
of Printers and Booksellers in England, Scotland and Ireland*, p. 81.

the punctuation and a number of substantive variants, however, none of them going beyond the scope of a compositor.[196] The fourth, D, presents a separate case. Its printing was shared between Bernard Alsop and T. Fawcet. The configurations of this edition most resemble C, suggesting that Alsop relied principally upon his own former edtion. D features further changes to commas, italics, and capitalization, as well as to sentences, the longer ones sometimes broken into several shorter ones. The running title in D, too, has been changed to "The most pleasant History, of ORNATUS and ARTESIA." Remarkably, however, there are several instances where D also follows A (without consultation of B) manifesting a kind of editorial frame of mind behind this edition. These changes are most apparent in chapters 5 and 6 (signatures D1^r–F2^v). For the record, the substantive variants appearing in D are recorded fully in the textual annotations.

The table on the next page records some selected variants among the four editions. From this sampling, it would appear that the compositor of C was the most innovative and that the compositor of D followed with a similar sense of license. Their "corrections" were sometimes inspired, sometimes indifferent, sometimes deleterious to the text. They are worth consultation, but lack more than incidental authority, leaving the editor with the primacy of the first two editions as the basis for a modernized copytext.

The following text of *Ornatus and Artesia* follows the basic rules for modern-spelling editions. Punctuation has been emended only for the sake of syntactic clarity; long sentences have been broken down into shorter ones, and I have added quotation marks around dialogue. I have kept the capitalizations of abstract nouns as they appear in the control text (e.g., Fortune), but I have changed capitals to lower case for titles not designating a specific person and substituting for a proper name (e.g., "King" has been changed to "king"). Occasionally, I have inserted a word in square brackets where it seemed absolutely

---

[196]Philip Gaskell (*A New Introduction to Bibliography*, p. 345) suggests that compositors demonstrated a fair amount of freedom in adding punctuation. Joseph Moxon (*Mechanick Exercises in the Whole Art of Printing*, London [1677]) concurs.

page line		A	B	C	D
A1^r	25	And I cease.	And so I cease.	And so I cease.	And I cease.
B3^r	16	intreat	intreat	entreate	intreat
B3^r	30–31	perpetuall bands of kind friendship	perpetuall bands of kinde friendship	perpetuall bandes of kinde loue and friendshippe	perpetuall bandes of kinde loue and friendshippe
C1^r	25	traill of lyaltie	traill of loyaltie	triall of my loyalty	tryall of my loyalty
D3^v	9	I enioy not Artesiaes loue,	I enioy not Artesiaes loue,	I enioy Artesiaes loue,	I enioy Artesiaes loue,
D3^v	9	as I am Ornatus	as I am Ornatus.	as I am Ornatus:	as being Ornatus:
F3^v	6	of with	of with	off with	off with
		on the Natolians sword,	on the Natolians sword,	thereof,	thereof,
		Whilst wreathe	Whilst wreathe	Whilest garland	Whilest garland
		these inhabitants	these inhabitants	the inhabitants	the inhabitants
		according to your	according to your	according your	according your

necessary, either to clarify the meaning or to supply a missing word. The italicization of proper names has been removed, along with the parentheses so frequently employed by Elizabethan stylists. Possessives have been standardized to modern usage. In two instances of names, where the original alternates between two variants, I have adopted the more frequently used spelling. For example, I have used "Thrasus" and "Phylastes," rather than such compositor's variants as "Trasus" and "Philastes."

Bibliography

Adams, Robert. "Bold Bawdry and Open Manslaughter: The English New Humanist Attack on Medieval Romance." *The Huntington Library Quarterly* 33 (1959): 33–48.

Aercke, Kristiaan Paul Guido. Theatrical Technique in Seventeenth-Century Prose Fiction. Ph.D. diss., University of Georgia, 1989.

Alpers, Paul. *What Is Pastoral?* Chicago: University of Chicago Press, 1996.

Amussen, Susan Dwyer. "Punishment, Discipline, and Power: The Social Meanings of Violence in Early Modern England." *Journal of British Studies* 34 (1995): 1–34.

——. *An Ordered Society: Gender and Class in Early Modern England.* Oxford: Basil Blackwell, 1988.

Ascham, Roger. *The Scholemaster.* London, 1570; repr. London: Bell and Daldy (1863); reissue, New York: AMS Press, 1967.

Baker, Ernest A. *The History of the English Novel.* Vol. II: *The Elizabethan Age and After.* London: H.F. and G. Witherby, 1937.

Bakhtin, M.M. *The Dialogic Imagination: Four Essays.* Ed. Michael Holquist. Trans. Caryl Emerson and Michael Holquist. Austin: University of Texas Press, 1981.

Barber, Giles. Daphnis and Chloe: *The Markets and Metamorphoses of an Unknown Bestseller.* London: The British Library, 1989.

Barbour, Reid. *Deciphering Elizabethan Fiction.* Delaware: University of Delaware Press; London: Associated University Presses, 1993.

Barker, W.W. "Rhetorical Romance: The 'Frivolous Toyes' of Robert Green." In *Unfolded Tales: Essays on Renaissance Romance.* Ed. George M. Logan and Gordon Teskey. Ithaca and London: Cornell University Press, 1989, pp. 74–97.

Bate, Jonathan. *Shakespeare and Ovid*. Oxford: Clarendon Press, 1994.

Bauman, Gerd. *The Written Word: Literacy in Transition*. Oxford: Clarendon Press, 1986.

Bawcutt, N.W., ed. "Introduction." Christopher Marlowe. *The Jew of Malta*, The Revels Plays. Manchester: Manchester University Press; Baltimore: Johns Hopkins University Press, 1978.

Beard, Thomas. *The Theatre of Gods Iudgements*. London: Adam Islip, 1597 (STC 1659).

Beecher, Donald, ed. *Critical Approaches to English Prose Fiction, 1520–1640*. Ottawa: Dovehouse Editions, 1998.

Beilin, Elaine V. *The Uses of Mythology in Elizabethan Prose Romance*. New York: Garland, 1988.

Bible. *The Geneva Bible, a facsimile of the 1560 edition*. Ed. Lloyd E. Berry. Madison: University of Wisconsin Press, 1969.

Blayney, Peter W.M. "The Publication of Playbooks." In *A New History of Early English Drama*. Ed. John D. Cox and David Scott Kastan. New York: Columbia University Press, 1997, pp. 384–422.

——. "The Numbers Game: Appraising the Revised *STC*." *The Papers of the Bibliographical Society of America* 88 (1994): 353–407.

——. *The Texts of King Lear and Their Origins*. Vol. I: *Nicholas Okes and the First Quarto*. Cambridge: Cambridge University Press, 1982.

Bond, Richard Warwick. *The Complete Works of John Lyly*. Oxford: Clarendon Press, 1902.

Bonheim, Helmut. "Emanuel Forde: *Ornatus and Artesia*." *Anglia* 90, 1–2 (1972): 43–59.

——, ed. *The English Novel before Richardson: A Checklist of Texts and Criticism to 1970*. Metuchen, N.J.: Scarecrow Press, 1971.

Bredbeck, Gregory W. *Sodomy and Interpretation: Marlowe to Milton*. Ithaca: Cornell University Press, 1991.

Breitenberg, Mark. *Anxious Masculinity in Early Modern England*. Cambridge: Cambridge University Press, 1996.

Breton, Nicholas. *The strange fortvnes of two excellent Princes: in their liues and loues, to their equall Ladies in all the titles of true honour*. London: P. Short for Nicholas Ling, 1600 (STC 3702).

Brewer, John, and Susan Staves, eds. *Early Modern Concepts of Property*. London York: Routledge, 1995.

Brooks, Peter. *Reading for the Plot: Design and Intention in Narrative*. Cambridge, Mass.: Harvard University Press, 1984.

Bullough, Geoffrey. *Narrative and Dramatic Sources of Shakespeare*. 8 vols. London: Routledge and Kegan Paul; New York: Columbia University Press, 1957. Vol. I.

Burke, Peter. *Popular Culture in Early Modern Europe.* New York: New York University Press, 1978.

Burnett, Mark Thornton. *Masters and Servants in English Renaissance Drama and Culture: Authority and Obedience.* New York: St. Martin's Press, 1997.

Bush, Douglas. *English Literature in the Earlier Seventeenth Century.* New York: Oxford University Press, 1952.

Canary, Robert H., and Henry Kozicki, eds. *The Writing of History: Literary Form and Historical Understanding.* Madison: University of Wisconsin Press, 1978.

Capp, Bernard. "Popular Literature." In *Popular Culture in Seventeenth-Century England.* Ed. Barry Reay. New York: St. Martin's Press, 1985, pp. 198–243.

Chambers, E.K. *William Shakespeare: A Study of Facts and Problems.* 2 vols. Oxford: Clarendon, 1930. Vol. I.

Chew, Samuel Claggett. *The Crescent and the Rose: Islam and England during the Renaissance.* New York: Oxford University Press, 1937.

Clegg, Cyndia Susan. *Press Censorship in Elizabethan England.* Cambridge: Cambridge University Press, 1997.

Cohn, Jan. *Romance and the Erotics of Property: Mass-Market Fiction for Women.* Durham: Duke University Press, 1988.

Conway, Eustace. *Anthony Munday and Other Essays.* New York: Privately printed, 1927.

Cooper, Thomas. *Thesaurus linguae Romane et Britannicae.* London: for H. Wykes, 1565 (STC 5689).

Craven, Alan E. "Simmers' Compositor A and Five Shakespeare Quartos." *Studies in Bibliography* 26 (1973): 37–60.

Cressy, David. *Birth, Marriage, and Death: Ritual, Religion, and the Life-Cycle in Tudor and Stuart England.* Oxford: Oxford University Press, 1997.

———. "Gender Trouble and Cross-Dressing in Early Modern England." *Journal of British Studies* 35 (1996): 438–65.

———. *Literacy and the Social Order: Reading and Writing in Tudor and Stuart England.* Cambridge: Cambridge University Press, 1980.

Curtius, Hans Robert. *European Literature and the Latin Middle Ages.* Trans. Willard R. Trask. New York: Pantheon Books for Bollingen Foundation, 1966.

Davis, Walter. *Idea and Act in Elizabethan Fiction.* Princeton: Princeton University Press, 1969.

Day, Angel, trans. *Daphnis and Chloe excellently describing the weight of affection, in a pastorall, and within the same pastorall. The shepheards holidaie.* London: Robert Waldegraue, 1587 (STC 6400).

de Certeau, Michel. *The Writing of History.* Trans. Tom Conley. New York: Columbia University Press, 1988.

Delumeau, Jean. *History of Paradise: The Garden of Eden in Myth and Tradition.* Trans. Matthew O'Connell. Urbana: University of Illinois Press, 2000.

Demetz, Peter, Thomas Greene, and Lowry Nelson, Jr. *The Disciplines of Criticism: Essays in Literary Theory, Interpretation, and History.* New Haven: Yale University Press, 1968.

Di Gangi, Mario. *The Homoerotics of Early Modern Drama.* Cambridge: Cambridge University Press, 1997.

Dipple, Elizabeth. "The Captivity Episode and the New Arcadia." *Journal of English and Germanic Philology* 73 (1971): 418–31.

Doody, Margaret Anne. *The True Story of the Novel.* New Brunswick, NJ: Rutgers University Press, 1996.

Dollimore, Jonathan. "Shakespeare, Cultural Materialism, Feminism and Marxist Humanism." *New Literary History* 21 (1990): 471–93.

Elliott, J.K. *The Apocryphal New Testament: A Collection of Apocryphal Christian Literature in an English Translation.* Oxford: Clarendon, 1993.

Esdaile, Arundell. *A List of English Tales and Prose Romances Printed before 1740.* London: The Bibliographical Society, 1912; repr. 1971.

Falke, Anne Amelia. Medieval and Popular Elements in the Romances of Emanuel Forde. Ph.D. diss., Michigan State University, 1974.

——— . " 'The Work Well Done that Pleaseath All': Emanuel Forde and the Seventeenth-Century Popular Chivalric Romances." *Studies in Philology* 78 (1981): 241–54.

——— . *Montelyon: Knight of Oracle, a modern edition. Salzburg Studies in English Literature* 99. Institut für Anglistik und Amerikanistik, Universität Salzburg, 1981.

Febvre, Lucien, and Henri-Jean Martin. *The Coming of the Book: The Impact of Printing, 1450–1800.* Trans. David Gerard. London York: Verso, 1990.

Ferguson, W. Craig. "The Compositors of *Henry IV, Part 2, Much Ado about Nothing, The Shoemaker's Holiday,* and *The First Part of the Contention.*" *Studies in Bibliography* 13 (1960): 19–29.

Fitz, Linda T. "'What Says the Married Woman?': Marriage Theory and Feminism in the English Renaissance." *Mosaic* 13, 2 (1980): 2–22.

Fletcher, Anthony. *Gender, Sex and Subordination in England 1500–1800.* New Haven: Yale University Press, 1995.

Frye, Northrop. *The Secular Scripture: A Study of the Structure of Romance.* Cambridge, Mass.: Harvard University Press, 1976.

Gaskell, Philip. *A New Introduction to Bibliography.* New York: Oxford University Press, 1972.

Gaunt, J.L. *"The Most Excellent History of Ornatus and Aurelia*: An Unusual Restoration Abridgement." *Studies in Short Fiction* 14 (1971): 399–401.

Goldhill, Simon. Foucault's *Virginity: Ancient Erotic Fiction and the History of Sexuality.* Cambridge: Cambridge University Press, 1995.

Greene, Thomas M. *The Light in Troy: Imitation and Discovery in Renaissance Poetry.* New Haven: Yale University Press, 1982.

Gubar, Susan D. Tudor Romance and Eighteenth-Century Fiction. Ph.D. diss., University of Iowa, 1972.

Hacket, Helen. *Women and Romance Fiction in the English Renaissance.* Cambridge: Cambridge University Press, 2000.

Halasz, Alexandra. *The Marketplace of Print: Pamphlets and the Public Sphere in Early Modern England.* Cambridge: Cambridge University Press, 1997.

Hall, Anne Drury. "Tudor Prose Style: English Humanists and the Problem of a Standard." *English Literary Renaissance* 7 (1977): 267–96.

Hamilton, A.C. "Elizabethan Prose Style and Some Trends in Recent Criticism." *Renaissance Quarterly* 37 (1984): 21–33.

———. "Elizabethan Romance: The Example of Prose Fiction." *English Literary History* 49 (1982): 287–99.

Hanning, Robert W. *The Individual in Twelfth-Century Romance.* New Haven: Yale University Press, 1977.

Helgerson, Richard. *Elizabethan Prodigals.* Berkeley: University of California Press, 1976.

———. "Lyly, Greene, Sidney, and Barnaby Rich's Brusanus." *Huntington Library Quarterly* 36 (1972/73): 105–18.

Henderson, Philip, ed. *Shorter Novels: Seventeenth Century.* London: J.M. Dent; New York: E.P. Dutton, 1930.

Hergest, William. *The right rvle of Christian Chastitie.* London: Richard Johnes, 1580 (STC 13203).

Hill, Christopher. "Sex, Marriage, and the Family in England." *Economic History Review,* 2nd series, 31 (1978): 450–63.

Hoskins, John. *Directions for Speech and Style.* Ed. Hoyt H. Hudson. Princeton: Princeton University Press, 1935.

Houlbrooke, Ralph A. *The English Family, 1450–1700.* London: Longman, 1984.

Howard, Jean E. "Cross-dressing, the Theatre, and Gender Struggle in Early Modern England." *Shakespeare Quarterly* 39 (1988): 418–40.

Hull, Suzane W. *Chaste, Silent, and Obedient: English Books for Women, 1475–1640.* San Marino: Huntington Library, 1982.

Hunter, J. Paul. *Before Novels: The Cultural Contexts of Eighteenth-Century English Fiction.* New York: Norton, 1990.

———. "The Young, the Ignorant, and the Idle: Some Notes on Readers and the Beginning of the English Novel." In *Anticipations of the Enlightenment in England, France, and Germany.* Ed. Alan Charles Kors and Paul J. Korshin. Philadelphia: University of Pennsylvania Press, 1987, pp. 259–82.

Hurrell, John Dennis. "*Loues Load-Starre*: A Study in Elizabethan Literary Craftsmanship." *Boston University Studies in English* 1 (1955): 197–209.

Hutson, Lorna. *The Usurer's Daughter: Male Friendship and Fictions of Women in Sixteenth-Century England.* London: Routledge, 1994.

———. "Fortunate Travelers: Reading for the Plot in Sixteenth-Century England." *Representations* 41 (1993): 83–103.

———. *Thomas Nashe in Context.* Oxford: Clarendon Press, 1989.

Ingram, Martin. *Church Courts, Sex and Marriage in England, 1570–1640.* Cambridge: Cambridge University Press, 1987.

Jameson, Fredric. "Magical Narratives: Romance as Genre." *New Literary History* 7 (1975–76), 135–63.

Jankowski, Theodora A. *Pure Resistance: Queer Virginity in Early Modern English Drama.* Philadelphia: University of Pennsylvania Press, 2000.

Jardine, Lisa, and Anthony Grafton. "'Studied for Action': How Gabriel Harvey Read His Livy." *Past and Present* 129 (1990): 30–78.

Jauss, Hans Robert. "Literary History as a Challenge to Literary Theory." Trans. Elizabeth Benzinger. *New Literary History* 2 (1970): 12–13.

Jones, Rosalind and Peter Stallybrass. *Renaissance Clothing and the Materials of Memory.* Cambridge: Cambridge University Press, 2000.

Jordan, Constance. *Renaissance Feminism: Literary Texts and Political Models.* Ithaca: Cornell University Press, 1990.

Jusserand, J.J. *The English Novel in the Time of Shakespeare.* London: Ernest Benn; New York: Barnes and Noble, 1966.

Kinney, Arthur. *Humanist Poetics: Thought, Rhetoric, and Fiction in Sixteenth-Century England.* Amherst: University of Massachusetts Press, 1986.

———. "Rhetoric and Fiction in Elizabethan England." In *Renaissance Eloquence: Studies in the Theory and Practice of Renaissance Rhetoric.* Ed. James J. Murphy. Berkeley: University of California Press, 1983, pp. 385–93.

——. "Rhetoric as Poetic: Humanist Fiction in the Renaissance." *Journal of English Literary History* 43 (1976): 413–43.

——. "Situational Poetics." *Prose Studies* 2, 2 (1988): 10–24.

Klein, Herbert-Günther. *Der Romanbrief in der englischen Literatur vom 16. bis zum 18. Jahrhundert. European University Studies Series* 14; *Anglo-Saxon Language and Literature* 154. Frankfurt-am-Mein: Lang, 1986.

Kloesel, Christian J.W., ed. *English Novel Explication: Supplement III.* Hamden: Shoe String Press, 1986.

Kronitiris, Tina. "Breaking Barriers of Genre and Gender: Margaret Tyler's Translation of The Mirrour of Knighthood." *English Literary Renaissance* 18 (1988): 19–39.

Lanham, Richard. "Opaque Style in Elizabethan Fiction." *Publications of the Philological Association of the Pacific Coast* 1 (1966): 25–31.

Leavis, Q.D. *Fiction and the Reading Public.* New York: Russell and Russell, 1965.

Levi, Giovanni, and Jean-Claude Schmitt. *A History of Young People in the West.* Vol. I: *Ancient and Medieval Rites of Passage.* Trans. Camille Naish. London: Belknap Press of Harvard University Press, 1997. 2 vols.

Levine, Laura. *Men in Women's Clothing: Anti-theatricality and Effeminization, 1579–1642.* Cambridge: Cambridge University Press, 1994.

Lithgow, William. *The Total Discourse of the Rare Adventures and Principal Peregrinations.* Glasgow: James MacLehose and Sons, 1906.

Logan, George M., and Gordon Teskey. *Unfolded Tales: Essays on Renaissance Romance.* Ithaca: Cornell University Press, 1989.

Loiseau, Jean. "Le récit dans le roman d'Emmanuel Ford: *Ornatus and Artesia.*" In *Récit et roman: Formes du roman anglais du XVIe au XXe.* Paris: Marcel Didier [n.d.], pp. 16–21.

Lucas, Caroline. *Writing for Women: The Example of Woman as Reader in Elizabethan Romance.* Milton Keynes: Open University Press, 1989.

Lyly, John. *Euphues: The Anatomy of Wit; Euphues and his England.* Ed. Morris William Croll and Harry Clemons. New York: Russell and Russell, 1964. [1916]

——. *The Complete Works.* Ed. R.W. Bond. 3 vols. Oxford: Clarendon Press, 1902.

Margolies, David. *Novel and Society in Elizabethan England.* London: Croom Helm, 1985.

Marlowe, Christopher. *The Complete Works of Christopher Marlowe.* 5 vols. Ed. Roma Gill. Vol. IV: *The Jew of Malta.* Oxford: Clarendon Press, 1995.

Maslen, Robert. W. *Elizabethan Fictions: Espionage, Counter-Espionage, and the Duplicity of Fiction in Early Elizabethan Prose Narratives.* Oxford: Clarendon Press, 1997.

McBurney, William H., ed. *A Check List of English Prose Fiction 1700–1739.* Cambridge, Mass.: Harvard University Press, 1960.

Meres, Francis. "School of English Literature, Painting, and Music, up to September 1598." In *An English Garner: Critical Essays and Literary Fragments.* Ed. J(ohn) Churton Collins. Westminster: Archibald Constable, 1903.

———. *English Prose Fiction 1700–1800 in the University of Illinois Library.* Urbana: University of Illinois Press, 1965.

McCoy, Richard C. *The Rites of Knighthood: The Literature and Politics of Elizabethan Chivalry.* Berkeley: University of California Press, 1989.

———. *Sir Philip Sidney: Rebellion in Arcadia.* New Brunswick, NJ: Rutgers University Press, 1979.

McKeon, Michael. *The Origins of the English Novel, 1600–1740.* Baltimore: Johns Hopkins University Press, 1987.

McKerrow, R.B., ed. *A Dictionary of Printers and Booksellers in England, Scotland and Ireland, and of Foreign Printers of English Books 1557–1640.* London: The Bibliographical Society, 1910.

Mercer, John M. "Adaptation of Conventions in the Elizabethan Prose Dedication." *Explorations in Renaissance Culture* 15 (1989): 49–58.

Mish, Charles C., ed. *English Prose Fiction, 1600–1700.* Charlottesville: Bibliographical Society of the University of Virginia, 1967.

———. "Best Sellers in Seventeenth-Century Fiction." *Papers of the Bibliographical Society of America* 47 (1953): 356–73.

———. "Black Letter as a Social Discriminant in the Seventeenth Century." *PMLA* 68 (1953): 627–30.

———. "Comparative Popularity of Early Fiction and Drama." *Notes and Queries* 197 (1952): 269–70.

Morgan, Charlotte E. *The Rise of the Novel of Manners: A Study of Euphuistic Prose Fiction between 1600 and 1740.* New York: Russell and Russell, 1963.

Morss, Robert Lovett, and Helen Sard Hughes. *The History of the Novel in England.* Boston: Houghton Mifflin, 1932.

Murphy, James J., ed. *Renaissance Eloquence: Studies in the Theory and Practice of Renaissance Rhetoric.* Berkeley: University of California Press, 1983.

Newcomb, Lori Humphrey. "'Social Things': The Production of Popular Culture in the Reception of Robert Greene's *Pandosto.*" *English Literary History* 61 (1994): 753–81.

Nicholl, Charles. *The Reckoning: The Murder of Christopher Marlowe*. London: Jonathan Cape, 1992.

O'Connell Stevenson, Laura. "The Elizabethan Bourgeois Hero-Tale: Aspects of an Adolescent Social Consciousness." In *After the Reformation: Essays in Honor of J.H. Hexter*. Ed. Barbara C. Malamet. Philadelphia: University of Pennsylvania Press, 1980, pp. 267–90.

O'Connor, John J. *Amadis de Gaule and Its Influence on Elizabethan Literature*. New Brunswick, NJ: Rutgers University Press, 1970.

Ong, Walter J. "Oral Residue in Tudor Prose Style." *PMLA* 80, 3 (1965): 145–54.

Orgel, Stephen. *Impersonations: The Performance of Gender in Shakespeare's England*. Cambridge: Cambridge University Press, 1996.

Orlin, Lena Cowen. *Private Matters and Public Culture in Post-Reformation England*. Ithaca: Cornell University Press, 1994.

Ovid. Ovid's *Metamorphoses: The Arthur Golding Translation*. Ed. John Frederick Nims. New York: Collier-Macmillan, 1965.

Parker, Patricia. *Inescapable Romance: Studies in the Poetics of a Mode*. Princeton: Princeton University Press, 1979.

Patchell, Mary. *The* Palmerin *Romances in Elizabethan Prose Fiction*. New York: AMS Press, 1966.

Patterson, Annabel. *Censorship and Interpretation: The Conditions of Writing and Reading in Early Modern England*. Madison: University of Wisconsin Press, 1984.

Percy, C.H. Herford, and Evelyn Simpson, eds. "An Execration upon Vulcan" (1640). In *Ben Jonson*. 11 vols. Oxford: Clarendon, 1947, Vol. VIII: 202–12.

Pettie, George. *A Petite Pallance of Pettie His Pleasure*. Ed. Herbert Hartman. London: Oxford University Press, 1938.

Pigeon, Renée Marie. Prose Fiction Adaptations of Sidney's *Arcadia*. Ph.D. diss., University of California, Los Angeles, 1988.

Plato. *Laches, Protagoras, Meno, Euthydemus*. Trans. W.R.M. Lamb. *The Loeb Classical Library* 4. London: William Heinemann; New York: G.P. Putnam's Sons, 1924.

Plomer, Henry R. *English Printers' Ornaments*. New York: Burt Franklin, 1924.

Prendergast, Maria Teresa Micaela. *Renaissance Fantasies: The Gendering of Aesthetics in Early Modern Fiction*. Kent, OH: Kent State University Press, 1999.

Pruvost, René. *Matteo Bandello and Elizabethan Fiction*. Paris: H. Campion, 1937.

Puttenham, George. *The Arte of English Poesie*. Ed. Gladys Doidge Will-cock and Alice Walker. Cambridge: Cambridge University Press, 1936.

Radford, Jean, ed. *The Progress of Romance: The Politics of Popular Fiction*. London York: Routledge and Kegan Paul, 1986.

Radway, Janice A. *Reading the Romance: Women, Patriarchy, and Popular Literature*. Chapel Hill: University of North Carolina Press, 1984.

Rainolds, John. *Th' overthrow of stage-playes*. Middleburg: R. Schilders, 1599 (STC 20616).

Randall, Dale B.J. *The Golden Tapestry: A Critical Survey of Non-Chivalric Spanish Fiction in English Translation, 1543–1637*. Durham: Duke University Press, 1963.

Relihan, Constance C. *Framing Elizabethan Fictions: Contemporary Approaches to Early Modern Narrative Prose*. Kent, OH: Kent State University Press, 1996.

———. *Fashioning Authority: The Development of Elizaberthan Novelistic Discourse*. Kent, OH: Kent State University Press, 1994.

Rhodes, Neil, ed. *English Renaissance Prose: History, Language, and Politics*. Tempe, Arizona: Medieval and Renaissance Texts and Studies, 1997.

Richardson, Brenda E. "Two English Francophiles: Some French Influences on Fashionable Elizabethan Fiction." *Proceedings of the Royal Irish Academy* 84 (1984): 225–35.

Roberts, Lewes. *The Marchants Mappe of Commerce*. London: by R.O. for Ralphe Mabb, 1638 (STC 21094).

Robertson, Jean. *The Art of Letter Writing: An Essay on the Handbooks Published in England during the Sixteenth and Seventeenth Centuries*. Liverpool: University Press; London: Hodder and Stoughton, 1943.

Ruggiero, Guido. "Marriage, Love, Sex, and Renaissance Civic Morality." In *Sexuality and Gender in Early Modern Europe: Institutions, Texts, Images*. Ed. James Grantham Turner. Cambridge: Cambridge University Press, 1995, p. 10–30.

Salzman, Paul. *English Prose Fiction, 1558–1700: A Critical History*. Oxford: Clarendon Press, 1985.

Scanlon, Paul A. "A Checklist of Prose Romances in English: 1474–1603." *The Library*, 5th series, 33 (1978): 143–52.

Schlauch, Margaret. "English Short Fiction in the 15th and 16th Centuries." *Studies in Short Fiction* 3 (1966): 393–434.

———. *The Antecedents of the English Novel, 1400–1600 (from Chaucer to Deloney)*. Warsaw: Polish Scientific Publishers; London: Oxford University Press, 1963.

Schleiner, Winfried. "Le feu caché: Homosocial Bonds between Women in a Renaissance Romance." *Renaissance Quarterly* 44 (1992): 293–311.

———. "Male Cross-Dressing and Transvestism in Renaissance Romance." *Sixteenth-Century Journal* 19 (1988): 605–19.

Schleiner, Louise. "Ladies and Gentlemen in Two Genres of Elizabethan Fiction." *Studies in English Literature, 1500–1900* 29 (1989): 1–20.

Seaton, Ethel. "Marlowe's Map." In *Marlowe: A Collection of Critical Essays*. Ed. Clifford Leech. Englewood Cliffs, NJ: Prentice-Hall, 1964.

Shakespeare, William. *Twelfth Night*. Ed. Roger Warren and Stanley Wells. Oxford: Oxford University Press, 1995.

———. *The Shakespeare Allusion-Book: A Collection of Allusions to Shakespeare from 1591 to 1700*. 2 vols. Originally comp. by C.M. Ingleby, L. Toulmin Smith, and F.J. Furnivall; re-ed John Munro. London: Humphrey Milford, Oxford University Press, 1932.

———. *Romeo and Juliet by William Shakespeare: The First Quarto, 1597*. A facsimile from the British Library copy. Ed. Charles Praetorius. Intr. Herbert A. Evans. London: C. Praetorius, 1886.

Sidney, Sir Philip. *The Countess of Pembroke's Arcadia (The Old Arcadia)*. Ed. Jean Robertson. Oxford: Clarendon Press, 1973.

———. *The Countess of Pembroke's Arcadia (The New Arcadia)*. Ed. Victor Skretkowicz. Oxford: Clarendon Press, 1987.

———. *A Defence of Poetry*. In *Miscellaneous Prose of Sir Philip Sidney*. Ed. Katherine Duncan-Jones and Jan Van Dorsten. Oxford: Clarendon Press, 1973.

Singer, Godfrey Frank. *The Epistolary Novel: Its Origin, Development, Decline, and Residuary Influence*. New York: Russell and Russell, 1963.

Smith, Rowland, ed. *The Greek Romances of Heliodorus, Longus, and Achilles Tatius*. London: Henry G. Bahn, 1855.

Smith, Thomas. *The Common-welth of England, and maner of government*. London: Iohn Windet for Gregorie Seton, 1589 (STC 22859).

Spufford, Margaret. "First Steps in Literacy: The Reading and Writing Experiences of the Humblest Seventeenth-Century Spiritual Autobiographers." *Social History* 4 (1978): 407–35.

———. *Small Books and Pleasant Histories: Popular Fiction and Its Readership in Seventeenth-Century England*. Athens: University of Georgia Press, 1981.

Staton, Walter F., Jr. "The Character of Style in Elizabethan Prose." *Journal of English and Germanic Philology* 57 (1958): 197–207.

Staves, Susan. *Married Women's Separate Property in England, 1660–1833*. Cambridge, Mass.: Harvard University Press, 1990.

104   ORNATUS AND ARTESIA

Stevenson, Laura Caroline. *Praise and Paradox: Merchants and Craftstmen in Elizabethan Popular Literature*. Cambridge: Cambridge University Press, 1984.

Stone, Lawrence. "Literacy and Education in England, 1640–1900." *Past and Present* 42 (1969): 69–139.

Stubbes, Philip. *The anatomie of abuses: contayning a discouerie, of vices in a verie famous ilande called Ailgna*. London: J. Kingston for Richard Jones, 1583 (STC 23376).

Thomas, Henry. "The Palmerin Romances." *Transactions of the Bibliograhical Society* 14 (1916): 98–144.

———. "The Romance of Amadis of Gaul." *Transactions of the Bibliographical Society* 11 (1913): 251–97.

Tilley, Morris Palmer. *A Dictionary of the Proverbs in England in the Sixteenth and Seventeenth Centuries: A Collection of Proverbs Found in English Literature and the Dictionaries of the Period*. Ann Arbor: University of Michigan Press, 1950.

Trimpi, Wesley. *Muses of One Mind: The Literary Analysis of Experience and Its Continuity*. Princeton, NJ: Princeton University Press, 1983.

Vinaver, Eugene. *The Rise of Romance*. Oxford: Clarendon Press, 1971.

Wall, Alison. "Elizabethan Precept and Feminine Practice: The Thynne Family of Longleat," *History* 75 (1990): 23–38.

Wall, Wendy. *The Imprint of Gender: Authorship and Publication in the English Renaissance*. Ithaca: Cornell University Press, 1993.

Weimann, Robert. "Minstrelsy and Author-Function in Romance." In *Authority and Representation in Early Modern Discourse*. Ed. David Hillman. Baltimore: Johns Hopkins University Press, 1996, pp. 120–32.

Wells, Stanley, and Gary Taylor. *William Shakespeare: A Textual Companion*. Oxford: Clarendon Press, 1987.

Whetstone, George. *Avrelia: The Paragon of Pleasure and Princely Delights*. London: Richard Iohnes, 1593 (STC 25338).

White, R.S. " 'Comedy' in Elizabethan Prose Romances." *The Yearbook of English Studies* 5 (1975): 46–51.

———. "The Rise and Fall of Elizabethan Fashion: Love Letters in Romances and Shakespearean Comedy." *Cahiers Élisabéthaines* 30 (1986): 35–47.

Williams, Franklin. *Index to Dedications and Commendatory Verses in English Books Before 1641*. London: Bibliographical Society, 1962.

Williams, Gordon. *A Dictionary of Sexual Language and Imagery in Shakespearean and Stuart Literature*. 3 vols. London: Athlone Press, 1994.

Wilson Richard. "Voyage to Tunis: New History and the Old World in the Tempest." *English Literary History* 64 (1997): 333–57.

Wilson, Thomas. *The Art of Rhetoric* (1560). Ed. Peter E. Medine. University Park: Pennsylvania State University Press, 1994.

Wolff, Samuel Lee. *The Greek Romances in Elizabethan Prose Fiction*. New York: Columbia University Press, 1912.

Woodbridge, Linda. *Women and the English Renaisssance: Literature and the Nature of Womankind, 1540–1620*. Urbana: University of Illinois Press, 1984.

Wright, Celeste Turner. *Anthony Mundy: An Elizabethan Man of Letters*. Berkeley: University of California Press, 1928; Millwood, NY: Kraus Reprint Co., 1977.

Wright, Louis B. "Henry Robarts: Patriotic Propagandist and Novelist." *Studies in Philology* 29 (1932): 176–99.

Yamada, Akihiro. *Thomas Creede: Printer to Shakespeare and His Contemporaries*. Tokyo: Meisei University Press, 1994.

T H E
MOST PLEASANT
Historie of Ornatus
and Artesia.

Wherein is contained the vniust Raigne
of *Thæon* King of *Phrygia*.

Who with his sonne *Lenon*, (intending *Ornatus*
death,) right Heire to the Crowne, was after-
wards slaine by his owne Servants, and
Ornatus after many extreame miseries, Crowned King.

LONDON
Printed by Thomas Creed, 1607.

TO THE RIGHT WORSHIPFUL
BRIAN STAPLETON OF CARLETON,
IN THE COUNTY OF YORK, ESQUIRE,
THE HEAVENS GRANT HEALTH, CONTENT, AND AFTER LIFE,
EVERLASTING HAPPINESS.

This unpolished history, Right Worshipful, wanting the ornament of eloquence fit for rare° invention, presenteth itself in his
natural and self-expressing form, in well applied words, not in
tedious borrowed phrases, wherein neither the lewd can find
examples to suit their dispositions, the virtuous no terms to discontent them, nor the well-affected any cause of offence. Here
shall you see lust tyrannizing, avarice guilty of murder, and dignity seeking his content with usurpation, yet all subverted by
virtue. Which I am bold to present unto you, not for the worth,
but to express my good will which is not unmindful in some sort
to gratify the manifold courtesies I have received of you. And although it be altogether not worth estimation, and to be accounted
no requital for so many good turns, yet I desire you to accept the
same instead of a better, and the sum° of that which my ability at
this time can afford: which being but a fancy,° vouchsafe to esteem, though not agreeing with your gravity, yet (as many both
noble and wise in such like matters have done) to be read for
recreation. As the value of the gift expresses not the affection of
the giver, nor the outward show the inward meaning, so I trust
you will esteem my goodwill, not by the worthiness hereof but
the quality of my well-affected° intent, which is devoted unto
you in the bands° of perfect good will, and will be ready to show
itself constant in any trial you shall make thereof. And for that
I know your wisdom and courtesy to be such as that you will

rare splendid, excellent.   **sum** fullest amount.   **fancy** light imaginative creation, bagatelle.   **well-affected** most friendly.   **bands**
bonds.

not misconceive me, but esteem well hereof, and my affection
to you to be expressed in the dedication, I have adventured to
dedicate the same to your protection though altogether undeserving the title of your patronage, which your further kindness
shall bind me hereafter to requite the same with some worthier
work collected° by my labors. Thus, being loath to be tedious
and troublesome unto you, I commit this silly° present to your
gentle acceptation, and yourself to the gracious protection of the
Almighty.

Your worship's most ready at° command,
Emanuel Ford.

THE EPISTLE
TO THE READER.

Gentlemen, I have published this history at the entreaty of some
of my familiar friends, being at the first with no intent to have
it printed, for as yet having taken but one flight I durst not too
boldly venture again lest my unskilfulness might cause my repentance. But being supported by the assistance of your gentle
favors, I shall grow hardy and hereafter labor to procure your
further delight the reward I expect being your kind acceptance.
But if, contrary to my thought, this my summer fruit be gathered
before it be ripe, I promise amends with old fruit that has been
a year in ripening and in the beginning of the next winter coming forth. In the meantime, peruse this history which savoreth
more of pleasure than eloquence, and although hastily compiled,
yet let it pass under your favorable censure, and by your courtesies be shrouded from the variable dislikes of Momus's[1] vain
imitators. The learned, wise, and courteous will, according to
the quality of their dispositions, esteem well of this unworthy
work, valuing the same, not by the worth but by the will of the

collected composed, assembled.   **silly** plain, simple.   **at** to.

writer. As for such as either rashly condemn without judgment, or lavishly dislike without advice, I esteem them like the down of thistles inconstantly disperst with every blast, accounting their discontent my content not caring for to please those that are pleased with nothing. But did my gains countervail° my labors, I would then frame my fancy to fit their humors, but getting nothing I can lose no less. Only to have a good opinion of the well-affected to learning is all I crave, and that I hope your good minds will afford.°

As at a banquet there are several kinds of meats, some pleasant, other sharp, yet all tasted, amongst grapes, some sour, some sweet, yet all esteemed so, with indifference amongst variety of eloquent histories, let this serve as one dish to furnish out a banquet and, like sour and sweet intermingled, make a pleasant taste by your courteous construing of my good meaning and your favorable opinion of Ornatus's love. So shall I account my debt to you great, my labors well bestowed, and myself bound to requite your kindness. You shall show your affection to learning, virtue in savoring good endeavors, and give encouragement to more worthy labors. I rest well contented, my reward rich, and hereafter be both ready and willing to deserve your courtesy. But if Ornatus's love breed my blame as it bred his banishment, then may I wish I had never known thereof, and cry out of mala fortuna° as my reward. With the bird Celos bred in Africa[2] who wandering far from her nest by forgetfulness cannot return and so forever after abandoneth company, so I too, boldly building on your courtesy, may be wounded with repentance and by my oversight be brought in despair unless your courtesy prevent the same on which my hopes depend. And so I cease.

E. Ford.

countervail equal, counterbalance.   afford to manage to give.
mala fortuna bad luck.

THE MOST PLEASANT HISTORY OF

ORNATUS AND ARTESIA

CHAPTER I

How Ornatus was Enamored of the Fair Artesia.

In the rich and renowned country of Phrygia,[3] in provinces not far distant from near neighborhood, dwelt two ancient knights, the one named Allinus, the other Arbastus, men of great possessions and much honored. Betwixt whom such extreme contention and hatred remained, by reason of the death of one Renon, brother to Allinus, long since slain in a quarrel by certain gentlemen belonging to Arbastus, that neither their own wisdom nor the sundry° persuasions of friends to either party allied were of any force to mitigate the same, both of them being enriched with innumerable blessings, especially in their fair progeny.

Allinus having a son of goodly stature and commendable gifts named Ornatus, and Arbastus a daughter called Artesia of exceeding comeliness, exteriorly beautified with abundance of gifts of nature and inwardly adorned with abundance of divine perfections, yet by reason of their parents' discord, they remained as far ignorant in knowledge one of the other as if they had been separated by an innumerable distance of strange countries.

Ornatus, above all things, delighted in hawking, and on a day, being weary, he wandered without company with his hawk on his fist into a most pleasant valley, where he shrouded himself under the shadow of a tuft of green trees with purpose to rest himself, and even when his eyes were ready to yield to slumber, he was revived from his drowsiness by the noise of a kennel of hounds that passed by him in chase of a stag, after whom Arbastus and divers in his company (though to him unknown) followed, who being passed by whilst he was in a deep study to think what they should be, he espied a beautiful damsel entering the same valley, who, being somewhat weary, liking the prospect

sundry various.

113

of that shady tuft of trees, alighted there, which Ornatus seeing, withdrew himself from her sight, whilst she, tying her steed to a bush, laid her delicate body down upon the cooling earth to breathe herself and dry up her sweat, which the sooner to accomplish, she unbraced her garments and with a decent and comely behavior discovered her milk-white neck and breast, beautified with two round precious teats, to receive the breath of the cool wind, which was affected with a delight° to exhale° the moistened vapors from her pure body. Ornatus seeing all, and unseen himself, noted with delight each perfect lineament of her proper body, beauty, sweet favor, and other comeliness, which filled his heart with exceeding pleasure, therewith growing into an unrestrained affection towards her, and a great study° what she should be, when suddenly his hawk feeling his fist unmoveable, thinking to perch herself with quiet, primed° herself, and with the noise of her bells made Artesia start, who as one half-aghast, with a fearful behavior arose from the ground. Looking round about her from whence that sound came, she espied Ornatus (who unwilling she should perceive he had yet seen her, lay as if he had slept), Artesia marvelling what he should be, and accordingly thinking he had slept, closed her naked breast with great haste and unloosing her horse thought to go away unespied. Which Ornatus perceiving, and unwilling without speaking to her to lose her sight, seemed to awake, and raising himself steadfastly beheld her, which infused such a red vermilion blush into her beautiful cheeks, and withal such a bashful confusion spread itself in her conceits,° that she stood like one half-amazed or ashamed. Which Ornatus perceiving, drew towards her, and greeted her with these speeches: "Fair damsel, be not abashed with my presence, though a stranger, which shall no way, if I can choose, offend you, but rather, command me° and I will be ready to do you any service." Artesia, notwithstanding his speeches,

---

affected with a delight moved by pleasure.   **exhale** draw forth.
study consideration.   **primed** roused.   **conceits** thoughts.
if I can choose . . . command me injure you, if the choice is mine to make, but instead, place myself at your command.

withdrew herself, leading her horse to a bank where with ease she mounted and so rode away, not giving him any answer at all. Ornatus marvelled thereat, yet rightly imputed her unkind departure to her fear, not discourtesy. And seeing himself deprived of her sight, the night approaching, departed home to his father's house. After supper, betaking himself to his chamber with intent to rest, he was possessed with such remembrance of the beautiful damsel he had seen that his sleep was transformed into continual cogitations of her beauty, form, and favor, and the pleasing sight he had seen in the discovery of some of her hidden beauties imprinted such a delight in his affectionate conceits that he could take no sleep, but continued all that night in those meditations.

The next day, thinking to shake off all further remembrance of her, he got into company of his most chosen friends wherein before time he took most delight, yet now by reason of his distemperature,◊ he rather seemed weary thereof. He had not continued long with them but he was saluted by a gentleman named Phylastes with whom he was familiarly acquainted. This gentleman belonged to an ancient duke named Turnus, who in honor of his birthday, from which Allinus excused himself of purpose because he thought he should meet Arbastus there, but because the duke should take no offence at him, he granted that his son Ornatus should go to do him honor. Which Phylastes acquainted Ornatus withal, who, glad thereof, departed thither in company of divers other gentlemen. The duke likewise had sent another messenger to request Arbastus's company, who being of a more mild nature than Allinus, willingly went, and with him, his lady and fair daughter Artesia.

distemperature disturbance of mind.

CHAPTER II

How Ornatus came to knowledge of Artesia and entreated
Adellena to make known his love to her, and of the rebuke
Artesia gave her.

After the feast was ended and the duke had honored his guests
with all manner of courtesy, he and the principalest, amongst
whom Arbastus was one of the chief, according to the custom
used in the country, seated themselves to behold certain games
and exercises to be performed by the young gentlemen: which
was, running, wrestling, and divers other exercises for trial of
the strength and nimbleness of the body. Amongst the rest, Ornatus (having never before made trial of himself) had such good
success, and behaved himself with such agility and strength, that
he won the chiefest honor and was presented before the duke to
receive a rich reward.

Which when he had received, casting his eyes upon the beholders, he espied Artesia whom he perfectly knew again, ready
to depart with her parents, who had bidden the duke farewell.
Ornatus, coming to Phylastes, asked if he knew that damsel,
showing him Artesia, who told him what she was. Ornatus was
glad of that small knowledge, which could add little means to
his hopes, yet somewhat discontented that she was daughter to
Arbastus. And thus the day being ended, everyone departed to
their abodes.

Ornatus, having again attained his chamber, spent his time of
rest in sundry cogitations of his love and how to give her knowledge of his affection, noting every danger, and pondering how
discontentedly his parents would take the same, if it should by
any means come to their knowledge, finding so many lets° to
hinder him that he was oftentimes in utter despair of attaining
to the least hope of good success, but finding his affections to increase more and more, and burning with a fervent desire, which
nothing but only her favor could extinguish.

lets obstacles.

After that night was passed, early the next morning he wandered towards the place where he had beheld her with such exceeding content, and by the way as he went he met with a gentlewoman named Adellena, of mean birth and small living yet of good education, who oftentimes resorted to Arbastus's house, and was going thither at that instant, into whose company he insinuated himself, for that he saw her alone, and said as followeth:

"Gentlewoman, I am bold to entreat a word or two with you."

"Sir," replied she, "with a good will I will satisfy you in what I can."

"Know you not," quoth he, "Arbastus?"

"I do," quoth she, "both know him and am very well acquainted with him, unto whose house I am now going."

"So would I," quoth he, "if I durst, for I serve Ornatus, son to Allinus, whom I do not doubt but you know well, of whom I would tell you more but that I fear to commit his secrets to them I know not and thereby unwillingly do him injury. But would you vouchsafe but to hear them, keep them secret, and withal add your help to further him, which you may with safety perform, you should do him an exceeding pleasure, and withal be so highly rewarded and thankfully gratified that you should think your labor very well employed. Do a deed of pity and bind him to you in the perpetual bands of kind friendship."

"Sir," replied Adellena, "I know not the gentleman, yet I have heard him much commended, in whom,° if I could any way pleasure, I would use both diligence and secrecy, promising you upon my faith and credit, if you will make me acquainted with your mind, I will either do my good will to further him or else conceal what you shall commit to my privity."°

Then said he: "My master not long since walking in yonder valley beheld Artesia, fair Artesia, daughter to Arbastus, to whose beauty he is exceedingly enthralled, that unless some means of comfort be found to ease his torments, I fear me it will

in whom who.   **privity** private knowledge.

endanger his life, whom you only may pleasure by making his love known to her in such sort as shall best agree with your wisdom. This is all, and yet so much that the revealing thereof may do much harm, and [yet] to effect such a contract might procure peace and unity twixt their parents. Therefore I entreat your aid and furtherance herein, with which good news, if I return to him, I know it will breed no little comfort to his disquiet heart."

"Sir," said she, "since I perceive his love is grounded upon virtue, not drawn thereto by any desire or reward, I undertake to be his assistant therein and will to the uttermost of my best endeavors labor to procure his content which this day I will in some sort put in execution. And if you return to me tomorrow, you shall know her answer."

"I will," said he, and so they departed. Ornatus, having left her, entered into many cogitations of this rash attempt, accounted himself overcredulous to commit his secrets to her privity of whose fidelity he had never made trial, sometimes comforting himself with hope of good event and again despairing of comfort for that he supposed Artesia would rather esteem him as an enemy than a friend by reason of their parents' hatred, and therefore would the more hardly be drawn to give any credit to his suit. And revolving a chaos° of these and such like confused cogitations, he attained his father's house, thinking the time tedious until his appointed meeting with Adellena which he overpassed° with great care. Adellena, after her departure from him, soon attained to Arbastus's house, using herself as she had formerly done, yet withal careful how to execute the charge she had in hand, which she could by no occasion utter till after dinner when she found Artesia all alone in the garden, insinuated herself into her company, which Artesia kindly accepted, entering into variety of discourses, and continuing some time in giving certain herbs their proper names. Amongst the rest, Artesia espied an herb with party° colored leaves, demanding

chaos state of utter confusion.   overpassed spent.   party diverse.

of Adellena if she knew the name thereof, which she told her she did not.

"I have oftentimes," quoth Artesia, "seen this herb, and it hath two pretty names: it is by some called love-in-idleness, and by some heart's-ease." With that Adellena fetched a deep, though counterfeit, sigh which Artesia noting, said: "What maketh you sigh to hear it named heart's ease?"[4]

"Marry," quoth she, "one way because those two names so ill agree, another, for by the same I call to remembrance the heart's grief I heard a young man complain of procured by love, which was not in idleness but I think in good earnest."

"Why," quoth Artesia, "can love procure such heart's grief to any, and not rather content?"

"Yea," said she, "because the party in love hath no hope to attain the good liking of the party he loveth."

"Then," quoth Artesia, "I account him a fool that will love so deeply without hope of reward, and that to be rather fondness than true friendship that placeth his affections with such inequalities. But I pray tell me, what is he into whose secrets you were so suddenly admitted?"

"Not admitted," quoth she, "for unawares I heard his complaints, which afterwards I promised him not to make any acquainted withal, but the party whom he so entirely loveth."

"Then," quoth Artesia, "I may not know, neither do I care, for it is but a vanity that troubleth one's cogitations."

"Yes," quoth she, "you may and shall, if you please, know who he is, conditionally you will neither be offended with me for telling you nor reveal what I shall impart."

"Why," quoth she, "am I the party or doth it any way concern me that I should be offended? If it be, then keep your counsels unrevealed, for it will prove unsavory to my stomach, for be it far from me to be troubled with the vain suits of doting lovers."

"Yet let me answer," quoth Adellena; "you bear too grievous a conceit° of love, which is the divine purity whereby hearts are

grievous a conceit heavy idea.

united in virtue. Without the which, neither mortals can attain
heaven, nor other creatures have their being, therefore not to be
abhorred. And for that any should love yourself, can that be an
offence to you, but rather be accepted in kind sort? We should
by nature love them that love us. Then will you, contrary to
nature, yield hatred for love? For you indeed are the party that
is beloved, and the party that is so far in love with you [is] every
way to be commended, and one way discommended, whose
name I will not reveal, and then I hope I shall breed no offence
to your ears."

"Do so," quoth Artesia, "for in concealing the same, you please
me, and if you will be welcome into my company, use no more
of these speeches."

"Had I thought," quoth she, "they would have been offensive,
I would not have uttered them, but in so doing, I did but fulfil
your request."

"Then at my request," again quoth she, "give over." After this
communication ended, they parted, Adellena home to her house,
and Artesia to her supper and afterwards to her chamber, where,
at first, some cold thoughts of those speeches passed in her fancy,
but afterwards she spent the rest of that night in quiet sleep.

CHAPTER III

*How Adellena conveyed Ornatus's letter into Artesia's cas-
ket, and with what impatience Artesia took the same.*

The morning being newly approached, Ornatus, who had long
expected the same, arose and soon got to Adellena's house where
he arrived before she was up, who, having knowledge thereof,
soon came down to him, taking him to be no other than Ornatus's
man to whom she declared the very truth of all her speeches had
with Artesia, which nipped him at the heart. But being put in
some hope by her persuasions, at last giving her a purse full
fraught with gold in recompense of her pains past and to entice
her to undertake more, he said as followeth:

"Good Adellena, be not dismayed to prosecute my suit for°
Artesia's first frown, for I am not Ornatus's man, but poor Ornatus himself that languish with desire to attain her love, which I
would myself prosecute if the discords betwixt our parents did
not hinder the same. Therefore, I beseech you once again do
something in my behalf, for you see how cruel destiny hath shut
me from all means to be put in practice by myself, and you may
pleasure me without any hazard° at all, for which I will rest so
thankful unto you as that you shall account your pains taken
well-bestowed.

"Sir," replied she, "I would undertake anything to further you
if I knew which way, but I perceive Artesia's forwardness° is
such that nothing I shall bring her will be welcome. But if you
will advise me what I shall do, I will once again hazard the loss
of her good liking for your sake."

Which said, Ornatus wrote a letter, which he desired her by
some means to convey to her sight, the contents whereof were
these:

To the fair Artesia,

Fairest of creatures, be not offended with my boldness, but
rather favorably censure of my good meaning, for being
bound to honor none but [the] most virtuous, I thought it
my duty to give you knowledge thereof, desiring you to pity
the extremity of my passions, procured by the attainture°
of your conquering perfections. I confess you may allege
many things as reasons to dissuade you from giving credit
to my speeches, or yielding me the least favor in your conceits. Yet I beseech you, make but trial of loyalty, love,
and duty so far as shall agree with your liking, and you
shall find me constant in the one and perseverant in the
other as one that hath submitted himself to your command,
vowed his devotions to purchase your favor, and everlast-

for because of.   hazard risk.   forwardness assertiveness, stub-
bornness.   attainture power to strike or touch and thereby cause a
mental affection or a physical disease.

ingly bound himself to be only yours unable to express my
humble meaning, unwilling to be offensive, and desirous
of favor then I beseech you be favorable to me, though
bearing the name of an enemy, in whom you shall find
the true heart of a constant friend, whose safety, comfort,
and preservation resteth in your power. The first view of
your beauty, which was in the valley when you were last
hunting, surprised my heart with such humble regard to
your virtues that, ever since my heart hath endured the
bitter torments of fearful despair which urgeth me to this
presumption, desiring from your sacred lips to receive my
sentence of comfort or affliction, rather than to spend my
life in languishing, unrevealed torment. Then be you gracious to him that is otherwise most miserable, and show
favor to an undeserving, unknown friend; so shall you not
only show that you are merciful, but also save a miserable
lover from utter ruin.

Your humble friend,
Ornatus.

Adellena, having received this letter, told him she would deliver the same, which the next day she performed in this sort:◊
being come to Arbastus's house, she continued most part of the
day in Artesia's company, not once renewing the least remembrance of the talk she had with her the day before, but espying
her open her casket wherein she put her works, whilst Artesia
was busy she privily conveyed the letter unseen into the same,
which by and by Artesia locked, for none but herself had the
use thereof.

Adellena thought long till she was gone,◊ fearing lest Artesia
should upon some occasion open the casket again and so find the
letter whilst she were there; therefore she soon found means to
depart. When the time of rest was come and Artesia alone in her
bed, taking book (according to her usual manner) to read awhile,

performed in this sort accomplished in the following manner.   **thought
long till she was gone** found the time long before she could leave.

she suddenly fell asleep, and in her sleep was possessed with a dream wherein her thoughts called to remembrance Adellena's speeches, which moved such a disquiet conceit of anger in her breast that thinking° she had chid° her, with the motions of her spirits she awaked, feeling an exceeding distemperature° in all her parts. And seeing the light still burning, she marvelled at her drowsiness that had before forgot to put the same out, and by this means called to remembrance Adellena's speeches, marvelling what he should be that was in love with her, and suddenly again reproving herself for giving her mind liberty to think of love, she would have banished all further remembrance thereof out of her mind. But the more she labored, the more unable she was to prevail in overmastering her fancies, that being both vexed with herself and Adellena, she uttered these speeches.

"What disquiet is this possesseth my heart, procureth such unwanted cogitations to rise in my fancies, and disturbeth my rest? I was not wont to trouble my thoughts with such vain cogitations which, the more I labor to suppress, the more they increase.

"Could Adellena's speeches have such force which I had wellnigh° forgotten as thus long to stick in my remembrance? Or what reason have I to regard them that were not worth the regarding, but rather tended to demonstrate the affection of some overfond lover that seeketh to entrap my chastity? Accursed be her lips for uttering them, and would to God I had been deaf that I might not have heard their enchanting sound."

This said, she catched up her book, thinking by reading to drive away all remembrance thereof, but her heart was so fully possessed with a kind of cogitation what he should be that she neither could read, or when she did read, remember what she did read; and finding this means not available, she started from her bed, opening her casket to take out her sampler° wherein she took most delight, when suddenly she espied the letter, and, reading the superscription, was half-astonished thereat,

thinking remembering that.   **chid** rebuked.   **distemperature** discomfort.   **wellnigh** nearly, almost.   **sampler** embroidery featuring designs or mottoes.

especially how it should come there and what the contents should
be, being oftentimes in mind to tear the same in pieces and not
to read it, which her heart would not suffer her to do before
she had seen what was the contents. Yet, striving to overmas-
ter her affections,◊ she tore the same in the midst, which done,
such a remorse rose in her fancy,◊ united with a desire to know
further thereof, that leaping into the bed she closed the same together, and betwixt a willing and unwilling mind, read the same
throughout. With that, fetching a deep sigh, she said:

"Aye me poor soul, how are my affections betrayed to mine
enemy? Was it Ornatus she meant? Can it be that he will prove
my friend that is my professed enemy? O no, he intendeth nothing less than love, but rather under color thereof seeketh my
ruin. Was it he that I beheld in the valley? Or is it possible
that he should be so deeply in love with me upon that small
sight? No, no, I will not credit his speeches, but still repute him
as an enemy, as indeed he is, and henceforward abandon Adellena's company by whose means this letter was conveyed into
my casket." Then tearing the same into a thousand pieces, she
abstained, so near as she could, from all thought of yielding the
least consent to love, and sought to increase her disdain and suspect of his falsehood, spending the rest of that night in confused
contrarieties of doubtful thoughts. Early in the morning she got
up and within short time met with Adellena (who was come as
desirous to know what issue her devise had taken) and finding
occasion fit when none was by, she uttered these speeches:

"Adellena, I marvel what folly ruleth your mind that you,
whom I had thought had been virtuously given, should seek
my ruin. Wherein have I shown myself so unkind that you
should requite me in this discourteous sort? You remember the
speeches passed betwixt us the other day in the garden, when
I, finding out your intent by your speeches, desired you to give
over to use any more talk to that effect, which you faithfully
promised, but now most unfaithfully have broken and more

affections emotions.   **fancy** imagination.

impudently have betrayed my quiet with your disquiet and ill-sounding news. If your rudeness had been such that you could not desist, you might then have delivered Ornatus's false and feigned enchantment into my hands and not so secretly have conveyed the same into my casket, wherein you have made me amends for my love to seek to betray my life into the hands of mine enemy, for otherwise° I neither can nor will esteem him. Therefore, henceforward come no more into my company, for I forswear your familiarity, hate your counsel, and will cause my father to banish you [from] his house, and alienate his friendship from you forever."

Adellena would have answered, but Artesia, refusing to hear her, departed, and left her so much grieved that for extreme vexation she immediately departed towards her own house.

CHAPTER IV

How Ornatus despairing, left his father's house and, disguising himself, was entertained of Arbastus.

Ornatus, desirous to hear how Artesia had accepted his letter, came to Adellena's house and found her weeping for anger, desiring to know the cause thereof, which she declared to him at large, which wrought such an exceeding passion of grief in his mind that, without yielding her either thanks for her pains or other speech, he departed, being so much overcome with inward sorrow that, finding a solitary place, he laid himself down upon the earth, uttering these lamentations:

"O miserable caitiff,° what hast thou to do but lament when thy ill fortune yields nothing but cause of lament? Why should thy life last to endure these torments and not rather to dissolve into unseen essences? Could anything have happened to me more miserable than to behold Artesia and now to endure her cruelty, or more fortunate if she had been merciful? But my destinies have drawn me to like her that hateth me, and to become

otherwise in no other terms.   **caitiff** wretch, slave.

thrall° to a cruel, unrelenting enemy. Well, my love is sweeter
than my life, and therefore I will venture life and all to purchase
her liking."

Having said this, he awhile sat silent, when suddenly to favor
his extremities, he beheld certain of his familiars° pass by, with
whom he departed home.

Early the next morning, being exceedingly troubled in mind
and impatient of delay, he left his father's house to visit Adellena
again, whom he had the day before left so unkindly, whom he
found ready to go to Arbastus's house again. Saluting her, [he]
said: "Adellena, be not offended at my last unmannerly departure, for my heart was so much disquieted at the ill success my
suit took that I could not use that behavior towards you your
pains deserved, but now I am returned to crave your counsel
what is further to be done herein."

"Sir," replied she, "I know not what further means to use,
neither dare I any more attempt to try Artesia's courtesy, who is
already so much offended with me that I fear to lose her friendship forever if I should utter that again that is so unwelcome
to her."

Ornatus, hearing her speeches, thought she was unwilling to
prosecute his suit any further, with a heavy heart left her, entering
into many thoughts and cogitations which way to comfort himself, oftentimes utterly despairing and yet purposing to leave no
means unassayed nor danger unattempted, though with hazard
of his life, to purchase some rest to his troubled heart.

At length he thought with himself: "What should make Artesia so hard-hearted as to give no credit to my speeches? It is not
her want of lenity, pity, or wisdom, for she is young and therefore subject to love; beautiful, and therefore to be won; wise,
and therefore will with consideration pity my sorrows. What
then should alienate her good liking from me more than from
another? My name, for by that she reputeth me an enemy? Then
were I not Ornatus, she would peradventure give some regard

thrall slave.   **familiars** intimate friends.

to my suits. Therefore I will change my name and be another than I am, that she not knowing me, may, if not love me, yet desist to hate me." Then began he to study what means to use to enjoy her sight (without the which he could not live) and yet not be known what he was. Amongst many other devices, this took deepest root. Within few days after, having provided all things necessary, he attired himself like a virgin of a strange country which he might well be esteemed to be by his youth. And taking with him his lute, whereon he could play exceedingly well, in the silent of the night he departed towards the sea coast which was near unto Arbastus's house, and seating himself upon the rocky shore, began to play upon his lute. Early the next morning, a shepherd happened to pass by that way, and espying° his strange disguise and hearing his sweet music was so exceedingly delighted therewith that he stayed to see what he was.

Ornatus, turning himself about, espied the old man stand gazing upon him, wherewith he drew towards him and said as followeth:

"Good father, muse not to see me in this unfrequented place, being by shipwreck cast on this shore and preserved from a grievous death by sea, to perish for want of comfort on the land in a strange place where I neither have friends nor know which way to get comfort. Therefore I beseech you, yield comfort to my distress and succor to my want."

"Fair damsel," quoth the shepherd, "if my homely cottage can yield you any comfort, so please you to accept thereof. It shall be at your command, whither so please you go; without more circumstance of speeches, you shall be most heartily welcome."

"I thank you," quoth Ornatus, "and I accept your gentle proffer."° So they departed together. And when they were entered, and the shepherdess in the best manner she could had welcomed him, and he had tasted of such food as was set before him, he told them his name was Sylvia, and telling a tale

espying seeing.   **proffer** offer.

of sufficient countenance to bear credit° of the manner of their shipwreck and the cause he undertook that voyage by sea, which the old folks believed, likewise framing himself to such a kind of behavior that it was almost impossible to discern but that he was a woman indeed. Where Sylvia, for under that name he shall awhile pass, stayed some two days, yet without any hope how to enjoy Artesia's company. But the third day it fortuned° Arbastus, being abroad hunting, was by a violent storm driven to seek shelter and most fortunately lighted on the shepherd's cottage where he boldly entered without calling, and suddenly espying Sylvia, was half-astonished to behold a damsel so beautiful and richly attired in that homely place, but after that he had awhile viewed her well, Sylvia being alone, with a courteous behavior he thus spoke:

"Fair damsel, pardon my boldness if I have disquieted you; I little thought to have found such guests in this homely° place." Sylvia, knowing him to be Arbastus, arose, but made him no answer, when presently the old shepherd came in, using great reverence to Arbastus, who demanded of him what damsel that was, whereupon the old man declared all that he knew.

Arbastus then thus said: "Damsel, I understand by this shepherd some part of your misfortunes, which I so much pity that I offer to do anything [that] resteth in me to do you pleasure. And for that this homely place is not agreeable to your birth, which may be greater than I can judge of, let me desire you to accept of such entertainment as my habitation° yieldeth,° whither you shall be welcome."

Sylvia, being glad of that proffer, yet fearing to be discovered by his willingness to yield,° made this answer: "Sir, this homely place is best agreeing to my poor estate, being by my fortune brought to misery, which I am also unworthy of for that I know not how to make my host amends, desiring rather to live

sufficient countenance to bear credit appearance plausible enough to be believed.   **fortuned** happened by chance.   **homely** plain, uncomely.   **habitation** dwelling.   **yieldeth** offers.   **yield** accept the invitation.

in this quiet palace void of care than in places of most dignity. But for that I shall be too chargeable to this poor man, and you so earnestly desire me, I will be so bold as to take your proffer, though unable to be so grateful as I would." Many other speeches passed betwixt them, and in the end they departed towards Arbastus's castle, where Sylvia was kindly and worthily entertained, having his heart's desire, which was to enjoy the sight of fair Artesia.

Ornatus, being alone by himself, began to meditate of the good success he had in this attempt, and how fortunately all things had fallen out to further him in his love. But most of all, he marvelled how the eyes of all that beheld him were blinded that they could not perceive what he was. In these and many such like comfortable meditations he spent some three or four days, taking most great content in beholding Artesia's perfections that he was more and more enthralled in the bands of vowed affection, hearing her speech, noting her behavior, admiring her virtue, commending her courtesy, affecting° her beauty, and imprinting each lineament of her divine form in his devoted affection with such immovable resolve of constant loyalty that he did not only love her but also honor her as an idol, being by Arbastus admitted [to] her company, that at all times he was with her. Artesia likewise took no little pleasure in Sylvian's[5] company, in whom so much courtesy abounded that everyone both liked and commended her.

CHAPTER V

How Adellena brought news to Arbastus's house of Ornatus's sudden departure. How he, naming himself Sylvian, a long time enjoyed her company, and what success he had in his love.

Adellena, having heard of Ornatus's departure from his father's house and of the exceeding care and grief his parents took, fearing

affecting imagining.

lest he might by some treachery be murdered, with which news she came to Arbastus's house, and soon published the same that the news came to Arbastus's hearing, who was exceedingly sorry to hear the same for that he esteemed well of Ornatus. And now coming into the garden where Artesia was walking with Sylvian, she could not withhold herself from speaking, but uttered her mind in these words:

"Artesia, be not offended with that I say, but rather be displeased with yourself who are the original° of this woe. Ornatus, whom you supposed your enemy, though indeed your most faithful friend, taking your unkind refusal most heavily and accounting himself not worthy to live if you despised him, either hath wrought his own untimely death or, despairing to find favor at your hands, hath abandoned both his parents, country, and acquaintance to live in exile. What will be said of you when the cause of this sorrow shall be known? How may your own conscience accuse yourself of hard-heartedness that would not yield pity to the distress of so worthy, virtuous, and courteous a gentleman, who for his humble suit was spitefully disdained, and his hearty good will disdainfully rejected? Which cruel deed of yours, no doubt, will be one day repaid with the like disdain where you shall most affect.° I know his love was firm, constant, and immovable,° which maketh me so much the more pity his estate.° I know his meaning was both virtuous and honorable; his birth you know; what virtues abounded in him, all can witness; and how heartily he loved you, the heavens can witness. Poor Ornatus, farewell. Hard was thy hap° to place thy true love so firmly where thou reapest so little reward."

Artesia, hearing her speeches, could not tell whether she might blame her or accuse herself, sometimes doubting whether she spoke this of policy to try her, or of truth, being as ready to blame herself as Adellena, and yet willing to do neither. For she thought if she spake true, she had good cause to say that she did,

original first cause.   **affect** place your love.   **immovable** fixed.
estate condition.   **hap** fortune.

and herself more to be blamed than any. For notwithstanding she had given Adellena so flat a denial, yet her conscience knew that some sparks of love were kindled in her breast, that her heart being somewhat oppressed with these thoughts caused the water to stand in her eyes. Ornatus, seeing all this, took no little comfort thereat, especially when he perceived Artesia's heart to relent. But for that by his disguise, being known no other than a woman, he kept silence when fain he would have spake lest he should discover himself. Adellena, seeing she had disquieted Artesia, being herself full of grief and unwilling to urge her any further, departed.

And Artesia, withdrawing herself from Sylvian's company into an arbor, uttered these speeches: "And can it be that Ornatus's love was so great that for my sake he hath done this? Could he love her so constantly that was his professed enemy? Is love of such a force to draw one into these extremes? Then may I compare it to the herb artas[6] found in Persia, who being but holden in the hand causeth a heat through all the body: so love but entertained in thought disquieteth all the senses. But why do I conceive so well of Ornatus when I know not the truth of Adellena's report? It may be he hath hired her to do this and thereby I may be deceived, yielding to pity when there is no cause, and with the bird akanthus[7] ready to come at every call. Admit it were so, I am not bound to favor him. Is he not my enemy and son unto my father's chiefest foe? What reason then have I either to give credit to his love or her protestation when both may be feigned? Well, I will be advised before I yield myself to love's entangling baits, and before I love I will know whom I love. Aye, but Artesia, thy fancy° yieldeth remorse already, and thy conscience bids thee pity him because he loveth thee, for love in a reputed enemy may be as constant and loyal as in an open friend, and an enemy becoming friend will be the more constant. Then what hast thou to do but make further proof of his constancy, and finding him true, yield reward to his desert?°

fancy imagination.   **desert** just merits.

Soft Artesia, wade not too far. If he be constant, if he be loyal, if he love thee so entirely, yet now thou hast made him forsake this country or procure his untimely death, then is there nothing else to be done for thee but to pity his death and accuse thyself of some discourtesy. All this while, Ornatus, shrouding himself from her sight by the thickness of the green leaves, heard her speeches to his exceeding comfort and again closely withdrew himself. Artesia, having ended her speeches, her heart being oppressed with many doubts, arose and came to Sylvian, to whom she said: "My mind is much troubled with the news Adellena told me of Ornatus's absence, whom, for that you know not, I will tell you what he was:

"There dwelleth not far hence one Allinus that mortally hateth my father and all that belong unto him, whose son Ornatus was, whom, if I should commend,° you might think me too cruel to refuse his love so unkindly. Only thus much I will say of him: he was every way worthy to be beloved, though my fancy could never be drawn to like of him, who, upon what occasion I know not, but as Adellena told me, made his love known to her which she likewise told me of. But I, refusing to hear her, answered her plainly that I was greatly offended with her for making any such motion and forbade her forever to speak of him again. But now this day you have heard what she hath told me, which I can hardly believe to be true, or that Ornatus would be so rash without wisdom to enter into such extremes. But if it be so, as I would it were not, it grieveth me for him, and I wish that I had not refused to hear his suit, though I am not willing to yield thereto. For I would not have it said of me, nor my name so much blazed,° that my cruelty procured him to that extremity, though his wisdom might have foreseen such mischief and he more moderately have tempered his love."

Ornatus, taking occasion, said: "I neither know the gentleman nor how constant his love was, but thus much my mind persuadeth me, that had not his love been great he would not

commend praise.   **blazed** revealed or made public.

have grieved so much at your unkindness. But love is of this force that it turneth the mind into extremes or utterly breaketh the heart, which force belike° it had in him, else would he not have done himself so much harm. But it may be, as you say, Ornatus hath not done himself outrage, but only abandoning company liveth in despair and so meaneth to die. Which, if it be so, then in my fancy you might do well to let him by some means understand° that you did pity him."

"Stay there," quoth Artesia, "you must first know whether I can do it or no, for if I should say I pity with my lips, and he not find it so, it would drive him to more despair, and therefore I will leave off to do that until I can find whether I can do so, or no."

These her speeches drave Ornatus into a perplexed doubt what to think, being no way assured of her love nor yet utterly despairing thereof for that° her speeches gave likelihood of both. Therefore he durst not speak too boldly lest° she should suspect him, but only rested in good hope to find comfort and by other means to try her.

Then taking his lute, he began to play so sweetly as would have ravished a comfortless mind with great content, to hear which harmony pleased Artesia so well that when he left she would request him, calling him Sylvian, to play again. Whilst he sat playing, Artesia, sitting close by his side, fell fast asleep, which he perceiving, left off his play to surfeit himself with beholding her sweet beauty, in which he took such delight as almost ravished her senses, sometimes thinking whilst she slept to imprint a kiss upon her sweet ruddy° lip, but fearing thereby to wake her and lose that delightful contemplation, he desisted, beholding each part of her visible form, which was most divine, his mind was affected with inward suppose° what perfections her hidden beauties did comprehend, which his fancy persuaded him he did in conceit° absolutely contemplate. Then seeing her stir, he suddenly caught his lute again, striking his sweet note to

belike it seems.   understand know.   for that insofar as.
lest for fear that.   ruddy red.   suppose conjecture.   conceit
image.

continue her in that slumber, and then again, laying by the same to enter into his former contemplation, comparing his delight to exceed all heavenly joy, and wishing, though Artesia could not love him, yet that she would always grant him so to behold her.

When he had a good while continued in these meditations, Artesia awoke, which somewhat grieved him, but when he beheld her beauteous eyes fixed upon him, he thought himself enriched with a heavenly happiness, to whom Artesia said: "I thank thee good Sylvian, for thy sweet music hath somewhat eased my heart by this quiet sleep. O what content do they enjoy that live void of care, and how happy was I before I heard Ornatus's name." With that she arose and they together went in. When night approached, which Ornatus thought too soon come for by that he must lose Artesia's sight, everyone betook themselves to their several lodgings.

Ornatus studying what means to use to further his love, wherein he found many difficulties, sometimes in thinking Artesia was in hope never to hear of him again, and sometimes supposing she did pity him, and being overcome with contrarieties of doubts, he uttered these complaints: "What should I do to procure my content when my miseries are one way great and my joys as exceeding, when my despair exceedeth and yet my comfort aboundeth? I enjoy Artesia's love, yet she loveth me not;[8] I enjoy her sight and yet not her sight. I have as much comfort as fills me with joy, and yet I am desperate with despair. How can that be? She loveth me as I am Sylvian, but hateth me because she loveth not Ornatus. Under the name of Sylvian I enjoy her sight, but not as Ornatus, and so am I deprived of her sight. I reap exceeding comfort by beholding her beauty, but I live in despair that she would shun love if she knew what I were. Though I enjoy many things by being Sylvian, yet am I deprived of all comfort as I am Ornatus. For she deemed him either dead or fled, hath no hope ever to see him, and if I should show any sign that he were living or near, she would presently° eschew my

presently immediately.

company, which, being as I am, I may enjoy. And thus am I void
of all means of attaining her love, yet, living as I am, I shall still
enjoy her love. Why Ornatus, thou hast better means to give her
knowledge of thy love in this disguise than if thou livest as Ornatus. Suppose thou shouldst make known to her what thou art,
thinkest thou she would bewray° thee, considering thou offerest
no other behavior towards her than that which agreeth with°
virtue? Or what if she did betray thee, wert thou not better to
endure the greatest extremity by her done than pine away with
grief in her absence? Yes, Ornatus, in being as thou art thou art
more happy, and therefore mayst thou be in some better hope of
comfort. What if she will not love thee? Yet for thy good will
she cannot hate thee. And though she know what thou art, she
will rather conceal thee than bewray thee. Then try whether she
loveth thee or no, but how? Make myself known? No, I will
write a letter which I will leave in some place where she may
find it and so by that means I shall see whether she will love or
no. And taking pen, ink, and paper, he wrote as followeth:

To the most virtuous Artesia, the forsaken
Ornatus sendeth humble greeting.

Were you but so merciful as fair, I would not despair of
pity. Or were you willing to know my truth and loyalty, you
would, though not yield to my suit, yet pity me. I cannot
use protestations nor dissemble grief, but be you most assured that what proceedeth out at my lips cometh from my
heart. Extremity maketh me overbold and despair maketh
me more desperate in uttering my mind. I cannot choose but
say I love you, for that I love indeed. I cannot set forth my
love with filed° terms, but in plain truth protest that my love
is constant, loyal, virtuous, and immovable.° And though
you hate, I must love; and though you forever deny to love,

---

bewray reveal, betray.   **agreeth with** is appropriate to.   **filed**
smoothed, polished.   **immovable** fixed.

yet will I persist in constancy, for the worst I can endure
is death and that my soul already inwardly feeleth. I have
forsaken my parents, friends, and all to become acceptable
to you, for whilst I was Allinus's son you did hate me. Then
I beseech you, now that I am not Allinus's son nor Ornatus,
pity me. For without your pity I die and little can my death
profit you. But letting me live, you shall forever enjoy a
faithful servant. So, most virtuous Artesia, I commit my
cause to your wise consideration.

Your inseparable, neither Ornatus
nor himself, but your poor
servant.

When he had written this letter and sealed the same, the next
morning he laid it in a place of the garden where he knew Artesia
would walk. And from thence coming to her chamber, he found
her ready to go forth.

Artesia welcomed Sylvian kindly and forth they went together, and walking up and down a pretty while, Artesia espied
the white paper, and desirous to see what it was, took it up, [and]
reading the superscription, marvelled◊ what the contents should
be and how it should come there. And turning to Sylvian:[9] "See
you this letter, it is directed to me. I marvel how it should come
here, unless it were laid of purpose. Well, howsoever that was, I
will read the contents and you shall be partaker of them." When
she had read the same and well understood that it was Ornatus,
at the first she was so exceedingly vexed that she said: "I now
perceive that Ornatus was wiser than I took him to be, for I see
he hath committed no outrage upon himself, but, wisely will try
me first, and if I will not yield to love him, what will he do?
Marry, return to his father again. This is Adellena's doing, and
according as I thought, they are agreed. She left this letter here,
and her may I blame and not him. For did not she promise him to
do it, he would never of himself attempt it. Sylvian, I pray thee

marvelled wondered.

counsel me what I should do herein, for my heart is oppressed with many thoughts that I will not utter until I know thy mind."

Sylvian thus answered: "Since you have given me licence to speak that which my heart thinketh, first I say, if Ornatus loveth according as he protesteth, as no doubt but he doth, you have good reason to pity him, for that by your own report he is every way worthy thereof, which if you do, you shall be sure of a constant friend, preserve his life, and make unity betwixt your parents. As for Adellena, if it were her deed, she did but the part of a friend. But it was very unlikely, for that she was not here since yesterday. Neither can I think any man can dissemble so much as to make these protestations and yet be false. For his words in my fancy bear an evident likelihood of truth. Therefore, if I may counsel you, yield to that which is virtuous, and in so doing, you shall purchase your own good, his content, and perpetual quiet° to both your families."

"Would you have me then," quoth she, "yield to love mine enemy?"

"How is he your enemy," quoth Sylvian, "when he loveth you?"

"He is mine enemy because, his father hating me, how can he love me?"

"Nay rather," quoth Sylvian, "his father not loving you, how can he choose but love you, because he seeth them hate you that are worthy to be beloved. Besides, their hatred being unjust, it showeth his virtue the more to love those his parents hate, and it is commonly seen where there is hatred betwixt the parents the children have loved most dearly, as in common experience it is seen. Have you not read the histories of Pyramus and Thisbe,[10] Romeo and Juliet,[11] and many other whose love was the more constant by so much the more their parents' hatred was deadly?"

"I remember such histories," quoth Artesia, "but what was the end of their love; was it not most miserable?"

"I grant it was," quoth Sylvian, "which was procured by their parents' cruelty, but not their love wherein, notwithstanding, they took such felicity that they rather chose to die together than

quiet peace.

to be parted, which argueth that the enmity twixt° parents cannot break off love twixt the children, yet might such tragical events have been prevented by wisdom."

"But how know I," said Artesia, "whether Ornatus's love be so constant or no?"

"Can you have any greater proof thereof than his own letters, the forsaking of his parents, and living peradventure in penury? But if you doubt of that, once again try him."

"Well," said Artesia, "I asked but thy counsel, but instead thereof thou usest persuasion. But seeing thou art so forward to do me good, which I hope is thy intent, if thou wilt keep my counsel thou shalt know both my mind and what I intend."

"Assure yourself," quoth Sylvian, "I will rather lose my life than prove unfaithful."

"Then," said she, "I confess to thee, Sylvian, that love hath made entrance into my heart, that I would willingly both pity Ornatus and grant him his request, for that with often remembering him I cannot forget him, neither doth any thought please me but when I think of him. But there are so many slips° to hinder our love, that though I love him I shall never enjoy him. For should my parents know hereof, they would pry so warily° into my actions that it were impossible for me once to have a sight of him, whom I do scarce remember I have so seldom seen him."

"You may," quoth Sylvian, "both love him and enjoy him, and since you have begun to like of him, he being worthy thereof and equalling you in affection, increase that love, and might I but once come to speak with him, I would not doubt but effect° all things with such secrecy[12] that you should with quiet enjoy him."

"Well," quoth Artesia, "I commit all to you — my life — for that dependeth on my love being willing to do anything that shall not disagree with modesty, desiring you to keep my counsels secret, for to bewray them may endanger both his and my life."

twixt between.   **slips** mishaps, accidents.   **pry so warily** look closely, investigate watchfully.   **effect** carry out, execute.

After many other speeches passed betwixt them, Adellena entered the garden. Artesia espying° her, at the first thus greeted her. "Good-morrow Adellena; I know not whether I may salute thee as a friend or a privy foe, for that by thy means I am brought into bondage. I pray thee tell me without dissembling, which I fear me thou canst do too well, when thou sawest Ornatus? And yet I know thy answer before I ask. Dost thou not know this letter? Didst thou not hide it in this garden that I might find it? Did not Ornatus hire thee to say that he was departed from his father's, whilst he lieth° at home in thy house? I know thy answer will be 'no,' but how may I believe that? Dost thou not likewise say he loveth me when thou knowest the contrary and dost but dissemble? If thou harborest any virtue in thee, tell me the truth and dissemble not, for in doing so thou shalt greatly content me, discharge thy conscience, and peradventure do Ornatus a good turn."

Adellena, hearing her speeches, was so astonished at their strangeness that for a good while she stood as one senseless, but at the last she made this answer: "Your demands are such as that I know not how to answer them, but heavens punish me if I dissemble. I saw not Ornatus since the time he came to me to know how you accepted the letter I conveyed into your casket. For that letter I am altogether ignorant therein, neither did I ever see the same before now. I never spake with Ornatus, saw Ornatus, or heard from him since I last gave him your answer, neither do I know where he is. But this I know, that he is not to be found, but poor gentleman languisheth in love, which I dare protest, loveth you most dearly. Neither need you misdoubt° that he is absent or think that he is hidden at my house, for it is too true he hath taken such grief at your unkindness as will, I fear me, endanger his life. I would it were not so, but that he were at my house, then would I counsel him rather to forget to love than endanger his life thereby."

"May I believe," quoth Artesia, "that this thou sayest is true?"

espying seeing.   **lieth** dwells, lodges.   **misdoubt** doubt.

"Heavens let me live no longer," quoth Adellena, "if I dissemble."

"Then," quoth Artesia, "how should this letter be conveyed into this garden but by himself?" With that the crystal tears fell from her eyes.

CHAPTER VI

How Ornatus's love was hindered[13] *by the news of Arbastus's death. How Floretus, to attain Sylvian's love, both confessed he slew Arbastus and intended to poison Artesia.*

To augment Artesia's tears a messenger, hastily running, came in and brought this news, uttering the same with a ghastly countenance: "O Artesia, hear my tragic discourse. Your father, as you know, rode forth this morning to chase the fearful deer, who wandering from his company at last by his long stay was missed, and all of us coming together, studied amongst ourselves what should be become of him. At last we were commanded by Floretus, your uncle, to post several ways in search of him, whom at last we found most grievously wounded and dead."

Artesia, hearing his words, with sudden grief fell down dead, which, when Sylvian perceived, caught her in his arms, rubbing her pale cheeks until she was revived again. Then they conveyed her to her bed in such extremity with that sudden grief that they feared to lose her life, which exceedingly tormented Sylvian to behold. Then was there such an uproar in Arbastus's house as all seemed in utter despair, one conjecturing this, another that, of Arbastus's death, but all in general concluding that it was done by Allinus in revenge of his brother's death.

Arbastus's wife likewise conceived such sorrow at this unexpected event that with very grief thereof she died. Artesia with both together[14] was ready to yield up her latest breath, and had done so had she not been carefully preserved by Sylvian and Adellena, who, by their counsel and endeavors pacified the extremity of her perplexity. This news was soon spread into most places of the country; but because there was no just proof of

the murderer there was no great question made thereof. Arbastus, having never a trusty friend to prosecute revenge, Floretus
now took upon him to rule and govern all that belonged to Arbastus, as his brother, and soon caused him and his lady to be
worthily interred° and built a sumptuous monument in their
remembrance. Which being overpassed,° he came again to Artesia as in the meantime he had oftentimes done and finding her
very weak used many speeches to comfort her, giving such as
were about her special charge to minister all things necessary to
restore her to her former health, seeming to be most careful of
her guard, promising and protesting to be unto her instead of
a father.°

Sylvian all this while was exceedingly grieved in mind to
see his love grown so weak and in such danger of her life, not
once forsaking her in all the time of her sickness, but continually
comforting her with hearty speeches, careful tendance,°15 not so
much as once departing her chamber, but taking exceeding pains
to pleasure her that she took great comfort in her supposed Sylvian, who oftentimes would steal a sweet kiss from Artesia's lips,
which she permitted, taking the same to proceed from a courteous mind, when Sylvian did it of deep affection, accounting
the estate wherein he lived to exceed all joys and his delight past
compare, proffering many familiarities° that Artesia took in kind
part, which otherwise she would have refused had she known
whom her companion Sylvian had been.

Ornatus marvelled that all this time she spake not of him,
which he devised to urge her to do by many occasions. But
these extremities had banished all remembrance of him out of
her mind, which exceedingly tormented Ornatus, fearing this
delay would some way turn to his ill. That whereas beforetime
he was pleasant, merry, and oftentimes would move Artesia
to mirth by his disport,° now that humor was alienated and

interred buried.   overpassed carried out, accomplished.   instead
of a father a father in the place of her own.   tendance attention.
proffering many familiarities offering many intimacies.   disport
wanton play, amusing frolics.

he became continually melancholy and sad, oftentimes when Artesia was from° him getting into a solitary place to bewail his hard fate, which she noted and wondered at, thinking the same had proceeded from being so long absent from his country and friends.[16] One day she found her deemed° Sylvian solitary, alone, and, coming unawares, heard her utter these words: "Oh how unhappy am I to love and not to be beloved."

Sylvian, espying her, left off, to whom Artesia said: "Why, how now Sylvian, are you in love? Can it be that your mind is attainted° with that venomous serpent that poisoneth the senses, altereth the complexion,° troubleth the head and heart? Shake it off and cast it out of your sight, for it never did any good, but hath brought many to perpetual misery."

"Since you have overheard me," quoth Sylvian, "I must needs confess I am in love, which doth not any way work any such effect in me as you speak off, but I take all comfort therein: my senses, heart, head, and all my parts take exceeding pleasure therein."

"Why then," quoth Artesia "sit you thus pensively alone, as it seemeth to me, bewailing your estate to be in love?"

"I do not," quoth Sylvian, "sorrow that I am in love, but that I am not beloved again, for being in love, I have vowed to live so ever, and sooner shall my life decay than forget my love, for with my love, my life shall end."

"What hard-hearted man," said Artesia, "is he that, knowing you love him, will not love you again?"

"Such is my hard estate,"° said Sylvian, "that the party whom I love knoweth I love, and yet causelessly doth hate me; neither am I far absent from him but enjoy his company, without which my life would decay."

"Is he in this house you love? Can it be you are entangled since you came hither?"

"No," quoth Sylvian, "I loved before I came hither."

from away from.   **deemed** supposed.   **attainted** corrupted, diseased.   **complexion** bodily temperament.   **hard estate** circumstance.

"How can that be when you are a stranger and cast in this country by shipwreck? Either you must needs be some other than we take you for, otherwise these things are impossible. But if you dare put trust in my secrecy, impart° your mind to me, and I promise you I will do the best I can to further your love."

"You may do much therein," quoth Sylvian, "and none more than yourself; but I beseech you pardon me for revealing the same before you assure me of one thing, which you may do without any harm to yourself, and be not offended with me if I ask you."

"Tell me what it is," quoth she, "and I will answer you."

"Then," said Sylvian, "I would first know whether you love Ornatus or no?" With that she started, saying: "Aye me, that name bringeth death to my heart, and thou woundest my soul with grief to hear him named. Dost thou think I have cause to love and not rather above all men to hate him? Dost thou not see my father lately murdered by him, or some by his appointment, and thinkest thou I can love so deadly a foe by whom I am brought to this misery? No, assure thyself Sylvian, according as I have just cause, I do hate him as the greatest enemy I have, whose very name affrighteth me with terror. And if thou hadst loved me, as I was persuaded thou didst, thou wouldst not have troubled my heart with that omnious° name. And yet for all this mischief that he hath done me, didst thou not see how he sued for my love and had so much prevailed that my heart began to yield to his suit?" With that she pulled out of her pocket the letter, saying: "These lines, the fruits of his dissimulation, were actors in his villainy." With that she tare them into a thousand pieces.

Sylvian, seeing the same, was ready to sound° with grief, breathing forth a heart-burning sigh, said: "O how is pure innocency suspected."

And being ready to say more, was disappointed by Floretus's coming, who even then entered the garden, and finding them out,

impart make known.   omnious a combination of enmity and omi-nous, hence bringing hatred and ill-fortune.   sound swoon.

used many courteous speeches to them both, especially comforting Artesia. To whom he said: "Dear cousin, since these mishaps cannot be remedied, let wisdom now oversway your passionate sorrow, and with patience remit° all further grief, for things past cure are not to be lamented. But now commit the care of your safety to my trustiness that will as tenderly regard your good as mine own life. Therefore, be of comfort, and whatsoever you desire shall be to the uttermost accomplished." Artesia yielded him many thanks, and so they went in. Artesia, being alone by herself, could by no means forget what speech she had with Sylvian, either thinking she did dissemble, or was some other than she seemed, or else that she was in love with Floretus. Then she remembered her speeches, saying: "How is innocency suspected," which she [Artesia] knew she [Sylvian] spake by her accusing of Ornatus,° which drave her into many doubtful cogitations and troubled her senses exceedingly. But by reason of her little suspect of Sylvian's disguise, she could not judge anything thereof. Sylvian, likewise not daring to offend her, and loving her so dearly that he could not endure to see her disquieted, used no more speeches tending to love, but frequenting her company wherein he took his whole felicity, accounting himself most happy to live and enjoy her sweet presence, being out of hope to attain her love, refreshing his heart with many solaces of sweet delight in beholding that which she little thought he had noted.

Many days continued Sylvian in this disguise, in which time Arbastus's death was almost forgotten. And Floretus, drawn by Sylvian's manifold virtues, began exceedingly to affect her, using such kind behavior towards her that she suspected that which afterwards she found true, for Floretus, concealing his love, felt the flame to burn the more inwardly, and living in that scorching penury thought it better for him to manifest his love than by hiding the same augment his torment, assuring himself to obtain his desire, for that Sylvian was a stranger far from friends and without his friendship likely to come to poverty, which he

remit cease, abate.　　**by her accusing of Ornatus** because she had accused Ornatus,.

thought would be means of importance to draw her to like of
him. Besides, he thought that he might do as he list with Artesia,
for that she was only in his custody.

And on a day, finding Sylvian alone in the garden, coming to
her with a submiss° behavior, he said as followeth: "My dear
Sylvian, I would gladly utter a matter of an importance if you
will vouchsafe me gentle audience. So it is, fair damsel, that
my heart hath long time been enthralled to your beauty, which I
have refrained to utter, fearing to be refused. But knew you how
faithfully my heart is devoted to your service, and with what
torment I have concealed the same, you would pity me. My
estate is sufficient to maintain you well, though not so worthily
as you deserve. You shall live with me in contented case, and
have so faithful and constant a friend as no torment nor affliction
shall alter. Therefore I beseech you, let me receive some hope of
comfort by your gentle speeches, which shall expel many cares
from my troubled heart."

Sylvian had much ado to abstain from smiling to think how
unfit he was to yield such a reward as Floretus expected; committing[17] further consideration thereof to time more convenient,
gave him this answer: "My mind, sir, is unapt to entertain love,
considering how far I am from my country and how soon I may be
overtaken; therefore, I pray you seek not that at my hands which I
will not grant, but if with your favor I may live so quietly as since
my coming I have done, I shall think myself more beholding to
you for that than for your proffered love which I cannot yield
unto." Floretus, thinking her soft answer was a sign she would
soon yield, still prosecuted his suit with earnestness in so much
that Sylvian told him that as yet she could not fancy him because
she had no trial of him, but that she would consider further
thereof. And so for that time they parted, Floretus in hope to
attain that which was not to be had, and Sylvian in hope by this
means the sooner to attain Artesia's love. First considering that
Floretus had the disposing of her, and therefore he must please
him lest otherwise he might be deprived of her company. Then

submiss submissive.

he began to think of Arbastus's murder, knowing assuredly that
it was not acted by his father's counsel but rather by some secret
foe that might as well be Floretus as any other, for that he was
the next heir, if Artesia hindered him not, which conceit° took
such effectual instance° in his fancy, that, with that his suspect,
comparing Floretus's behavior, countenance, and little inquiry
for the murderer, he plainly suspected him, which by the divine
providence rather than by any evident proof was stirred in his
opinion.° Such murder is never unrevealed, and though never
so closely done, yet God by some extraordinary means or other
revealeth the same. So came it to pass with Ornatus, although
he was no way privy to any such act or had any probability
thereof, yet he thought that Floretus's countenance bewrayed°
his treachery, and therefore he longed to have some conference
with him to see if he could gather the truth, whereby he thought
both to discharge himself of that suspect Artesia had of him, and
also when she saw his innocency and constancy, she might yield
to love him, purposing to leave no means unattempted to try
him, which he did the next time he spoke with him in this sort.

Early the next morning, Floretus not unmindful of his love
which kept him from his sleep that night, never left° till he
had found Sylvian, and coming to her with manifold submiss
speeches solicited his suit. Whom Sylvian cunningly handled,
still putting him in hope and yet making no promise, which set
him the more on fire, being so far overgone with affection that
he purposely determined either to win her love or hazard his
own life and to leave no means unattempted, were it never so
dangerous, to procure his own content. That the more unwilling
he saw Sylvian, the more importunate he grew, till at last Sylvian
said as followeth: "Floretus, I know no reason you have to be
so importunate when I see in you no token of fidelity. But once
having attained your purpose, you will esteem me as lightly as
easily won. Besides, I see not wherein you can perform any such

conceit idea.   effectual instance strong impression.   stirred in
his opinion aroused in his mind.   bewrayed revealed.   never
left did nothing else.

matter as you promise, for I, being in a strange country, have
nothing and you, for ought I see, as little. Then by matching
with you, I shall but bring myself to poverty and misery, and
then your love now so hot will be as cold and I rejected, cast off
to utter misery."

Floretus, not suffering her to proceed any further, made this
answer: "Sylvian, do you not see Arbastus's wealth, will not that
be sufficient? The great possessions I now enjoy by him are of
substance to maintain you in all quiet and yield you your heart's
content."

"Arbastus's wealth," said Sylvian, "that is Artesia's by right.
Then how can you possess the same, she living?"

"Do but grant me love," said he, "and I will quickly satisfy
you in that. I have a mean to get all into mine own hands and
therefore I beseech you, let no such matter trouble your mind,
but be assured that in enjoying me you shall have all happiness
and quiet, by my humble, dutiful, and constant loyalty."

"Do but assure me of this," quoth Sylvian, "and you shall
know my resolution afterwards."

Artesia, entering the chamber, broke off their speeches, whose
presence vexed Floretus at the heart, being scarce able to speak
by reason of his inward rancor. For indeed he hated Artesia because she only kept him from possessing his brother's living, the
want whereof kept him from attaining Sylvian's love. Therefore
he resolved by some means to work her downfall which, within
short time, he acquainted Sylvian withal by this occasion. One
day, finding her alone in a secret place in the garden, after many
speeches passed betwixt them whereby he perceived the chiefest
things that hindered him was his want of wealth, and after that
Sylvian had in some sort made him a grant only to try him, he
began to utter his full intent in this sort: "My dear Sylvian, I
am so well persuaded of your virtue, and put such confidence
in your trustiness, that I will reveal to you the very depth and
secrets of my heart, would you but swear to keep my counsel.
For to purchase your content, I have determined to put in practice

a matter of secrecy which concerneth my life to be° revealed."

Sylvian, hearing that, thought it better to swear a thousand oaths and break them all than by niceness° to endanger the life of Artesia, which she supposed he aimed at, promised him by many protestations to keep secret whatsoever he told her. Whereupon Floretus, urged with hope to win her love and emboldened in mischief, cared not what he did to attain his will, said as followeth: "Sylvian, you see Arbastus is dead, which was one stop that kept me from enjoying great possessions, and my purpose is, so you will but vouchsafe to aid me therein, to be rid of Artesia, and then all that belongeth to her by her father's death shall be yours to dispose of."

Sylvian's heart throbbed to hear his speeches, but determining to sift him to the full,° said as followeth: "Floretus, I am sure you speak this only to try me and so entrap me, and not of any intent you have to perform the same, wherein you shalt do me great wrong, and yourself no good, for I cannot believe you bear the least thought to do it."

"By heaven," quoth he, "it is my full intent, and for that you may be assured thereof. It was I that slew Arbastus, howsoever the matter is imputed to Allinus, and purpose likewise to be rid of Artesia, only for your sake. Therefore make no doubt of my resolution, for I am absolutely purposed to do it."

O, thought Sylvian, rather shalt thou see my blood than spill one drop of hers. "Why Floretus, would you have me do anything therein?"

"You only may do it," quoth he, "with more safety than any other, and the manner how is this: within some mile from this castle, Arbastus hath a banqueting house in his park, where oftentimes he would for his recreation lie; whither I will persuade Artesia to go for a season to take the air and to recreate° her senses dulled with grief, and none but you to keep her company, and some two servants whose trustiness I am assured of. This done, I

to be were it to be.   **niceness** scruples.   **sift him to the full,** discover all his thoughts.   **recreate** refresh.

will get a drink to be made, the force whereof shall expel life and yet by no means nor any cunning or skill be found out. Which you shall think it most convenient, give unto her, and being once dead, who will make any enquiry but that she died of a natural sickness? And so this matter may without the least suspicion be effected, and then you shall be mistress both of her heritage and myself."

Sylvian said, "When shall this be put in practice?"

"Within these two days at the farthest," said he. "In the meantime, frequent° you Artesia's company in such similar sort as heretofore you have done, and myself will use her with no less kindness." Many other speeches being past betwixt them at that time, they parted.

CHAPTER VII

How Ornatus told Artesia of Floretus's intent, and upon what occasion he discovered° himself.

Floretus, being by himself, began to consider how rashly he had committed his secrets to Sylvian, entering into these meditations: "Doth Sylvian think that my policy° exceedeth not her shallow capacity? Poor simple stranger, she hath undertaken a matter of great importance for me that means nothing less than good will to her. She for my love hath promised to poison Artesia and is likely, that once done, to taste of the same sauce, for loved she me never so well, I will not trust her with my life. But peradventure she hateth me and will reveal my drift to Artesia."

"No Floretus, thou art deceived; she is so far in love that she doteth,° and would, I am sure, do anything at my request. What a world is this, what villainy can be intended, that some either for favor or reward will not execute? If I should trust her that is so easily won to do such a heinous deed, might I not be accounted mad? Yes, and therefore I will not trust her. Artesia being once

frequent keep.   **discovered** revealed, disclosed.   **policy** capacity for intrigue, cunning.   **doteth** gives me all her affection.

dispatched, she shall follow next. Ornatus, on the contrary part, was glad that he hath felt the depth of Floretus's counsel, thinking likewise that he was so far in love with him, taking him for a woman, that for his sake he sought Artesia's death, which was the only means to help him attain her [Sylvian's] love, which he likewise determined to give her [Artesia] knowledge of, and discover himself, hoping that when she saw his innocency, his faithful love, and how by his means her life was preserved, she would yield him due guerdon° for his good will."

Whilst he was in the depth of those cogitations, he espied Artesia enter the garden, and, taking his lute, found her seated upon a flowery bank under the shade of a myrtle tree, and perceiving that she was somewhat heavily inclined,° he sat down by her and with his sweet melody brought her asleep. When she had slept a good while, being exceedingly affrighted° with a dream, she started up, looking earnestly upon Sylvian, saying: "I pray thee Sylvian do not poison me."

Sylvian, seeing her so affrighted, was exceedingly amazed, and she herself not yet fully recovered, seemed to be afraid of him, till at last Sylvian said: "I beseech you what is it that affrighteth you?"

"O Sylvian," said she, "I dreamt thou wouldst have murdered me."

"Heavens forbid," quoth he, "that I should attempt so heinous a deed. But would you vouchsafe° to hear my tragic report you should be rid of that doubt, though Sylvian is much tempted to do such a deed, who esteem your life more dearer than mine own, and would rather with my own hands tear out my woeful heart than think the least thought to wrong you. But because I have so fit occasion, and I hope your patience will permit me, I will rehearse a most monstrous and heinous intended mischief. The other day I remember you were exceedingly offended with me for naming Ornatus, for that you supposed him to be an actor

guerdon reward, recompense.   **heavily inclined** drowsy, sleepy.
affrighted terrified.   **vouchsafe** permit, allow.

in Arbastus's death, but both he and Allinus are innocent and far from any such thought, for your uncle Floretus was his murderer, which he told me himself. He hath been oftentimes importunate[◊] to win my love which another possesseth but I, suspecting as much as I now find to be true, held him off with this delay — that he had not wealth to maintain me. Which, when I had often alleged, he told me all that belonged to Arbastus was his. Then I demanded how that could be since you were living? Quoth he, "swear but to be secret, and I will tell you how." With that, upon my protestations, he told me that he had murdered Arbastus and meant to poison you, persuading me to consent thereto for that he said I only could do it. With that, I, not purposing to do it but to preserve you, promised him my uttermost assistance, which he told me should be done in this manner. 'I will,' quoth he 'persuade Artesia to forsake this castle and to sojourn some few days in a house Arbastus hath in his park where none but you and two other servants, whose secrecy I nothing doubt, shall keep her company, where I will give you such a potion as shall end her life and yet by no means be perceived, neither can there be any doubt[◊] thereof, for that I and none else am left of her kindred to search the truth.' This is the sum of that he told me."

Artesia, hearing her words, sat like one without sense a good space, being so far overcome with grief and fear that she could not speak a word, but at the last burst forth into these lamentations: "Aye me, unkind, and most unnatural uncle, canst thou speak me so fair and intend me so much harm? Who would have thought so foul impiety had been shrouded under so fair pretext? Couldst thou be so unnatural[◊] as to murder thy own most natural, loving and dear brother, and, not contented with his tragedy, to seek my untimely death? What frenzy or folly doth possess thy breast that I esteemed replete with virtue? How canst thou suffer[◊] so impious and heinous a thought to sink in thy breast, much less to act such a notorious outrage against him that loved thee as his

---

importunate persistent in solicitation.   **doubt** suspicion, fear.
unnatural inhuman.   **suffer** allow.

life, and her that honoreth thee as her friend? O Sylvian, may
I credit thy words and not rather accuse thee and excuse him?
May I think him so simple to trust thee with his secrets? No, I
fear me this is some policy invented by thee to some bad end.
Yet I pray thee pardon me, for what canst thou get by telling me
so unless it were so? Or not rather have kept his counsel and
then thou mightest have been my heir. And pardon I ask of thee,
good Ornatus, though thou art absent, for that I accused thee as
accessary to my father's death when thou art innocent."

With that, a flood of tears stopped the passage of her speech
and Sylvian said: "Artesia, yet vouchsafe to hear my counsel,
which shall prevent all these imminent evils. You may peradventure make some doubt of the truth of that which I have spoken,
but I take heaven to record no word is false, for I regard your
good above all things and your quiet above mine own content.
For should you die, I could not live, for by you I draw my breath.
I dived into Floretus's counsels not to aid him but to prevent
them, for that I knew Ornatus was no way guilty of any such
treason but would have ventured his own life to have preserved
your father's whom he both loved and honored as himself, of
whom I could have told you more but that fearing to offend you,
and partly seeing how vehemently you accused him, I durst not,
whose love is loyal and thereon I will pawn my life."

"Sylvian," quoth Artesia, "thou tellest me things of wonder,
but especially that thou art so privy to Ornatus's thoughts, and
that thou darest so boldly affirm he loveth me when thou mayest
be deceived."

"Most virtuous Artesia," quoth he, "were you but so privy to
the thoughts of his heart as I am, you would say as much as I,
and believe all that I tell you. And to put you in assurance of
what I know, I give you knowledge that I am Ornatus that in this
disguise have sought to attain your love, for which boldness I
most humbly beseech you to pardon me."

With that, a ruddy° blush spread itself in Artesia's cheeks,
before pale with fear, being so much ashamed that he had been
ruddy red.

so privy to many of her actions that she could not tell with what
countenance to behold him. Then Ornatus said: "I beseech you
pity my torment which hath urged me to this boldness, being
frustrated of other means to enjoy your presence, my meaning
being no other than virtuous, but resting at your merciful disposition, desiring you to put assured confidence in me for preventing
Floretus's intent, which you need not doubt of, for to my grief I
know it to be too true."

Artesia marvelled exceedingly at the strangeness of these
news, but most of all admired Ornatus's love, which she could
not tell how to reject for that she both well knew he deserved
love and the necessity of time was such that her safety rested in
his secrecy. Yet being not willing at that instant to yield without
further assault, said: "I know not by what name to call you when
neither I know whether you are Sylvian or Ornatus, but which
of both your words bear great show of true friendship, which I
fear me is not grounded in your heart, neither do I greatly care;
for since my uncle seeketh my life, let him take it, for I am weary
thereof."

"Let not your gentle heart," quoth Ornatus, "make any doubt
that I am Ornatus, though my counterfeit disguise doth show me
other, but either vouchsafe me love or give me leave to die for
Artesia, for that potion that should dispatch you shall end my
life, for my life is bound to your command, and all my felicity
resteth in your favor, which, unless you grant, my life without
the same will be but short and the time I have to live an endless
labyrinth of sorrow."

Adellena, by occasion,° entered the garden and found Artesia
weeping and Sylvian in a heavy dump,° ready to torment himself
to see her sorrow. But Artesia espying her, said: "Adellena, dost
thou love Ornatus so much as thou wouldst hazard life and credit
to do him good, for that I know him to be a most virtuous and
honest gentleman?"

occasion a particular juncture of circumstances.   dump cheerless
state.

"Aye, but wouldst thou," quoth she, "keep my counsel if I reveal a secret of importance to you concerning Ornatus?" And upon Adellena's promise, she said: "Do you know Ornatus if you see him? Behold, there he is." Adellena was at the first half astonished at her speeches, but at last she perfectly remembered that was he indeed, rejoicing most exceedingly to see him there, especially with Artesia. Then they declared unto her all that had happened, and of Floretus's intent, desiring her to be secret and make no show of discontent lest he should suspect Sylvian had bewrayed° his secrets. And after some other speeches passed, they went in together.

CHAPTER VIII

How Artesia departed to the lodge with Sylvian and from thence secretly departed to Adellena's house, and how Ornatus, taken to be Sylvian, was by Floretus's accusation and Artesia's want,° banished.

It fell so out the next day that the king, with divers of his company, amongst whom was his only son and heir Lenon, being wearied with travel, arrived at Arbastus's house, thinking to have found him there. But the king, hearing of his sudden death, was exceedingly sorry, persuading himself, as all men else did, that he was slain by some of Allinus's house, which made him make small tarriance° there, but departed to his palace. Now it fortuned that Lenon beheld Artesia's beauty and was, with the first view thereof, exceedingly bewitched° that, after he was gone, he could by no means forget her, but determined ere long to return to see if he could attain her love. Now the time was come that Floretus had appointed to set abroach° his villainy, and, according as Ornatus had before told Artesia, he came to her, persuading her for a season to lie in the country which she, as forearmed, consented unto, and so the next morning she, with

bewrayed revealed, disclosed.   **want** absence, disappearance.
small tarriance short stay.   **bewitched** enchanted.   **to set abroach** to set afoot.

Sylvian, Floretus, and divers others, departed. At night Floretus
returning and leaving with her, according as he had promised,
Sylvian and only two servants that were to provide them necessaries but knew no part of the conspiracy. When Ornatus and
Artesia were alone together, for that she was undoubtedly assured of his love, faith and fidelity, she used these comfortable°
speeches to him: "Ornatus, whereas always before this time too
unkindly I have reputed you as foe, I now crave pardon, being
sorry that my heart hath done you so much wrong, which now
I will requite with kindness. I confess it was strange to me to
entertain love, but now I willingly yield myself to be her subject
and your true and faithful friend, committing my life[18] to your
custody, and my love and self to be yours to dispose of."

Ornatus, hearing her speeches, was ravished with a heaven of
joy, with a gentle and kind behavior folding her in his arms and
imprinting a sweet kiss upon her rosiate° lips, he said: "Never
was poor wretch exalted to more happiness than I am by being
enriched with this inestimable treasure of your love. O how
rich a reward have I now reaped for my cares, and what glory,
joy, or wealth can be compared to the riches of your love. O
heavenly Artesia, how fortunate have you made Ornatus. How
have you blessed Ornatus. How full of joy is Ornatus by your
sweet consent. Was ever any so unworthy, so exalted? For
this kindness and love I will perform more than my tongue can
utter and be more faithful than your heart can wish." Then
began they to embrace each other and to surfeit themselves in
the solaces true love yieldeth. He sometimes lending her a kiss
and she with interest paying two for one, for one sweet look two,
and so many embracings as are not to be explicated; their hands
and hearts joined in such firm bands of true affection as is not
to be dissolved, and surfeiting with such exceeding content as
is impossible to be described. These storms of love somewhat
mitigated, they began to consult of their dangerous estate° and
to devise how to prevent the intended mischief. In this place they

comfortable comforting.   **rosiate** rosy, red.   **estate** condition.

continued some two days in exceeding content, still expecting to hear from Floretus, who, the third day, fearing to trust any with a matter of such weight, came himself to bring the potion, yet in show of kindness to visit Artesia, delivering the same to Sylvian, willing her the next night to give it her, which she promised him faithfully to accomplish.

When he was gone, Artesia came to Ornatus to know what news Floretus brought, who told her all and showed her the poison in a glass, which he had charged should be given to her the next day. With that Artesia began to wail and exclaim against her uncle in most extreme sort. But Ornatus entreated her to cease such vain grief, which could not hurt him but herself, promising her to prevent the same if she would follow his counsel, which she willingly yielded unto. Then quoth he: "Let us presently depart hence to Adellena's house, which you know is not far off, who you know is agreed with us already, where I will leave you and return." Which said, while the servants were absent upon some special occasion, they departed, with little labor arriving at Adellena's house, who was ready to receive them. And after many farewells, Ornatus returned back to the lodge. And when it was suppertime the servants brought up meat, but Ornatus told them that Artesia was scarce well and therefore they would not sup that night. And being alone by himself, he studied what excuse to make for Artesia's absence when Floretus should come, spending that night in much care and many unquiet cogitations,[◇] which took away his sleep.

Floretus was no sooner returned from the lodge but he met Lenon, who of purpose came to meet Artesia, whom Floretus kindly saluted, marvelling much wherefore he came — to ease which doubt, Lenon said: "My friend Floretus, I come to visit the fair Artesia, to whose beauty I am enthralled, not as regarding her wealth but her sweet love of whom you only have the government. Therefore I pray, befriend me so much that I may come to speech with her." Floretus was so exceedingly amazed

cogitations thoughts.

to hear his speeches that he could not tell what answer to make, nor how to excuse her absence. Lenon, seeing him in such a study,° continued his speeches, saying: "Floretus, be not unwilling I should match with Artesia, for that shall no way hinder your preferment, who think peradventure the longer she liveth unmarried, the more wealth you shall get by her. But to rid you of that doubt, be but a means to win her consent and I vow by heaven I will not take one pennyworth of Arbastus's substance° from you, but freely give it you all. For it is not her possessions I regard, but her love; therefore I pray, resolve me of your mind° herein."

"My Lord," replied he, "your offer is so bountiful. Besides my duty urging me, I am ready to perform your will to the uttermost of my power."

"I thank you, good Floretus," quoth Lenon, "then I pray thee bring me to her, for my love is impatient of delay."

"My lord," replied he, "that can I not do instantly, for Artesia some two days past, with the strange° damsel Sylvian departed hence and are now at the lodge, whither, if you please to take such entertainment as this place yieldeth, we will both go tomorrow morning."

"Agreed," quoth Lenon, "I will accept your proffer." When the time of rest was come, Floretus being alone by himself entered into these cogitations. "What inconveniences hast thou run into Floretus? Thou hast hired one to murder Artesia in hope to get her wealth and made Sylvian acquainted with thy counsel, which wealth thou mayest now attain by preserving her life; and besides, winning her to love Lenon, thou shalt find him thy faithful friend forever. What wert thou then best to do? If thou shouldst murder her, he would make enquiry of her death and so thou be undone. If not, then will Sylvian be displeased and so bewray thy drift,° that the mischiefs thou by folly hast run into are so intricate that thou knowest not which way to shun them.

study distraction.   **substance** wealth.   **resolve me of your mind** let me know what you think.   **strange** foreign.   **bewray thy drift** reveal your intention.

Were it not better to save her life and win her love for Lenon than
to poison her and so to die myself? If I save her life, Sylvian will
be discontented. What of that? Then let Sylvian smart for it,° for
if she will not be contented with that I shall do, she shall never
live to bewray my counsel. And therefore will I first try her, and
finding any suspicion thereof, I will stab her myself, whose death
I may easilier answer than Artesia's."

Early the next morning Lenon and he rode to the lodge, where
no sooner arrived but he met with Sylvian, to whom he said:
"How now, Sylvian, I have news of importance to bewray to
thee. Lenon, whom thou here beholdest, is son to the king, who
is deeply in love with Artesia, and hath given me assurance of all
Arbastus's livings if I can win Artesia to match with him. Now I
think it good to defer our purpose as concerning her death until
we have made trial whether she will love him or no. Which if we
can effect, we shall be quit of so cruel a deed, enjoy her heritage,
and have an assured friend of Lenon whilst we live. Therefore
let me know your opinion herein." Sylvian was exceedingly
amazed to hear his speeches, thinking that if he did tell him
where Artesia was, she should be wrested from his possession
and so himself disappointed of her love. And on the other side,
he thought what mischief would arise if he should say he had
already given her poison. Yet his love, overmastering the fear
of any danger, made him say: "All this I like. But Floretus, it is
now too late, for I have caused Artesia to drink the poison you
delivered me and she is dead, which was of such force that all her
body purpled into blisters and swellings, which because I knew
would bewray what we had done, I took her body and conveyed
it into a deep pit where it is impossible to be found."

Floretus, now fearing to have his treason bewrayed, thought
to stab Sylvian and so to rid of them both, that in a monstrous
rage he drew his dagger and unawares struck Sylvian in the
left arm, who feeling the smart, with violence more than Floretus expected, stepped to him and, in spite of his uttermost

smart for it feel the pain.

strength, wrung the dagger out of his hands, and with the same
wounded him in three places, and had not Lenon stepped betwixt
them, Floretus had been slain. With that Lenon, parting them,
demanded what the matter was. Floretus, thinking rather to
accuse than be accused himself, and terrified with affright, said
that wicked woman hath murdered Artesia. Sylvian made no
answer until Lenon laid hold on her, demanding where Artesia
was, she answering: "By the enticement of that wicked Floretus
I gave her a drink that unknowing to me hath poisoned her."[19]

"O wicked creature," said Lenon, "thou hast condemned thyself, and therefore worthily shall thy accursed life make satisfaction for her death." With that he began to draw his sword,
but Ornatus thinking it no time to dally lest he might by them
be murdered, caught hold on Lenon's sword, having such advantage that he easily wrung it from him, and said: "Worthy
Lenon be advised, do not thou seek to spill my innocent blood
without further consideration lest for the same thou lose thine
own. Thinkest thou I am as faulty and guilty as Floretus is? Be
assured I am not. But if thou lovest justice, lay hands on that
traitor, for he, not I, is capable of shedding her innocent blood."

By this time Lenon's servants, perceiving their contention,
came running in with their swords drawn by their lord's commandment, apprehending Floretus and afterwards seeking by
violence to take Sylvian, but he, standing in his own defense, resisted them, alleging innocence till Lenon vowed and protested
[that] if he were not accessary thereto he should have no other
than justice, and that his cause should be heard before the king.
Ornatus thought it better to yield by fair means, rather than by
compulsion, and esteeming it less grief to be made a prisoner
than to bewray where Artesia was and so have her taken from
him, yielded, both of them being conveyed to the palace and for
that night committed to several prisons. Floretus's conscience so
deeply accused him of villainy that he continued cursing and ex-
claiming against his hard fortune, with bitter bannings,◊ raging

bannings cursing.

against himself for trusting Sylvian, seeming with extreme fear of death, desperate.

Ornatus, on the other side, took that trouble patiently as endured for Artesia's sake, fearing nothing, for that he knew himself innocent and could easily acquit himself of such accusation, purposing rather to hazard the worst than bewray what he was, which to conceal was his greatest care. The next day they were brought before the prince, where Floretus, upon Sylvian's accusation, confessed the truth both concerning Artesia and how he slew Arbastus, for which he was adjudged to die within two days. And quoth he to Sylvian: "For that thou art a stranger and by his counsel rather than of thine own inclination wert drawn unwittingly to do that deed, I will pardon thy life, but adjudge thee to be banished this country."

"And," quoth he, "because I fear that some will seek thy life, thou shalt presently be conveyed hence, which doom shall stand irrevocable." Then gave he commandment he should be conveyed to the haven presently, committing her to the custody of certain rude Moors, who, not staying to hear what answer she would make, whereof poor Ornatus was not readily provided of in that extremity, immediately carried her away. To whom Ornatus would have told the truth of all, but he spake to them that understood him not, who, with speed executing their sovereign's command, rudely haled him aboard and hoisting sail never rested until they arrived near the coast of Natolia[20] where they were commanded to leave her.

CHAPTER IX

Of the sorrow Artesia took for Ornatus's banishment, and of the several adventures [that] befell him in Natolia.

Artesia, remaining in Adellena's house, marvelled she heard not from Ornatus according to his promise, which drove her into some doubt of his safety, that, coming to Adellena, she desired her to haste to the lodge to entreat him to come to her for that by her heart's misdoubt she suspected some heavy news. Adellena immediately hasted thither, finding the servants in great sorrow, whom she asked for Sylvian. "Aye me," quoth one of them, "by this time she is past speaking withal, for such heavy news is befallen since your departure as grieveth me to utter." Yet, notwithstanding, he told her all that was happened.

Adellena, brooking° no delay,[21] which in those affairs was dangerous, stood not to imitate of those griefs and how contrarily everything fell out, but with all haste returned to Artesia, who, espying her coming, thought her countenance bewrayed some unwelcome accident, hastily enquiring how Ornatus did. Adellena, for want of breath, could not speak a good space, but at the last she said: "Artesia, tedious lament is not now to be used but speedy counsel how to save Ornatus, for he is carried before the king, is accused by Floretus to have murdered you. For coming to the lodge with Lenon, the king's son who pretendeth° great love to you and not finding you, Ornatus told Floretus he had given you the poison, whereupon Floretus would have slain him, but Ornatus taking his dagger from him had done the like to him had not Lenon stepped betwixt them. Then Floretus accused him for your death and he, Floretus, and both were yesterday carried before the king."

"Alas, poor Ornatus," said Artesia, "what misery is befallen thee for my sake. How art thou rewarded for preserving my life? Good Adellena, counsel me what is to be done. Ornatus, being amongst them a reputed stranger, having no friend to plead for him and peradventure overswayed by Floretus's perjury, may have his life endangered, and the rather for that he is taken to be a Natolian. Therefore, Adellena, if thou lovest him or me, wilt save both his and my life and discharge him of that false accusation, run to the court and finding out Lenon tell him of my safety and request him for my sake to pity poor Sylvian." Adellena, according to her commandment, mounted a horse, and with great speed, by that time it was night, attained the court,

brooking tolerating.   **pretendeth** professes.

and finding out Lenon, uttered these speeches: "Most worthy Lenon, vouchsafe to hear me speak. The fair Artesia, whom you suppose dead, is alive and in safety at my house, who hath sent me unto you in the behalf of Sylvian, fearing some wrong might be done to her as suspected to be her death when she only hath preserved her life."

Lenon was so amazed at her speeches that he could not tell what to say, being exceedingly grieved for Sylvian, but at length told her what his father had done, which appalled her senses with deadly fear. Lenon, notwithstanding it somewhat grieved him for Sylvian, yet his heart was glad to hear of Artesia's safety, and therefore he determined to go with Adellena to visit her, which likewise he performed, and entering where she was, making exceeding lamentation, he said: "I beseech you grieve not fair damsel for Sylvian, for no harm is done to her; only my father, upon her own confession and Floretus's accusation, hath banished her to her own country."

Artesia, hearing his speeches, with very grief fell into a deadly trance, both Lenon and Adellena having much ado to bring her life again. And being conveyed to her bed, when her senses were come to their perfect use and Lenon standing by her, whose sight was most grievous to her, she turned her head from his sight, shedding such abundance of tears that she bedewed the place where she lay. Lenon, perceiving that she was displeased with his presence, withdrew himself, giving Adellena this charge. "Adellena, since Artesia is in thy custody, I charge thee let her not depart hence until thou hearest of me again, for if thou doest, thou shalt answer the same. But if thou wilt stand my friend and in my behalf entreat my favor, I will prove so grateful a friend as thou shalt account thy labor well employed."

He was no sooner gone but Artesia uttered these lamentations: "Most accursed wretch that I am, to be thus separated from my dear love, whose courteous mind is the fountain of all virtue. How unfortunate am I made by my father's death and my uncle's cruelty, but especially by his loss that is unjustly banished into a strange country where he, poor, true and loyal gentleman, never set foot. How unhappy was he made when he first began his love, but now most miserable, by seeking to preserve my life hath cast away his own, and fearing to be disappointed of my love hath quite dissevered himself from my sight to hazard his person by sea and land. Is it possible that he should ever return, being so far conveyed from his native soil and left to the mercies of strange people that will be ready to destroy his guiltless life? No, I fear me, never shall I be so happy as [to] behold him, and though I do not, yet shall my love to him remain immoveable. Therefore, now will I arm myself to endure all perils, to live in care and continual lament for want of beloved Ornatus, whose heart I know is replete with sorrow and peradventure misdoubteth my loyalty, having been so unkind to him before and knowing Lenon's affection may suppose his dignity might alter my constancy. But sooner shall Ornatus hear of my death than that I have altered my love or yielded his right to another, were he the greatest potentate in the world."

Which said, another flood of brinish° tears overflowed her eyes, and her passage of speech was stopped by heart-piercing sighings, which, in confused multitudes, issued with her sweet breath, never ceasing her laments but still bewailing her true love's absence that it pierced Adellena's heart with such sorrow that she wept as fast as Artesia, both being so much grieved that they seemed to strive how to exceed one another in laments. In which sorrowful estate Artesia remained so long that she waxed extreme sick and grew to that extremity that Adellena feared her death.

Lenon, likewise being come to the court, got pardon° of his father for Floretus's death, but notwithstanding he remained in prison all the days of his life. Lenon, likewise hearing of Artesia's sickness, refrained from visiting her, only he would oftentimes repair° to Adellena's house to enquire how she did.

Ornatus, being left in the country of Natolia, took his misfortunes in such heavy sort that, had not his hope to see Artesia

brinish salty.   **pardon** release (for Floretus) from the death penalty.
repair go.

again withheld him, he had offered himself some outrage, for a season giving himself to forlorn and careless desperation, neither regarding which way to provide for his safety nor otherwise respecting what danger he might run into in that strange country, for the Moors had landed him in a waste and desolate coast of the country.

Thus careless° did he continue a whole night and a day, not so much as seeking food to preserve him from famine. But in the end, hunger constrained him to seek succor,° but when his stomach served him, he could find no meat, that with the extremity thereof, calling to remembrance his estate, he uttered these plaints: "Thus contrary is Nature to her subjects, sometimes hoisting them to the top of all felicity, and then with violence tumbling them down headlong into the depth of extreme misery. Was ever [one] more fortunate and suddenly [more] miserable than I am? Could ever any man whatsoever attain more heavenly felicity and happiness than I did by being possessed of Artesia, and now again more accursed being thus far absented from her and banished my native soil into a strange country, ready to be famished or devoured by wild beasts, or that which is worst, never likely to see Artesia again? How could any man contain himself from desperateness being so miserable as I am? How can I withhold my hands from murdering myself, when, by doing it, I should be rid out of a wretched life? What should I do, which way should I go? Here I am in a desolate and unfrequented place where no human creatures inhabit but wild beasts, without food, without weapons, in woman's apparel, and without hope of comfort. Shall I stay here, then shall I be famished; shall I leave this place and travel further, then I go farther from my beloved, and meeting with some ravenous beast may be devoured. Now being hungry I want food, and there is none, unless I will eat the earth, leaves of trees, and roots of the grass. Well, I will seek my fortune, be it good or ill." And in this desperate mood he travelled on, and by good fortune found a tree laden with exceeding,

careless heedless.   **succor** shelter, relief.

pleasant and goodly fruit, with which he stanched◊ his hunger not far from which place he took up his night's lodging.

Early the next morning he arose, first filling his belly and then his lap◊ with that pleasant fruit, the taste whereof was like pleasant wine that being drunk in abundance will make the head light, which made Ornatus's heart merry that he travelled on apace. But fortune, not contented with the misery he endured already, sent him another affliction. He entered into a place like a forest beset with trees of huge proportion scattered here and there, where he met with a wild and fierce boar that haunted those deserts, who, espying◊ Ornatus, with a terrible groaning bristled himself◊ coming towards him. Ornatus, being now driven to his uttermost shifts, began to run with all his force from the beast, but he making the more speed had almost overtaken him when one of the apples Ornatus carried about him fell down and the boar, espying the same, stayed his haste to take it up, whereby Ornatus had gotten some little ground of him, and seeing him so much affect◊ the fruit, cast down another apple after which the boar ran, with greediness devouring the same. Ornatus was glad of this poor shift and still cast down one apple and then another that in the end he had almost thrown away all, and, notwithstanding that, feared to be destroyed, but the boar, feeling his belly full and his hunger stanched, left off his eager pursuit and followed him more carelessly, whom he still fed with apples so long as his store lasted, that in the end the boar being drunk with the pleasant fruit began to reel and stagger, and lying down fast asleep, which Ornatus seeing, having no other than a knife about him, with the same approached the boar and without fear violently thrust the same so deep into the boar's bristled side that it pierced his heart and he, after some struggling, died.[22]

Ornatus then held up his hands to heaven for joy, exceedingly applauding this his fortunate and unexpected escape, which he

stanched satisfied.   **lap** a small pouch.   **espying** seeing.
bristled himself the bristles standing upright in preparation for a fight.
affect like.

took as a fortunate presage° of good success. But yet, before he could determine what to do, fortune once again showed her mutability, for when Ornatus had parted the boar's head from his huge body and with the same was ready to depart, there passed by as it seemed a knight gallantly mounted in green armor, who, espying a woman bearing the boar's head, drew towards her and said: "Woman, where hadst thou that boar's head? I pray thee deliver it me."

Ornatus made this answer: "Sir I need not do either unless I know more cause than as yet I do."

The knight, hearing that short answer, alighted and said: "I will show no other reason but that I will have it." With that he began to strive for the same, but Ornatus, having more mind to his sword than to keep the boar's head, suddenly caught hold on the Natolian's sword and drew the same out, which when he had gotten, he said: "Disloyal and discourteous knight, now will I keep the boar's head in despite of thee. With that he thrust at him, and contrary to his thought, wounded him so deep that he left him for dead, wishing that he had not done that deed, but not knowing how discourteously he would have used° him, let pass all further remorse, and casting off his woman's apparel put on the knight's apparel and armor, mounted the steed and, with the boar's head, rode back the same way he saw the knight come, and within a little space found a beaten way that conducted him to a goodly town whose turret tops he saw long before he came to the same. Then began he to study what to do, sometimes thinking it best not to enter into the town from whence it is likely the knight he slew came, and so he being taken for him might be known and so afterwards endangered for his death. For peradventure° the knight might be of good estimation° and of purpose sent to slay the boar, and if it should be known that he had slain him, his friends would for the same, and the rather for that he was a stranger, prosecute sharp° revenge against him. Whilst he was

presage indicator, foreshadowing.   **used** treated.   **peradventure** as it happened; by chance.   **estimation** reputation.   **sharp** harsh, severe.

in these meditations he came near the town, not fully resolved what to do, where he was soon espied of some of the people, who, seeing the boar's head, came running towards him making exceeding joy. Which when he saw, he thought it too late to turn back, but that he must go on and hazard the worst. And being entered the town, a number of the inhabitants flocked about him, some with garlands, some with praises, and all with joy, uttering these speeches: "Welcome home most brave Alprinus."

Ornatus then perfectly knew that the knight's name was Alprinus, and went of purpose to slay the boar, whom they took him to be and that he must of necessity be known, which drave him into exceeding care what excuse to make to avoid the danger of death. Then presently he beheld a troop of beautiful damsels, with the sounds of sweet music, coming towards him, amongst whom one as chief and more beautiful than the rest was crowned with a wreath of flowers, bearing another in her hand, who all at once applauded his victory, dancing before him, until he came into the midst of the town where sat the chief magistrates, where the damsel that was crowned thus spoke to him:

"Sir Alprinus, your conquest hath released these inhabitants of care, extolled thy fame, preserved thy life, and won me for thy love. You have well-performed the task you undertook, and according to your desert I come to crown you with these flowers and to yield myself as yours for ever."

Ornatus, hearing her speeches, thought to try the end of this adventure, which could be no worse than death, which of force he must now hazard,° alighted, laying down the boar's head upon a table that stood before the ancients, with humble and comely behavior kissing the damsel's hand, who set the wreath of flowers upon his head, and, taking him by the hand, brought him before the ancients, one of whom stood up and said: "Worthy gentleman, whereas before thou wert by us adjudged to die, as worthy thereof, for this thy valiant deed we freely pardon thee and acquit thee from all the trespasses that thou hast committed against any whomsoever until this present hour."

hazard risk.

And taking the damsel by the hand, said: "Lucida, according to thy desire and his desert, I yield thee up to be his wife."

"And gentleman," quoth he, "take her as thine own, as freely as she was by birth adopted mine, and after my death, be thou inheritor of my land."

To all this Ornatus gave a reverent°23 consent, and the night now approaching, he with Lucida went to her father's house where was a great feast provided, from which Ornatus excused himself in this sort. When he was entered the house, being still armed, only lifting up his beaver he took Lucida by the hand and withdrawing her aside, said: "Lucida, I now find your love to be infallible and your constancy to excel all women's that I have known; and that Alprinus is so far indebted unto you as that he shall never, might he live a thousand years, be able to recompense this inestimable favor of your love which hath preserved my unworthy life from destruction. But notwithstanding your love — Alprinus his debt is so great as can no way be gratified,° — I request one further favor at your hands, whereon my chiefest felicity dependeth, yea my life, your love, and perpetual good, which I fear to utter lest you should misconceive the same, there being no other thing to hinder the content Alprinus seeketh but only your favorable consent to banish all mistrust of my faith."

Lucida marvelled at his speeches, indeed loving him so well that she would have spilt her own blood for his sake, saying: "Alprinus, what need you make doubt of my consent to anything whatsoever it be for your sake? Know you not how faithful I have continued, though you slew my only brother, and that I esteemed your love far dearer than his life, and when you should have died for that deed, obtained this at my father's and the rest of the ancients' hands, that slaying the boar that destroyed many people you should save your own life and win me as your love. And notwithstanding all this, do you make a question whether I will yield consent to anything that shall be for your good? O Alprinus, if your love were so constant as mine, if you intended

reverent respectful.   **gratified** requited.

to continue my love forever, if your heart felt so deep a sting of love as mine, you would not make such a doubt of my loyalty, of my truth, true love and constancy. For you know whatsoever you should ask, I will grant; whatsoever you should request, I will perform; and wherein soever a lover may show infallible tokens of her truth, I will do as much as any. But since you will not believe me without an oath, I swear by my love, my unspotted virginity, and by all the good I wish my heart, I will consent, agree, perform, or do anything, not be offended with anything, be the news never so unwelcome, so it be for Alprinus's good, nor leave anything unperformed you shall require."

Ornatus, hearing with what constancy her speeches proceeded from her, and how grievously she conceived it that any doubt should be made of her loyalty, thought most certainly that he might put his life into her hands, and therefore having already studied a device, said: "It ill agreeth with my nature to dissemble, and hardly could I have been drawn thereto but that desire to preserve love drew me thereto. For know, most worthy Lucida, that I am not Alprinus, but one that for his sake hath undertaken this; the truth whereof, if you will hear with patience, I will declare."

"Yesterday, I travelled through the forest, or desert, where I met Alprinus sore wounded and flying° from the boar that pursued him with celerity, which when I beheld, to rescue him from death, I sat upon the boar and by good fortune slew him; which, when he beheld, he declared to me the cause of his coming. Which when I heard, pitying his estate, I bid him take the boar's head and withal helped him to mount his steed, but his wounds would not suffer him° to ride, [so] that I was in some fear of his life, when presently we beheld an ancient hermit coming towards us, who lived in a cave in those woods and undertook to cure his wounds, being glad of the boar's death. To whose cell I conveyed Alprinus, at whose request I have performed this which you see,

flying running away, fleeing.   **suffer him** allow him.

and have undertaken to hazard my life to discharge him of death and to win the assured possession of your love."

"Now I most humbly entreat you for his sake to conceal what I am that I be not known and so both disappoint yourself of his love and him of safety. Only devise a means to excuse me from this feast, which I trust you will do for Alprinus's sake, and then we may have time to study for your further content."

Lucida's love made her believe that all he said was true, and therefore said: "Sir, I trust there is no cause why I should mistrust you, and therefore relying upon the truth of that which you have said, I will tell my father you are wounded and desire rather to go to your chamber than to the feast, who I know will deny me nothing." This said, she went to her father and so prevailed with him that he was contented she should have the tending of him whom she took to a chamber, suffering none to come at him but her maid, whom she trusted and well might trust for her fidelity. Afterwards, Lucida came to Ornatus to determine how she might come to see Alprinus, being most careful of his health, and amongst many other speeches they concluded that Ornatus, the next morning, should depart towards the forest to Alprinus, and that she, by some means, would come thither the next day after, if he would meet her to give her directions where to find him, which he promised to do. According to this agreement, Ornatus very early the next morning armed himself, and as Lucida had instructed him, took his leave of her father, who little suspected he had been any other then Alprinus, gave his consent, and so Ornatus in Alprinus's armor again departed the town, being glad that he was escaped from death, which he was sure to have endured if it had been any ways known that he had slain Alprinus.

And being now alone by himself, having the wide world to travel into, but never a friend to go to, void of fear but not of care, he studied whither to direct his journey. Sometimes his conscience accusing him of too much disloyal dealing towards Lucida in betraying her virtues by his dissimulation, in telling her Alprinus was living when he knew it to the contrary.

Then he contrarily thought it was lawful for him to dissemble with her to save his own life, and, though he had slain Alprinus, he did it but in defence of his honor.

Amongst all these, this cogitation seemed most to acquit him of dishonor, that Fortune and the Destinies had by that means ordained him to escape. Whilst he rode on in these deep meditations, he met with an ancient hermit, who, coming towards him, said: "Discourteous gentleman, how camest thou by that armor; and yet I need not ask thee, for I know thou slewest the worthy gentleman Alprinus, which I beheld to my grief."

"Father," quoth Ornatus, "if thou didst behold the same, thou canst witness I did it against my will and in mine own defense, for whose death I am as sorry as thyself, and would as willingly have done anything to preserve the same as any man living."

"Will you then," said the Hermit, "do this for him: vouchsafe to come and speak with him who is in reasonable good estate in my cell?"

"I would to God," said Ornatus, "thy words were true, for if he be living, it will revive my heart with joy that is almost vanquished with care, desiring nothing more than to see him."

"He is living," said the hermit, "and if you will go I will bring you to him presently."

Ornatus, being come to the cell, accordingly° found Alprinus very weak by reason of his grievous° wound, to whom Ornatus declared all that happened between him and Lucida, which added no little comfort to Alprinus's heart that he thought himself of sufficient strength to go and meet with her, and therefore told Ornatus he would go and meet with her, and withal yielded him so many thanks as if by his means his life had been preserved.

In the meantime they continued in the old hermit's cave, Alprinus in great [dis]comfort, and Ornatus in no less care for the absence of his dear Artesia, breathing forth many a scalding sigh and uttering many a sad and mournful lamentation, sometimes

accordingly as expected.   **grievous** dangerous.

utterly despairing of attaining her love and then again, by remembering her virtues, growing into some better confidence of
her constancy. Yet most of all, fearing that Lenon's love to her
might either by persuasion of his death, force, affect of dignity,
or other means, win her to consent to him, especially for that she
had no parents to govern her, nor he never a faithful friend to
counsel her.

The next day Alprinus and he went out to meet Lucida, whom
they met at the entrance into the forest, and after many kind
salutations passed betwixt the two lovers, they all together went
back into the town to Lucida's father's house, who that morning
was departed to a haven about business of importance.

Ornatus was most kindly used° of them, remaining there until
Alprinus had wedded Lucida. But then he thought it high time
for him to depart, and, on a time, finding Alprinus alone, who
had shown sufficient tokens of his friendship, he declared unto
him the whole truth of his forepassed° love to Artesia, requesting
his help for his passage into Phrygia.

Alprinus, with great regard, attended the whole discourse,
promising his uttermost assistance, "which," quoth he, "none can
effect so well as Lucida, whose father is a merchant and sendeth
forth ships into sundry provinces, who only may pleasure you,
which charge I will undertake and cause her to deal so effectually
with him that you shall attain your desire." Ornatus continued
in good hope, somewhat abandoning his former despair, whom
for a time we will leave, attending the time that some of the ships
should depart, to speak of Artesia, his careful° lover.

---

used treated.   **forepassed** earlier, previous.   **careful** anxious,
troubled.

CHAPTER X

*How Lenon caused Artesia by violence to be carried from
Adellena's house to the green fortress; of the miseries she
endured there. How she was rescued from thence by Allinus and from him taken by pirates. And how Allinus,
accused by Lenon for her death, was imprisoned.*

After that Artesia, by Adellena's careful tendance,◇ had somewhat recovered her health, Lenon began to visit her again, being
unable to endure the heavy burthen of burning love, thinking
her sickness had proceeded from fear of Floretus, not for want
of Ornatus's company, finding an occasion, saluted her in this
sort: "Most fairest Artesia, my heart is so firmly enthralled to
your beauty and my affections so admire your virtues that I
am constrained to utter my mind and to tell you, I love your
beauty,[24] virtues, and other most rare perfections wherewith you
are adorned, that I humbly sue to you for favor and prostrate
myself your thrall,◇ desiring to be enriched with those jewels
of inestimable price, which, having once attained, I shall think
I have more wealth in my possession than all the world besides
myself doth contain. Your unkind uncle's cruelty you need not
fear, nor other misfortune; neither have you any parents to over-
rule you in making your choice. Then vouchsafe to accept my
suit and yield consent to my love."

"My Lord," replied Artesia, "I thank you for your good will,
but I know not how to accept of your love, being yet so far
from knowing what it is that if I should but dream thereof my
heart would be out of quiet. Besides, many cares continually
attend the same, and my mean estate so far unworthy thereof,
with innumerable other discontents and cares that I should make
myself subject unto, that I had rather a thousand times remain
in the estate I am now in. Therefore, I entreat you to settle your
love elsewhere more agreeable to your estate and fancy, for I shall
think myself most fortunate if I never fall into that labyrinth of

tendance attention.   **thrall** slave.

disquiets, but will, during my life, labor to keep myself free from love's bands."

Lenon would not take this for an answer, but with many other speeches continued his suit, whom Artesia still put out of hope, that he departed for that time exceedingly discontented, leaving her no less disquieted in her thoughts how to avoid his love.

In this sort° did he daily visit her, still growing more importunate. Amongst many other, this conference passed betwixt them: "Artesia," quoth he, "how long shall I sue and be frustrated in my hopes by your unkindness? Is your heart hardened against me? Or am I of so base conditions that you cannot conceive well of me? Or is it possible you bear so hateful a conceit of love as you make show for? Then may I acurse mine eyes that have betrayed my senses in making them your thrall, then may I think my woe began when I first began to love. O Artesia, be not so cruel as to punish me with this disdain."

"My lord," replied she, "I seek not your disquiet, for at the first motion° I told you my mind, which shall never alter, neither is my heart hardened against you more than others, for I am determined not to love. Then seeing you see my intent, it were a point of wisdom in you to shake off this fond and foolish love, which is but a toy° and an idle fancy that is bred by vanity, and do not seek to make love grow without a root, for in my heart it shall never take root. But rather, when it is rooted I will pull out heart and all, but I will root it out."

"Then," quoth he, "you are led by obstinacy and not by reason, for that you are subject to love you cannot deny; then why not me before another, considering my love is more faithful than any other? And I, being most worthy, why should I not be first accepted?"

Artesia was weary of his speeches, having her constant thoughts only bent on Ornatus. Therefore to rid him from her, she said: "It is in vain to use many words; neither am I like to those that will at the first seem coy but afterwards yield. But I desire you

sort manner.   **motion** impulse.   **toy** trifle.

to be satisfied with that which I have already said, that I cannot love."

"Fair damsel, how can I be satisfied with that unreasonable answer when my life dependeth on your consent, which your denial will finish? Then give me leave to say, I cannot be so satisfied, but being extremely refused, I must grow perforce to be as unreasonable in my requests. Consider you not what dignity I might advance you to by making you my wife? Consider you not the pleasures, joys, and abundance of all contents you might enjoy with me, and how faithfully I love you and with what humility I seek your love, and yet notwithstanding you remain obdurate? My power is great that whereas I sue I might command and by authority compel you to consent; then be not so overconceited° as so obstinately to reject your good. And think that if my love were not constant, I might use extremes which would soon alter your mind."

"Suppose," replied Artesia, "I were so peevish as you term me, yet being born free I am not to be made bound by constraint; and were you the greatest king in the world, you could not rule the heart, though you might by injustice punish the body. For it is not kingdoms, wealth, nor cruelty can turn hatred to love, but it may sooner turn love into hatred. But by your speeches I may partly know your thought, and the lips utter what the heart intendeth. Do with me what you will, I cannot love, neither will I love you were you monarch of all the world."

Lenon was so much grieved and vexed at her speeches that he was ready to tear his hair, his love's extremity making him rather mad than sober, that presently he departed, saying no more but this: "Farewell, hard-hearted Artesia."

She was glad he was gone, presently telling Adellena all that had passed betwixt them, and how peremptorily° she had answered his importunate suit, telling Adellena that since Ornatus was for her sake banished, she would never love any but him and preserve her life in hope to see him once again.[25] But the

overconceited opinionated.   **peremptorily** decisively; categorically.

first knowledge of his death should be the latest date of her life, both she and Adellena thinking that Lenon would never return to prosecute his love. But he being come to the palace betook himself to his chamber, raging more like a mad man than a passionate lover, sometimes swearing, cursing, and stamping, yielding so much to that mad fancy that in the end he vowed to obtain Artesia's love, though he hazarded his life, honor and good name that, ranging in his sort up and down his chamber, he espied an old gentlewoman named Flera going by his window, whom he called unto him and thus said: "Flera, because I have assured confidence in thy fidelity and purpose to reward thee liberally, I crave thy counsel and with it thy consent to be faithful in concealing my secrets and diligent in doing my command."

The old hag, making an evil-fashioned low courtesy, said: "My dear son Lenon, be it to do you good I will hazard my life, and rather be torn into a thousand pieces than reveal what you shall vouchsafe to tell me."

"Then," quoth he, "counsel me which way I should begin to win a fair damsel's love." "Marry my lord," quoth she, "give her knowledge thereof and then with fair speeches woo her. If that will not prevail, give her gold, and there is no doubt that fair bait will catch her."

"No, no," quoth he, "these are of no force. I have made my love known to her by humble suits, submiss behaviors, and by all kind of courteous means entreated her consent, yet for all that she remaineth obstinate; she is rich and therefore gold with her is of no force; she is fair, virtuous, noble, and chaste, then what engine hast thou to undermine that chastity?"

"Means enough," quoth she. "Peradventure she is ruled by other's counsel, which may prevail more than your suit. But might I have access unto her, I would not doubt but to alter her mind, for being fair, young, and rich, she cannot choose but delight to be praised, subject to love, and therefore yield to desire."

"Dost thou think," quoth he, "thou couldst win her, wert thou her keeper?"

"I warrant you," quoth she, "I would do it."

"Then shalt thou be her keeper. See that thou beest tomorrow at my father's castle in the green forest where tomorrow by night this damsel shall be, whose name is Artesia, daughter to Arbastus lately dead. Use her kindly, let her want nothing, nor be not in any wise known that thou knowest me, nor that the castle belongeth to my father, nor speak not of love in any case. Use her in this sort until I speak with thee, for thou only shalt have her custody." Flera, being gone about her business, he found out two of his trustiest servants to whom he imparted both his mind and intent, willing them the next morning with speed to go to Adellena's house and either by force or fair means to take Artesia from thence and carry her unto the green fortress in the green forest where they should find Flera, to whose custody they should commit Artesia, and themselves should remain there to provide all things necessary until his coming.

Early the next morning, the servants rode to Adellena's house wereinto they boldly entered, and coming to Artesia first spake her fair,◊ but afterwards told her she must go with them, if not willingly, by constraint. Artesia then began to burst into tears, weeping and lamenting exceedingly, upon her knees entreating them not to offer by violence to carry her from thence, but if they would needs◊ that they would take Adellena with them. But all was in vain, for they constrained her to mount up behind one of them, and away they rode in great haste. This heavy parting was so sudden that Artesia could not bid Adellena adieu but with tears, nor Adellena speak a word for grief, their senses being so far confounded with care that their hearts were ready to burst therewith. Artesia thought this was Lenon's doing and therefore sorrowed the more: not that he used her unkindly but that he loved her, not fearing his cruelty but his lust; not regarding what cruelty he could use by hatred but fearing his love would make him seek her dishonor. Being come to the fortress and committed to the custody of Flera, the old woman began to speak her fair and

spake her fair reasoned gently.   **would needs** were compelled to do it.

use her kindly, yet her very words and countenance bewraying her guilty conscience, to whom Artesia would not speak a word lest thereby she should give her occasion to prate.° Meat she brought unto her but she refused to taste thereof, and when she came to her chamber she lay on the rushes, refusing the bed, tormenting her heart with care, vexing her head with thought and busying her senses, or meditating to what issue this usage would sort,° sometimes calling on Ornatus's name for comfort, sometimes accusing Lenon of barbarous cruelty and cursing her crooked° destinies, uttering such plaints as would have turned tyrants to ruth,° weeping her eyes dry and her garments wet, tearing her hair and tormenting every one of her senses with vexation, refusing sleep, rest, ease, or quiet.

The next day Lenon came hither, asking Flera how she fared, who told him that she would not speak, eat, nor sleep, but fared like one mad and senseless. "But let her alone," quoth she, "and you shall see this fit will soon be over, the extremity whereof being once past I will use my skill to try her."

Lenon, giving order to have all things necessary provided, departed. Dinner time being come and meat set before Artesia, she refused to eat. Likewise, supper time being come, she determined to do the like, which Flera perceiving, said: "Fair gentlewoman, to behold your outward appearance would make one judge your mind harbored many hidden virtues, but I, comparing your actions with your apparent show, suppose that you are either mad or careless. This behavior to seem dumb, to refuse sustenance, and to refrain from sleep are instances of folly, not of wisdom. What if you speak, what if you did eat or take rest, should you be ever the worse? Or refraining, can that do you good, or banish grief, and not rather make your estate worse? Do you think to prevent anything by doing yourself harm? No, fond child, eat thy meat, and preserve thy life, for living thou mayest attain thy desires, but dying thou art past hope." With that she departed, smiling.

prate talk idly, chatter.   **sort** result in, arrive at.   **crooked** false, perverse.   **ruth** pity.

Artesia, hearing her speeches, began to consider indeed what folly it was to refuse her meat, and for fear to shorten her life by distempering herself, which might be the means to further Lenon's intent, whom she knew would seek her life if he could not win her love, she presently left off such desperate behavior, and with well weighed consideration attended the event of the worst misfortune, that from that time she both eat her meat and did all that she could to comfort herself, still living in good hope of Ornatus's return.

Some few days after Lenon came to the fortress again, enquiring of Flera how Artesia fared. "Well," quoth she, "but you willed me to conceal that it was your doing to bring her hither, and somebody else hath told her thereof, for she knoweth the truth as well as yourself or I; and therefore I would wish you visit her, and after that let me alone to persuade her."

Lenon was ruled by the old woman and came where Artesia was, saluting her, but she, disdaining either to look on him or hear him speak, withdrew herself from his presence. Wherewith he departed, willing Flera to do that which she had undertaken. And Flera, finding her as she thought in a fit mood, began to commune° with her of many things, amongst which love was one. Artesia awhile heard her, but in the end, perceiving her drift, cut her off with these speeches.

"Old iniquity, I know whereto thy talk tendeth. Thinkest thou I will ever harbor a thought of Lenon that hath used me thus dishonorably? No, rather will I rent my woeful heart from out my breast before his face. Neither needst thou tell me that he hath entreated thee to speak for him, for I know too well both his and thy intent, which shall nothing prevail but harden my heart against him. Therefore, do not speak to me, for I will not hear thee nor answer thee, but hate him, thee, thy council, and remain so constant in despising him that a thousand deaths shall not alter me. Is it love hath made him with violence carry me from my friends, make me a prisoner, and commit me to the custody of such a hellish hag as thyself? If that be his love, let him turn

commune converse.

it to hatred and never trouble me but with hating me, for in so doing he shall better please me."

Often Flera would have replied but Artesia would not suffer her, that she began to wax° angry and in the end to plain fury, that running to Artesia, she caught hold on her and began to tear her garments from her body, and withal caught sometimes such firm hold on her pure flesh with her nails that the blood followed that Artesia began to cry and shriek for fear and smart.

When the old beldam° had executed some part of her intended revenge and cruelty upon her in this sort, she said: "Proud girl, thinkest thou to bear it away with out-facing me? No, do not think I will leave thee thus, but thou shalt repent that ever thou camest here, and before I go I will have my mind of thee." Then pulled she out a knife and catching hold on her swore that unless she would promise to use Lenon kindly when he next came she would cut her throat, which drove Artesia into that fear that she began to entreat her and speak fair, promising to condescend to anything that agreed to her honor. "Stand not upon those nice terms with me," quoth Flera, "but here swear to yield to love him, for so thou mayest delay him and frustrate his hopeful expectation whom thou art not worthy to touch, much less to bear such a presuming mind as thou doest in scorn of his love. Therefore, yield to that which I request or stand to my mercy. Canst thou bestow thy love better than on so honorable a prince? Canst thou attain more dignity, reap more content, or enjoy more quiet with any than with him? Then do not deny me, for I purpose not to be denied."

Artesia, trembling for fear, made this answer only to satisfy her: "I am contented to be ruled by Lenon, whose meaning I know is honorable. Therefore, I pray do not offer me this outrage,° but suffer° me to live in quiet until his coming. If this will not satisfy you, then do the worst you can for death is more welcome to me than life in these extremities."

wax grow.   **beldam** aged woman, witch.   **outrage** violence, indignity.   **suffer** allow.

"Well," quoth she, "I will try you. But if you dally,◊ beware what will ensue, for I am resolved what do to." Artesia was glad she had satisfied her, though it were with uttering words which she never intended to perform.

Adellena, seeing how suddenly Artesia was taken from her, caused one of her servants privily◊ to follow them to the green fortress, who returning, told her what he had seen. Then Adellena began to study how to release her from thence and with all haste rode to Allinus's house, where, being arrived, she declared all that she knew as concerning Ornatus and how Lenon had carried Artesia by violence into the green fortress. Allinus, being glad to hear that Ornatus was alive, promised to redeem Artesia from Lenon's custody, and that to effect, the next evening caused his men to mount themselves, and himself with some five of them, disguised from being known, came to the green fortress, and one of them knocking whilst the other[s] hid themselves. The servants, little suspecting any such ambush or intent, opened the gate, when presently they rushed in and soon found out Artesia, whom Allinus told who he was and to what intent he came. Artesia was glad thereof and willingly yielded to go with him, but the old woman made such an outcry that all the place rung thereof. One of Allinus's servants, seeing she would not be pacified, drew his sword and thrust it through her body and so with a yelling cry she gave up the ghost. Then presently Allinus departed with her, intending to carry her to his own house to keep her there unknown until he could hear of Ornatus. And remembering that the two servants were fled and would no doubt certify Lenon what was done, would not go back the same way he came, though the readiest, for then he thought he should meet them, but went a more secret way, thinking by that means to pass unseen. And entering into the plains where cattle fed, Allinus espied a company coming towards them whom he presently suspected to be Lenon, which in reason he could not think but that fear persuaded him thereto. The company likewise espying

dally trifle, deceive (me).   **privily** secretly, quietly.

them, who were certain pirates that were wandered from their
ships to steal cattle, wondered what they should be that were so
late abroad, and being ready to any mischief set upon Allinus and
his company, who [Allinus] thinking it had been Lenon, would
by no means yield nor speak, fearing he should descry them,
but resisted the pirates, who, being used to many such meetings, soon slew two of Allinus's servants and had given himself
[Allinus] many grievous wounds, enforcing him to yield. Who,
taking from him all that was good, constraining Artesia to go
with them, and hasted to their ships; when having conveyed
her aboard, to prevent the worst, hoisted sail and launched into
the deep.[26] Then was Allinus left in most miserable estate,° with
all speed hasting to his house. Lenon's servants likewise were
(by that time it was midnight) gotten to the palace and called
their lord out of his bed to certify him what was happened, who
presently mounted himself and with a sufficient company rode
to the fortress, and entering, found Flera slain and all else fled.
Then began he to muse° who should do that deed and what
they should be that had carried away Artesia. By this time it
was daylight and Lenon rested in exceeding vexation to be dis-
possessed of his beautiful love, yet he commanded his men to
post by companies several ways, if it were possible, to find those
that had done that deed, whilst he himself remained there bewailing that misfortune. His servants had not rode far but, by
the light of the day which discovereth things done in darkness,
they found Allinus's two servants whose dead bodies they carried back to the fortress. Lenon, seeing them, presently assured
himself that Allinus was a party in this action, and that he had
taken away Artesia to seek her death, to prevent which mischief,
as he thought then or never to be done, he presently rode home
to the court and humbly upon his knee entreated his father to
grant him licence with a sufficient power to rescue Artesia from
Allinus, who intended to murder her, declaring how he himself
found her in Adellena's house and how that he had placed her in

estate condition.   **muse** ponder, wonder.

the green fortress to defend her from Allinus's and others' cruelty, being left fatherless, and how that night Allinus had taken her from thence by treason and intended no less then her ruin. The king, hearing his son's speeches, granted his request. Then presently divers° to the number of three hundredth men, with as much speed as could possibly be, armed themselves, and in haste with Lenon went to Allinus's castle into which they violently and unawares to any within, entered. Lenon presently laid hands on Allinus, whom he found sore wounded, asking him for Artesia, who, thinking some of his servants had before bewrayed° what he had done, presently confessed the truth of all, both of his intent and how Artesia was rescued from him, but by whom he knew not, and how at that time two of his servants were slain.

Lenon, giving no credit to his speeches, never left till he had searched the whole castle throughout, but not finding her accused Allinus that he had murdered her, commanding his men to bind him and carry him as a traitor to the court. Who, being come before the king, confessed the truth as before he had done, utterly denying that he never° sought Artesia's death, but her safety. But yet notwithstanding, the king was so overruled° by Lenon's accusations and persuasions that he committed him to prison, his goods and lands were seized upon as a traitor, his lady wife turned out of doors in poor array, and all cruelty and outrage committed against his servants and kinfolks, and commandment given that none should succor them. Allinus, being in prison laden with irons and hardly used,° yet endured that affliction patiently, but hearing of his lady's calamity and how she was unjustly constrained to beg that all her life long had been tenderly brought up, thought those sorrows would soon bring her to an end, and entered into many bitter lamentations for her and his own misfortune which were too tedious to recite. His servants were constrained to disguise themselves and travel into

divers many.   **bewrayed** revealed.   **never** ever.   **overruled** swayed.   **hardly used** harshly treated.

farther places of the country to live unknown, otherwise none would have entertained them. His lady was compelled to seek out a kinswoman of hers that lived in the country, of whom she was entertained, and there lived a poor life, far differing from her former life, which she took most patiently. And thus was Allinus's house defaced, his goods and lands seized upon, himself imprisoned, his wife in poor estate, his servants driven to wander from place to place, ready often to perish for want of succor,◊ and all his dignity turned to misery only by Lenon's malice who had no ground for those accusations he used against him, but only of a vain suppose◊ and mad, frantic affection that overruled◊ his heart, which so much prevailed with him that he [Lenon] sought by all means he could his [Allinus's] death.

CHAPTER XI

How Ornatus got shipping into Phrygia, how Allinus was set at liberty, and how the pirates cast lots who should possess Artesia.

Ornatus all this while remained in the country of Natolia with Alprinus and Lucida in great grief for want of means to depart into Phrygia to see what was become of his dear love, Artesia. But being a long time frustrated by reason none of the ships that were at sea came home, he began to despair, thinking that Artesia, supposing him to be dead by reason of his long absence, would now marry Lenon, which grief and many other doubtful thoughts oppressed his heart with such passion that he began to wear sick and afterwards fell into an exceeding fever which held him for the space of three months in great extremity, which surely had abridged◊ his days had he not been most carefully nourished by Lucida, who had an especial care of his good. During which time of his sickness, certain ships of Phrygia arrived on the coast of Natolia some fourteen miles distant from the

succor relief.   **suppose** conjecture.   **overruled** swayed.   **abridged** shortened.

town where Ornatus was, of which he had intelligence by certain factors° belonging to Lucida's father, which news revived his spirits with joy (before drooping with care) that within few days he recovered his former health, which greatly rejoiced Alprinus and Lucida whose hearts were linked unto him in bands of inseparable friendship, who likewise dealt so effectually for him that they attained warrant for his passage and furnished him with all kind of necessaries and sufficient store of gold to bear his charges.

Lucida likewise intreating her father to agree with the Phrygian merchants for his convoy, for that himself would not be known, disguising himself into the habit° of a pilgrim, which kind of people might without disturbance pass unexamined and without molestation. And the time of his departure being come, he took his leave of Lucida, who took his departure with such exceeding sorrow that the abundance of her flowing tears stopped the passage of her speech. Alprinus likewise with many courtesies bad him farewell and wished his prosperous success. Thus departed he the confines of Natolia, where he was in so short space so well beloved and so kindly used° that, had not his love to Artesia and hope to find her in safety constrained him, he could have been contented to have spent the term of his life in that place.

The merchants of Phrygia had not sailed many days but they arrived in a haven some ten miles distant from the court whither Ornatus determined to travel, and having taken his leave of the mariners and paid them their due, furnished with all things fit for his disguise, he took his journey and the first night lodged at a village near-adjoining to his father's castle, the custom of which place he well knew before and therefore framed his behavior accordingly. And being set at supper amongst such guests as lodged in that house with him, the host named Mylo suddenly sighed, which one of then noting, demanded what inward grief drave him thereto. "Marry sir," quoth he, "if you have not

factors merchants.   **habit** attire.   **used** treated.

already heard the news, I will tell you so much as I know, which I would I had never known. Within few days there dwelt an ancient knight hereby named Allinus, exceedingly well beloved of all men, who is lately fallen into great misery, the occasion whereof was this." Then did he declare the manner of all that had happened unto Allinus, how Artesia was taken from him, but by whom no man knew, himself in prison, his goods confiscated, and his wife and servants turned out of door with command that none should succor them.

Ornatus's heart was so pinched with this news that he was ready to fall under the table, which old Mylo and the rest noted, perceiving such a change of countenance in him that they all deemed him to be exceedingly sick. But he, fearing to discover himself, told them it was but an ordinary course with him to be so troubled. But being unable to mitigate that passion, he rose from the table and got to his chamber, where, being alone, he began to meditate the depth of these mischances, imputing the original thereof to proceed from himself, that he entered into these bitter plaints:◊ "My misfortunes are without compare and I more miserable than any wretch living. By my evil destinies Artesia was first left in misery, afterwards imprisoned, and now surprised by those that will intend her ruin or dishonor. My father imprisoned, my mother banished, all his lands, livings,◊ servants, and friends taken from him, and he subject to Lenon's mercy, that is merciless, cruel, deceitful, and malicious. Only by my folly are these mischances befallen. Can there then be any more wretched than myself? Hath not my father cause to wish that he had never begotten me and my mother that she had never borne me? Hath not Artesia cause to accuse me, hate me, and forsake me, when for my sake, by my folly and want of wisdom, she is brought to so many miseries? What shall I do, or what remedy shall I seek, when all things is◊ past recure?◊ Whom may I blame but myself? Is there any that is interested

plaints laments.   livings income from rents.   is meaning: are.
recure remedy.   interested in concerned with, has a share in.

in° the cause of these woes but myself? Lenon, Lenon, as well as myself, hath procured these evils. His affection to Artesia hath caused my banishment, my parents' woe, and her loss. To travel in her search and leave my father in prison, the one would be in vain when I know not whither she is conveyed, and the other dangerous to his safety, for Lenon, no doubt, of malice will seek his death."

In these and such like plaints he spent most part of that night. Early the next morning, coming out of his chamber, he heard a great tumult in that village, the occasion whereof was this: such as were tenants and friends to Allinus, hearing of his unjust imprisonment and with what cruelty Lenon sought his overthrow, assembled themselves together with purpose to entreat the king for his release, that in the end there was three hundred of them assembled. The common people and such as were idle persons and ready to any attempt, misconceiving their intent and bearing a mind desirous of liberty, which they thought they were restrained from by certain strict laws the king had made, gathered unto them, that, contrary to their expectation, there was a multitude, the intent of whose assembly being demanded, they answered that they meant to redeem Allinus amongst whom Ornatus, in his disguise, thrust himself, using many forcible persuasions to urge them forwards to that attempt that they were ready to run confusedly to the court, not regarding danger nor the displeasure of the king.

One of Allinus's friends named Thrasus, standing up amongst the rest, craved audience, to whom they all listened whilst he said: "I perceive your intent is to release Allinus, wherein you shall show your love to him and do a deed worthy to be eternized,° for that he hath not at all deserved to have such injustice ministered unto him. Therefore be wise in this attempt and first know against whom you bear arms, that is, against your lawful king who may punish this fact with death, for that we undertake to break those laws which he hath ordained. But follow my counsel

eternized remembered forever.

and I will set you down a course whereby you shall attain your desire and be void of any such danger, which is this. First, let us all repair to the court and humbly entreat the king for his release. If he will not grant that, then that he would have his cause tried by the rest of the peers of the land. Which, if he also deny, then may we with good cause venture our lives in his rescue."

The multitude, hearing Thrasus, in sign of consent all cried: "Thrasus, Thrasus shall be our captain!"

Then presently everyone, with such furniture° as they had, hasted to the court, and coming together would not seem to enter by force but with a full consent yielded to Thrasus's directions, who desired one of the guard to certify his majesty that there were a number of his subjects gathered together with no intent of evil, but only humbly to crave a boon° at his highness's hand. The king, being certified hereof, was much troubled in his mind what the thing should be they would demand, and being persuaded by Lenon, would not himself come out, but sent one of his knights to demand what was their request. Thrasus declared unto him the cause of their coming and what they demanded, which, when the king understood, being exceedingly enraged at their boldness, had the knight make them this answer, that he was not by his subjects to be controlled, and therefore denied to perform the least of their demand, commanding them presently to depart every man to their several place lest he punished their presumption with death. The messenger had not scarce ended his words, but presently the unruly multitude began to rush in at the court gates, some carelessly ruinating° whatsoever came next hand, some breaking down windows, some assailing such as resisted them, and everyone bent to do mischief. The king, fearing the people's unruly rebellion would turn to some greater mischief than could suddenly be prevented and might also endanger his person, not knowing who had instigating them thereto, with the queen and Lenon fled. Which, when Thrasus knew,° calling

furniture equipment.   crave a boon ask for a favor.   ruinating destroying.   knew realized.

to the multitude, he willed them in any wise° not to destroy
the king's house nor attempt anything more to displease his
majesty, for that the king was departed and he had Allinus at
liberty. But notwithstanding, some, bent only to enrich themselves, spoiled the King's treasure and utterly defaced the house,
by which time the night drew nigh and everyone began to with-
draw themselves. Allinus seeing what exceeding mischief this
attempt had bred, which was done contrary to his thought and
without his consent, yet thought it best not to trust to the king's
mercy, though he were never so innocent, for notwithstanding
that he would suppose it was done by his procurement. Therefore, after Thrasus had willed the unruly multitude to depart as
secretly as they could, every one to his house to prevent further
danger and save their lives by keeping themselves unknown, he
and Thrasus that night, without delay, disguised themselves and
fled towards the coast to get shipping for Armenia, whither they
intended to travel.

Ornatus was by and beheld all this, glad of his father's escape, not purposing at all to discover himself until he had found
Artesia, in whose search he meant presently to travel. But such
confused thoughts whither to direct his steps did so overwhelm
his conceits that he rested like one metamorphosed, not knowing
whether he would[27] seek her by sea or by land. By sea he thought
his labors would be in vain, and if he should go to find her by
land, he knew not whether she might be at sea and so conveyed
into foreign countries. At last, remembering he had heard Mylo
say she was rescued from Allinus in the desert where his cattle
fed, he determined to travel thither, though he had little hope to
find her there. And being come thither, sometimes bewailing her
absence, accusing his hard fortune, breathing forth bitter sighs
in remembrance of her loss and renewing the remembrance of
their love, he spent some three days in that place uttering those
plaints to the trees and birds, for otherwise there was none to
hear him where for a while we will leave him.

wise manner.

The pirates having, as is before said, taken Artesia from Allinus, and with her such wealth as they could find about them, having withal furnished themselves with the spoil° of such cattle as fed in those places, returned to their ship and with haste hoisted sail, the night being now passed.

One that was chief amongst the rest named Luprates went down to view Artesia, having as yet not seen her beauty by reason of the night, and now coming near her and beholding her divine form, his mind was presently ravished with that sight and he thought that none but himself should enjoy her, which took such efficacy that whereas before he intended nothing but her dishonor, his mind was now altered, and he intended to use her in most reverent and decent sort and, not by cruelty, but courtesy to win her love. But beholding her tears and exceeding lamentation and how impatiently she endured the extremities she was driven unto, coming towards her with a most submiss° gesture, friendly countenance, and gentle speech, he said: "Fair lady, be not anything° disquieted that you are made captive to such as delight in spoil, for though our minds are otherwise bent to all incivility, yet to yourself shall no wrong be offered—such virtue hath beauty imprinted in my heart. And whereas heretofore without mercy both I and the rest of my consorts have not regarded the plaints, distress, nor what wrong we have offered either to lady or damsel, yet towards yourself is my heart altered and my meaning° honestly bent, that I assure you not only of quiet and to be void of all wrong by us to be done, but also, wherein soever I may work your will, quiet, ease, or desire, I will most willingly employ my uttermost endeavors. Then I beseech you mitigate these cares, banish this sorrow, and dry up your tears, for you have no cause of care nor occasion of sorrow, but rather to say this virtue resteth in me to alter rude and barbarous minds to civil and virtuous behavior."

spoil loot, booty.   **submiss** subdued, humble.   **anything** at all.
meaning intention.

Artesia, looking earnestly upon him, being indued◊ with an exceeding wit, and thinking it best to speak him fair that used her so kindly, said: "Sir, I know not how to mitigate my grief when it increaseth, or how can I be void of care unless I should grow altogether careless, being only subject to woe, and none so unfortunate as myself, having endured so many afflictions and crosses in all respects that I know not how to assure myself of the least quiet? Then give me leave to continue my endless plaints and do not blame me of impatience, nor think I suspect your speeches, or distrust your fidelity, if in some sort I continue my sorrows, for I have so long continued in them as I can better away with them than mirth, for that to me is a stranger. Yet notwithstanding, my heart will harbor some quiet if by your courtesy I may rest in security and be sheltered from wrong."

By this time they were arrived at their place of harbor, which was betwixt the hollow of two rocks, or rather rocky islands, where their ship lay safe from weather and so far under their shadow that it could not be seen, themselves conveying such wealth as they from time to time got into hollow caves of great largeness, where was all things necessary. And the rest of Luprates's fellows called him up. When having fastened their ship, Luprates brought Artesia into the cave, who, beholding the same, was surprised with an exceeding discomfort of ever getting from thence.

Some of the ruder sort, liking Artesia, began their rude behavior towards her, but Luprates, stepping unto them, uttered these speeches: "My masters, thus long have I lived your captain in this place, with care respecting your good◊ as much as mine own, and taking but an equal share with you of such prizes we have taken, and rather the least part, now only in respect of my faith and fidelity, I request to have this damsel as my prize, the rest of the wealth take you. In doing which, you shall bind me unto you forever."

indued endowed.   **good** well-being.

One of the rest, liking Artesia's beauty as well as he, and of a more rude mind, disdaining that he alone should have her possession, said: "Captain, all which you say we confess to be true; neither hath our care been any way less than yours. Therefore, there is no reason why you should claim any peculiar privilege above any of us. Besides, you know we made a law and bound ourselves to perform the same by oath, which was that none should possess anything without the general consent of us all. Then perform those conditions and let her belong to us all, or to the chiefest of us, and in so doing neither of us shall sustain wrong."

Thus began they to contend about Artesia, every one desirous to possess her and yet neither willing any should have her but himself that they were likely to mutiny and fall out, till at the last they concluded to cast lots and she fell to Luprates's share, that was the most worthy of that privilege for that he bare the most virtuous mind. Thus for a time this strife was ended and Artesia was by Luprates kindly used° for many days. In the end their victuals began to waste, and they thought it high time to seek for more, that they determined to fetch in some as before they had done. But then began Luprates to take care in whose custody to leave Artesia lest in his absence they should do her wrong. Amongst the rest he chose out one whom he thought fittest, and to him he committed her, by whose means Artesia rested void of disturbance, though not void of exceeding care that continually tormented her, fearing never to see Ornatus again nor to be released from that place of bondage.

used treated.

CHAPTER XII

How Ornatus found Artesia and preserved her life, and
how she was again taken from him by Lenon, and what
afterwards befell.

Luprates and the rest, being landed, came in the night into the
plains to steal cattle and by chance lighted on the place where
Ornatus haunted, being directed to him by the sound of his
lamentations. Luprates demanded what he was. "I am," quoth
he, "a most miserable forlorn creature by misfortune drawn to
all extremity."

"Then," quoth he, "art thou not for our company," and with
that they departed, leaving him there. Ornatus's heart began
presently to misdoubt° that they were the very same that had
taken Artesia from Allinus, which made him presently study
how to have them apprehended. Remembering that he had
heard many complain that their cattle were often stolen, he supposed verily° them to be the thieves, that with all the haste he
could, he ran to the next village and raised the townsmen, telling
them what he had seen, who presently issued out and with such
weapons as came next [to] hand followed the pirates, and soon
found them, setting upon them took two of them, and the rest,
some sore wounded and hurt, fled to their ship and with all the
haste they could got to their harbor.

Early the next morning the inhabitants conveyed the pirates
to the court, who, being come before the king, confessed the
manner of their life and where they lived. Then Lenon presently
supposed that they were the very same that had taken Artesia
from Allinus, and demanding the same of them, they told him
that there was such a damsel in their cave, and that she told them
her name was Artesia. Then Lenon without delay, strongly accompanied, rode to the next haven and there got shipping, by the
pirates' directions, to find out their fort. Ornatus, likewise, after
he had raised the people, secretly followed the pirates unto the

misdoubt suspect.   **verily** in fact, in truth.

place where their ship lay, and amongst the rest entered the same who, by reason of their haste and exceeding fear, regarded him not° who thrust himself into that danger only to see if Artesia were in their custody, not recking° how his life might be endangered thereby. But the pirates by Luprates's directions hasted to the fort and from thence took Artesia into their ship, not daring to stay there, for that they knew some of their fellows were taken who might by compulsion be constrained to reveal the place of their abode.

Ornatus no sooner espied Artesia but he knew her and his heart leapt within him for joy to see that happy sight, but he durst not speak to her nor scarce settle his eyes to behold her for fear of suspect for that Luprates marvelled how he came amongst them, demanding what he was and what he made there.

"I am," quoth he, "a poor pilgrim that against my will was by some of this company constrained to come aboard." Luprates, believing he said true, made no further question, but with haste sailed from Phrygia, conveying Artesia into his cabin, using many speeches to comfort her.

They had not sailed many hours but a contrary wind began to arise and the heavens were darkened with thick clouds, and such a mighty tempest arose that the ship was by violence driven back, their main mast broken and thrown overboard and all in danger of destruction had not the land been near. For the ship, driven by violence of the sea, ran aground and there split in sunder and the pirates with great hazard escaped drowning, none of them, nor Luprates, once regarding° Artesia. But Ornatus, seeing in what peril she was, caught hold on her, and getting on to a plank, being withal somewhat skilful to swim, with much ado got onto the firm land and preserved her from a miserable death by drowning.

He was no sooner past danger but Luprates would have taken her from him, but Ornatus, seeing none but himself there and all the rest fled for fear, told him, since he had forsaken her in

regarded him not took no notice of him.   **recking** considering.
regarding looking after.

extremity, he was not worthy of her and therefore should not have her.

"Villain," quoth Luprates, "yield her me with quiet or else thy life shall not detain her." With that Ornatus caught hold on a board which he cleft in sunder with his foot, and with the same gave Luprates so sudden and deadly a wound that the brains fell about the place and he died. By this time the storm was quite overpassed, and Ornatus, seeing his dear love very weak with fear and distemperature,◊ by the arm led her unto a mossy bank where the sun's bright beams had full force to dry her garments dropping with wet.

Artesia, seeing how tenderly this stranger regarded her and with what pain he had preserved her when she was of all but him forsaken, being willing to show that she was grateful, said: "Sir, the pains you have taken and friendship you have shown to me deserve more thanks and recompense then I am able to give, and therefore I desire you to think that if I were able, I would requite the same; but my misfortunes are so exceeding that they withhold me from doing that I would; only thanks is the small requital I can yield in token of a grateful mind, being by your means at more quiet than many days I have been, though more disquieted than you would judge. But now I rely upon your virtues with hope thereby to be preserved and not driven to further misery."

"Fair lady," quoth Ornatus, "my life shall be spent in your defence, neither will I part from you until I have brought you to the place which you desire, requesting you to make no doubt of my loyalty. I suppose your name is Artesia, because," quoth he, "in my travels I have met a gentleman of this country named Ornatus of whom I learned the truth of many of your misfortunes, who I assure you is in good health."

"O blessed news," quoth she, "then will I hope once again to see my dear Ornatus, whose absence hath been my only cause of woe."

distemperature mental anguish.

She had scarce ended those words, but Ornatus espied a ship even then come ashore where theirs was cast away, most of the men landed, which was the ship wherein Lenon was, who beheld the other ship cast away, and the storm being ceased, arrived there. From whom Ornatus knew not how to hide himself, and Artesia, not so much as thinking Lenon had been [in] it, but that it was some ship that likewise by the storm was driven to land there. Presently the men began to spread themselves every way, and some of them soon espied Artesia, giving Lenon knowledge thereof, who immediately came towards her, most kindly saluting her. But she, being exceedingly dismayed with his sight whom she most mortally hated, for very grief burst into tears that in abundance gushed from her eyes.

Lenon, marvelling thereat, and little thinking how much she hated him, and how unwelcome he was, rather expecting thanks for his pains than reproof, said: "My dear Artesia, be not now discomforted, since there is no further cause of care. I have most diligently labored to release you from grief ever since Allinus by treason conveyed you from my custody, taking your absence in great heaviness for that it pinched my heart to think you should fall into such distress. But now that all those misfortunes are passed, I beseech you go with me to the court where I will labor to procure your content."

Artesia's heart was vexed to hear his speeches that she made him this answer: "Most discourteous Lenon, none but yourself are cause of my woe, whose sight more tormenteth me than all the afflictions I ever endured. Allinus carried me indeed from the green fortress, not by treason but to shelter me from dishonor which you did intend, else would you not have suffered me to endure such misery as I did by my hellish keeper. Think you I have cause either to think you intend my good, or take any comfort by your presence when you only disquiet me, not suffering me to enjoy my liberty, but would perforce constrain me to that I cannot like? Had you left me in Adellena's house, then had I not fallen into such misery as since that I have endured, nor Allinus for his virtue have been brought to poverty, that being before my professed enemy, seeing my misery, it so mollified◇ his heart that he hath pitied me and sought my liberty, and only by cruelty, not by justice, have you sought his overthrow. Then I beseech you leave me here, for I had rather endure the hazard of my misfortune than live to be tormented with your importunacy."◇

Lenon was so amazed to hear her unkind reply, little thinking he had been so much out of her favor, that he could not tell what to say, sometimes thinking to leave her there and utterly to forsake her. But that thought was soon overcome by his affection or violent sting of desire to enjoy her love, that once again he said: "Why Artesia, do you regard my good will no more than for my pains to yield me rebukes, and for my love, disdain? That I caused you to be brought from Adellena's house was for that being there you were subject to many misfortunes. And if I imprisoned Allinus, it was for that I supposed him your enemy and feared he would have done you wrong, so that whatsoever I did with intent of good you repay me with dislike and convert all my doings to the worst meaning, wherein you show yourself too cruel, that will not yield me the least favor for my constant love. O Artesia be not so hard-hearted."

Artesia, notwithstanding many fair promises, vows, and pro-testations he made, would not yield to go with him, but desired rather that he would leave her there. Lenon told her, though not for his sake, yet for her safety, it were best for her to go, which said, he commanded his servants to place her in a litter. Which when she saw she must needs do, she called to Ornatus, saying: "Good Palmer go along with me that for the kindness you have shown in preserving my life I may yield you some recompense." And, quoth she, to Lenon, "I request nothing of you for myself, but for this strange pilgrim who, when by the storm the ship was cast away, I ready to perish, caught me out of the water and preserved my life. And do not, for his good will to me, use him as you did my dear Sylvian, whom you banished, for that she

mollified softened.　　　**importunacy** urgent requests.

preserved my life from my unkind uncle." With that she wept exceedingly.

Then Lenon asked Ornatus what he was. "I am," quoth he, "as you see, a pilgrim that was forced to come aboard the pirates' ship, and, amongst the rest, was ready to perish but that by the Divine Providence I was ordained to preserve that virtuous damsel's life."

"For that deed," quoth Lenon, "I will reward you most kindly; therefore, go along with us." Then they all departed to the court. Lenon presently caused Artesia to be lodged in a most sumptuous place of the court, appointing divers damsels to attend her, thinking by those means to win her to consent to love him. But all proved vain, his care was cast away, his cost to little effect, and his kindness unregarded. For Artesia was so constant to Ornatus that she hated Lenon, her heart was wholly employed to wish his good and Lenon's ill. For she determined never to love him, though she were assured of Ornatus's death, that she spent her time in continual care and sadness, showing no sign of joy, no show of comfort, but even as one that regarded no rest, nor took felicity in anything, that Lenon both admired the same and labored by many means to alter that humor. But the more he sought to please her, the more she was displeased and more discontented at his kindness than anything else. In this sort° she continued many days without the least show of alteration.

Ornatus all this while remaining in the court, making the cause of his stay to receive Lenon's promised reward, whereas indeed he stayed to see what would become of Artesia, or by what means to get her from thence. To effect which he saw no possible means, nor could in many days come to see Artesia, which filled his heart with grief, only comforted[28] himself with remembering her constant loyalty. And one day being by himself alone, he entered into these cogitations: "Ornatus, thou hast remained many days in this place kept from thy love and sought no means to set thy heart at rest or her at liberty. Dost thou make no more account of her love than to attempt nothing to attain the same?

sort way, manner.

Or are thy spirits of no more courage? Then they will do nothing. Thy wit so shallow thou canst devise no stratagem, or thy mind so cowardly thou darest not revenge the wrong Lenon doth thee? What though he be the prince and heir of this land? Is not both he and his father hated, ruling by usurpation and with cruelty, not with justice, hath sought the downfall of thy house? Can Artesia think either valor or virtue to rest in thee when she shall know how near thou art [to] her foe, but darest not touch him? Will she not esteem thee a coward and unworthy to enjoy her love? Nay, when she knoweth this, will she not alter her love? Why shouldst not thou seek thy own content, though it be with his discontent? Thou art every way as good as he by birth though he now rule the land. Hath not thy father said that his father was but a captain in the last king's days and by treason put his lawful king to death and so won the rule? Then Ornatus, revive thy spirits, seem not dismayed with any danger, fear not misfortune, seek to release thy love and venture thy life therein, for living thus thou shalt be deprived of her love. Lenon will by force or fair means overcome her, and then mayest thou blame this delay. The king is now sick, and he being dead Lenon must reign, who then may do what he list. Then take the advantage of the time and do not frustrate thy blessed hopes with slothful delay."

Having ended this meditation, he then began to study how to perform his will, wherein he found many contrarieties.◇ But presently he beheld Lenon entering the court, before whom he stood so opposite that he [Lenon] could not choose but note him, and withal remembered how earnestly Artesia had entreated him on the pilgrim's behalf whom he thought she esteemed, and therefore suddenly this cogitation arose in his fancy to use him as an instrument to win her love, that calling Ornatus unto him, he said: "Pilgrim, I pray thee blame me not for forgetting to perform my promise made to Artesia as concerning thee, which I have not neglected for want of good will, but by reason of thousands of cares that daily torment me, only procured by her unkindness.

contrarieties obstructions.

But if thou wilt undertake on my behalf to persuade her to yield to my just request, for that I think thou mayest prevail with her above any, I will not only reward thy former kindness so shown to her, but also for thy pains herein promote thee to high dignity. Therefore I pray thee give consent to follow my counsel herein."

Ornatus was willing to be employed in that business which fell out according to his heart's desire, and therefore made him this answer: "My noble lord, for that I perceive your intent is good, I will be ready to follow your directions and do you any service I can, wherein I know not whether I shall prove fortunate or no, but assuring you that I will deal both faithfully and effectually in that which I shall undertake."

Lenon was as glad as he that he yielded to do that which he thought least to perform, and therefore presently gave command that the pilgrim only should have her in custody. Artesia marvelled that her keepers were changed, misdoubted° some intent of hard usage, but seeing it was the pilgrim that now had her custody, her heart was comforted.

CHAPTER XIII

How Ornatus had the custody of Artesia; how he discovered himself unto her; how Allinus and Trasus arrived in Armenia and got the king to send ambassadors into Phrygia.

Ornatus, at his first coming, found her sitting in the darkest corner of the chamber bewailing her misfortune with salt tears, bedewing her purple cheeks, her ornaments disorderly put on and her golden tresses hanging carelessly down, which added beauty to her sweet beauty, and though disordered, most comely leaning her arm upon a chair and her cheek laid upon the back of her hand. When he beheld her sitting in this discomfortable sort, his heart was ready to melt with remorse, and he breathed forth so bitter a sigh that she heard the same, which he perceiving came towards her with humble behavior, saying: "Most virtuous

misdoubted suspected.

lady, pardon my presumption in presuming thus unmannerly to interrupt your quiet. Lenon the prince hath appointed me to be your attendant; therefore I beseech you, notwithstanding I am his substitute, command me in any dutiful sort and I will most willingly employ my uttermost endeavors to purchase your content."

Artesia, raising herself from the ground, said: "Pilgrim, I thank you for your kind proffer and am glad you are my keeper for two causes: one, for that I trust your virtues will not suffer me to be injured; the other, for that I would hear out your discourse of my dear friend Ornatus, which I was hindered from by Lenon's sudden finding me."

"Lady," quoth he, "you shall be assured of the one, and hear more of the other, if first you will vouchsafe without offence to hear my speech and suffer me to execute the charge Lenon hath given me and I have undertaken."

"Why, what is that?" quoth Artesia, "I will not be offended."

"Lenon hath made known to me his love, and how long and with what constancy it is grounded, commanding and entreating me in his behalf to become an humble suitor unto you. He telleth me that still you ungently disdain him without cause, reason, or consideration. Therefore, I humbly desire, both for that he is constant, a prince, and of good and virtuous gifts, [that you] yield to his love or else to[29] satisfy me of the chiefest reasons that withhold you from the same."

"Pilgrim," quoth she, "for that my mind persuadeth me you in wisdom will conceive of reason, and will be faithful in concealing that which I shall disclose, I answer you thus: first, admit Lenon did love me, yet by his usage I find the contrary nor I cannot fancy him, for that I already have plighted° my faith to another more worthy than himself, which is that most virtuous and kind gentlemen Ornatus, who likewise equaleth me in affection, and therefore I should dishonor my name, break my faith, and reap perpetual infamy if I should show myself so inconstant. These I think are reasons to a reasonable creature sufficient and of such

plighted pledged.

force as none can contradict, and therefore no more can be said therein. Besides, were not all this so, you have no reason to persuade me to that which I have so often denied and will never yield unto."

"Your reasons indeed," quoth he, "are great, and the cause such as should no way be violated. But now you are subject to his mercy, and he may enforce you to that which you are most unwilling to have done. Then what remedy have you but rather to yield than endure such extremity as he may use?"

"Yes," quoth she, "when I can preserve myself no longer from his lust, death shall rid me from his power, which I will execute upon myself rather than condescend to yield him so much as an outward show of favor. Therefore I pray use no more words tending to the breach of my faith and furtherance of his love, for knew you but how hateful his name were unto me and how odious to think of his doting love, you would of pity desist to torment me with the sound of that ominous monster, but rather seek to comfort my distressed estate and poor pining heart almost drowned with sorrow, being more unfortunate than ever any was by these afflictions and the loss of my dear Ornatus, whose presence should release me from this thraldom and labyrinth of discontent. Of whom, if you can tell me any tidings, I beseech you impart them unto me, thereby to add comfort to mitigate my care."

Ornatus was so ravished to hear her utter such heavenly speeches that he had much ado to refrain from embracing her, uttering these speeches: "How happy is Ornatus by attaining the love of so virtuous and constant a lady, worthy to be admired, eternized and for ever honored. What comfort may these pleasing words bring to his heart? What torment can he not account pleasure, endured for so sweet a lady's safety? And what pains should he refuse to procure her sweet content? O Artesia, divine Artesia, Ornatus is not able to express his content nor your desert, unable to recompense your kindness, and everlastingly bound to you in all firm bands of faithful loyalty. In your heart is the harbor of true loyalty grounded upon virtuous love. Then how happy is he by being enriched and possessed of such a love. His reward is greater than his pain, his pleasure more than ever his sorrow could be, and his gains a thousand times beyond his loss. Why should I then conceal the truth of his safety from you?" With that he said: "Behold Artesia, your Ornatus."

With that he discovered himself unto her and she perfectly knew him, being almost amazed with that heavenly sight, when with a sweet behavior they both embraced each other, intermingling their kisses with tears of joy that in abundance distilled from their eyes, surfeiting so much in that sweet delight that they were loath to part but that fear to be espied compelled them, taking such exceeding comfort in each other's presence as is not to be expressed, withal using many kindnesses usual betwixt faithful friends to express their joy, he sometimes embracing her, and she again with a sweet kiss welcoming him, being so many, so kind and hearty as would ask a skilful description. At last, having somewhat recreated themselves and with sudden joy banished some part of their care, they thought it time to study how to procure their happiness, lest the same might again be crossed by Lenon, who by that time expected to hear from him.

Therefore Ornatus said: "My most dear and kind Artesia, by whose love my life is preserved, I am not able to express the joy my heart conceiveth by this fortunate meeting, being likewise as sorry to think of the misfortune you have endured by my careless oversight, and how to get you from this place and from Lenon's affection, whom I know to be of such uncivil a disposition that he will leave no disloyal means unattempted to further his intent. Therefore, in this urgent extremity, if you will be contented to esteem me as your friend and follow my directions, I will labor all that I can to get you from this place."

"My true friend Ornatus," said Artesia, "I have dedicated myself to your disposition and made myself all one with you, both in heart, body and mind, that whatsoever you would with yourself you do to me, and whatsoever pleaseth you cannot displease me, for I am your self. Therefore, I commit all things to your wisdom, and rest to be ruled, counselled, and ordered by you in whatsoever you shall think convenient, and will do anything you shall counsel me unto, both for our escape from hence, or otherwise, accounting my bliss yours and yours mine, your care mine and your quiet my content. Lenon's love is most hateful unto me and injury to you. Then what means can you work to rid me of that and revenge your own wrong, perform, for my consent is ready to yield to anything you shall think convenient."

"I most humbly thank you," said Ornatus, "and first I think this is the best course to procure my good liking with him and to rid us from hence, that at his next coming you show a little more friendly countenance unto him than heretofore you have done, as shall best agree with your wisdom, and he, perceiving that my service hath done more for him than ever he could attain, will not only credit me, but also be ruled by me in anything I shall counsel him unto. Which if you will perform, commit the rest to me."

"My dear Ornatus, at your request I will do this, which otherwise I would never of myself yield unto, for that my love to you and hate to him would not suffer me so much to[30] dissemble. But I pray God deliver me well from forth of his power that I may in quiet enjoy your sweet company."

These speeches being ended, they parted with a sweet kiss, he sighing and she for grief shedding tears. Not long after, Lenon came to Ornatus requesting to know whether he had prevailed anything with Artesia in his behalf.

"My Lord," quoth he, "I have used many persuasions to her, which in some sort have prevailed, but hereafter I do not doubt by my persuasions but to win her full consent if you, with wisdom, will be directed by me and not with rashness mar all.° Therefore go in unto her, but not too rashly, and see if she be not altered."

Lenon embraced him in his arms, saying: "Thou bringest me tidings of exceeding comfort for which I will reward thee most bountifully." With that he gave him a purse of gold, which

mar all spoil everything.

Ornatus took, thinking that should be a means to further him and hinder the giver. Lenon entered Artesia's chamber using many kind speeches and submiss behaviors, whom she used more kindly than ever she had before done, which both filled his heart with joy and made him according to the pilgrim's directions more careful of his behavior, lest by any boldness he might offend her, that having passed some small time with her, he departed.

Now was Ornatus studying how to release Artesia, to further whose intent the occasion thus fell out.◊ Allinus and Trasus, as is before said, gat shipping for Armenia and arrived there with safety, first directing their course to the king's palace where Allinus was most honorably entertained being somewhat allied to the king, to whom he declared both the cause of his exile and the injury done to him by Thæon, king of Phrygia. Turbulus, the Armenian king, comforted him all that he could and bade him withal request anything at his hands and he would grant it him. Allinus, alleging many things to persuade Turbulus to yield thereto, requested him to send ambassadors into Phrygia, either to request performance of certain articles or else to give him open defiance for war. The articles were these: that Allinus should be restored to his lands, and the damage and loss he had sustained should be repaid to the full, that his wife should be recalled from banishment, and that he should yield up Artesia to Allinus, if she should be in his custody, and that the king and Lenon should be sworn to perform all this. Turbulus was easily won and therefore presently sent four of his noblemen as ambassadors to request the performance of those conditions, who even at that instant were landed in Phrygia, and news thereof brought to the court.

The king, being himself somewhat sickly, sent Lenon to meet them and give them entertainment, who was loath to go from Artesia's sight, but assuring himself of the pilgrim's faith committed her wholly to his custody. Ornatus thought it now the fittest time to seek to escape, but he was hindered by other of Lenon's servants whom he had secretly appointed as overseers to look into the pilgrim's action that it was impossible for him to **fell out** occurred.

attempt anything that way but it must needs both be discovered and prevented. Ornatus, seeing himself disappointed of his purpose that way, made Artesia acquainted with what he intended and how he was prevented, spending the time of Lenon's absence continually in her company. But having met the Armenian ambassadors, brought them to the court where they were honorably entertained, and having declared their embassage, Thæon the king told them they should receive answer within two days.

Lenon, hearing the articles, counselled his father not to yield to perform any such conditions, but rather to send Turbulus defiance. "For," quoth he, "your majesty are[31] as absolutely king of Phrygia as he of Armenia, and then what dishonor were it unto you to stoop to his command and show yourself, as it were, afraid of his threats; for to bind yourself to this were to become his subject, which would soon be published through the whole world to your dishonor."

The king, being overruled by his persuasions, gave the ambassadors this answer, that he meant not to perform the least of those articles they demanded, nor feared their king's threats of war, for that he was able to deal with a mightier foe then he, using many other words, and some of reproach, that the Armenians denouncing° open war according as they were commanded, departed.

CHAPTER XIV

How Ornatus, staying too late in Artesia's chamber, was accused by Lenon's servants, whom he slew. How Allinus with a band of Armenians landed in Phrygia, and how Ornatus was imprisoned.

Thæon knew that the king of Armenia would perform his word and therefore gave Lenon charge to muster up men throughout the whole land, committing the chief charge of the army and ordering of these affairs unto him, who, more hardy-bold than

denouncing proclaiming.

wise, undertook all and within short space had gathered an exceeding great army and furnished certain ships to meet with the Armenians by sea, if it might be possible, to vanquish them before they should land.

These troubles filled the commons' hearts with grief and their mouths with murmurings, for they, understanding that the king of Armenia did offer war to Phrygia in the behalf of Allinus that was generally beloved, there was° few of those that were pressed to those wars but came unwillingly and rather by constraint, being more ready to turn their sword points against Thæon than against Allinus.

Ornatus, likewise hearing of these wars, by his wisdom found out the opinion of the multitude and with what unwillingness they came to the wars, which, when he was in some sort assured of, he came to the camp and amongst all the rest of his familiars espied Phylastes, who always loved him most dearly; him he knew to be of a most faithful and constant resolution in performing his promise, and was by Lenon appointed one of the chiefest leaders.

Ornatus, finding him remote from the camp, came to him and after salutation said: "Sir Phylastes, I am sent unto you by a dear friend of yours named Ornatus, who trusteth so much in your virtues that he is willing to put his life into your hands, which you shall hazard,° in denying him one small favor which with safety you may grant. First, therefore, I request but your promise for your warranty and then I will declare what I have in charge."

"My friend," quoth Phylastes, "thou tellest me news of wonder when thou sayest thou comest from Ornatus, whom I fear is long since dead. But if thou knowest the contrary and canst resolve me thereof, I promise and swear to perform whatsoever thou shalt demand, for I am sure Ornatus knoweth that I love him, nor maketh any doubt thereof, which if he do, he injureth that love and friendship that hath passed between us."

was meaning: were.   **hazard** put at risk.

"Then kind sir," quoth he, "that Ornatus is not dead but in safety, and I am that Ornatus that, notwithstanding my speech, make no doubt of your love."

Phylastes, beholding his countenance, knew him well and for joy caught him in his arms: "My dear friend Ornatus," quoth he, "I am glad of your safety, and accursed be my soul if I do not anything that you shall command."

"I thank you," quoth Ornatus. "To enter into the tedious discourse of my afflictions would be tedious, but in few words I will tell you all. I loved Artesia long but found no hope nor means to attain my love, which made me disguise myself into woman's apparel, naming myself Sylvian, and was fortunately entertained by Arbastus, whose death I found to be acted by Floretus, who, falling into love with me, told me for my sake he would poison Artesia at the lodge, whither he conveyed her. I, fearing to have her taken from me, and having won her love, told her his intent and conveyed her to Adellena's house. Then Floretus and Lenon came thither, demanding her of me, whom I told I had poisoned her according to his counsel. We, striving, were brought before Thæon, who banished me into Natolia, from whence I came back and by good fortune have the keeping of Artesia in this disguise, the manner I will tell you at more leisure. Now my dear friend Phylastes, my desire is to change my place with you, you to have the custody of Artesia in my palmer's weeds, and I to march into the field in your armor, which if you grant, you shall bind me unto you forever."

Phylastes yielded to fulfil his request, and so for that time they parted, appointing° to meet the next day. Ornatus, being come to Artesia, told her where he had been and what he intended, which made Artesia sad, dissuading him from his purpose in this sort: "My dear love, what need you venture your person in the dangers that are incident to war? Will you leave me here in doubt and not rather stay with me to my comfort; there are enough besides and too many in the field, and Phylastes is able

appointing arranging.

to execute his own place. Then I beseech you, do not leave me in discomfort, for how can I be void of care when I shall think you are amongst so many enemies ready to be slaughtered?"

"My dear love," quoth he, "that which I will do shall be without any hazard at all, but shall procure both your and mine own content. Then I beseech you, remit this care for my safety, for I will preserve myself from danger for your sake. Besides, Phylastes's virtue is such that you need not once so much as think amiss of him, who I know would venture his life for my sake. Besides, my honor urgeth me; revenge of injuries done to yourself and me and my father's safety are reasons sufficient to persuade your consent, besides many other causes more forcible than these too tedious to recite. Then I beseech you deny me not, for when it shall be known that my father was in armor in the field and I in this place not regarding to aid him, it will turn to my great dishonor, and those which before did esteem well of me will then begin to hate me. Then let not your doubt and true love to me hinder my determination, for on that mine honor, your safety, and my father's life dependeth."

Artesia, seeing she could by no means dissuade him, thought not to let him depart so suddenly, but clasping her tender arms about his neck a thousand times kissed his lips, whilst with her abundant tears she bedewed his manly cheeks. Ornatus took great sorrow at her heaviness and delight in her embracings, that the contrarieties of his conceits° were exceeding, pleasure itself seeming more pleasant intermingled with care and care a pleasure to be endured with such delight. Artesia was loath to let Ornatus depart that night for that she deemed he should be in danger the next day, and he as unwilling to leave her in sorrow, she on the one side solacing herself in his company, and he by her kindness making him forget to depart, that before they were aware, night was come and well spent, and Ornatus then bethinking himself thought it was too late to depart.

conceits conflicting thoughts.

And Artesia hearing him make a motion to be gone, desired him to stay. "And yet my dear Ornatus," quoth she, "do not endanger yourself for my sake, for should Lenon's servants find you here, it might redound to our great disquiet." Ornatus likewise, well considering the inconvenience, took his leave of her and left her shedding abundance of tears.

Ornatus being gone, found the servants awake, and watching his coming out, one of them saying: "Pilgrim, what maketh thee so saucy as to court my master's love? Is this a fit time of the night to be in her chamber? My lord shall understand your behavior and what familiarity is betwixt you. We take you to be some counterfeit, else would not such behaviors pass betwixt you as we have beheld. Therefore, here shall you stay until we give him knowledge of your doings and fidelity." With that they locked fast the door, not suffering him to go out or in.

Ornatus by that perceived that they had seen the kindness betwixt him and Artesia, which he knew if Lenon should understand, he would find out what he was. These thoughts troubled his heart exceedingly that he was assured unless he could be rid of them, there was no means to escape death if Lenon should know him. With these studies he sat a good while silent till he perceived them inclined to sleep, and casting his eye aside, espied a bill hanging by the wall to which he stole secretly, and taking hold of the same he drew towards them, entering into these meditations: "And shall I now commit murder and endanger my soul by so heinous a sin? What will Artesia say if she [should] know thou art so bloodily bent° and that thy heart is so hard as to shed thine own countrymen's blood? Ornatus, be well advised before thou do this deed and bethink of some other mean; avoid the danger thou art ready to fall into. Other means, Ornatus? Yea, but what other means hast thou? None at all. Dost thou not see how they have betrayed thee and made thee prisoner? What then needest thou make a question to save thyself and by their deaths preserve thine own life, which, they

bloodily bent inclined to bloodshed.

living, will be endangered. And being once done thou art safe, but by delay thy own life may perish."

With that, lifting up his arms with more than wanted force, he smote the one on the head and beat out his brains, wherewith the other began to awake. But in his awakening, he stroke him so full on the breast that the bill pierced his heart and he lay breathless sprawling in his gore. This done, Ornatus found a vault and into the same he conveyed their dead bodies, purposing never to reveal what he had done. Then returning, he bethought himself of the keys of the doors that he had thrown into the vault with their bodies, devising how to get out without suspicion of the deed he had done, that he was enforced to take the bill and by main force and often striving, wrung asunder the locks. His mind being exceedingly affrighted with these cares, he entered into Artesia's chamber to see whether he had disquieted her or no with the noise. Her he found in bed and fast asleep, with the light still burning by her bed's side, her breast uncovered down to the waist, and nothing to shroud her from his perfect view but the single sheet that lay carelessly cast over her tender body, her arms cast to either side of the bed, and her head leaning on the one side with so sweet an aspect as would have ravished a thousand beholders. Ornatus's heart was revived to behold this sweet sight that the remembrance thereof had banished all remembrance of his troubles past, and affected his heart with incomparable delight, that he stood like one amazed to behold her sweet beauties and to take a surfeiting view of those her perfections so amiably laid forth. Artesia suddenly awaking, blushed to see him so nigh, yet therewith more comforted than dismayed, she caught the clothes and covered herself, whilst he, folding his hand in hers, desired pardon for his boldness. But she viewing him well, beheld his pale and ghastly countenance, which drove her into fear, and raising herself upright in her bed, caught him in her arms, asking what he ailed to look so pale.

"My dear Artesia," quoth he, "since I parted from you I have endured great danger and passed through a hell of calamities, which now I fear not." With that, he let his head fall into her

sweet bosom, and there made the period° of his speech, feeling
her tender heart pant with the motions of her troubled spirits.
In which palace he rested it a good while, whilst she, with her
soft hand, curled his hair, and with sweet kisses mollified his
lips, using many other familiarities and sweet favors proceeding
from the depth of kind love, wherewith Ornatus was so ravished
that he not only took heavenly comfort therein, but also desired
a further content and possession of her love, which he never before asked nor thought she would grant, but being heartened by
the assurance of her love, he used more bold behavior, which
she permitted. But at last growing more bold than she thought
convenient for her modesty to permit, with a kind and lovely
behavior she both blamed and hindered him, but the motions of
affection so far prevailed with them both that he desired and she
inwardly yielded, though outwardly she refused. But his behavior, her own love, the present occasion, so fit opportunity, their
heart's unity, and other sweet enticements so far prevailed that
she yielded up her unspotted body and pure chastity to his possession, and the impression of his attempt dissolved her virgin
zone, giving full interests of her heart, love and body to him, that
pursued the possession of those riches with earnestness. Sometimes blushing, sometimes shrieking, and yet yielding, denying,
and yet granting, willing and unwilling, yet at last she gave that
[which] she could not recall, and let him possess her spotless
virginity, which being passed, her heart panted with the motion
and she felt her senses sad, a little repenting, yet not altogether
sorry sighing for sadness, and yet not sad at all, whilst he bathed
himself in that heaven of bliss, passing the rest of that night in
such unspeakable pleasure as cannot be deciphered. Early the
next morning he arose, taking his farewell with a sweet adieu,
leaving Artesia sad for sorrow and lamenting his absence, but yet
with earnest and hearty prayers invocating° his happy success,
bathing her heart in lukewarm tears, thinking she had been too
prodigal of her favors to him, and yet esteeming him worthy of a

period end.   **invocating** calling for.

thousand times greater gift if she had it in her possession, with repentance rejoicing though deeming herself metamorphosed and other than she was wont◊ to be, being glad she had no more company to converse withal lest her guilt should make her blush and so bewray◊ her fault.

And when Phoebus[32] began to lighten the chamber with his splendor, she hid herself within the bed, as if the daylight had accused her of that she had done in the dark. Ornatus, being come to the camp, found out Phylastes and brought him to Artesia's lodging, by the way instructing him how to order their business when Lenon should come. Where, being entered, Phylastes having saluted Artesia and a while conversed◊ about their affairs, they changed their habits,◊ Ornatus with many a sorrowful sigh taking his leave of her whilst her heart bled warm drops of blood. Ornatus again took his leave of Artesia and entered the camp, framing himself to such kind of behavior that he was of all taken for Phylastes.

News came that the Armenians were landed and had brought their forces within a day's march of Thæon's camp. The king assembled all the chief leaders together to appoint every man his charge and consult what to do. Ornatus, in Phylastes's stead, had under his charge four thousand men, whom, by his own seeking, he was appointed to convoy◊ into a wood that stood fitly to offend◊ the enemy, and the rest appointed to other places that seemed for most advantage. Ornatus, having his soldiers alone, thought it time to execute what he intended, and therefore called unto him such as were captains and chief under him, uttering these speeches: "Fellow soldiers, I would willingly utter my mind which is troubled in some sort with remembrance of the injuries Allinus hath already causelessly endured, against whom now we address ourselves to fight; wherein, in my mind, we deal unjustly, for he was never traitor to his country nor now cometh to disturb the land with oppression, but only to claim his own

wont accustomed.   bewray reveal.   conversed talked.   habits clothes.   convoy escort, convey.   stood fitly to offend was an advantageous position from which to assault.

inheritance and liberty, which ourselves do permit. Therefore I think it best, before we draw our weapons, to consider against whom we draw them and whom we offend: one that loveth us, his country, and people, and would not willingly shed a drop of our blood. Now if I could find a remedy for all this, which standeth with equity, would you follow my directions?" With that they all at once said they would be ruled by him. Then he said: "Thæon, that is now our king, destroyed all his family and such as are in any degree near to him in blood, the last of whom is Allinus, whose utter ruin he now seeketh, not by justice, but that neither he nor any of his progeny should hinder his succession. Therefore, if you will follow my counsel, when the armies are met, let us not offer to offend the Armenians, but keep ourselves from sight until Lenon, affrighted therewith and fearing the people's revolt, will peradventure yield to perform the articles the Armenian ambassadors demanded, and by this means shall we restore Allinus to his right, save the effusion of blood, and yet not wrong our reputation."

The people, hearing his speeches, generally gave their consent, crying: "Phylastes, Phylastes!" With that, Ornatus bestowed the gold among them that Lenon had before given him, which prevailed with the multitude exceedingly. Ornatus, having effected this according to his desire, went unto the Armenian camp, desiring to speak with Allinus the general, to whom he declared what he intended in his behalf, not discovering° him to be other than Phylastes, for which Allinus yielded him many hearty thanks. Whilst Ornatus was absent, a captain named Ortonus, drawn by desire of reward and above the rest favoring Lenon's party, stole from the wood, and, coming into the camp to Lenon, bewrayed° what Phylastes intended and how that he was now gone to the Armenian camp to confer with Allinus.

Lenon, hearing that, thought it best not to send for him by warrant, but amongst the rest to assemble him to counsel, and to that effect sent a herald. Ornatus, being returned, had knowledge

discovering finding.   **bewrayed** discovered.

of the general assembly and willingly went, little suspecting what Lenon intended, and being entered the camp and Lenon's tent, he was before all the estates by a herald arrested of high treason. Ornatus then thought his intent was bewrayed, demanding what they could lay to his charge. Whereupon Ortonus, before them all, declared what he had done, which he could not deny, upon which accusation he was presently° sent to the court and there imprisoned.

CHAPTER XV

How Ornatus was delivered out of prison and carried Artesia from the court. How Ornatus in a single combat overcame Lenon and caused Thæon's flight. And how Artesia, to escape Thæon, fled to Adellena's house.

The news of Ornatus's imprisonment was soon blazed° through the whole camp, court, and country, and at last came to Artesia's hearing, who, with exceeding lamentations, bewailed his misfortune. But Phylastes, coming unto her, comforted her all that he could, promising to set Ornatus at liberty, "if," quoth he, "at Lenon's next coming you will request his signet to keep as his warrant for your safety." The next day the armies should meet, and therefore Lenon that night visited Artesia, finding her very sad, demanding[33] the cause thereof: "My lord," quoth she, "how can I be otherwise than sad when I am ready every hour to fall into more misery, not knowing whither your life may be endangered by these wars and I thereby subject to some misfortune. Therefore, in sign you love me, grant me your signet to be my warrant and privilege against all injury that may be offered me." With that she kissed him, which she had never before done, not drawn by any good will but with desire to help Ornatus. Lenon's heart was so overcome that he presently gave her the same, staying some time with her, entreating her consent to his love. He was no sooner gone but Phylastes, taking the

presently instantly, immediately.   **blazed** spread rapidly.

ring of Artesia, went unto the place where Ornatus was, and coming to the jailer told him that he must deliver Phylastes to his custody, showing him the prince's signet as his warrant. The jailer seeing the same, and knowing that the pilgrim was of great credit and trust with Lenon, made no doubt but presently delivered Ornatus unto him, both departing together to Artesia, who seeing her beloved so fortunately delivered, shed tears of joy for his escape. After salutations in the kindest sort passed, Ornatus declared what he intended and how he was betrayed by Ortonus. Phylastes then counselled Ornatus that night to convey Artesia from thence unto some place of better security, who sometimes thought to carry her to Adellena's house, but he thought Lenon would misdoubt° the place. At last he concluded to convey her to her castle where Arbastus her father dwelt, which was still kept to her use by certain of her father's servants. Both Artesia and Phylastes liked this well, and therefore leaving the court they departed thitherwards. Artesia, not wanted° to travel, could scarcely endure to hold out, but by their help they arrived there at midnight, and knocking, awoke the porter, who, looking over the battlements, demanded who was below at that unreasonable time of the night.

"My friend," quoth Ornatus, "it is Artesia that cometh in time of her most need for harbor in this place." The porter, viewing her well by the bright light of Cynthia[34] and knew her, calling up the rest of his fellows, came running down and opened the gate where he and the rest received her in with great joy.

Ornatus was glad of this happy escape but yet exceeding sad that he could not assist his father against Lenon, but that he must perforce° be absent from his rescue, which filled his heart with such care that all that night he could take no rest. And though he enjoyed Artesia's company without control, he could harbor no rest or quiet to his distempered thoughts, that Phylastes demanded the cause of his sadness.

misdoubt suspect and thus discover.   **wanted** accustomed.   **perforce** of necessity.

"My assured friend Phylastes," quoth he, "the remembrance of my father's estate and fear of his mishap maketh me thus sad, and grief's exceeding torment possesseth me that I cannot be present to aid him against Lenon that, by cowardly malice, not with valor, will seek his ruin before any others. O were I but present to defend him; though I offended none my heart would be at quiet."

Artesia, hearing his speeches, said: "Good Ornatus, do not again hazard yourself as you lately did, for had not fortune and Phylastes's wisdom assisted us, both your life and with it mine had been cast away."

"My dear Artesia," quoth he, "that misfortune hath taught me wisdom, and by remembering it I will learn to eschew such mischiefs and know whom I trust. Therefore, I beseech you, grant I may once again go to do my duty in aiding my father, which I will now do without danger for that I will make none privy to that I intend, nor attempt more than I am able to perform."

Artesia, seeing how fully he was bent° to go, preferred his will before her own desire, knowing her duty not to contradict but to counsel him, and therefore said: "My dear Ornatus, my duty bindeth me to consent, but my love willeth me to deny; fear of your mishap maketh me unwilling, but will to fulfil your desire maketh me give an unwilling consent. Only let me request this, that you will take Phylastes in your company and leave me to the custody of my servants whose fidelity I am assured of, for having him with you, his aid and counsel may much avail to preserve your life, which if you lose as heavens forbid with the same shall mine expire, for it is impossible Artesia should breathe, Ornatus being breathless."

Ornatus, with a few tears that by exceeding grief were wrung from his heart, participated [in] her laments. First, requesting the servants to be careful of her good, and then, without delay, both furnishing himself and Phylastes with rich armor and horse, of which there was great choice in that castle, and for that the day began to appear they thought it time to depart lest their coming

bent inclined.

from thence might be discovered. There might one behold sorrow at parting in his right form, heart-breaking sighs, breathing sad farewells, and sorrowful tears at so sad a parting; when their lips were parted, their hands still fast; [when] their hands disjoined, then their voices oftentimes uttering that woeful word, "farewell." And when they were past hearing, their eyes unwillingly leaving each other's sight, he being without looking back, and she within looking after so long as she could perceive the glimmering glance of his bright armor; and he being past sight of her, with watery eyes beholding the place of her abode, thus parted they as if they had parted never to meet.[35]

Drawing nigh the armies, they beheld them met and in hot skirmish, standing still a good space to see to whether° party it was likely the victory would incline, and in the end they beheld the Armenians begin to retreat, and Lenon with Thæon his father in the midst of the throng making exceeding slaughter and proud of their deemed conquest, which set Ornatus's heart on fire that he rushed amongst the thickest of his countrymen, yet not once offering a blow nor shedding a drop of the blood he loved, but only making way to come to Lenon, which made them not offer to stay his passage, but admiring what he was, let him go free, after whom Phylastes hasted. The soldiers seeing these two new-come knights offend none, admired what they should be, not one of them all offering a blow, because they offered none. By this time Ornatus was come to the place where Lenon was, who, even then and not before, had met Allinus, betwixt whom many blows and some wounds were given and received; but Allinus had the worst by reason of his age. Ornatus, knowing his father by his armor, came betwixt them with his sword drawn, saying: "Lenon stay thy hand, let age go free, and let thy youth cope with me that am come to challenge thee before both the armies. And therefore as thou art the king's son, a knight, and honorest arms, give order by thy herald to stay the fury of the battles till thou and I have tried our valors. Otherwise, this knight and I

whether which.

have vowed to hunt thee from place to place and never give over until we have spilt thy blood."

Lenon, hearing this champions' proud challenge, said: "If thou art a knight, a gentleman as I am, and canst show wherein I have wronged thee, I will answer thee; otherwise know that I scorn thee, although I know myself of sufficient strength to abate thy haughty presumption, were it never so great." With that, two heralds were sent from either general to part the soldiers, which done, Ornatus before the open assembly said: "Lenon, first I say I am a gentleman, as absolute and as good as thyself. Prince I am none, neither art thou by right, but that by tyranny and usurpation thou holdest the same. I come as Artesia's champion to challenge thee of disloyalty, as the outrages thou hast committed by detaining her liberty do manifest.◊ I challenge thee for doing injustice against Allinus, whom thou withholdest from his right by treacherous malice. I challenge thee as a partaker of Arbastus's death, for that thou sufferest and upholdest his murderer, Floretus, that hath deserved death. I challenge thee for oppression laid upon this whole land, and, lastly, for detaining Ornatus's living,◊ who never was impeached of treason. And therefore, if thou darest answer my challenge, I am here ready; otherwise, I here pronounce thee for a coward and miscreant, not worthy to bear arms."

Lenon made this reply: "Being accused by a stranger, without cause, I regard it not, and being judge myself will not by thee be adjudged. But for thy proud challenge I will answer thee, as little regarding what thou canst do as thou boastingly dost vaunt of thy valor. Therefore, even now before I depart, I will without delay abate thy haughtiness, though thy accusations are manifestly false, for I both love and esteem Artesia as dearly as I do myself; my title to the crown is just; for Allinus, he is both a traitor at home and abroad, first in causing his complices◊ to seek my father's life, and lastly, for bringing these Armenian bands to destroy this country. For Floretus's pardon, it is mercy,

manifest reveal.   **living** castle and estates.   **complices** associates in crime.

not injustice. As for oppression done to Ornatus, all know I never injured him; but if he take the injustice that is done to his traitorous father as done to him, I cannot help that, but revenge it thou since thou art his champion."

Ornatus had much ado to stay to hear out his speech which galled◊ him to the very heart, that without speaking a word more he smote at Lenon, and Lenon, with courage answered his blows, beginning a most fierce and forcible encounter, and with like fury continuing the same till both had received many wounds, and their steeds began to be furious and mad with the smart of some strokes that missed their right aim.

Ornatus, calling to remembrance first the injuries he had received, and that Lenon and none else could dispossess him of Artesia's love, and many other wrongs he had done him and his parents, thought now to revenge them all and dispossess Thæon of the crown by Lenon's death, revived[36] his spirits with such courage that he began with renewed strength to assail Lenon, who even then began to faint, and would have yielded but that shame withheld him. Which when Ornatus perceived, he thought at once to end the strife, that with one forcible blow he gave him so deep a wound on the right arm where the armor was broken away that he let fall his sword and fell senseless in his horse's neck. Thæon, perceiving his son in that danger, with his guard came rushing in and rescued him from Ornatus's sword, which otherwise had parted his head from his body. With this, both the armies joined battle again, the Armenians with new courage rushing upon their enemies, whose hearts began to fail seeing Lenon so near death, which made such a confusion among them that they were readier to fly or yield to Allinus than to fight it out, that of a sudden the Armenians had slain an infinite number of them and all the earth was dyed to a purple color with their blood. Ornatus's heart was vexed to see so much of his country's blood shed that he entreated Phylastes to persuade the solders to give over, and himself rode betwixt the two armies with a herald, desiring them to stay their fury for a while. Long

galled irritated.

it was before they would give over, but at last by the drums
and trumpet sound, having called back the Armenians, Ornatus
placing himself in the midst of his countrymen that a multitude
might hear him, said: "Renowned people of Phrygia, hear my
speech, that am tormented to see so much of your blood shed,
the effusion whereof I seek by all means to stop, having, as you
see, for the love I bear to you, not lifted my hand against any of
you but only Lenon; the causes that urge me to challenge him is
the manifest wrongs he and his father hath done to yourselves,
this country, and all the nobility, for the true testimony whereof
let everyone inwardly examine his own conscience and they will
not deny my words, but find themselves exceedingly grieved
with his oppression. Do you not see what destruction he hath
brought upon this land? Are not almost all the nobility slain
and destroyed? Are not your liberties, goods, and friends taken
from you? Is not the whole land in an uproar, and everyone
driven from his quiet at home to venture his life in the field,
and all this for satisfaction of his will and self command, not
grounded upon law nor justice? Examine your consciences: is
he your lawful king? Did he not murder your lawful king, only
to make you his vassals? Again, doth Allinus seek to do his
country wrong? Doth he come to oppress you? Doth he seek to
abuse your liberty? No, he only cometh to claim his possessions
by injustice taken from him; he cometh as urged by grief, not
to live as a banished man, being himself, his wife, children, and
family driven to live in misery and slavery for the satisfaction of
his lust. Then I beseech you good soldiers, consider well what
you do, whom you defend, a traitor, and whom you resist, a
dear friend that loveth and tendereth your lives as dear as his
own, whose estate the Armenians pity, to whom he was never
gracious; but his own countrymen's hearts are hardened against
him, repaying cruelty for his love and resistance to withhold his
right. I could allege so many reasons to dissuade you from following Thæon's will as would ask a tedious recital, but I know
you are of wisdom to conceive the right, your hearts merciful to
pity him, and your minds apt to do justice. Then give him over,

discharge your minds of care, and disburden yourselves of his oppression. I stand here as an advocate to plead for Allinus's right that hath endured too much wrong. I stand here as Artesia's champion that is imprisoned by Lenon, abused by Lenon, and withheld from her liberty by Lenon. I stand here to entreat you save your own lives, to preserve your liberty, to execute justice, and to do Allinus right. Then I beseech you, lay aside your arms taken in defence of wrong, and turn your hearts to pity innocence, whereby you shall save many of your lives, show yourselves men that are ruled by wisdom, not by rage, and purchase liberty, freedom, and peace forever. Then you that hear the true hearts of Phrygians follow me and give over to follow that usurper, and stay such ruin and destruction as are like to ensue by your refusal. And let the rightful heir possess the crown, who will love you, cherish you, and seek his country's peace."

The people's hearts were so altered with his speeches that many came running to him, crying: "Allinus, Allinus!" And the rest that were not yet resolved, stood in a doubt what to do, whilst Duke Ternus commanded his forces to follow him, who withdrew himself from the camp, espying so fit occasion, determined likewise not to follow Thæon longer, whom he neither hated nor loved, but yet esteemed as unlawful usurper of that kingdom, and rather desiring Allinus should possess his right of inheritance than any way willingly contradicting the same, being, as many others were, forced to come to those wars fearing Thæon's displeasure, who cared not in what sort his will was performed. Ternus therefore drew himself apart with this policy, that if Thæon prevailed, yet he could not impeach him, and if Allinus had the best, yet he could not allege that Ternus withstood him, thinking it the greatest point of wisdom to keep himself upright. Thæon had no sooner conveyed his son to his tent and with much ado recovered him to his senses but there came a messenger posting from the court with news that Phylastes was two days since escaped out of prison. And presently after him another brought news that Artesia with the pilgrim was fled, but no man could tell whither. Lenon, hearing the news, became almost mad and raged so extremely that his wounds burst into fresh bleeding, and to fill up his heart with sorrow and vexation, another messenger from the camp came running in, crying: "Fly Thæon, fly, we are betrayed to the enemy! The leaders, captains, and soldiers are revolted, and the enemy is near at hand to surprise thee. Fly and save thy life, for thine own subjects have left thee and refused thy government!" Thæon was so amazed and terrified with fear that without regard of Lenon's life he fled to save himself. Everyone, saving those that were fled with Thæon, with haste running to their revolting fellows to save themselves. This news was brought to Allinus, who hearing the same and being past fear of Thæon's rage, sent a herald to Ternus to know whether he were his friend or still continued those bands to resist him as his foe, who returned this answer, that he was never foe to him but always wished his good.

Afterwards, dismissing his soldiers and sending everyone well rewarded to his own house, himself coming back to his tent where he met Allinus, whom he kindly saluted. Thither were assembled the chief states° of the land, to whom Allinus said: "My lords, since Thæon and Lenon are fled, and none left but your honors in place of justice, with right and equality° to minister the same to such as have sustained wrong, I, as one that have abode° the greatest loss, commit my cause to your wisdoms. You know what injuries I have endured by his malice; only for that I sought to set Artesia at liberty that was by Lenon imprisoned and badly used,° requesting nothing of you but that which by right is mine and belongeth to me by inheritance." The nobles, with a general assent, granted that he should enjoy his former possessions, and that his loss should be repaid out of the king's treasure.

Ornatus, standing by, said: "Most noble peers, you stand here debating matters whilst the cause of your woe is living and far enough from yielding to that you grant, who now, peradventure, is mustering new forces to make frustrate what you intend and

states land holders.   **equality** fairness, impartiality.   **abode** endured.   **used** treated.

to work revenge. Which to prevent, give me your consents to pursue him, and he being once taken, then may you, without control, either establish him or choose a new that should by right be your king."

To this all the nobles gave consent, and Ornatus with three thousand horsemen followed Thæon, who first took the green fortress with five hundred men who continued firm, won by great rewards but hearing of the Armenians' approach under the conduct of the stranger that slew Lenon, in the night he fled with a hundred of his nearest friends and allies to Arbastus's castle, where he thought to live secure and unknown, for that he thought his enemies would least of all suspect that place. He arrived there in the dead time of the night, but knocking, was denied entrance, which made him almost desperate, that he assayed to enter by force, and prevailed so that he got in with the rest of his company, making fast the gates again after them.

Artesia's servants, knowing what he was, some ran one way, some another, to hide themselves from him. One amongst the rest came running into Artesia's chamber declaring to her what had befallen and how that the king had taken the castle. Artesia, having not yet heard of Lenon's death nor what success Ornatus had in the camp, wringing her hands, made this lamentation: "Twice hath my dear Ornatus left me in this danger and hazarded his own life hoping to attain good success, but cruel fortune hath still crossed his laudable attempts and left both him and my poor self in extreme misery. Now am I assured he is taken prisoner again and myself am like not long to go free, for I am sure the king hath heard of my being here, which maketh him come thus late. Well, might I but be made prisoner in the same place my Ornatus lyeth enthralled° that I might yet enjoy his sight, then should I think myself happy in misery. But I fear me too much they will privily° murder him and never let me know thereof, whereby I shall be held with long frustrated hope to see him and in the end be deceived. Never was poor maiden brought

enthralled deprived of liberty.   **privily** secretly.

to such misery, nor I think true love never crossed with such bitter adversities, which both he for me, and I for him, have been continually subject unto ever since our first acquaintance."

As she was still continuing her laments, the same servant whose name was Thristus came running in again, saying: "Dear mistress, I have found a means for your escape from hence unespied if you will attempt the same, which is without any danger at all."

"Never tell me what it is," quoth she, "but be thou my guide and I will follow thee, for I will attempt anything to escape from him."

"Then," quoth he, "fear nothing, but follow me." Then took he her by the hand, leading her out of that room into a dark entry where by reason of the night there appeared not the least glimpse of light, and through that into many back rooms and unfrequented places of the castle, until he came to a postern gate° which he opened, and after he was out shut the same fast again, saying: "Now mistress you are out of the castle and past fear of the king, who little knoweth you can pass out this way, therefore I pray tell me whither I shall conduct you?"

"I thank thee, good Thristus," quoth she, "for this thy good assistance, for which I will one day be thankful unto thee, and now I pray thee direct me to Adellena's house who is my faithful friend and will rather die than discover me." This said, they began their journey, which was but three miles, and therefore they soon overcome the same, even by the morning light arriving at the wished place. Adellena, hearing some knock at the gate, commanded her maid to rise to see who it was; the damsel coming down, before she would open the gate, asked who was there? Artesia knowing her voice, said: "It is Artesia, good Anna, let me in."

With that the damsel opened the gate, conducting her to her mistress's chamber, who espying her was so surprised with joy that she, embracing her, shed abundance of tears, saying:

postern gate small side, or back door.

"Welcome my dear Artesia. I was afraid I should never have seen you again, you have been so long time absent."

"Indeed," quoth she, "I have been long absent from thee, though still not far from thee.

But I have news of importance to tell thee, which I will forbear to speak of until I have refreshed myself, for care and travel hath made me exceedingly weary." Then Adellena brought her unto a sweet and pleasant chamber where she laid her down to rest.

CHAPTER XVI

How Ornatus surprised Thæon in Arbastus's castle, who was slain by one of his own servants.

Ornatus, hearing the king had taken the green fortress, beset the same round with horsemen who took certain of the king's followers, that, being brought before him, told him the king was fled with some hundred in his company to Arbastus's castle, which, when he heard, without delay he rode thither, fearing lest Thæon, getting in and finding Artesia, should offer her some injury. He was no sooner come but he found it so, for he was denied entrance, nor could [he] see one of Artesia's servants whom he left as keepers of the same, which so much disquieted his heart that he could not tell what to do, thinking it best to entreat Thæon kindly lest he should seek revenge against Artesia, though she were innocent and no way to be blamed for anything. And such a multitude of contrarious fears arose in his fancies that he seemed therewith metamorphosed.

Which Phylastes soon perceived and, coming to him, said: "How now Ornatus? What, hath fear taken away your courage?"

"O my friend Phylastes," quoth he, "Thæon is within and thereby possessed of Artesia whose mind is so far from the least thought of virtue that no doubt he will seek revenge on her."

"Fear not that," quoth he, "but summon him to the walls by the sound of a trumpet and will him to yield himself, and stand to the courtesy of his nobles, and promise him with safety to conduct him thither."

Ornatus allowed his counsel and therefore commanded a trumpet to sound a parley,° and thereupon one from the king appeared on the walls demanding what he would have. To whom Ornatus said: "Tell Thæon the king that we come to him from the peers of the realm." The messenger told the king what he said, whereupon Thæon came in sight, demanding what he would have.

Quoth he, "I would have you yield, lest by resistance you procure a greater mischief to yourself than is by us pretended."

"Suppose I should yield," quoth he, "how would you use me?"

"Like a king," quoth Ornatus, "honorably."

"I have found," said he, "so small cause to trust you that it were fondness° to put my life within compass of your mercy. Therefore I will keep myself where I am, not doubting ere many days to have so many friends as shall both chase thee and the Armenians from the walls, and so out of this country," which he spoke upon the confidence he had in certain friends that had promised to gather new forces, but meant never to perform the same.

Ornatus was much troubled in his mind to think what was become of Artesia, marvelling that he spoke not of her, nor could hear of any of her servants that might give him knowledge how she fared. But seeing his fair words would not prevail, said: "Thæon, since thou refusest the courteous proffer I make thee, know that my intent is altered, and since thou wilt not by fair means yield, I will enforce thee to submit thyself to my mercy or abide my rigor; for not all the friends thou canst find shall shelter thee from my revenge, for I have sworn thy death and nothing but that shall satisfy me. Which vow I will once again revoke if you will yield without enforcement and deliver me Artesia in safety that is in that castle."

"Artesia," quoth Thæon, "had I her in my custody, I would be revenged on her because thou wishest her safety, but she is

to sound a parley to call a meeting.   **fondness** foolish.

far enough from me. Therefore thou seekest her in vain at my
hands, who would as readily deliver her to thee as thou couldst
ask, for that I [e]steem her not. But for myself, it shall never be
said my mind would stoop to base submission nor that a king
yielded to a slave and base vassal as thou art. Dost thou think
that a royal mind can put on so degenerate a habit? No, I tell
thee. Whatsoever thou art, I had rather by enforcement die than
by submission live. But be thou advised what thou dost, nor
stay long before these walls, for there are so many whetting their
swords and putting on armor in my defence as ere the morning's
sun arise will scare thee from hence."

Ornatus's heart could not endure these braves,◊ and being
withal vexed for fear that Artesia should sustain some injury,
thought speedily to work revenge. Which, by Phylastes's counsel, he remitted until it were night, that then unawares◊ they
might by some means get entrance into the castle and so surprise them.

Ornatus, thinking to walk alone by himself to breath forth in
sighs some part of the fear that possessed his heart, and withal
determining to view the castle how he might with conveniency
get into the same without destroying it, for that it belonged to
his beloved, he espied the postern gate whereat, thrusting, it
presently flew open, which way as yet neither Thæon nor any of
his company had found. Ornatus's heart was glad he had found
so good a means to accomplish his will, putting[37] the same to◊
again, came to Phylastes and told him thereof. Then both of them
presently agreed to enter that way and surprise them, conveying
a hundred of the best soldiers secretly under the wall unto that
postern and placing the rest in the open view of the castle as if
none of them had been wanting.

Ornatus and Phylastes entered and after them the rest, who,
passing along through the waste rooms, at last came to the place
where they had left Artesia, but found her not, and such success
had they in their attempt that Ornatus, coming behind Thæon,

braves vaunts, affronts.   **unawares** unnoticed.   **to** closed.

smote him with his hand on the back before he had any knowledge of his approach. Thæon therewith starting and looking
back was amazed, but running forward drew out his sword,
crying: "My friends save and defend yourselves!"

Wherewith those that were about him drew their swords, to
whom Ornatus said:

"How now usurping king, where are those mighty forces
should chase me hence? Will you yet yield or stand to the trial
by fight?"

"I yield," quoth Thæon, "but much against my will, for had
friends dealt faithfully, I had not been left in this misery. But
since fortune so much favoreth thee as to make me thy prisoner,
use me well for that I am a king and to none but thyself am
enthralled."

"Tell me," quoth Ornatus, "what is become of Artesia, that not
many days since I left in this place?"

"I saw her not," quoth Thæon, "nor know I where she is, only
I found certain servants in this place whom I have put to death
lest they should bewray my being here."

"Tyrant," quoth Ornatus, "thinkest thou their deaths shall go
unrevenged? Couldst thou be so cruel as to murder those that
were innocent, with whom, I fear me, thou hast made away
Artesia."

"Why, what art thou," quoth Thæon, "that usest such unde-
cent° words to a king, that art thyself not worthy to speak to a
king? And why makest thou such enquiry after Artesia, that, for
ought I know, hast no interest in her? Suppose I have slain her
that was the cause of all this woe? What canst thou challenge at
my hands for her? It had been good she had never been born,
for she only hath caused the original of these troubles."

"Art thou a king," quoth Ornatus, "and bearest so unkingly a
mind as to slander true virtue? No, thou art a villain, a murderer,
a traitor to this land, an usurper of the crown, and a most wicked
and cruel homicide. But for that thou wouldst know what I am,

undecent inappropriate.

know that I have more interest to the crown than thou hast; my name, Ornatus, and thy enemy, to whom by right that crown belongeth and which thou shalt no longer enjoy."

"Therefore," said he, "such as are my friends, lay hold on this traitor." He had no sooner spoken these words, but Thæon's own servants were the first that apprehended him, being weary of his government. And one amongst the rest, thinking that he had commanded them to slay him, and withal hoping for reward for that forward exploit, having his sword ready drawn, suddenly whilst Ornatus did but turn back to confer with Phylastes thrust the same through Thæon's body, that giving a piteous groan he gave up the ghost. Ornatus, turning back, demanded who had done that deed; with that the murderer drew back, fearing to come before him until he was compelled. To whom Ornatus said: "What art thou that hast done this deed? Art thou not one of his servants? Hast not thou been maintained by him? Did he not trust thee with his life? Was he not thy king? Then how durst thou presume to strike thy master, be ungrateful to him that gave thee gifts, prove false to him that trusted thee and slay thy anointed king?"

"My lord," quoth he, "I did mistake your words and hope to preserve my own life, made me to do that deed, which I thought would have pleased you."

"I am not," quoth he, "sorry he is dead, but for that thou slewest him whom thou in all duty oughtest to have defended, for which thou shalt die a miserable death." Then he commanded that he should be drawn in pieces with horses, which, before he departed thence, was performed.

CHAPTER XVII

How Ornatus was chosen king. How he departed un-
known in search of Artesia. How Lenon sought again
to betray him, was disappointed.[38] *How he was banished.*
Tyresus pardoned. And Ornatus and Artesia royally mar-
ried.

The king dead, Ornatus, with Phylastes, returned to the court
where all the peers were assembled, who before his coming had
by a voluntary messenger understood the manner of Thæon's
death, the care whereof was already past, for that few or none
at all loved him but now their care was whom to choose as their
king. But first they welcomed Ornatus, none of them all knowing
him nor once° suspecting what he was, who now could find no
further occasion to conceal himself, but humbling himself before
Allinus, he said: "My renowned lord, the cause I have so long
concealed myself hath been fear of the king's cruelty and Lenon's
envy, who both would have endangered me, but now being void
of that misdoubt, your poor son Ornatus submitteth himself,
humbly craving pardon for my neglect of duty."

With that he unarmed his head, and his father knowing him,
in most loving wise embraced him, shedding tears for joy of
his safety whom he thought had been long since dead. Duke
Ternus and the rest rejoiced to see him, and with embracings expressed their joy, entering into admiration of his honored parts
and noble chivalry. Phylastes, being likewise known, was much
commended, whom they deemed had been murdered in the
prison by Lenon for that he could not be found. Allinus beholding Ornatus, and with what valor he had behaved himself,
rejoiced exceedingly. The commons clapped their hands for joy
and the peers amongst themselves began to relate how virtuously, valiantly, and prudently he had behaved himself in all
that he had undertaken. After many welcomes past, Ternus,
craving audience, stood by uttering these speeches: "My lords,

once ever.

we need not now defer giving of Allinus his right, because there is none to contradict what we establish. Besides, we being all now assembled together and our late usurping king dead, there can be no fitter time to choose a new king, and such a one as by right of blood and by our general consents may rule us. Thæon, you know, was no way interested in the crown° but by usurpation, and hath rooted out almost all that he knew to have any title or interest in our late king's blood, of which house Allinus's issue is the last by marriage of the lady Aura, niece unto our late king. Therefore, the right being in him, if there be any man in this assembly that can contradict that which I have said, let him speak." Which, when he had said, he again sat down. Upon his speeches the nobles conferred, the people consulted, and at last the common soldiers cried out: "Let Ornatus be our king, Ornatus is our king!" The nobles likewise gave consent to that the multitude liked, and Ornatus was chosen king, whom they would have crowned. But at his desire they deferred the day of his coronation for a month. In the meantime, esteeming him as their king, and that day with great royalty setting him in possession thereof.

All business for that day being ended, the Armenians richly rewarded, feasted, and with joy ready to return, Allinus in quiet but for the want of his lady, and all things in good order, Ornatus being alone by himself endured much disquiet for Artesia, marvelling what was become of her, sometimes thinking she was slain by Thæon, and then supposing she was escaped out at the postern gate which he found open, that in these contrarieties of doubts he continued, sometimes despairing, and then again feeding himself with hope.

After Artesia had rested herself and received some part of her sleep she had lost that night, though but with broken slumbers, she began to declare to Adellena what miseries she had endured and troubles she had passed since she was by Lenon carried from her house, how she met with Ornatus again, and everything that

was no way interested in the crown had no right to the crown.

was befallen, with the cause of her flight at that instant. "But Adellena," said she, "I fear me I shall never see him again, for had he not been taken and his father overthrown, Thæon could not have had so much leisure as to come to surprise me there, but the heavens granted me a fortunate escape. And if I could be so happy as to hear that Ornatus were in safety, though he had not that success his desires did aim at, my heart would be at some rest which is now pinched with suspicious torment. His adventurous valiant heart could not be withdrawn by any persuasion to leave to aid his father, but notwithstanding infinite perils hung over his head, yet to show the duty of a loving son and the mind of a virtuous valiant gentleman, he would not desist to hazard his person, which now I fear me is fallen into the hands of his enemies. But yet Phylastes I hope will, by his good and friendly counsel, be a means to keep him from danger."

Many other speeches Artesia used, and Adellena used as many on the contrary part to persuade her that Ornatus was in safety, the truth whereof she told her, she should soon know, "for," quoth she, "I have sent one of my servants to learn the truth of all that is happened, who I know will shortly return." Which fell out even as she had told, for the servant returned bringing news of Lenon's death acted by a strange knight, and how that[39] Thæon was fled, and being likewise by the strange knight surprised in Arbastus's castle, was slain by one of his own servants. Which knight was now known to be Ornatus and was elected king by the peers, but he had deferred his day of coronation by reason of some special grief that troubled him. Artesia's heart was revived with these news, knowing the grief Ornatus endured was for her absence, that presently she determined to send him word of her safety, and wrote a letter, the contents whereof were these:

My dear Ornatus, no news could have come more welcome to me than your safety, and nothing more unwelcome than to hear of your heaviness, which I would entreat you to cease for that I am in safety at Adellena's house, being by

one of my servants the same night the king took my castle
at a postern gate in safety brought hither, where I trust ere
long to see you which will replenish my soul with exceeding
comfort, for on your safety my life and felicity dependeth.

Yours for ever, Artesia.

Having wrote this letter, she gave it to Thristus, willing him to
deliver the same to Ornatus with all speed.

Destinies do allot many to exceeding misfortunes, and some
men are of that dishonorable and unmanly disposition that they
account all means to attain their desires lawful, not regarding
the shame and peril [that] will ensue thereon. Of which nature was Lenon, who, being conveyed from the camp by his
friends, soon recovered, and kept in a secret place lest he might
be known, having no other means but by absenting himself to
save his life, whose supposed death caused Thæon's flight to
the green fortress from whence likewise he was departed before
Lenon could come to give him knowledge of this safety, and
knowing that it was then too late to salve° those miseries, he
still concealed himself, following Ornatus, though unknown to
him, with intent to murder him if he could by any means take
him at advantage. But he was still disappointed, and withal
saw the death of his father done by his own servant, still intermingling himself amongst the soldiers that he was taken to be
one of them and never suspected.[40] But Ornatus, being returned
to the court, Lenon was then compelled to leave to follow him,
and harbored sometimes in one place and sometimes in another;
having knowledge of Artesia's absence, he could not tell whether
she were alive or dead; but dead he thought she could not be,
but rather by some means escaped. And even when Thristus
was newly come out of Adellena's house, Lenon espied him,
and knowing him to be one of Artesia's servants, he suspected
his mistress was there, to whom he came, saying: "My friend
well met. I take you to be one of Artesia's servants, unless I be

salve alleviate as a wound with ointment.

deceived, which, if you will resolve me of, I will do a message to you that I am willed to deliver to her from her dearest friend Ornatus."

"Indeed," quoth Thristus, "I serve Artesia and am now going to Ornatus with a letter from Artesia, who is in safety in Adellena's house." Lenon hearing his speech, being before determined what to do, drew out his dagger and suddenly stabbed him, casting his body into a pit, and taking the letter from him broke up the seal and read the contents, which, when he had done, he began to study which way to revenge himself on Ornatus and afterwards to get Artesia into his possession. And for that he thought delay might hinder his intent, he first wrote a letter in Artesia's name, the contents were these:

Ornatus my dearest friend, the news of your happy victory and conquest of your enemies is come to my knowledge, than which nothing could have been more welcome unto me. Likewise, I hear that much heaviness possesseth you for my absence, that am in safety, and desire you to meet me tomorrow night, and you shall find me with Adellena at the lodge in the park near unto my castle. In the meantime, remitting all further report of my escape and manifestation of my love, until the happy time I may meet you.

Yours in all love, Artesia.

When he had written this letter and imitated therein Artesia's own hand so near that it could hardly be discerned, he went to the court, and behaved° the matter so cunningly that he was no way suspected, but was admitted into Phylastes's presence, to whom he delivered the letter for Ornatus himself, being exceedingly troubled in his mind, had left the court with some three in his company to go in search of Artesia and left Phylastes in his chamber, and in his stead to answer such as should come with any suits to him. Phylastes, being taken [for Ornatus][41] of all, but of

behaved performed.   **but of some certain** except for a few.

some certain° that attended him,[42] received the letter, promising
to meet Artesia there at the same time appointed, giving the
messenger a reward. Lenon, being departed, went to a place
where he found a certain kinsman, of his named Lucertus, to
whom he declared both what he was, and what means he had
wrought for his revenge on Ornatus, who without respect° joined
hands with him, and promised with many oaths to explore his
life in pursuit of revenge, who, with Lenon included, before
Ornatus's coming, to be in the lodge with a sufficient company
to surprise him and work the premeditated revenge. Lenon,
being assured of his aid, next determined to take Artesia from
Adellena's house and to bring her to Lucertus's castle, until the
time appointed staying with Lucertus to see him depart with his
ambush to the lodge, which he saw effectually performed.

Phylastes presently, upon the receipt of that letter, sent out a
messenger to seek Ornatus and to certify him that Artesia would
meet him at the lodge with Adellena that evening, and that he
should find Phylastes there who, being by Artesia's messenger taken for himself, had appointed to be there lest he should
not conveniently be found. The messenger with great haste
departed, and enquiring after four pilgrims, for in that habit Ornatus and such as were with him went — by that time the day
drew near to an end — the messenger found Ornatus, to whom
he declared what Phylastes had given him in charge, only mistaking the place, for whereas he should by his direction have
said at the lodge, mistaking Phylastes's words, he said at Adellena's house. Ornatus, hearing that heavenly tidings, leapt for
joy, presently hasting towards Adellena's house, which was not
far off. Lenon, to further his attempt, which he thought he could
not with[43] violence execute, for he thought if he should carry
her away perforce in the day time he should be prevented, devised an answer of the letter which he had taken from Thristus,
which he determined to deliver to Artesia, as from Ornatus, the
contents whereof were these:

without respect without deliberation.

My most dear and beloved Artesia, I have received the letter
you sent me by your servant, whom I have employed about
a matter of great importance that none could so fitly execute
as himself, which news was most welcome to the comfort
of my heart that was almost overcome with despair of your
safety, whereon my chiefest felicity dependeth. Therefore,
omitting further recital of my joy for your safety, which this
paper cannot express, therefore I will meet you soon where
this my servant will bring you, whose fidelity I assure you
to be such as that he will do nothing but what I have given
him in change. Until which time of meeting, I cease all
further circumstances of speeches.

Yours, Ornatus.

With this letter Lenon went to Adellena's house, and knocking
at the gate, was brought to her, to whom he delivered the same,
who reading the contents, and being before not well acquainted
with Ornatus's hand, nothing at all suspected the contrary but
both believed that it came from him and determined to go with
the messenger to meet him. Whilst she was preparing to go with
Lenon, Adellena's maid came in, telling her that there was another to speak with her from Ornatus. With that Lenon changed
countenance, and Artesia willed her to bring him in. Ornatus,
beholding her, had thought to have embraced her and discovered
himself, but seeing a stranger there and a letter in her hand, he
stood in a study.◊ Artesia noting well his countenance, thought
it was Ornatus himself, but standing in a doubt thereof, said: "I
have received this letter from Ornatus already, and therefore if
you have any further message from him, tell it me, for any news
from him shall be most welcome."

Ornatus thought that it was sent by Phylastes, but not knowing the messenger marvelled thereat, saying: "I cannot believe
that it came from him, for while within this hour he had not
knowledge of your being here." With that Artesia gave him the

study state of reflection.

letter, willing him to read the same. Ornatus soon knew that it was invented by some treachery, and therefore said: "I know this comes not from Ornatus, for this is not his hand, nor he that brought it any of his servants, for himself sent me before, appointing° to be here within this hour."

Lenon, hearing his speeches, wished himself a thousand miles off, fearing to be discovered for that he could not tell how to excuse himself, nor by any color avoid that[44] danger. To whom Ornatus said: "My friend, when did he deliver thee this letter?"

"Yesterday," quoth he.

"Thou liest," said Ornatus, "for he hath not been at the court these three days."

Lenon, thinking with impudency to outface, having no other means left that was likely to help him, and therefore said: "This letter came from Ornatus, and thou liest in saying the contrary, being some villain that art set to betray this lady. Therefore," quoth he, speaking to Artesia, "believe him not, for he is come with some evil intent."

With that Ornatus bad those that were with him lay hands on him, who presently apprehended him, and pulling off his hat and a subtle disguise that he wore, knew him to be Lenon, at the first being half afraid to touch him for that they would have sworn he had been dead. Ornatus, seeing Artesia in an exceeding fright, discovered himself and with great joy embraced her, desiring her to fear nothing. Artesia, knowing him, soon forgot her fear, embracing him with exceeding joy. To whom he said: "Fear him not, my dear Artesia, for be it himself or his ghost, I care not; it shall go hard if he now escape my hands."

To whom he said: "Most discourteous and cowardly villain, couldst thou not be contented to live in quiet, having once escaped my fury, but that thou must by further complots° and treacheries seek to betray this lady that never did injure thee? How often hast thou interrupted her quiet and from quietness brought her into misery? And knowing that she could not like

appointing determining.   **complots** plots, trickeries.

thee, yet thou wert so impudent as never to give over thy suit; but, to attain thy desire, first depriveth her of liberty, banishest me in the disguise of Sylvian, and soughtest to betray my father's life; and not satisfied with all these, like a cowardly miscreant° seekest by villainy to betray her. And notwithstanding thou hast beheld thy father's woeful downfall and meritorious punishment, thou seekest to betray this lady's life by some unknown treachery not yet revealed. For all which thou shalt suffer such punishment as I have devised and have power to execute."

Lenon, seeing himself discovered, grew desperate, and scorning to be so rebuked at his hands, whom he still esteemed his inferior, but especially vexed that it was he that had so long hindered his love to Artesia, said: "Ornatus, I think thou hast either forgotten thyself, or else what I am, that at thy pleasure rebukest me in such uncivil and ill-beseeming terms. Am I not thy better, and one that not long since might have commanded thee? And is thy mind so much elevated and proud that thou wilt not acknowledge it? Thou makest brags of thy victory when thou mayst rather with shame keep silence, and with remorse repent that thou hast sought the death of thy lawful king, being thyself but a traitor."

As he would have spake more, Ornatus interrupted him, saying: "Hold thy peace and do not stir my mind to more sharp revenge by thy reply, for I scorn to hear thee speak. Therefore give over lest I punish that tongue of thine for uttering such high° words in defence of vice."

"Since," quoth Lenon, "thou wilt not hear me speak in defence of myself, let me be conveyed from thy presence, for thy sight is as odious unto me as mine to thee."

Whilst they continued in Adellena's house, a messenger came running in breathless, uttering these speeches: "Behold most worthy Ornatus, I bring a message of much woe and heavy import. Yesterday there was a messenger came to the court that brought a letter in Artesia's name to Phylastes, as supposing him

miscreant vile wretch.   high inflated.

to be yourself, wherein she requested you to meet her this night at the lodge in her park. Phylastes, who presently sent out a messenger to give you knowledge thereof, but not hearing of his return, went himself with some twenty in his company to the place appointed, and entering, he found not Artesia there but a crowd of rebels, amongst whom Lucertus was chief, who all at once set upon him and his followers, taking him for yourself, having so many above the small number that were with Phylastes that they had soon slain most of them that were with him. And himself, not able to withstand such a multitude, had received many grievous wounds and had been surely slain but that the heavens sent them this aid. It fortuned that day that Duke Ternus was going from the court to his own house, who, by great fortune, hearing the noise, with his men hasted thitherwards and having knowledge of what was done, most valiantly doth himself and his men set upon Lucertus, whom they soon vanquished, having first slain many of his complices, and him hath he carried prisoner with the rest of such as were alive unto the court, and with them Phylastes in great danger of death."

Ornatus's heart was exceedingly vexed to hear of his dear friend Phylastes' hurt, but especially to think that he had not before attacked Lucertus, which he was once in mind to have done, which would have prevented all these mischiefs. The night now being come, Ornatus caused Lenon to be bound hand and foot and put into a strong place of the house with some to watch him lest he should do himself violence, himself with Artesia spending that evening in many speeches relating the manner of all these misfortunes, but especially comforting themselves in each other's love, with Adellena calling to remembrance the whole manner of their troubles only procured by Lenon, which sad relations made the renewing of their love more pleasant and delectable.

Early the next morning, Ornatus putting himself in his palmer's weeds, and covering Artesia's face with a veil, and carrying Lenon with them bound, departed towards the court. The next morning the peers of the land, being still there, assembled them-

selves, amongst whom was Allinus, that likewise had found his
lady, who, hearing of his happy success against Thæon, was that
morning newly arrived at the court and by him entertained with
exceeding joy. By that time they were assembled and had called
Lucertus before them, Ornatus with his company were likewise
come, though unknown and standing by, heard Lucertus confess
that Lenon had instigated him to work that revenge against Ornatus, himself being likewise gone to betray Artesia. The whole
assembly marvelled when they heard him say that Lenon persuaded him to it, that Allinus stood up, saying: "Is not he dead,
then how can this be?"

"Lenon," quoth Lucertus "is not dead."

With that, Ornatus stepping in, thrusting Lenon before him,
said: "Here is the man that hath procured him to all this mischief." The nobles, beholding him, were amazed at his sight, but
being assured it was he by the perfect knowledge they had of
him, Ternus said: "Lenon, I had always thought thou hadst born
the mind of a gentleman, but now I find the contrary in thee, and
that in the most shamefulest degree. What fury led thee to such
mischievous attempts to hire Lucertus to slay Ornatus, which he
hath almost performed, and thyself to seek the death or misery
of that virtuous lady that hath already endured too much wrong
by thy folly?"

Allinus had not as yet heard of Ornatus's hurt, nor any knew
the contrary but that Phylastes was he, for he, according to the
mind of a most virtuous and constant friend, still concealed himself. Nor the Lady Aura had yet seen her son, whom she had
but heard of, that Allinus said: "Is my son Ornatus almost slain?
O traitorous villain!" With that, Aura likewise began to make
exceeding lamentation, which Ornatus was not able to behold,
and therefore pulling off his disguised habit, humbly reverenced
himself before them upon his knee. Both his parents knew him
and with exceeding joy embraced him, shedding abundance of
tears for his safety. With that, Duke Ternus and all the rest came
to him, using him with such behavior as belonged to him they
had chosen king, seating him in an imperial chair.

He being set thus, said: "My noble lords, I thank you for entitling me with this exceeding honor. Therefore my desire is, since you have elected me of your free and bounteous hearts to be your king, let me this day and instantly be installed with possession of the diadem for that I have now no further cause of care to cause me defer the same, and likewise that I may give judgment against these most wicked conspirators."

The nobles, with joyful hearts, gave consent and immediately crowned him, with bended knees doing him reverence. Which done, Ornatus rising from his imperial seat came to Artesia, taking her by the hand and leading her up the throne, seated her in the chair, placing the crown upon her head, saying: "My lords, I pray likewise be contented with that I do, and as you have elected me king, make this your queen."[45] Then pulled he off the veil from Artesia's face, and her clear beauty appeared to the admiration of all, who beholding in humble sort did her reverence, making exceeding shouts for joy, their hearts being all exceedingly glad of her safety.

When this was done, she came down and embraced them, yielding them many thanks, who all showed such exceeding kindness as expressed their hearty good will, and rejoiced both her and Ornatus to behold especially Aura and Ternus's duchess, who with many embracings which they thought they could not sufficiently express, rejoiced to see her in that safety. By that time Ornatus was again seated and Artesia by him, Phylastes hearing of Ornatus's return, being though grievously wounded, yet in no great danger of death, as well as he could came into the presence, where he, beholding Ornatus and Artesia crowned, kneeled down before them, his heart conceiving exceeding joy to behold that heavenly sight, whom Ornatus kindly embraced, rejoicing to see him in that good estate, after Artesia's salutation, willing him to sit down amongst them. Then Ornatus, first commanding Floretus to be sent for out of prison, thus said:

"Now there resteth nothing but to give sentence against these that by conspiracies have been murderers, which fact is so heinous that it maketh them both odious to God and man, in which offence both thou Lenon, Lucertus, and Tyresus, are guilty."

"Therefore, Lenon," quoth he, "still declare[46] what moved thee from time to time to commit so many and grievous acts as thou hast done?" Lenon's heart was dead with vexation to see him crowned and Artesia chosen his queen, that hanging down his head he would not speak. But Lucertus, humbling himself upon his knee, asked pardon. By this time, Floretus was brought in, looking with such a meagre and pale countenance, by reason of his long imprisonment, that Artesia wept to behold him and could not choose but run and embrace him, upon her knee entreating Ornatus to pardon the offence he had committed, which was against none but herself. Ornatus, seeing her kneel, suddenly caught her up, embracing Floretus, and commanding his bands to be unloosed, withal saying:

"I not only with a willing heart pardon you, but also give unto you forever all those possessions that belonged unto your brother Arbastus."

Floretus, before expecting nothing but death, which was turned to such exceeding joy, humbly upon his knee yielded many thanks.

Then Ornatus, seating himself again, said: "Because this day is the first of our reign which should begin with mercy and not with rigor,◊ there shall not a drop of blood by our command be spilt. And therefore, Lenon, though thou hast deserved no favor but a most miserable death, we pardon thee. And Lucertus, commanding thee upon pain of death, within ten days to depart this land, for that we banish thee hence for ever, which doom◊ is too merciful for thy fact.◊ For thee Lenon, we only banish thee [from] this court, where, on pain of death, set not thy foot lest thy life ransom thy presumption."

This said, taking Artesia by the hand, he was by the peers, with the noise of trumpets and exceeding joy, conducted to a chapel and in royal sort that day married to Artesia, and from thence to an imperial feast, spending all that day in great pleasure, and

rigor harshness.   **doom** judgment.   **fact** crime.

at night taking lawful delight in her love, both then, and during the time of both their lives, living in most pleasant, loving and virtuous sort that most places of the world were filled with the report of their virtuous life and peaceable government.

FINIS

Textual Annotations

1. Momus, one of the Greek gods, is remembered for his ridiculing of the faults of other gods. He is usually represented lifting a mask from his face and holding a figurine in his hands. Thomas Cooper (*Thesaurus linguæ Romanæ et Britannicæ*, London, 1565) describes Momus as "the carpynge God of reprehension, sonne of Nox and Sommus, whose propertie it is . . . neuer to doe or make by thynge himselfe, but with curious eyes to beholde the doynges of others: and if any thynge weare let passe, to carpe the same. Whereof all curious carpers of other mens doinges are called Momi" (sig. M2^r).
2. A spelling variant of the name of the mythical bird Celeus, also spelt as Celes or Celos. According to Pliny (*Natural History*, X.60, 79) Laius, a Cretan, with three other thieves, Aegolis, Celeus, and Cerberus, attempted to steal honey from the sacred cave of bees in Crete and accidentally came upon the cradle of the infant Zeus. The god wanted to destroy them with a flash of lightning but was dissuaded by the Moirae and Themis, because no one was allowed to be killed on the sacred spot. He metamorphosed them into birds instead; hence the name of the bird.
3. Phrygia is a large ancient country within Natolia, that is, Asia Minor. The map in the 1560 edition of the Geneva Bible shows it stretching in the west to the coast of the Sea of Marmara, and bordering on Pontus, Bythinia, Galatia, Cappadocia, Pisidia, and Mysia. These countries may be the "provinces not far distant from [Phrygia's] near neighborhood" in Ford's text. Lewes Roberts (*The Marchants Mappe of Commerce*, London: by R.O. for Ralphe Mabb, 1638; STC 21094) divides Phrygia into Phrygia Minor, which "affordeth the place where the ancient and famous Citie of Troy was seated" (sig. L6^v), and Phrygia Major, which includes most of the

rest of Asia Minor, in which "doth not remaine any thing note wor-
thie" (sig. L6ᵛ). Pliny (*Natural History*, V.xli) says that Phrygia "lies
behind Troas and ... between Cape Lectum and the river Echelus,"
suggesting that it was originally an important commercial city in
Natolia, powerful enough to give its name to both a region and a
nation north of Troy. In romances, Phrygia occasionally appears as
a city too: for example, as the centre of action in the first part of
Richard Johnson's *The most famous history of the seuen Champions of
Christendome* (London: for Elizabeth Burbie, 1596; STC 14677).

4. The name of a song popular in Shakespeare's time, of which, according to Sternfeld, only the music has survived. See F.W. Sternfeld, *Music in Shakespearean Tragedy* (London: Routledge and Kegan
Paul; New York: Dover Publications, 1963), p. 102. In *Romeo and
Juliet*, Peter, clown and servant to Juliet's Nurse, requests that the
musicians play the song:

> Peter: Musicians, O musicians, "Heart's ease," "Heart's
> ease!" O, an you will have me live, play "Heart's
> ease."
>
> First musician: Why "Heart's ease?"
>
> Peter: O, musicians, because my heart itself plays "My
> heart is full." O play me some merry dump to
> comfort me.
>
> (4.4.126–30)

Sternfeld posits that "the clown [Peter] underlines the unsuitable
presence of merry musicians" (102). The text of *Romeo and Juliet*
is quoted from the Oxford Shakespeare edition of that play, ed. Jill
L. Levenson (Oxford: Oxford University Press, 2000).

5. From this point on, Ford uses the form "Sylvian" throughout the rest
of the text, signalling the male body under the female disguise, and
thus avoiding any connotation of illicit erotic titillation that might
be incurred in situations in which Ornatus-Sylvia and Artesia are
together.

6. A mythical exotic herb which, when held, tells of joy or sorrow in
the future.

7. The bird "akanthus" exists, but there is some disagreement about
which bird it corresponds to. Aristotle mentions it in *Historia ani-
malium* (IX.i.610a) as the acanthis, enemy to the ass, because the one
lives on and the other eats thistles. The "us" at the end no doubt
derives from Aelian who, in his *On the Characteristics of Animals* (X.
Sect. 32), derives the name of the bird from the acanthus plant on
which it feeds. Among Ford's contemporaries, only Lodge (in *A*

Margarite of America and elsewhere) spells it in this way. There are further reasons than this to suggest that Ford had Lodge's work of 1596 on his desk, insofar as several of these comparisons are shared by these two authors — but the fluidity of these images among writers renders proof difficult. The bird has been variously identified as the goldfinch, the thistle-finch, the linnet and the siskin.

8. "not" in [1599] and 1607; missing in 1619 and 1634. But in [1599] "not" ("I enjoy not Artesia's love, yet she loveth me not") is probably a compositor's error, for the sentence means "I do not enjoy her love since she does not love me."

9. "Sylvian:" in [1599] and 1607; "Sylvian, said:" in 1619 and 1634.

10. The source of the story of Pyramus and Thisbe is Ovid (*Met.*, IV.55–201). Pyramus and Thisbe were next-door neighbors in Babylon. Because their parents did not allow them to marry, they talked to each other through a crack in the wall that separated the two houses. Finally they arranged a meeting at Ninus's tomb. There Thisbe was frightened by a lion returning from its hunt; she ran away, dropping her cloak, which the lion mouthed, leaving blood stains on it. Pyramus, finding Thisbe's bloodstained cloak and supposing her dead, killed himself. Thisbe returned, found Pyramus's body, and killed herself. Their blood stained a mulberry tree, whose ripe fruit remained black ever since. Their tragic story, popular in the Renaissance (see Calderón, *La dama duende* I.i.), emblematized young love constrained to disaster by parental opposition.

11. Ford may refer to one of the printed versions of the famous story, perhaps Arthur Brooke's translation of Bandello entitled *The Tragical Historye of Romeus and Juliet* (1562), but he may also have in mind one of the earlier productions of Shakespeare's play.

12. "secrecie" in [1599] and 1607; "sincerity" in 1619 and 1634.

13. "How Ornatus loue was hindred" in [1599] and 1607; "How Ornatus was hindred" in 1619 and 1634.

14. "both together" in [1599] and 1607; "both of them together" in 1619 and 1634.

15. "tendance" in [1599] and 1607; "attendance" in 1619 and 1634.

16. "friends." in [1599] and 1607; "friends and country." in 1619 and 1634.

17. "committing" in [1599] and 1607; "but committing" in 1619 and 1634.

18. "life" in [1599] and 1607; "selfe" in 1619 and 1634.

19. The 1607 edition is here different from the [1599], 1619, and 1634 editions. The 1607 edition reads: "That by the enticement of that wicked ... her."; the 1619 and 1634 editions read, "By the enticement

of that wicked Floretus, I gave her a drink, that unknowing to me, hath poisoned her."

20. In the section "Of Anatolia, or Natolia in generall" in *The Merchants Mappe*, Lewes Roberts states that "Natolia is limited on the East with the River Euphrates, on the West with Thracius Bosphorus, Propontis, Hellespont, and the Egean; on the North with Pontus Euxinus, on the South with the Rhodian and Lician Seas. In this country was anciently accounted 4000 Cities and Townes . . . but now the ruines of them are hardly to be seen . . . " (sig. L4^V). Although Renaissance cartographers and geographers considered Natolia a large land mass incorporating various other countries, including Phrygia, by making the Moors' ship carrying the banished Ornatus sail from Phrygia to Natolia, Ford treats Phrygia and Natolia as two separate countries. He makes that division even more pronounced when he later makes Natolia Phrygia's enemy.

21. "brooking no delay" is a version of the proverbs, "Delay breeds danger (is dangerous)" and "Delay in love is dangerous," quoted by Tilley (p. 149).

22. The episode of Ornatus's running in skirts and throwing apples to the boar draws on one of several versions of the myth of Atalanta and Hippomenes (or Melanion). According to Ovid, Atalanta determined forever to live in celibacy ("O Atalanta, thou at all of husband hast no neede. Shonne husbanding . . . / . . . She being sore afrayd / Of this Apollos Oracle, did keepe herself a mayd, / And lived in the shady woods" (*Met.*, X.654–57). Yet her beauty attracted many suitors, and to free herself from their impositions, the swift-footed Atalanta proposed to run a race with them. In the race she was to carry a dart in her hands, while her suitors were to run unarmed and to start first. Whoever arrived at the goal before her was to be given her hand as a reward, but those whom she overtook were to be killed with the dart that she herself carried. Many suitors died in the race, until Hippomenes proposed himself as a suitor. Venus gave him three golden apples from the garden of Hesperides, and as soon as he started the race, he threw the apples at a distance one from another, thus delaying Atalanta, who stopped to pick them up. Hippomenes remained ahead of her, and, arriving at the goal first, he obtained her as a wife. In some versions there is no race, but Hippomenes wins Atalanta's love while hunting with her (*OCD*). In another version of the myth, one that may have also influenced Ford, Atalanta, an experienced huntress, took part in the hunting of the Calydonian boar. She first wounded the boar and then received its head as a gift from Meleager, a celebrated hero,

who was in love with her. Ford's reworking of the Atalanta story is a parody.

23. "reuerent" in [1599] and 1607; "feruent" in 1619 and 1634.

24. "I loue your beauty" in [1599]; "I love your Beautie" in 1607; "I so love your beauty" in 1619 and 1634.

25. "to see him againe" in [1599] and 1607; "to see him once againe" in 1619 and 1634.

26. This part of the narrative may have been inspired by an episode from Longus's *Daphnis and Chloe* (I.28–31), where Tyrian pirates plunder the crops, steal the cattle from Daphnis's island, and carry him away. Another similar instance of plunder and abduction occurs in book II (20–24), when the Methymenians ravage the coast, seize Daphnis's herds, plunder the crops, and carry off Chloe, forcing her to flee into the cave of the Nymphs.

27. "would" in [1599] and 1607; "should" in 1619 and 1634.

28. "comforted" in [1599] and 1607; "comforting" in 1619 and 1634.

29. "to" in [1599] and 1607; missing in 1619 and 1635.

30. "to" in 1607, 1619, and 1634; missing in [1599].

31. "are" in [1599] and 1607; "is" in 1619 and 1634.

32. Another name for Apollo, the sun-god.

33. "demanding" in [1599] and 1607; "demanded" in 1619 and 1634.

34. The goddess of Mount Cynthus, i.e. Diana, who was believed to have been born there; also the moon.

35. The source of the parting motif may have been the departure scene in Ovid's story of Ceyx and Alcyone (*Met.*, XI.537–28). Shakespeare seems to have drawn on the same passage in the scene of Posthumus's parting from Pisanio in *Cymbeline* (I.3.8–13). A parting motif, resembling the departure scene in Ovid, can also be found in the story of "Cephalus and Procris" in George Pettie's *A Petite Palace* (1576).

36. The [1599] and 1607 editions read "revived," while the 1619 and 1634 editions read "reviving."

37. "putting" in [1599] and 1607; "& putting" in 1619; "and putting" in 1634.

38. "was disappointed" in [1599] and 1607; "& was disappointed" in 1607; "but was disappointed" in 1616 and 1634.

39. "that" is used disparagingly here, in a demonstrative and emphatic sense.

40. Lenon is thinking about the servant who murdered his father, and who cannot be recognized as the murderer because he is still mixing with soldiers and is therefore believed to be one of them.

41. "for Ornatus" in 1619 and 1634; missing in [1599] and 1607.

42. Everyone took Phylastes to be Ornatus, and those who were in his attendance were certain that he is in fact Ornatus.
43. "with" in [1599] and 1607; "by" in 1619 and 1634.
44. "that" in [1599] and 1607; "the" in 1619 and 1634.
45. Missing in [1599]: "My Lords, as you haue elected me king, I pray likewise be contented with that I do, and make this your queen."
46. "still declare" in [1599] and 1607; "first declare" in 1619 and 1634.